FURY
IN HER EYES

a Novel

PHILLIP VEGA

First edition 2024
Published in Canton, GA, USA by *thewordverve*
(**www.thewordverve.com**)

eBook ISBN: 978-1-956856-51-4
Paperback ISBN: 978-1-956856-52-1

Library of Congress Control Number: 2024914465

Fury in Her Eyes

A Book with Verve by *thewordverve*

Cover and interior design by Robin Krauss at Linden Design
www.bookformatters.com
www.LindenDesign.biz

eBook formatting by thewordverve

"Just as water reflects the face, so one human heart reflects another." – Proverbs 27:19 NRSV

"The first to apologize is the bravest. The first to forgive is the strongest. The first to forget is the happiest." – Unknown.

PROLOGUE

Modern Day

What was that old saying, "Time heals all wounds"?

I'm going to need a bigger watch.

"Get him!" someone shouted.

I scrambled. "Derek, go get help!"

"But Ollie—"

A blow to the back of my head. Blood streamed down my face, and I remembered my boss's words, *"C'mon, Ollie, do me this favor. Your wife's out of town anyway."*

"Run, Derek! Go, go, g—"

I fell to the cold, hard January grass and curled into the fetal position. Alleged patriots dressed head to toe in combat gear held barbwire bats, wooden signs, and metal pipes. Treated me like a preschooler's piñata.

One moment I was a Pulitzer Prize-winning photojournalist doing my editor a last-minute favor, showing a newbie how to *document* the news, and not *become* it. The next, I fought for my life.

Wham!

"How's *that* feel, ya *nigger*?" one guy shouted.

Over the ruckus, I heard a woman. "Fuckin' *fake* news . . ."

For what felt like an eternity, the ass-kicking continued. A masked woman armed with a two-by-four and garbled accent, shattered my right ankle.

In the distance, I heard, "They got into the Capitol."

"Whoo-hoo! 'Bout fuckin' time."

A man wearing a *Don't Tread on Me* shirt pointed at me. "What about this guy?"

The masked woman delivered her final love note with a hard boot to my face and parting comment, "Fuck him."

Wham!

Liquid fire coursed through my body. I arched my back as my eyes flew open, and I attempted to gasp for air, but something obstructed my passageway. Every nerve ending cried for relief as gloved hands pressed down on my flailing body.

"Hold him down!" a familiar voice shouted.

"I'm trying," another replied.

"Try harder."

I bit down. The crunch of plastic. The taste of blood. I wanted to throw up.

"Hit him with the morphine!" A familiar voice shouted over blaring electronics.

"He just came out of his coma."

"I don't care. Hit him, or I will."

"But Doctor . . ."

"This is my *fucking* brother! Do it. *Now.*"

Jaime?

I blinked. Tried to focus. Above me, an off-color tile, slightly stained ceiling, followed by a warm rush of pain relief.

Fade to black . . .

A voice echoed.

"Ollie? Can you hear me?"

A sharp light hit my eyes. I tried to knock it away but couldn't.

Velcro straps tightened around my wrist, restricting any movement.

"It's okay, Ollie. I'm here."

Where the hell am I? Where's Derek?

I tracked the voice. It's Jaime, my kid brother, dressed head to toe in personal protective equipment, or PPE. I tried speaking but couldn't. A foreign object in my throat prevented me.

What the fuck happened?

I scanned my surroundings. Between my muted voice, the electronic leads connecting my body to various monitors, and the straps restricting my movement, I felt like Frankenstein's monster. The only thing missing were metal bolts sticking from my neck.

"Easy, bro. We put you in restraints for your own good."

The familiar stench of floral antiseptic hit my nostrils. I was in a hospital. On the wall behind Jaime hung an ink-stained greaseboard with the name *Delphine* written in red eraser marker. My brother attempted to explain where I was and how long I'd been there, but I barely heard a word.

All I wanted to do was sleep...

Alarms blared.

Oh, my God, the pain.

A door burst open. A nurse rushed in. Even behind her blue mask, she looked like a kid playing dress-up. Shut off the alarms. Checked my vitals. My eyes blurred as I tried reading her name badge. A warm, spicy blend of roses and something exotic hit my exposed nostrils. It took me back in time. Brought me comfort.

In a slight French accent, she cooed, "Shh . . . you're okay. My name is Delphine."

She sat me up. Slipped my hospital gown off my shoulders,

revealing scars from my past. A bullet wound in my left bicep while covering Afghanistan. The remnant from a knife wound to the back under my right shoulder blade.

"These must have hurt," she commented.

You have no idea.

She finished her gentle torture and carefully laid me back onto my pillow. Like a Vegas magician, a plastic syringe appeared in her hand. She flicked the tip, removing errant air bubbles before injecting the clear contents into my IV.

Liquid salvation.

Images swirled in my mind's eye. Jaime now wore old-timey film director's garb. Gone is his PPE. He stood next to television cameras on a soundstage with a bullhorn in his hand. A crisp white button-down shirt, black vest, matching beret, and pencil-thin pornstache completed his look.

He held the bullhorn to his mouth and shouted, *"Roll film."*

Visions from a lifetime covering the many travesties our planet had to offer flashed before my eyes. Blood from innocent children dripped off machetes. African war lords soon transformed into innocent migrant workers. They now stood in line, stripped naked from the waist down, while gold-toothed thugs bent them over tables, converting them into drug mules. One of the misfortunates convulsed as a baggie burst inside his intestines, killing him instantly. More blood. More terror. A scream caught in my throat.

A technicolor wave transformed my visions. Politicians replaced the mules, but not the horror. Clad in the finest garb, men and women casually reclined on the backs of starving constituents, eating caviar while sipping expensive champagne. Tears rolled down my cheeks. A puff of smoke. A new vision.

A shadowy figure approached. Her hazel eyes emitted a fiery

glow. Vibrant. Youthful. Full of hope, wonder, and something else.

A secret ache—an agony.

A fury.

Auburn hair framed her delicate face.

Her ethereal voice called out to me, "Ollie."

Drew me in.

Slender arms wrapped around my neck.

Pouty lips and a freckled nose pressed against me.

I held her and whispered a name.

"Navil."

CHAPTER ONE

Winter 1986

"Y ou're going to miss your bus," Tía Carolina shouted in Spanish over Bella's constant barking.

Crest spat from my mouth, and I shouted, "I'm coming."

I scrambled to my room, gathered my crap, and hoofed it out the front door. My dutiful Aunt Carolina held it open while my long-haired miniature dachshund leaped about like an idiot. In the distance rumbled the diesel-powered engine from my school bus.

Shit, I'm gonna miss it.

After kissing my aunt goodbye, I burst out the door and began my morning routine, racing three houses down to my bus stop. Ahead of me, disappointedly shaking her head, was my next-door neighbor and best friend since elementary school, Fiona Sullivan. A five-foot-two, raven-haired, blue-eyed, didn't-take-shit-from-anybody, perpetual-pain-in-my-ass spitfire.

Breathlessly, I hopped onto the musty, stinky, adolescent-scented bus and thanked the driver for waiting. I received a grunt for my troubles and made my way to my seat across from Fi.

"Every morning, Morales." Fi snickered. "It's called an alarm clock, ya know."

I waved her off.

She gestured toward my driveway at my piece-of-shit blue

two-tone 1982 Ford Granada. "I still don't understand why we can't just drive to school."

"You *know* why."

"It's not like you started World War III. It was only a speeding ticket."

While Fi droned on, Pop's lecture played in my head. *"If you can't follow the simple rules, how can I trust you with the difficult ones? Give me your keys."*

By 7:45 a.m., we headed to our lockers before our first-period class, AP Bible English 12, with Mrs. Chase. A few hundred teens filled the cavernous hallway with chatter, laughter, and squeaks from rubber-soled shoes on highly polished floors.

Twenty feet or so from my blue painted locker stood my latest obsession and the shiny new object every guy in school wanted on their arm—Navil Laurent. An auburn-haired, hazel-eyed recent arrival from Europe.

Belgium to be specific.

There was something different about her.

Special.

The daughter of a diplomat or something, she gave off a worldly vibe. Elegant. Sophisticated. A Princess Diana-like quality. Beautiful yet approachable. Never one to walk around like her shit didn't stink. Tastefully stylish in her full-length black winter coat with matching leather gloves and blood-red crimson scarf. Like her style, her interests seemed to differ as well.

Word on the street that after attending last summer's *Live Aid* concert at Wembley Stadium in London, she became obsessed with humanitarian organizations like *Amnesty International* and *Human Rights Watch* and their efforts around the world.

Tucked in the crook of her arm were copies of *The New York Times, The Guardian,* and some newspaper called *Le Soir.*

Rumor had it that she wanted to work for one of those human rights groups. Of course, she'd first have to pass AP Calculus and graduate high school, but more on that later.

From my locker, I watched as girls from her clique surrounded her. Hung on to her every word, like ladies-in-waiting, giggled at her wit and sometimes self-effacing comments.

In my six years at this school, from seventh through twelfth grade, I had never seen anyone make this quick an impact. Everyone was enamored by this girl. At least, that's what it felt like. My infatuation blinded me to reality.

But not to her brief glimpse and ever-so-slight smile in my direction. In that moment, her essence cut through the air and straight into my soul. And just as quickly, her attention returned to her new friends. Mid-conversation, Davis Warner, a six-foot-two, blonde-haired, basketball-playing pretty boy approached, flashing his million-dollar, trust-fund smile.

I overheard his singsong greeting. "Navil, how's it going?"

They quietly bantered back and forth. Her friends listened intently. I wished I'd ignored the whole interaction and gone about my business, but I didn't. I couldn't. She mesmerized me. I so wanted to walk up and talk to her.

Slicked back my brown curls. Flashed a crooked smile. Told a quick joke. Heard her laugh. Took in her exotic perfume. Watched her almond-shaped hazel eyes sparkle as she nervously shifted back and forth.

The bell rang, and she dispersed everyone, including Davis, with a chuckle. Before stepping into class, Navil glanced back in my direction, presumably to make sure she still had an audience.

She did.

And as a parting gift, tossed me a warm smile.

"Seriously, dude, you need to ask her out," Fi remarked.

"Don't start."

"I'm just sayin'."

"Pfff . . . like she'd say yes."

She shook her head. "Morales, you're an idiot."

Tell me something I don't know.

I shut my locker and followed Fi to class. Crossing the threshold, I passed through the alluring scent of youth left behind by my European fixation. A spicy blend of roses and something exotic. Reminded me of the cocktails Tía Carolina sipped on while sunbathing on the beach last summer in Puerto Rico.

I quietly scanned the student-filled classroom and found my target seated in the far-back corner. She stared out the back windows, seemingly lost in thought. Golden rays gently painted her porcelain skin. I grew jealous of the sun.

As I took my customary desk, second-row center, I remembered my first encounter with Navil. Fresh in my mind as a warm towel pulled from the dryer on a cold winter morning.

I was the lead student photographer. The school asked me to take yearbook pictures for late-year arrivals, along with the select few who were back for reshoots—like Jacqueline Leigh Woodley, or Jackie, our school newspaper editor and perpetual pain in my ass. She was also Navil's roommate.

Over break, she lost her braces, got contact lenses, and updated her look from frumpy JC Penney Catalog to L.L. Bean preppy, not that it mattered much. Jackie was still obnoxious and had perpetual *RBF*, resting bitch face. If RBF were an Olympic event, she would have taken home the gold.

My next subject, a mousy, new tenth grader from who-knew-where, April Paxton, shifted back and forth on the stool while I focused my lens.

"Okay, look this way," I instructed. "Great, now smile."

She smiled but turned her gaze elsewhere.

Fucking tenth graders.

Annoyed, I traced her glance, and standing there, lost in thought, was an auburn-haired, hazel-eyed stunner, looking out the bay windows just like in class. I couldn't take my eyes off her. The moment I saw her, I knew.

She was the one. Like a Disney princess brought to life. The curtain dust seemingly came to life and swirled around her body. The only things missing were cartoon birds and animals scurrying about.

She had this air of casual confidence, like she knew who she was but was not ready to share it with anyone. Certainly not with a slightly overweight Hispanic photographer. I glanced at the sign-in sheet and spotted her name.

Navil Laurent.

Twelfth Grade.

I turned back to April, took a couple more shots, and called for the next person. Three students and one new teacher later, she was up. My new fixation.

I mispronounced her name. "Navel?"

She rolled her eyes. "That's Nah-*vil.*"

French accent.

Sexy.

"Sorry about that. Why don't you get set while I make some adjustments?"

She removed her black overcoat, revealing a form-fitting, lavender, calf-length dress with matching shoes. Adorning her neck, an elegant strand of white pearls.

After adjusting the lights, I went back and stared through my Nikon camera lens. Gazing back were these orbs, vibrant, full of life, and giving off the impression that they held the secrets of the universe. Those eyes, mixed with the slightest upturned smile, caused my spontaneous reaction.

"Woah," I loudly whispered.

Nearby, students chuckled while Navil arched her shapely brow. My flushed embarrassment placed a brief and wicked smile on her otherwise angelic face. Stunned by the image, I snapped off a few shots and captured the moment for all eternity.

Like an addict, I needed more.

"Don't . . . move," I ordered.

I found my muse. The Sedgwick to my Warhol. Threw caution to the wind and posed her like my personal mannequin. Phil Collins's hit tune, *Sussudio,* played in my head as I snapped away.

"Okay, now look this way. All right, now look down. Good. Smile."

Shorthand developed between us. With a mere hand gesture, she twisted and turned. In that moment, I knew her limits, and she mine.

And aside from Fi, I hadn't connected this fast with anyone. I could have spent hours taking action shots had Jackie not walked over and interrupted the impromptu photo session.

Like fingernails on a blackboard, she hissed, "Wrap it up, *Jimmy Olsen.* Some of us have class."

In the time it took for me to turn and tell Jackie to chill out, Navil had put on her coat and made her way toward the exit. I watched as wisps of auburn hair floated gently behind as she stepped outside the door.

"Thank God," Jackie huffed. "Now hurry up, Ollie, I don't have all day. And remember, get my good side."

You mean, the back of your head?

The second she hopped up onto the stool, I snapped her picture.

"Okay, next," I shouted.

"What do you mean, next? You just spent—"

"*Next*. C'mon, Jackie, people have class, remember?"

"That *better* be a good one," she barked.

Then get a different face.

CHAPTER TWO

After the final bell, I raced to my *Fortress of Solitude,* as I dubbed the photo lab, hung the *Developing Film* sign on the outside of the door and went to work.

And the results were—

Perfect.

Meanwhile, back in class, the second bell rang at 8:10 a.m. Another start of a new day at *The Stony Brook Institute for Higher Learning,* or *SBI,* as students called it.

"Okay, everyone, pens out and books away. Time for a quiz," Mrs. Chase announced over groans. "Hope you finished your last reading assignment."

"Shit, you ready for this?" Fi whispered.

I smiled confidently.

"*Of course,* you are."

As I passed the exam back to Jackie Woodley, I noticed Navil. She glared at the quiz with quiet contempt. Mumbled something under her breath. Must not have read the material.

I scanned twenty questions on *A Separate Peace,* a novel by John Knowles.

Piece of cake.

Thirty-five minutes later, I turned in my quiz, returned to my chair and quietly enjoyed a favorite pastime . . . daydreaming.

Aside from taking pictures, watching Mel Brooks or Burt Reynolds marathons on HBO in my basement with Fi, listening to my favorite radio station, *WBAB*, or sucking down Giuseppe's pizza, nothing was better.

I glanced around the institutionally pale green painted classroom for inspiration. Apart from the stunner in the back corner furrowing her sexy brows, there wasn't much to check out.

"Turn around, Ollie," Jackie quietly hissed.

Especially not that harpy.

After class, Mrs. C handed back my results.

B+.

Meh, good enough.

From my locker, I noticed Navil down the hall. She frowned at her results, crumpled up the paper, and shoved it into her bag.

"I guess she tanked hers," Fi commented over my shoulder.

I shrugged.

"How'd you do?"

"B+. You?"

"An A."

"Wait, *you* got an *A*? But you were all . . ." I made a face.

"And you fall for it every time, Morales." She popped my arm. "See you at lunch."

After the final bell of the day rang, I attempted to escape from my AP Calculus with the ever-loving, ball-busting Professor Michaels. However, . . .

"Excuse me, Mr. Morales, have a moment?" he called out to me.

Like I had a choice?

"Hey, Professor Michaels. What's up?"

"*Hay* is for *horses*, young man. I need your . . . assistance."

"With a picture or something?"

"No, young man, nothing like that. Have you ever . . . tutored?"

"Like, in calculus?"

He sighed, "Yes, Mr. Morales, like in calculus."

"No, but—"

"Well, I think you would do a fine job, as a matter of fact."

Even a blind man could see where this was headed.

Destiny awaited.

The following day after school, as usual, my fellow photogs and I were down in the lab developing film, listening to the Eagles sing *Hotel California* on the boom box while Fi sat on the stain-covered sofa doing homework.

"Ols . . . door," Fi shouted over the din.

"Hey, shut up you guys. Yeah, come in."

The door swung open, and like an ethereal vision, she entered our domain.

Light from the hallway cast a shadow across her face.

All I could see were a pair of piercing hazel eyes.

I wanted to drink them in.

In the background, *Don Henley* sang, "*This could be heaven, or this could be hell.*"

She spotted me. Smiled. Made her approach.

In that moment, I knew—this girl was heaven.

Navil Laurent.

Forever my muse.

The blended scent of teenaged sweat and vinegary developer chemicals caused her to crinkle her freckled nose.

She glanced at the slip in her hand and looked up at me. "Oliver Morales, non?"

The way she pronounced my name, *O-lee-ver Mor-alees.* Her French accent made me sound exotic.

I nodded. "Yep, but everyone calls me Ollie."

"Ollie." She tasted my name for the first time and smiled. "I'm—"

"Navil. I know. We're in—"

"Mrs. Chase's class together."

"Right. Anyway, welcome to—"

She glanced over my shoulder. "Mon Dieu."

She brushed past me toward an eight by ten black and white print sandwiched between posters of David Bowie from his *Modern Love* video and the Police from their gold and blue *Zenyatta Mondatta* album cover hanging on the wall.

"C'est moi," she whispered.

One of the photos from our impromptu photo session. I forgot to take it down. I lowered my head, embarrassed.

She quietly inspected the enlarged print. Traced her slightly upturned lips with the tip of a finger and nodded approvingly.

From there, she moved on to the other prints hanging on the wall. Like a gallery owner, I followed closely behind, watching as she casually admired the various action shots captured during the fall and previous spring.

Soccer superstar Jean Paul Michael, mid-air bicycle-kicking a ball deep into a net. Dylan O'Donnell's bat connecting with a baseball during last year's playoffs against Hampton Bays. A ponytailed B Karlsson tossing up a tennis ball before nailing a winning ace. And Fi throwing a runner out from shortstop as Allison Nilsen watched from the mound after pitching another shutout in softball.

"Did you take all these?"

"Some."

"You have . . . a great eye."

Yours are better.

"Thanks." I smiled.

"They remind me of Bobby Williams or Erwin H. Hagler's pictures."

"You know—"

"Their work? Oui. I especially love Hagler's cowboy prints. So, how do you say—rugged? Realistic."

I nodded. "Yeah, totally. My favorites, though, are Robert Frank and Richard Avedon."

"Ah, so you like well-lit pictures." She smiled.

We stood there, lost in our own private Idaho. Chatted about photography. Even though words passed between us, it was her eyes and smile that spoke volumes. I felt . . . seen. Special. Like I was the only person in a room full of people. There was an intimate casualness in the way she spoke.

A small gesture here. A touch to my bicep or forearm there. We connected, just like during our photoshoot. Like an invisible current flowed from her soul to mine. Held us in place. Forever trapped. I was hers, and she was mine.

Unfortunately, just as we grew closer, Fi's allergies kicked in. Her sneeze dissipated our impromptu moment of closeness like mini marshmallows melting in hot chocolate. I merely turned and shot her a look.

I received a shrug and apologetic *sorry*.

"Oh, hello, Fiona, ça va?" Navil seemingly noticed her for the first time.

In addition to Mrs. C's, the pair shared AP chemistry and gym class.

"Doin'." Fi smiled. "You?"

"Same," Navil replied.

"What are you doin' down here?"

"Right, yes. Professor Michael . . ." She turned to me.

"Said I would help you with Calc?"

"*Oui.*" She nodded.

"Not a problem. If you want, we can work down here." I gestured to the sofa and coffee table, only to receive a scrunched nose. "The smell?"

She nodded.

"Yeah, you eventually get used to it."

"The library?" Fi coughed.

Navil chuckled, "That would work."

I nodded. "Grab yourself a Coke from the fridge while I clean up my stuff."

She squeezed my forearm. "Merci, Ollie."

She grabbed a soda and plopped down next to Fi. The pair chatted away while I cleaned up. Periodically, they glanced my way and giggled. Caused me to feel self-conscious, something I mentioned to Fi later. After wiping down the counter, I tossed Eddie Robbins, a junior and fellow photog, the keys, and asked Navil if she was ready to go.

"Oui."

As we ducked out, Fi cooed, "Have fun."

Fi, I swear to God.

CHAPTER THREE

An orange and crimson sky greeted us as we stepped outside. The temperature dropped as the sun dipped behind the massive oak trees dotting our campus. Navil snuggled into her black winter coat and crimson red scarf.

Her reddened cheeks put a smile on my face for some reason. Maybe it was because I found it cute, or that I was just happy to be this close to my latest fascination.

On our walk over to Goldberg Hall, the two-story home of our science building and library, Navil nonchalantly wrapped a hand around my bicep, steadying herself from slipping on various patches of black ice.

"You don't mind, do you?"

I'd carry you naked through an inferno.

"Nah, I don't mind."

We chitchatted on our way to the library.

"So, what brought you to our school?"

"The usual," she remarked. "What about you? How long have you been here?"

"Forever," I grumbled, and earned the side-eye. "Sorry, I meant since seventh grade. Fi and me both."

She nodded approvingly.

"How do you like it so far?" I asked.

She pursed her slightly chapped lips.

"That good, huh?"

She chuckled as we crossed the street.

"It's just that—" she tucked a strand of auburn locks behind her left ear "—everyone here is so . . . nosy, *non*?"

Given her meteoric rise in popularity, her comment surprised me. Although, with just under 400 students ranging from seventh to twelfth grade, the grapevine tendrils were surprisingly vast.

The moment *fresh meat*, as some called new students, stepped onto campus, the gossipmongers kicked into high gear.

By the time someone reached the dean's office, people like Jackie Woodley had already documented their demographics: where they were from, who their parents were, their net worth, and, most importantly, were they dating anyone.

"I think the only thing people don't know is my blood type."

"Sorry about that," I replied.

"B-positive, by the way."

"I am positive."

"No, my blood type. It's B-positive. You know, just in case."

"Ohhhh . . ."

"*Mon Dieu*, Ollie, are you always so serious?" She elbowed my ribs.

"Me . . . serious? Nah. I'm Mr. Laughs."

She chuckled.

We got to the library and took the elevator to the third floor.

"So, uh, where are you from . . . you know . . . exactly. I mean, you're clearly from Europe, right?

"What gave it away?" She smirked.

"I'd say . . . your attitude," I joked as the doors opened.

She slapped my chest and let out a guffaw. It echoed across the foyer. We stepped into our library. It was modernly designed, spacious and circular—yet functional. It held the traditions often found at prep schools. Columns and rows of floor-to-ceiling mahogany bookshelves filled with first- and second-edition hardcover classics.

Lemon oil-polished wooden tables and chairs strategically placed throughout the floor, along with oversized leather sofas and coffee tables in the center of the room.

"Where do you want to sit?" I asked.

Students were seated everywhere, including people like B Karlsson, the girl from the black-and-white picture in the lab playing tennis. A group seated on the sofa were friends of Navil's from her dorm. The moment they spotted us, they waved her over.

"Do you mind, Ollie?"

"Not at all." I spied an empty table near the windows overlooking the quad. "There's an empty table over there. I'll go set up."

"*Merci*, Ollie. I'm sure they just want to know why I'm here."

With a loser like me, you mean.

She walked over and did the kiss-on-both-cheeks thing while I unloaded my backpack. Navil soon joined me and settled in. Rested her coat and scarf on the empty seat to her right. Her perfume drifted up my nostrils, placed a smile on my face. She looked up at me with her hazel eyes.

"So, what now?" she asked.

I gulped. It was my first time tutoring and didn't want to screw things up. I thought about her crumpled test from Mrs. C's class.

"Do you have a copy of our last test?"

She pursed her lips and handed me the crumpled copy from her bag.

At least she's consistent . . . a D+.

"Ouch."

"Oui."

"Look, it's no big deal."

"If you say so, Ollie." She sighed.

"Let's see where you messed up, and then we'll do tonight's homework."

She patted my forearm. "You're le tuteur."

I'm something, all right.

CHAPTER FOUR

We spent the next hour going over her exam, followed by some homework. We also got to know one another.

"Okay, you see right here. You take this derivative and . . ."

"Mon Dieu, Ollie." She quietly sighed. "I don't know how you remember all this."

"I guess I just have a thing for numbers."

"Most artists do, from what my grand-mère says."

"You think I'm an artist?"

"Oui. Don't you?"

I shrugged. No one had ever called me an artist before. Hell, no one had ever called me anything except *idiot, moron, spic, or nigger.*

"Well, I think you are, and so would Mémé. That's what I call her."

"Pretty name."

"She's a pretty woman, Ollie. Très élégant. And her eyes are full of life . . . of fury."

"Sounds familiar," I smirked.

My compliment flustered her for the first time.

"Thank you, Ollie," she whispered demurely. "I would love to be just like her one day. She's so . . . *mondaine.*"

I furrowed my brow, unsure of her expression.

"How you say . . . worldly," she explained. "You would love her. Everyone adores Mémé."

The crimson sunset that shone through the bay windows reflected in her hazel eyes. Its allure added to the nearly perfect beauty that sat to my left. She spent the next few minutes sharing stories about the matriarch of her family.

"And at Christmas, people come from everywhere for a slice of her Bûche de Noël."

"I'm sorry . . . *bush?*"

She chuckled, "It's the most delicious chocolate cake."

I nodded. "That makes sense."

She spoke with her hands. "It's shaped like a . . . yule log. It is filled with homemade whipped cream and topped with the sweetest Belgian chocolate, meringue mushrooms, and sugared cranberries."

I salivated at her description and glanced out the windows. "Crap."

"Is everything okay?" She followed my gaze.

"Yeah, no. It's my dad." I pointed at the Cadillac that just pulled up.

Her eyes expressed disappointment, "You have to go?"

"Sorry."

She squeezed my hand. "It's okay, Ollie. Can we meet again tomorrow?"

"Absolutely." I smiled. "Same bat time, same bat channel?"

She arched a brow.

I shook my head, "Never mind. Meet here . . . same time?"

"Oui, same bat channel." She chuckled.

I *so* wanted to stay, but knew if Pop waited too long, I would have heard about it all night. I quickly gathered my stuff, said good night, and left, but not before looking back one last time.

The moment I stepped away, her girlfriends surrounded her, no doubt asking about our study session. Lord knows I was about to get the same from Fi, who sat in the back seat of Pop's car.

The passenger door barely closed before she asked, "How'd it go?"

"Went okay." I nonchalantly responded.

Pop chucked me a curious look, "What went well, bub?"

"Hmm? Oh, nothing, Pop."

"Nothing?" Fi chortled. "You're kidding me, right?"

Pop glanced into the rearview. I wrenched my neck to look back at her and received a shit-eating grin.

"Fi . . ." I growled.

"Settle down, Ollie," Pop smirked. "Go on, Fiona."

Like a toddler with a secret, she couldn't wait to share the news. "Ollie has this *huge* crush on this new girl at school, and he just started tutoring her."

Pop looked over at me. "Really, Ollie?"

I mouthed, *You motherfucker*, to Fi before answering Pop. "I guess."

"Well, that's great, bub. Good for you."

"Thanks."

"So, when do we get to meet her?"

I rolled my eyes. "I don't know, Pop."

"You should take her out this weekend," Fi chimed in.

I mouthed to Fi, *I'm going to fucking kill you.*

"You could even use your car if you want," Pop offered.

I gasped. "*Really*, Pop?"

Fi smiled.

"Sure, why not. I think you've been punished long enough, don't you?"

"Uh, yeah, definitely. Thanks, Pop." I beamed brightly.

"Of course, if you get another ticket . . ."

I sighed. "I know, Pop, I know. You're going to get rid of the car."

He smiled flatly. "Exactly. So, what's she like, this girl?"

"Her name's Navil . . ."

We spent the rest of the ride talking about her. By the time we pulled into my driveway, Pop seemed satisfied with the update. He hopped out and went inside while Fi and I hung out in the chilly evening on my driveway.

"Not too long, Ollie. Carolina will have dinner on the table," Pop called as he entered the house.

"Yeah, okay, Pop," I replied before turning to Fi. "What the hell was *that*?"

"What are you talking about?"

"The car. Ollie has a crush . . ." I mimicked. "I can't believe you blabbed."

"Hey, you should be thanking me."

"Really?"

"You got your car back, didn't you?"

"I suppose, but still . . ."

"Whatever. You'll get over it."

"I guess."

"Are you guys meeting again tomorrow?"

"Heck yeah," I replied. "In the library."

"Good." She looked at her watch. "I've gotta get inside. Get dinner going for Gramps and me."

"What're you making?" I asked as she walked away.

"Meatloaf," she called over her shoulder. "Call me later?"

"Yep."

I got my car back!

CHAPTER FIVE

Modern Day

Dressed in PPE, the ever-cheerful Delphine entered. "How are we feeling today, Mr. Morales?"

The smart-ass in me wanted to flip her off, but I know she's only doing her job. It wasn't her fault I was stuck in this lousy bed with a tube shoved down my throat. I had others to thank for that. Plus, I was taught to be nice to those caring for me.

I grunted.

"Are we in pain?"

I nodded.

"Well, we can't have our favorite patient in distress, can we? Let me check your vitals first, then we'll deal with your pain, okay?"

Delphine checked me over, head to toe, every crack, crease, and crevasse. It was less invasive than the first few times, but still my least favorite part of my stay.

While entering notes into her tablet, she stated, "I do have some good news."

I looked up.

"We're taking you off the ventilator today."

I gave her a thumbs-up and pointed toward the wall clock.

"Oh, what time?" she asked. "Mmm . . . probably within the hour."

I smiled.

"Unfortunately, though . . ."

My smile dropped.

" . . . this means I can't give you anything for the pain at the moment, since we're going to need you somewhat . . . lucid."

I rolled my eyes and tried to stop my leg from shaking.

"I know. I'm sorry. We're going to have to tough it out for a little while longer."

We?

"I'll see you around four thirty, okay?"

What felt like an eternity later, Delphine arrived with my kid brother in tow, another nurse, and a respiratory therapist.

Jaime came to my side. "Ready to get that thing out?"

I gave him a thumbs-up. The team positioned themselves around my bed. I felt anxious. Without warning, beads of sweat dripped down my forehead. My heart pounded like a jackhammer. The monitors began to wail.

"Doctor Morales?" Delphine called out.

I clamped my eyes shut.

Jaime yelled at me over the noise, "Ollie, we need you to calm down."

"Doctor Morales . . ."

"Get me the morphine," Jaime ordered.

"But Doctor . . ."

"Get me the goddamn . . . You know what? I'll get it myself."

Air . . . I need . . .

A back spasm hit me hard. A muted scream of pain.

"Get out of the way," Jaime ordered.

A warm rush.

What the hell is happe . . .

I blinked myself awake, still in a fog. Noticed I'm no longer on the ventilator. I heard snoring. I glance to my right. Asleep in a lounge chair, an unmasked Jaime. Drool dripped down his unshaven mug.

I tossed an empty Styrofoam cup at him. Hit his chest.

"Oh, hey, you're up."

He yawned. Wiped the sludge from his face. Stretched as he came to my side. Planted a quick, wet kiss on my forehead.

"You really scared us for a second there."

"Sorry."

"It's okay."

"What happened?"

He looked away. "I . . . don't know."

He's the world's worst liar.

I grunted his name, "Jaime."

"I think . . . you had . . . a panic attack."

Surprised, I chucked him a look.

He pulled up a chair. "Look, Ollie, I'm no shrink . . ."

No shit.

"But have you ever thought about seeing someone . . . you know . . . professionally?"

"Like a hooker?" I joked. "You do know who I'm married to, right?"

"You're an idiot." He shook his head. "I'm trying to be serious here, Ollie."

"Jaime . . ."

He leaned in all doctor-like and began a lecture I'd heard a million times.

"First of all, you eat like a fifteen-year-old . . ."

Diet . . . check . . .

". . . and when was the last time you took a walk, for like, fifteen minutes?"

Exercise . . . check . . .

He pointed at my body. "You've been stabbed, shot . . ."

Check…

" … and now nearly beaten to death. Broken leg. Punctured lung. A bruised heart."

And check…

"Don't you think it's time to hang up the camera?"

"And get like … a real job, you mean?"

"What about going back to the White House?"

I laughed and hurt my throat.

"Aren't you tired of chasing ghosts?"

I hissed, "I'm not chasing—"

"All I'm saying is, I'm worried about you."

"I … know."

"We all are." The familiar new voice put a smile on my face.

"There she is," I replied. "How's my favorite sister-in-law?"

"You mean your *only* sister-in-law." Cheryl kissed Jaime hello.

"Same difference."

"How's he doing?" she asked before grabbing my chart.

He threw his hands up. "Ask him."

"Ollie?"

"I'm fine, *Doctor* Morales."

What's worse than having two doctors in your immediate family? Try having three. The pair met in medical school. She's a blonde-haired, blue-eyed Argentinian endocrinologist. Specialized in something called Addison's disease and spoke perfect English, something that impressed my wife, Pop, and Tía Carolina.

In other words, she was damn-near perfect.

"He had a panic attack while we were trying to remove his ventilator," Jaime informed her.

"It *wasn't* a panic attack."

The pair ignored me.

"To be honest, it makes sense. We surrounded his bed—" He began to pace. " . . . it probably brought back memories of his . . . incident."

Is that what we're calling it now?

"Maybe we *should have* given him something beforehand. You know, to keep him calm."

"So, why didn't you?" she asked. "I thought that was normal protocol?"

"I don't know. I guess I just thought . . . he could handle it. That he was . . . okay."

She held his hand. "It's all these hours we're putting in. It's a wonder we're thinking straight."

Fifty layers of PPE couldn't hide his embarrassment or their exhaustion.

"Hey," I grunted. "It's okay. I'll be . . . okay."

His cellphone alarm went off. "I've got rounds."

"I can stay for a bit." Cheryl kissed Jaime before grabbing a chair.

"Delphine will stop by and take care of you."

"Take care of me?" I quirked a playful brow. "You know Cheryl's right there."

"You're a moron," a weary Jaime chuckled. "Later, Ols."

"Later, James."

As the door closed, Cheryl informed me, "Oh, I got ahold of your wife . . ."

Oh boy.

CHAPTER SIX

I t's been two days, and my throat still felt like shit. My voice made me sound like a poor man's Demi Moore, all raspy. Jaime joked that the nurses found it sexy. I thought it was annoying, but at least I got out of the ICU.

Thanks to the post-pandemic protocols, my semi-famous wife was stuck overseas in Australia. Her TV show was on hiatus for a month, so she used the time and her celebrity status to visit the kids. Her plan was to spend a couple weeks visiting our youngest, Anne-Marie, in Australia, who was there working on her bachelor's in art history at the University of Sydney.

From there, she was going to fly to Denmark to see our son, Gabriel. His second year of medical school at the University of Copenhagen. Unlike his uncle and grandfather, his area of focus was internal medicine, but they didn't care. There was another medical doctor in the family.

Between the two kids, I found keeping track of the time zones a constant struggle, and it seemed I inevitably end up calling at the most inopportune time, like when they slept.

Anyway, when my wife heard about my incident, she tried leaving the country, but because of their strict protocols, she was stuck in quarantine. And even though Pop, Jaime, and Cheryl visited often, I still felt alone.

Also, I couldn't believe I got stuck sharing a room with someone. The dude, whoever he was, desperately needed a sleep apnea machine or pillow shoved over his face. If he snored any harder, he was going to suck the marrow from my bones. I couldn't wait to get the hell out of this joint.

>Knock, knock<

"Come in," my neighbor shouted.

Two guys in N95 masks and power suits entered. The lead wore a navy-blue pinstripe blazer, muted red tie, brown leather wingtips, and slicked-back, salt-and-pepper hair. Behind him was another guy in a similar outfit. The only exception was an evil glint, shiny bald head, and large manila envelope under his armpit. They didn't need to hand me their business cards. I knew who they were the moment they slithered into the room.

With a quick scan, they found their mark.

Yours truly.

Salt-and-Pepper came to my bedside. "Mr. Morales? Oliver?"

"Guilty," I whispered.

He went to shake my hand before awkwardly switching to a fist bump at the last moment. "Sorry. I keep forgetting the protocol."

I ignored his faux pas. "How can I help you?"

"Is there someplace we can go that's a little more . . . private?"

I pointed to the cast on my leg. "Not really."

He gestured to his partner to draw the curtain between my neighbor and me. It allowed a semblance of privacy, even though my neighbor heard everything we discussed.

Salt-and-Pepper pulled over a chair and took up residence at my bedside, while Baldy stood watch behind him and glared. Thank God for fluorescent lighting. Otherwise, the sheen from his forehead would have blinded me. Salt-and-Pepper leaned forward.

Lifted his mask and began his spiel. "We're here representing . . ."

The global media conglomerate I worked for wanted me to sign off on paperwork shielding them from any litigation that may have arisen from my recent on-the-job injuries.

The still-masked Baldy handed me a thick, yellow-highlighted document and Montblanc pen while Salt-and-Pepper stated, "If you could sign here, here, and here, we'd appreciate it."

I held the pen and blinked at the pair.

"Don't sign a thing," my neighbor coughed.

"Excuse us, sir, but please mind your own business," Baldy remarked back.

"Hey kid, I don't know what they're trying to get you to sign, but I'd tell them to fuck off."

Just as Baldy began to reply, Jaime entered the room. "Can I help you?"

Salt-and-Pepper replaced his mask and stood. "It's all right, Doctor . . . ?"

"Morales, as in . . ." Jaime pointed, "*his* brother."

Guilt oozed from their pores.

"Who are you, and what do you need?"

"We're just here checking on . . ."

"Bullshit. They're . . ." my roommate coughed . . ." scumbag attorneys."

Jaime's eyes flared.

"And they're trying to get him to sign something."

"Really?" Jaime squinted.

Salt-and-Pepper gets all syrupy. "Doctor Morales—"

"Save it." My brother then gestured toward the door. "Get out."

Baldy glared as the man behind the curtain laughed.

Salt-and-Pepper pleaded, "Listen, this will only take a moment, and—"

"You heard the man." More coughing. "Hit the bricks."

Jaime held the door open.

"Fine. "We'll be back at a more convenient time," Salt-and-Pepper stated.

Baldy, in the meantime, retrieved the paperwork and pen from my hands. I smiled as my kid brother gave the bum's rush to the pair. After the door closed, Jaime ducked behind the curtain. Thanked my nosy neighbor.

"Thank you, Judge Watson."

"Think nothing of it," he wheezed. "You'd be surprised at the nonsense I see in my courtroom. When it comes to lawyers, I agree with Shakespeare."

The judge began to cough uncontrollably, and from behind the curtain, I watched a silhouette of my brother administer care. I heard him pull over a chair and adjust the judge's breathing apparatus.

"That's it. Slow and steady breaths," Jaime soothed.

After a few minutes, a nurse entered, walked past my bed, and took over for my brother, who slipped from behind the curtain and came to my bedside.

"Hey," he greeted.

"Hey."

"How're you feeling?" He yawned.

"How am *I* feeling? How are *you* feeling?"

He waved off my comment, brushed his hair back before melting into the chair recently occupied by Salt-and-Pepper. I'd seen wounded soldiers in Afghanistan in better shape.

"Are you sure you're okay?" I asked.

"Yeah, just . . ."

"Tired?"

Without warning, there was a knock on the door. A nurse holding a tablet. She spotted my brother in the chair and walked over.

"Excuse me, Dr. Morales?"

"Hey, Penny, what's up?" He took the proffered tablet.

No rest for the weary.

CHAPTER SEVEN

1986

I t'd been about three weeks since I began tutoring Navil, and she was doing great. She'd caught up and was ready for next week's mid-terms. At least, I thought so. She, on the other hand ...

"I'm going to fail." Navil sighed.

"You're *not* going to fail." I handed her assignments to her. "Yesterday, you got a ninety-two. On this one, you got a ninety-eight."

"Sounds to me like you're kicking ass," Fi chimed in.

"Yeah, Navil, I don't know why you're worrying so much," Alli said.

Soon, everyone around the table offered their opinions, which was another issue. We'd suddenly become the *popular* table. What started as a twosome blossomed into a too-many-some. By the middle of our second week, Fi joined us.

I think, in part, to check on my progress with Navil, which was intrusive but manageable. She kept to herself for the most part, busting my balls periodically to keep me on my toes, as she later told me.

By the end of that week, a pair of Navil's friends from the dorm joined as well— Ginny Collins, a junior and all-star softball pitcher from Alabama , and her best friend, Allison (Alli) Nilsen, a senior and tennis player from Minnesota. Like Navil, they struggled with calculus, so she offered my services without my permission.

"As my grand-mère says, *when people need help, you help them.*"

It bothered me, but what was I going to say? *No?* Soon, we were about a dozen strong. Some were there for tutoring assistance, some to catch up on homework, some to gossip, like her roommate Jackie Woodley, and others, just to hang out at the *cool* table.

"Okay, guys, I think she gets your point," I commented.

"You know what you need?" Fi asked as heads turned.

"What?" Navil replied.

"A night out," Fi replied. "Hey, dumbass."

"Yes?" I sighed.

"Are we still doing that Giuseppe's pizza and Mel Brooks marathon this weekend?"

My eyes grew the size of saucers. "Yeah . . . why?"

"Perfect. Navil . . ."

Fi . . .

"Are you busy Saturday night?"

Fi-i-i-i . . .

"No."

"Great. It's settled. You're joining us."

Navil turned to me. "It does sound like fun. You don't mind, do you, Ollie?"

Those eyes. Those *goddamn* eyes. They were like hazel orbs. Drew me in like a mosquito to a sweaty, fat kid.

How could I say no?

Not that I wanted to.

"Yeah, no, it's okay," I whispered. "You *sure* you want to come?"

Navil nodded.

"Great. It's a date," Fi said as I continued to stare deeply.

"Bon." Navil smiled. "It's a date."

Date?

I sprung out of bed first thing Saturday morning without Tía Carolina's usual umpteenth prodding. I cleaned my room, put away my clothes, made my bed, or at least my version of it, vacuumed my carpet, took out my trash, and sprayed the shit out of my room with Lysol.

And the look of shock on Tía Carolina's face?

Priceless.

I didn't stop there. After finishing my room, I hit the basement. I swept the floor, put away Jaime's Legos, neatened up the VHS video collection, and filled another garbage bag full of junk. It took me a while, but by midday, both were, as Tía Carolina put it, presentable. Pop's interrogation began the moment I plopped down on the couch for lunch.

"So, what's going on, bub?"

I bit into my peanut butter and jelly sandwich. "Nothing, why?"

"Nothing, hmm? So, you just had the sudden urge to clean?"

"I guess." I swallowed.

"Uh-huh." His eyes narrowed. "This wouldn't have anything to do with that girl you're tutoring, would it?"

I stopped mid-bite. "What? No. Why would you say that?"

"Mm-hmm. Hey, aren't you having Fi over tonight for some movie marathon thing?"

I put the sandwich down on my paper plate. "Yeah."

"So just Fi then, right?" He prodded. "No one else joining you?"

I silently stared at my lunch.

"I guess it'll be okay that I join you? You know how much I love Mel Brooks."

"Pop . . ." I began.

"And if *History of the World, Part One* is on, I can sing along to *The Inquisition*."

I threw my hand up and stood, "Jesus, *fine*, you win, all right? Yes, Navil is coming over, too. Happy now?"

He smiled. "Well, why didn't you say so?"

I grumbled under my breath as I stormed off, "I didn't think I had to."

"Sorry, what was that?"

I turned around. "Nothing."

"I'm just glad to see your room clean for a change. I imagine your aunt is too."

I wanted to say something back but didn't. I was annoyed. Not stupid.

"We'll try and stay out of your hair tonight," he informed me. "And Ollie, remember . . ."

I flatly stared back.

"No . . . hanky-panky."

I hate my life.

"It's good to be the king." He smiled.

CHAPTER EIGHT

Here was the plan. I'd swing by school around five, pick up Navil, hit Giuseppe's for the pizza, and be home by six in time to kick off our first movie, *Young Frankenstein,* a black-and-white classic comedic masterpiece based on the Mary Shelley novel, followed by either *Blazing Saddles* or *History of the World, Part One.*

By 4:45 p.m., I headed out the door and ran into Fi, who wanted to ride shotgun, just in case I said or did something stupid.

"Fine, but you're sitting in the back seat when we pick her up."

That night, it felt like the universe was against me. First, I hit every red light on my way to school, making me late picking Navil up. Second, she wasn't alone when I arrived. Waiting with her on the steps of the auditorium were three other girls—Ginny, Alli, and my smiling nemesis, Jackie Woodley.

So much for this being a date.

"You don't mind, do you?" Navil asked as I held the door open for her.

"He doesn't mind, do you, Ollie?" Jackie interjected.

"No, not at all." I glared.

The three girls hopped into the back seat while Navil and Fi slid into the front. The moment Jackie got in she turned into her usual pain in the ass.

"Can you turn up this song? It's my favorite."

"Can you turn down the heat?"

"Ginny, where'd your boyfriend fly to this weekend?"

"Alli, can you roll down the window?"

It felt like Chinese water torture, just one comment after the other.

Then she leaned forward and sniffed my neck. "Eww, what are you wearing?"

I wanted to drive us into a telephone pole, and almost did till Navil snuggled close and commented she liked how I smelled.

"You would," Jackie scoffed.

At the pizzeria, I held the door open for everyone and entered behind Navil. I took the opportunity to enjoy the view, and she didn't disappoint. The way her jeans hugged her body, and the way she moved . . . like she was gliding on glass.

Tony, the mustachioed proprietor and maestro of all things pizza, greeted me when we came to the counter.

"Hey, there he is. Whatcha say, kid? Here for your order?"

"Hey, Tony. Yeah, but I think we're going to need a few more pies."

"Not a problem," he replied, giving Navil a brief once-over.

"Oh, uh, Tony, this is Navil."

"How ya doing, sweetheart?" He smiled.

"Bonjour, Tony."

Based on his expression, I could tell he liked her accent.

I leaned in. "She's from Belgium."

"Ya don't say?"

"Yeah, it's in Europe."

"I *know* where Belgium is. I served overseas, remember?" He pointed to a grease-stained picture from his youth during his time in the U.S. Army.

"Sorry, Tony."

"So, how many more pies are ya gonna need?"

I turned and asked Navil and Fi, who joined us at the counter.

"What do you think? Two? Three?"

"Why don't you get three, just in case," Fi replied, and Navil nodded.

Thirty minutes and five pies later, we pulled into my driveway. I grabbed the pizzas from my trunk because, heaven forbid, anyone in the backseat got grease on their designer jeans. Tía Carolina and Jaime stood watch at the front door while Bella leaped about barking. My brother bum-rushed Fi the moment she stepped inside.

"*Fi!*" Jaime bear-hugged her while Bella continued barking.

"Bella, settle down," Pop chastised as he joined them.

I went straight to the dining room table and put the boxes down while Fi took care of the introductions. After the obligatory nice to meet you's, Pop joined me.

"I thought it was only going to be you, Fiona, and that girl?"

"So did I," I grumbled.

"Well, did you have enough cash?"

"Yeah."

"You *sure*?" He grabbed his wallet and held out a twenty.

I snatched it. "Thanks, Pop."

Navil stuck her head into the room. "Ollie, do you need help?"

It was like the world stopped, and everyone else disappeared.

"We're good." I smiled.

In the distance I heard Pop say, "I'm just going to grab a few slices."

Navil came to my side.

"Hungry?"

"Oui, starving."

As he left, Pop shot me a thumbs-up and mouthed, *Wow*.

I ignored him.

I didn't know what smelled better that night. The hot, delicious scent of perfectly blended marinara and pepperoni, or the fresh-faced girl with a high ponytail and exposed neck, which seemingly begged for me to unleash my fangs and feed on her like a vampire in desperate need of nourishment.

As if she were reading my mind, Navil tilted her head slightly, almost like she was inviting me in to sample the merchandise.

She took my hand. "Thanks for letting everyone come tonight."

"Sure, no problem." I smiled.

As we chatted, Tía Carolina entered the room with my kid brother in tow, followed by the girls.

"The fridge downstairs is full of soda," she informed us as she and Jaime grabbed slices.

"Gracias, Tía."

The girls filled their paper plates with pizza and followed me to a cleaner-than-I-left-it basement.

"The fridge is over there. Make yourself at home," I said, setting up the movie.

After getting sodas, Alli and Ginny took the lounge chairs situated on either side of our big, comfy couch while Fi sat in the beanbag chair next to the coffee table. The only two options left were oversized throw pillows on the area rug, or the aforementioned couch.

Care to guess where Jackie sat?

CHAPTER NINE

Seated on the middle cushion, a smiling Jackie turned to Navil. "You don't mind, do you?"

It pissed me off.

The ever-friendly Navil just smiled back. "Not at all."

After jamming the cassette into the VCR and hitting play, I joined the pair on the couch. The moment I got comfortable, Jackie slid closer.

Are you fucking kidding me?

Her annoyance didn't stop there.

"Oh, this movie's in black and white?" Jackie asked.

"Yeah, shhh . . ." I replied.

"I thought we were watching a Mel Brooks movie?"

"*Young Frankenstein is* a . . ."

"And this is supposed to be . . ."

"*Jack* . . ."

"Jackie?" Navil interjected. "Why don't you and I clean up?"

"Yeah, okay."

The girls hopped off the couch and gathered everyone's trash.

"I'll come with . . ."

Navil placed a hand on my shoulder and smiled. "Stay. Enjoy the movie."

"But . . ."

"It's okay." Her warm hand caressed my face. "I've seen it already."

Not with me, you haven't.

As the movie played, Alli excused herself and went to the bathroom. I kept glaring at the stairs, praying for Navil to return, solo if possible. That's when Fi joined me on the sofa.

"You okay?" she whispered.

"Peachy," I grumbled.

"Sorry."

I pursed my lips.

"Why did she have to come?"

She rubbed my arm.

I pointed to the TV. "Ah, man, she's missing the best parts."

As I sat there stewing in self-misery, I heard Bella barking outside. There was something different about it. Unusual. Like a Timmy-fell-in-a-well kind of bark.

"I'll be right back."

As I shut the door behind me, I overheard horses whinny from the basement TV, letting me know that Cloris Leachman just delivered a favorite line, "I am Frau Blücher."

With a sigh, I made my way through an empty family room to the sliding glass door overlooking the patio.

By the pool stood a worried Navil with Jaime at her side, along with a barking Bella. Pop, meanwhile, was bent over someone, giving them what looked like CPR. The drapes blocked my view, and all I could make out were a pair of jeans and sneakers.

What the hell?

I ripped the door open, ran out, and found Pop administering mouth-to-mouth to Jackie, who lay in a pool of blood, with Tía Carolina delivering chest compressions. I'd never seen anything like it before.

I panicked and yelled, "What happened?"

"Get back inside and call 9-1-1," Pop ordered, "and take your brother and that damn dog with you."

I scooped up Bella and took Jaime inside. Within minutes, pandemonium broke out. Emergency services were soon in my backyard, caring for Jackie. Police officers sat in my family room, taking statements from Pop, Tía Carolina, and Navil. The rest of us remained in the dining room, trying our best to eavesdrop on the conversations.

"We were taking the trash out, and the dog wanted to ... how do you say, go out and do its business, non?" Navil explained.

"Go on," an authoritative voice replied.

"Jackie threw a ball for the dog to retrieve, and it went into the pool."

What a fucking idiot.

"I told her to leave it alone, but she ignored me."

"What happened next?"

"I'm not sure. I was playing with the dog." She sounded nervous. "I heard her scream, and when I turned around, I saw her on the ground ... bleeding. That's when I yelled for help."

"Unbelievable," I scoffed.

"Shut up, Ollie," Fi chided. "She could really be hurt."

I slumped back into my chair.

After the interviews, Pop drove to University Hospital—where they transported Jackie—while I took a visibly upset Navil back to school, along with Ginny and Alli, who sat with her in the backseat, consoling her.

The moment I parked the car in the quad, the three girls made a beeline straight to their dorm. I tried to say something, but they barely acknowledged my presence.

I watched as they went inside. Instead of standing around, I got back into my car, drove home, and went straight to bed.

With a pit in my stomach and a heaviness on my heart, I drifted off that evening with images of Navil holding back her tears. I so wished I could hold her. Comfort her. Be there for her.

Why the hell did Jackie have to come tonight?

CHAPTER TEN

P op's crow's feet were more pronounced that morning. He slumped into his chair while Jaime and I ate scrambled eggs and crispy bacon.

Tía poured my dad some coffee. "How's the girl?"

"Thankfully, she only needed a few stitches and has a mild concussion."

"So, she'll be okay?" I asked.

"She'll be fine. It looked like she got hit in the head with something."

That's weird.

"Any ideas?"

"Beats me, Pop. I was in the basement, remember?"

"I'm going to grab a shower. I've got to head back to the hospital later for rounds. I'll look in on her while I'm there."

Crunching on bacon, I thought of Navil. I knew they held Sunday chapel at school but didn't know what time or when it ended. Plus, it's not like I could simply pick up the phone and call her.

There weren't any phones in the dorm rooms. The girl's dorm shared two pay phones between approximately four dozen girls. You're lucky you got through on a weeknight. On a Sunday, it was damn near impossible, regardless of the time.

By midday, after watching *Abbott and Costello*, I called Fi.

"Whatcha doin'?" she asked.

"Nuthin'. You?"

"Same. Watching TV and doing homework."

"Gotcha."

"Any news on Jackie?"

"Yeah. Pop said she has a concussion but will be okay. He just went back to the hospital and said he'd check on her between rounds. It's just . . ."

"What?"

"Why did she have to come over last night, Fi?"

"It's not like she was looking to get hurt, Ols."

"Yeah, I know, but still."

"But still what?"

"That bitch ruins everything. Plus, she can't stand me."

Fi laughed.

"What's so funny?"

"You don't know?"

"Know what?"

"Oliver . . ."

"Fiona . . ."

"How can anyone be so clueless?"

"Clueless about what?"

"About Jackie."

"What about Jackie?"

"Ollie, she's had a crush on you since like tenth grade."

"Ewww . . ."

"Everyone knows."

"Well, she's got a stupid way of showing it. Always bossing me around. Writing crap in that notebook of hers."

Fi chuckled, "I'm not saying she's smooth about it, but she does like you. Also, she writes stuff down because she wants to be a reporter one day."

"Whatever."

"So, what are you going to do about it?"

"About what? Jackie?"

"Yeah."

"*Nothing.* Lois Lane doesn't end up with Jimmy Olsen, remember?"

Fi laughed.

"Besides, I like Navil."

"Oh, trust me, I think the entire planet knows that at this point."

"What's *that* supposed to mean?"

"Nothing, Ollie, nothing."

"No, go ahead. Say it?"

"Ols, look."

"Look what? She's out of my league? She's too pretty for me? Too good for me? You don't think I know all this?"

"I never said that."

"What is it, then?"

"It's just whenever you're around her, you get all . . . I don't know . . . intense."

"What do you mean, in*tense*?"

"Like the whole world around you vanishes."

"And?"

"What do you mean, and?"

"*Why* is that bad? I'm crazy about her, Fi."

Her subsequent sigh annoyed me, "I've got to go."

"Ols . . ."

"Talk to ya later." I hung up.

I brooded and stared at the phone. I wanted to talk to Navil. See her. Make sure she was okay. And while I had a better chance of hitting the lottery than getting through on the pay phones, I rolled the dice.

To my surprise, I got through on my third attempt.

" . . . so, all she has are some stitches and a concussion."

"Mon Dieu, that's wonderful news, Ollie."

"I thought you'd be happy." I smiled. "Are you doing okay?"

"Oui. I'm fine. I was just so worried about Jackie, you know?"

"I get it."

"One minute she's standing there, the next . . ."

"Must have been scary."

"Very. And all that blood."

"It *was* pretty nasty. I took some pictures this afternoon while Tía Carolina sprayed down the pool area."

"That woman is a saint," she replied. "Reminds me of my grand-mère."

"What are you doing this afternoon?"

"Nothing special. You?"

"Same."

Hmm . . .

"You know, we do have pizza left over from last night," I informed her. "If you want to, uh, you know, come over. We can eat some pizza, do our homework, and even finish watching the rest of the movie."

"That does sound like fun, but won't your father mind?"

"Nah, he's cool."

"Well, I will have to get permission from my dorm parents."

"Okay. Want to call me back?"

"Oui. Are you *sure* it's okay?"

"Go get permission and call me back."

An hour later, Navil and I settled in the basement. The Police's *Synchronicity* on the record player. Chilled Cokes and warm slices on the coffee table. Jaime was off somewhere playing or watching TV, Pop was still at the hospital, and Tía Carolina was busy doing laundry before heading out for her Sunday evening canasta with friends.

About an hour and a half later, Navil and I wrapped up our

respective homework assignments, along with our lunch, and settled onto the couch to watch the rest of *Young Frankenstein*. She grabbed the blanket off the back of the couch and snuggled in next to me while I sat there, not knowing where to put my arm.

Should I wrap it around her shoulder?

Do I rest it in my lap?

How 'bout I go neutral and rest it on the back of the couch.

Argh, why is this so tough?

CHAPTER ELEVEN

Navil lay there enjoying the movie while I continued with my arm struggle. I felt so stupid. So inexperienced. I wished I could pause time and call someone like Ernie, my neighbor across the street.

The dude was about a decade older than me and cooler than an October morning. A car mechanic by trade, he owned a shop in Nassau County and worked on exotic imports like Mercedes Benz and BMWs.

But his pride and joy? A fathom-green 1969 Stingray Corvette convertible that sat in his home garage, so clean you could lick ice cream off the floor.

Every Friday night, like clockwork, he'd race home, change out of his mechanic's wear, and hop into his Corvette. He'd hit the town, searching for his next conquest, as he'd put it.

Sure enough, Saturday mornings, you'd see him drive off with a hot blonde or brunette wearing their previous evening's garb, presumably heading off to the girl's house or car parked overnight in a bar parking lot.

I once overheard Fi's Gramps tell Pop at a summer block party, "That man could charm the skin off a snake."

He wasn't just a ladies' man, Ernie was also one of the nicest guys on the block. A prince of the neighborhood. Like that Billy Joel song, always ready with a smile or a joke. And whenever he saw Fi, he'd tease her, which I loved but drove her crazy, although deep down, I think she liked the attention.

"You okay?" Navil looked up and whispered.

"Hmm? Yeah."

"You're not bored with me already, are you?

I jerked my head back. "*What*? No."

"Just checking." She giggled.

We sat in silence and watched the movie. Well, she did. I kept staring at the top of her head, which was now nestled on my chest. The mixed scent of *Herbal Essences* shampoo and hairspray filled my nostrils, as did the warmth of her body pressed comfortably into mine.

Even though we both laughed while watching Gene Wilder and his lovely assistant, Inga, battle an unruly bookcase, I kept thinking: *What would Ernie do? What would Ernie do?*

I think Navil grew tired of my lack of moxie.

Mid-laughter, she nonchalantly rose from my chest and sat upright, continuing to chuckle along to the movie. Like a faucet slowly shutting off, her laughter died down.

Hearty laughs became faint giggles.

Giggles to subtle glances.

Glances to a fiery stare.

My lopsided smile.

I attempted to lean back to take her in.

She wouldn't have it.

Her manicured fingers pulled me forward.

Our lips were inches apart.

The scent of spicy marinara fresh on her breath blended with her sweet perfume.

Her head tilted left, as did mine.

I closed my eyes and leaned forward.

Her lips brushed mine.

"Hey, Ols, you guys down there?" Fi called from the top of the stairs.

You've got to be kidding me.

CHAPTER TWELVE

Navil sat back, snickering in disbelief.

"Yeah, come on down," I groaned.

"Hey, guys."

"Bonjour, Fiona."

"Oh, watching the rest of the movie?"

"Something like that." I received an elbow from Navil. "What's up?"

"Nothing. I was bored, so I figured I'd come over."

Of course you did.

Fi grabbed a soda from the fridge and hopped onto the beanbag chair before bringing up the events from the previous evening.

I paused the movie.

"It all happened so fast," Navil explained. "One moment she's standing there, the next—"

"You heard her scream and fall down," Fi chimed in.

"What's weird is when I was out there taking pictures, I couldn't find any black ice or anything."

"What the hell caused her to slip?" Fi asked.

Navil shrugged.

"And all that blood. It took a while for Tía Carolina to spray it down."

"Well, at least Jackie's okay, non?" She turned to me. "Just a concussion, oui?"

"That and some stitches," I added.

The more we talked about the incident, the more my bur-geoning photojournalistic sixth sense kicked in. I felt like I missed something but left it alone for the moment. I didn't want to ask questions I was afraid to have answered.

Fi hung out, and I drove Navil back to school.

"Thank you for a nice afternoon."

"Any time."

"Walk me to my dorm?"

"Sure." I smiled.

At the front door, I received a warm hug and a kiss on the cheek.

"Oh . . . uh . . . thanks."

She smiled.

"And, sorry about . . . well . . . you know."

"Next time." She caressed my face.

Over dinner, I asked, "So . . . how's Jackie doing, Pop?"

"Better, Ollie. She'll be back at school this week. Her parents came up from Maryland. Nice folks."

"That's cool," I replied. "But she's . . . you know . . . okay?"

His eyes narrowed. "Yes, Oliver. Why the concern?"

"I don't know, Pop. Something about this doesn't seem . . . right."

He leaned forward on his elbows. "What about it doesn't seem right?"

The problem was, I didn't know. My only clues were my gut feelings. And, while they've served me well as a professional photojournalist, at eighteen, I was way out of my depth.

I put my fork down and looked out the back window. "I don't know."

"Well, when you figure it out, let me know, okay? In the meantime, stop worrying so much and pass me the salt."

"All right, Pop."

By midweek, life went back to normal. A moderately bandaged Jackie returned to school, her bitch-on-wheels self. I walked around like a lovestruck pup pining after Navil. And Fi busted my balls.

In class, I checked on Jackie and apologized for her injury. She damn near bit my head off.

"Turn around and go screw yourself, Ollie," she snapped. "You're probably just happy that my parents didn't sue you."

"What? No, I'm not. I mean, I am, but no, I was worried about you."

"I could tell by all the times you came to visit me in the hospital."

"Okay, everyone, turn to page . . ." Mrs. C announced.

I turned back around, followed Mrs. C's instructions, but thought about what Jackie just said, and she was wrong. Yes, it's true. I didn't visit her in the hospital. But I wasn't the only one.

No one did, except Pop, and from what I heard, the dean and the headmaster. Hell, not even the school nurse stopped to check on her.

I was lost in thought when Jackie leaned forward and whispered, "By the way, I know you were the one who threw that rock."

Her comment twisted my spine.

"*What?*"

"Oliver, is there a problem?" Mrs. C asked.

"Um, no ma'am. Sorry."

I ignored Jackie and paid attention to class, but her comment pissed me off, gnawing my insides like that creature from the movie *Alien*.

After class, I followed Jackie to her locker and confronted her.

"What's your problem?"

"This." She pointed to her head wound. "You hit me in the head with a rock."

"You're out of your mind. I didn't—"

"Yeah, right."

"Seriously, Jackie, I thought—"

"What? That I slipped on something?"

"Yeah."

"You know what?" She searched for the right words but came up empty. A first for her. "Just . . . leave me alone."

She slammed her locker shut, stormed off, and left me speechless. I watched as she plowed her way down the hall with zero regard for anyone in her path, which pissed me off further.

Navil tapped my shoulder. "Are you o—"

I waved her off and ran after Jackie.

There's no way I'd let her have the last word on this.

"Jackie . . ." I shouted as she turned the corner.

She stopped and turned around. "What?"

"Look. I'm sorry you got hurt, I really am, but I—"

"Well, if it wasn't you, then it was probably . . ." she pointed at Navil, staring at us from down the hall. " . . . that *French* girlfriend of yours."

Her accusation reverberated down the hallway.

"She was the only one outside with me, except for your stupid dog, and I doubt he did it."

"First of all, my dog's a *she*. Second, Navil's *Belgian* . . ."

"Same thing."

"And she's *not* my girlfriend—"

"Whatever. Who cares?"

"And third, why would she hit—"

"I don't know, Ollie. That's a good question. Go ask *her*."

"Fine. I *will*."

"*Good.*"

"*Fantastic.*"

She stormed off to her next class, pissy as a soaked cat. Navil came to my side, but I told her I had to get to my next class and didn't have time to talk. I felt bad for walking away but was so ticked off . . . I didn't want to take out my anger on her.

I couldn't believe Jackie thought I hit her with a rock. I mean, if someone did, she had every right to be ticked off, but it wasn't me. And it couldn't have been Navil.

Didn't make any sense.

Even if she was acting like a pain in the ass that night, it wouldn't justify her getting nailed in the head. Something weird was going on.

I had to get to the bottom of it.

CHAPTER THIRTEEN

After the last bell, we had our weekly school newspaper meeting in the classroom located at the back of the auditorium. Jackie, our lead reporter and editor, sat next to Mrs. C, our academic advisor and sponsor.

With her poison pen and notebook in hand, Jackie sat there barking out comments. And when the conversation turned to photography, she ripped me a new one.

"How many times do I have to tell you—"

"What now?"

"You call these action shots?"

"What would you call them?"

"Garbage," she barked and flung the prints at me like a stack of playing cards.

"*Mrs. Chase,*" I called out.

"*Jackie.*"

"What?"

"You may be editor-in-chief, but that's no way to treat a colleague."

"A colleague? Please."

"Young lady, if this behavior continues, I *will* remove you from this paper. Understood? Now apologize to Ollie."

I'd never seen a more pained expression. "Fine. I'm . . . sorry."

"Yeah, whatever."

Of course, Jackie got in the last word.

"Oh, and Mrs. C?"

"Yes, Jackie?"

"Please tell *Peter Parker* over there that he has till Friday to get me new prints, or we go to press without him."

My lips curled as I shot her the stink face.

Fifteen minutes later, we wrapped up the meeting. I left the auditorium, grabbed my gear from the photo lab, and went to work, stopping first at the boys' varsity basketball game, already in progress.

I grabbed a seat in the stands and loaded fresh film into my Nikon. By halftime, I'd captured a fast break, a few three-pointers, and Stefan Sutherland, Ginny's boyfriend, ripping the ball from an opponent's hands.

Satisfied, I left the game and went to the pool to take more shots. My first was of B Karlsson practicing her butterfly stroke. I then got Giles Denton, Alli's boyfriend, mid-pike off the diving board.

Between the smell of chlorine and my lens fogging up, I didn't stick around long. I thought about walking around and taking nature shots, but noticed it was getting late, so I made a beeline back to the lab and developed my roll.

Eddie was there working on prints as well.

"Hey, bud."

"Hey, Ollie."

"How'd things go at the pap—"

"Don't ask."

"That good, huh?"

"Let's just say, Jackie was in rare form."

Eddie snickered.

I cranked up the radio and got to work. An hour or so later, I was clipping prints up to dry next to Eddie's shots of faculty members playing with their kids.

"Guess it's time to clean up," he commented.

I nodded.

He and I were old pros at this point. I grabbed the developer trays while he began storing away the chemicals. Within fifteen minutes, we were done.

As I finished wiping down the counters, a commercial for a *Hot Tuna* rock concert at the local state university played on the radio. Even though it was six weeks out, they were already giving away tickets.

Upon hearing the commercial, Eddie asked if I'd received any acceptance letters yet.

I sighed. "Not yet."

"Damn. Sorry, man."

"It's all right." I waved him off.

The thing was, I wasn't all right with it.

Fi had already received three acceptance letters, and I hadn't received my first.

Of course, Pop had a rational take on the matter. After seeing my reaction to Fi's third letter, he sat me down.

"Ollie, you're worrying about nothing."

"How can you say that, Pop?"

"Because I've been there."

Here we go.

"Look, worst case scenario, you go to Suffolk Community."

I shut my eyes and shook my head.

"You knock out your prerequisites, then matriculate to whatever college you want, as long as you keep your GPA up, and I can afford the tuition."

"Yeah, okay, Pop," I replied before going to my room.

My dad just didn't get it. People at my school equated community college to attending thirteenth grade. You might as well run out and join the circus. At least there, you get paid to shovel shit.

At our prep school, we had an unwritten rule. Graduates went Ivy League or attended a handful of prominent Christian colleges. Prestigious universities like Duke, Stanford, M.I.T, or Georgetown were also acceptable. The latter was my first choice because of its journalism program.

After wiping down the counter, I grabbed my gear and noticed the undeveloped roll of film from the previous weekend. Bloody images of Jackie's injury swirled my head, along with the chaos from the emergency workers flooding our backyard and house.

I turned to Eddie. "Hey, listen, I know we just cleaned up, but I've got another roll to develop."

"That's cool. Want some help?"

"Sure."

With his help, we quickly set things back up, and I got down to the business at hand, developing my mystery roll of film.

Normally, I didn't mind waiting for the chemicals to process the negatives. In this case, though, I wished there was a quicker process than the manual one we were stuck with in our lab.

"C'mon . . . finish already," I commanded the processor.

"Why so impatient? What's on there?" Eddie asked.

The timer went off as I started to explain, allowing me to multitask. As I processed the developed negatives, I shared with Eddie the whole story.

"Wait, you had chicks over, and *I* wasn't invited?" he replied.

"*That's* what you got out of that story?"

"What?"

"*Eddie—*"

"All right, I'm sorry. But next time—"

I shook my head. "I promise."

I finished developing the contact sheet, blew it dry, so I could start inspecting the results.

"Hand me the magnifier, would you?"

I sat on the stool and checked out every single frame.

"Find anything yet?"

"Not ye . . . hold on." I handed him the magnifier. "Check this out. What do you see there?"

He bent over and examined the sheet.

"Well?"

"Looks like a rock lodged in your pool cover."

I thought so too.

"And . . . is that blood?"

Fuck.

CHAPTER FOURTEEN

Modern Day

"**T**wo *weeks?*"

"Oh, quit being such a baby," Jaime replied. "It's only rehab."

I flipped him the finger.

"Real mature. Listen, I've got rounds." He patted my arm. "I'll swing by before heading home."

I grumbled and watched him leave.

"You've got a good brother there," Judge Watson chimed in from his bed behind the drawn curtain.

"Thanks, Judge, he's okay. Just don't tell him I said so."

"Secret's safe with me. I have a brother too."

A few days later, Jaime delivered me to an inpatient rehab facility in the *burbs*.

"What? Didn't trust me?" I asked as he helped me get into bed.

He laughed at me as the facility director entered the room. "Hey, Sharon."

Looking to be in her mid-to-late-forties, Sharon wore a dark blue blazer and matching pants, a crisp white shirt, and black loafers. She had shoulder-length, salt-and-pepper hair and sported a pair of stylish pink and purple cat-eye eyeglasses.

"And how's my favorite doctor doing?" Sharon asked with a COVID-appropriate elbow bump.

"Doing just fine."

"And whom do we have here?"

"Sharon, this is my older brother, Ollie."

"The photojournalist you're always talking about?"

"You mean the pain in the ass?" Jaime joked.

"Oh, you." She playfully swatted his shoulder. "It's very nice to meet you, Mr. Morales. Your brother here speaks highly of you."

"Good to meet you too. And please call me Ollie."

"Ollie, it is." She reviewed her clipboard. "Looks like you're going to be with us for a couple of weeks."

"So they tell me," I muttered.

She smiled warmly. "I promise we'll take good care of you."

Famous last words.

She stuck around for a few minutes, bullshitting with Jaime before excusing herself. Once she left, Jaime kicked into Doctor Morales mode and spent the next few minutes giving me instructions.

"I spoke with your orthopedist, and he's transmitted his instructions to the facility. Starting tomorrow, you'll be meeting with a PT twice a day."

"Why so much?"

He patted my belly. "I asked for three, but at your age . . ."

"You're so lucky I'm stuck in this bed."

He snickered. "And before I forget, I left a strict do not disturb order in place. We don't need another repeat with those lawyers showing up unexpectedly."

"Any word from—"

"Yes, she should be out of quarantine and back in town in a few days. In the meantime, if you need anything—"

"You told her I'm here, right? And not at the hospital."

He rolled his eyes.

"And she has the—"

"Jesus, Ollie, relax. We've got it all covered, okay?"

"What about the kids? Do they—"

"Everyone knows, Ollie. You're going to drive yourself—"

Mid-sentence, the evening nurse entered.

"Hello, my name is Edyta," she stated with a bit of an accent.

Eastern European?

"Please, call me Ollie." I smiled and gestured to my brother. "And this is Jaime."

"Dr. Morales," Jaime corrected. "Nice to meet you, Edyta."

"You too, Dr. Morales."

She printed her information on the grease board mounted on the wall.

"If you need anything, just call this number, okay? Or you can press the button."

She came to my bedside, wrapped the long remote-control cord around the bedrail, and instructed me how to use the hardwired controller.

"You can control everything with this," she explained, "but if you need anything, just call for me, okay?"

"How about an Uber?" I mumbled.

"Sorry?"

"Ignore him, Edyta," Jaime chimed in. "Listen, may I speak with you in the hallway?"

"James, leave her alone."

He waved me off, and the pair walked out the door.

"What'd ya do, tell her that I'm a flight risk?" I asked upon his return.

"Something like that."

"Unbelievable."

"Hey, if the shoe fits—" he joked as his cell rang.

"Smell it. I know."

He looked at his phone and answered, mouthing that it's his hospital.

"Dr. Morales," he stated. "Uh-huh. Uh-huh. Okay, I'll be there in a few minutes."

"Dude, you just left."

"Tell me about it."

I watched my exhausted kid brother leave after he kissed my forehead. I grabbed the hard-wired remote and turned on the TV. Out of habit, I flipped to one of the cable news channels. Four talking heads spoke about the Capitol riots and showed highlights from the event.

Suddenly, my throat dried as beads of sweat dotted my forehead. My hands began to tremble as tension crept across my chest. Slowly, I curled into the fetal position. As I did, the remote slipped from my hand and landed hard on the slick linoleum floor, changing the channel to a loud soccer match.

"Water . . . I need . . ."

I reached for the Styrofoam jug and knocked it over. Spilled ice water across the entire floor. I couldn't think straight.

Where's . . . Jaime?

Over the speaker, Edyta called, "Mr. Morales, is everything okay?"

I tried to respond.

"Ollie? Are you okay?" I heard her call out.

I can't . . . breathe . . .

. . . need . . .

My door burst open, and Edyta ran in. She slipped on an ice cube and skidded ass first into the wall, leaving a unique imprint in the cheap drywall.

On the TV an announcer shouted, "G-o-o-o-a-l!"

Chaotic cheers filled the room.

Turbulent images from my past swirled in my mind's eye.

Explosions.

Distant gunfire.

"Man down, man down!" screamed a U.S. Marine.

The room continued spinning.

"Ambush . . . ambush," someone cried.

The taste of dust, sand, sweat, and blood flooded my senses.

I grabbed onto the bed railing.

I held on for dear life.

Breathe, Ollie . . . breathe.

CHAPTER FIFTEEN

1986

I should have left things alone. Things at school were back to normal. And with any luck, a new scandal would soon rock the place, and this Jackie incident would be a distant memory.

Unfortunately, it's not how I rolled, and I couldn't let it go. It was like an itch on a sweaty afternoon that needed scratching. The moment I got home, I grabbed a flashlight and went straight to the pool area.

Within seconds, I found the rock sticking out from under the pool cover, just like in the picture, speckled with blood and strands of hair.

"Ollie, dinner," Tía called from the sliding glass door.

Foolishly, I picked it up and stuck it in my front pocket.

After dinner, I called the one person I trusted.

"What'd you do with it?" Fi asked.

"Shoved it in my pocket, why?"

"Jesus, Ollie, don't you watch *Hill Street Blues* or *Quincy*?"

"What?"

"Dude, you *never* handle the evidence."

"What was I supposed to do? Leave it there?"

"Yes, then get an adult."

I groaned. "How could I be so *stupid*?"

"Beats me."

"What should I do now?"

"I don't know. Talk to your dad."

"He's at the hospital, delivering another baby."

"What about your aunt?"

"And play Twenty Questions? No thanks."

"Well, ya gotta do something."

"I'll figure it out." I sighed.

"Ols?"

"Yeah?"

She asked the one question I refused to consider.

"What if Navil did it?"

"She didn't do it, Fi."

"But, what if she *did*?"

I grew silent and stared out my bedroom window.

"You still there?"

"Yeah, I'm still here."

"Well?"

"Fi. I . . . don't know."

The following day, Fi's question played on a mind loop and caused me to avoid Navil like she was contagious.

And after lunch, I spotted Jackie walking out of the auditorium, gold and blue notebook in hand, sporting a smug look on her face.

I wanted to share what I'd found with her but wasn't in the mood for an "I told you so" lecture.

After last bell, I tracked down Fi and told her I needed to get out of Dodge.

"Ols, you're going to need to face her sooner or later."

"I know," I replied. "Just not tonight, okay?"

That evening, Navil tried calling, but each time, I made up an excuse not to come to the phone. Eventually, she got the hint and stopped calling. That, or she ran out of change.

The following morning, she waited for me at my locker.

"Ollie, are you okay? You didn't come to class yesterday and missed our study session."

"Yeah, sorry about that."

"And when you didn't come to the phone, I thought I'd done something . . ."

My head reared back. "*What*? No, not at all."

"Then why didn't you come to the . . ."

I held my stomach and whispered, "I wasn't . . . um . . . feeling well, ya know?"

"Oh." She cautiously stepped back. "But you're feeling better?"

"Yeah. It was probably something I ate for breakfast."

She rubbed my back. "Well, take it easy today."

"I will."

I grabbed my books, then allowed her to escort me to class. The moment we crossed the threshold, I locked eyes with Jackie and felt the blood drain from my face. I felt like such a traitor. Such a fraud. She glared but didn't say anything.

Instead of taking her usual back corner spot, Navil grabbed the seat to my left while Fi took her customary one to my right.

Talk about feeling trapped.

During class, I felt Jackie's eyes burn a hole in the back of my skull. Periodically, Navil glanced over and offered a friendly smile to her roommate. Based on the look on her face, Navil either received a sneer or the finger. Maybe both, knowing Jackie.

"Jackie, what's wrong?" Navil whispered.

"Why don't you ask your *boyfriend*."

The comment shocked Navil, and pissed me off, but I left it alone. After class, she attempted to speak with Jackie, but the bitch shoved past us and stormed off without saying another word.

"Just ignore her," I advised.

"But she seems—"

"That's just Jackie being Jackie. One minute she's fine. The next she's—" I gestured to the girl stomping down the hallway.

"If you say so." She shrugged. "Well, I've got to get to French class."

"I still don't understand how you get away with taking that class."

"Well, you take English, non?"

I smiled, "Fair enough."

She squeezed my bicep. "See you in the library later?"

"Absolutely."

"Good." She then teased. "See you later, *boyfriend*."

I knew she was joking, but the comment set me back on my heels. My eyes grew, and my mouth opened. She snickered, turned, and sauntered away, glancing back every so often to make sure I watched, and I didn't disappoint her.

The way her body sashayed down the hall caused a stirring in my nether regions. Before turning the corner, she tossed me a wink, causing my heart to skip a beat.

Of course, I wasn't the only one to see the exchange. Behind me stood our Dean of Students, Mr. Digman. He leaned into my left ear and cleared his throat.

"Ahem, aren't we going to be late for our next class, Mr. Morales?"

I leaped out of my skin and nearly cursed but caught myself. Instead, I hightailed it to my next class.

"See ya later, Mr. D."

I heard his jovial chuckle halfway down the hall.

***

After school, I met up with my *girlfriend* in the library as promised. I wanted to pull her aside and talk to her about the rock but pussied out. Instead, we took our customary table near the bay windows overlooking the front of the building and were soon joined by the rest of our study crew.

Everyone, that is, except for Jackie. And sadly no one else seemed to care.

"Where's Jackie?" I asked the group.

"Who cares?" Alli sniped.

"She's always poking around everybody's business," Ginny chimed in.

I pursed my lips as others giggled and added their insults. Navil must have seen the expression on my face. She took my hand and leaned closer.

"Should we go look for her?" she whispered.

I shook my head no. She shrugged, took out her homework, and began studying. I did the same but couldn't stop thinking about Jackie.

On the ride home, I complained to Fi, "Can you believe those assholes?"

"Those assholes?" she shot back. "What about you?"

"What about me?"

Fi shook her head. "Have you talked to her yet?"

"Oh, that."

"Unbelievable."

"Fi—"

"Ollie, save it." She held her hand up.

"She didn't do it, Fi."

"You don't know that."

"And neither do you, *okay*? So, let's drop it."

"Ollie . . ."

I ignored her and drummed my fingers on the steering wheel.

"Oliver . . ."

I then fiddled with the radio.

"Do you want *me* to talk to her?"

I slammed on the brakes, nearly causing a pileup.

"*What*? No."

"I can, you know."

Cars behind me blew their horns. Some drove past and flipped me off.

"I'll take care of it, all right?" I informed her, jamming the accelerator.

God.

CHAPTER SIXTEEN

That night, I hardly touched my meatloaf, and it didn't go unnoticed.

"You okay, bub?" Pop asked.

I shrugged, and my dad and aunt exchanged glances.

Pop gestured to Jaime. "Hey, kiddo, why don't you take your dinner into the family room so I can talk to your brother."

"Sure, Pop."

He hopped off his chair and walked to the family room with Bella in tow. The dog scarfed down errant morsels that fell from Jaime's plate. Tía shook her head, took her meal, and followed the pair.

"What's going on, bub? It's not like you to not eat your dinner."

I poked at my peas. "Nothing, Pop."

His eyes narrowed, and he sipped his ice water, patiently waiting for me to crack.

It didn't take long.

I spent the next ten minutes fessing up.

"Coño, Ollie, why didn't you tell me?"

"I don't know, Pop," I whined.

"Where's the rock now?"

"In my room."

"Go get it for me, please."

When I returned, Tía Carolina had as well, and the second I sat down, they tag-teamed me.

"You're eighteen years old, Oliver. When are you going to grow up?"

"Your father's right, hijo de mi vida. We won't always be here—"

"You need to be more responsible—"

"Think of the example you're setting for tu hermanito."

And Fi wondered why I didn't say anything.

"Give me the rock." Pop held out his hand.

I handed it to him. "What are you going to do with it?"

"Don't know yet, but I feel safer with it in my possession," he replied. "Now, finish your dinner and take out the trash, please. It's pickup day tomorrow."

After dinner, I rolled the cans to the curb and stood in the cool evening, taking in the night sky. I prayed for Scotty to beam me up from this place but to no avail.

Instead, a '60s doo-wop sound caught my ear, coming from Ernie's garage across the street. This only meant one thing. He was taking care of his baby.

I looked both ways, crossed the street, and walked up his driveway. I stood at the entrance of his open two-car garage and appreciated his homage to late-1950s décor.

Plastered on the walls were images of James Dean, Marilyn Monroe, and Marlon Brando. All in their prime. The image of Brando—dressed in leather—showed him leaning against his Harley Davidson.

Placards, vintage license plates, and other accoutrements hung throughout this automotive place of worship.

He had a vintage Wurlitzer jukebox in the corner full of 45s from the '50s, '60s, and early '70s. Currently, the Platters were singing their classic, "The Great Pretender," the song I heard from my curb.

From under the hood of his car, Ernie sang along. I let him finish before interrupting his evening.

"Knock-knock," I called out.

He popped up from behind the open hood, his brown hair slicked back. The moment he saw me, he flashed his pearly whites.

"He-e-y, there he is. How's it going, Ollie?"

I shrugged. "It's going. Whatcha doing?"

"Just getting her ready for the weekend."

I walked over to admire his handiwork.

"You just stopping by to say hi, or . . ."

I looked away.

He snickered and wiped his hands off on a greasy towel lying on the floor.

"What's her name?"

Surprised, I asked, "How'd ya know?"

"You think you're the first guy to darken my doorstep with that mug on his face?"

"No, huh?"

"Not by a longshot." He walked to his nearby fridge. "Beer?"

"Sure." I smiled.

"Wait a minute. How old are you again?"

"Um . . . twenty-one?"

He raised a brow.

"Eighteen."

"Just don't tell Carolina. She'd kill me if she found out."

He isn't wrong . . .

"I won't," I promised as I cracked the can open.

"Here's to making them laugh," he toasted before sucking down half his beer.

I sipped mine and remembered how much I hated the taste.

"So, what's going on?" Ernie asked after a throaty belch.

I opened my mouth but didn't know where to start.

"It's not Fiona, is it?"

"*What*? No! Why does everyone always think—"

"Sorry, kid, but the way you two hang out together—"

"Yeah, well, it's not her."

"Who is it?"

"It's this chick from school. Her name's Navil."

"Pretty name."

"Prettier girl."

I took another sip of the disgusting swill while he shut off the jukebox, allowing me to unburden myself without any disruptions. To his credit, he sat there patiently and never interrupted. Ernie allowed me to finish my story before asking questions.

"I wondered what happened."

I nodded.

"And she called you her boyfriend?"

"Yeah, but I think she was joking."

"How do you know? Ya ask her?"

"No." I sighed. "I felt, I don't know . . . stupid."

"We've all been there, kiddo," he replied. "Sounds to me like you need to have a conversation."

Et tu, Brute?

"Yeah, but what do I say?" I asked. "Did you try to kill Jackie the other night?"

He laughed. "Well, I wouldn't put it *that* way."

"So, what do I say?"

"Ease into it. Start with the facts."

"What do you mean?"

"Well, tell her that your friend . . . Jackie, was it?"

"She's not my friend."

"Whatever. Tell her that Jackie said someone hit her in the head with a rock."

"And?"

"*And* would she know anything about it?"

"What if she says no?"

"Without accusing her, merely tell her you found the rock. You said you found it, right?"

"Uh-huh. I gave it to Pop."

"Gotcha." He finished his beer and tossed the can into the nearby bin. "Then tell her Jackie thinks she did it. See how she reacts. Again, you're not the one accusing her."

"Okay."

"Just remember, Ollie. Be honest with her. Chicks dig honesty."

"Understood," I replied before finishing my beer.

"All right, you better get back home before Carolina sends out a search party."

I laughed. "Thanks, Ernie."

"Door's always open, kiddo, unless it's not. Know what I mean?" He winked.

Like I said, the man's a prince.

CHAPTER SEVENTEEN

I'd love to admit that I went to school the following morning, threw the skunk on the porch, and talked to Navil about the rock, but the moment I saw her, my stones shot up my sphincter, and I lost my courage.

Between her dazzling smile and general glow, all I could think about was her *boyfriend* comment.

She stood outside the classroom waiting to go in and looked so fine. She wore a stylish blue outfit with a crisp, white collared shirt. Her hair was clipped up, and the moment I approached, her sensual perfume enveloped me.

"Bonjour, Ollie."

"Morning."

Her eyes reflected the sunshine peeking through the distant windows. It was like staring into a prism. Flecks of brown, green, and gold.

When Fi learned later, she let me have it. "*Jesus*, Oliver."

"I just haven't found the right—"

"How many times have you seen her today?"

"I don't know."

She chucked me a similar look of disappointment Tía Carolina had given me.

"Okay . . . three or four."

"And you *still* haven't talked to her?"

"Not about that, no."

She shook her head. "Unbelievable."

I held my hands up. "I'll talk to her . . . I'll talk to her."

"If you don't—"

"I know . . . I know."

She walked away, and I wondered why she gave a shit about Jackie. It's not like they were best friends. She found her as annoying as everyone else did. Regardless, she was right, as usual. I needed to grow a pair; so, after school, I pulled Navil aside in the library.

"Can we . . . uh . . . talk?"

"Oui, Ollie. What's up?" She smiled.

That goddamn smile.

She placed the back of her hand on my forehead. "Still not feeling well?"

"No, no, I'm fine. Let's"—I pointed to a secluded alcove—"go over there."

We walked over, and based on her devilish grin, she expected something else to happen. Sadly, she was wrong.

"Remember what I told you about Jackie?"

She looked around and wrapped her arms around my neck. "Is *that* really what you want to talk about right now?"

I caught a glimpse of Fi's reflection in the window overlooking the parking lot, chucking me the stink-eye.

Damnit.

I stepped out of her embrace. "Sorry, but this is important."

Surprised, she raised her brows.

"Remember how I told you about Jackie's concussion?"

She nodded.

"Well, that's not all."

"What do you mean?"

I mumbled and looked at the ground, "She thinks that . . ."

Navil raised my chin, and we locked eyes.

I swallowed hard and whispered, "Apparently, someone hit her in the head with a rock."

"Mon Dieu, Ollie," she gasped. "That's terrible. Who would do such a thing?"

My glance away told her everything she needed to know.

"You don't think that . . ." She placed a hand on her chest.

I shut my guilty eyes.

"Oliver, you can't be serious," she said, and muttered something in French.

"I'm sorry, but you and Bella were the only ones out there."

"But why would I do such a thing?"

"I don't know, but someone did, and I found the rock."

"Well, it wasn't me."

It was moment-of-truth time. She could deny and tell me to fuck off or prove me wrong.

Instead, pain filled her hazel eyes, and conviction filled her voice.

Through gritted teeth. "I . . . didn't . . . do it."

I took her hand.

"You have to believe me."

My heart melted.

"I do, Navil. I do." I stared deeply into her aching orbs.

"Well, it doesn't feel like it." She yanked her hand back.

I placed my right hand over my heart. "I swear."

"Is this why you avoided me the other day?"

I nodded.

"Incroyable."

"If it wasn't you . . . and it wasn't me . . ."

She came to the same conclusion.

"Then we need to figure out who it was."

I nodded.

"Where's Jackie now?"

"No clue," I replied.

She turned and left the alcove.

"Where are you going?"

"Where do you think?" She grabbed her things and made a beeline to the exit.

"Wait. I'll go with you."

I chucked my backpack over my shoulder and ran after her.

"Where're you two going?" Fi asked.

"To talk to Jackie."

"You sure that's a good idea?"

I shrugged and kept running.

CHAPTER EIGHTEEN

Navil was halfway down the stairs when I caught up with her. She wore a fierce look of determination on her face and clearly meant business, shoving her way past students saying hello.

"What's her problem?" I heard someone ask as we stepped outside.

We scanned the campus and started in the gym. Navil searched the girls' locker room while I checked out the basketball court and swimming pool area. We came up short.

"Do you think she's in your room?" I asked.

"I don't know, but that's where I'm going next."

"You mean where *we're* going."

I reached for her hand, but she swatted it away.

We quickly crossed campus and entered the lobby of Lawrence Hall, one of the two girls' dorms on campus.

"I'll wait here."

I watched her leave, and once alone, felt like a fish out of water. Every few seconds, I'd check my watch, wondering what was taking so long. I imagined the pair fighting. Rolling around on the floor, surrounded by a crowd of girls cheering them on as they pulled each other's hair and punched each other's face.

Of course, if that were happening, I would have heard the commotion, even from the lobby. I noticed a magazine rack and perused old copies of student newspapers, some with Jackie's exposés on the front cover. While thumbing through the selections, I heard a nearby door open and footsteps approaching.

I turned and found Navil sporting a frown on her beautiful face.

"No luck?"

She shook her head. "And I asked around. No one knows where she is."

I glanced at the newspaper in my hand.

"You know . . ." I held it out. "She could be working on—"

"C'est possible . . ."

Within minutes, we stepped into the auditorium and walked toward our makeshift newsroom. As we approached, I noticed the light on from under the door and the sound of Jackie arguing with some dude.

Not wanting to get caught in her crossfire, Navil held me back, and I abided, which was my first mistake. The argument soon took a heated turn.

"I warned you to mind your damn business. Now give it," I heard the guy order.

Jackie shrieked, "Get the hell away from me!"

We heard a scuffle, followed quickly by an audible thud.

Navil and I exchanged looks.

Instead of running in, I called out to Jackie, my second mistake.

"Hey, is everything okay back there?"

I heard things getting knocked over inside the makeshift office, followed by the screech from a wooden window opening.

After waiting a beat, Navil ran toward the danger. I took off behind her, and as we entered the room, some guy in gray sweatpants and blue school hoodie leaped outside.

I ran to the window and slipped on some spilled water. I leaned out and searched for the guy, but all I heard were distant echoes of pounding feet and breaking branches. A draft blew in, and the stench of chlorine from my time in the pool area briefly filled my nostrils.

Behind me, Navil screamed.

"Jackie!"

Not again.

I went around a desk and found Navil kneeling by Jackie's side. She gently tried to shake her awake but to no avail.

A small pool of blood slowly formed under Jackie's head. I bent down and checked her pulse.

"Anything?"

"Barely," I replied. "Looks like she's breathing, though."

"We need to get help."

I agreed but didn't want to leave Navil alone. It didn't feel safe, but she insisted, so I grabbed the heaviest object I could find, an electric stapler, and handed it to her.

"If the guy returns—"

"Go, Ollie."

I squeezed her hand and ran toward the door.

"But make it quick," she called as I left the room.

Once outside, I sprinted toward the gym, praying I'd run into an adult. Thankfully, Coach Connors, our Director of Athletics, was just leaving.

"Coach . . . Coach . . ."

"Whoa, calm down, son. Where's the fire?"

"Ya gotta . . . Jackie Woodley . . . she's . . ."

"Where?"

"Newsroom." I pointed.

He tucked his clipboard under his right arm and ran to the auditorium, with me close behind. Adrenaline rushed through my body as I entered the newsroom.

Navil stood guard over Jackie, her weapon at the ready.

"What happened?" Coach demanded.

We quickly explained what we heard.

"Why didn't you call 9-1-1?"

"I don't know."

He rolled his eyes and tossed me a quarter. "Go . . . now."

As I left, Coach ordered Navil to step aside.

Fifteen minutes later, cherry tops lit up the quad. Suffolk County's finest prevented the burgeoning crowd from contaminating the scene.

EMTs tended to Jackie while Coach, Navil, and I watched. After taking her blood pressure, they wrapped her in a blanket, placed her onto a stretcher, and wheeled her out of the building.

Minutes later, police detectives arrived on the scene, separated Coach Connors, Navil, and me, and began taking statements.

CHAPTER NINETEEN

Navil walked to the stage with a gruff and slightly over-weight detective I learned later was named Detective Chao. A cop named Wallace escorted Coach to Aaron Doherty's office, head of our Theater Arts program.

Yours truly had the pleasure of speaking with Detective Gallagher, a tired-looking guy with bags under his eyes and needing a shave. He smelled like coffee and cigarettes.

Instead of going into a classroom or the newsroom, we stepped into a cluttered green room behind the stage. Students used the poorly lit area to change costumes between performances. The aroma was a perfect blend of mothballs and stinky feet.

Detective Gallagher placed a hand over his nose and mouth. "Is there a window in this place?"

"Yeah, I'll get it."

I wedged myself behind stacked chairs and a pile of old costumes and opened a back window. Upon my return, I found that the detective had placed a couple of folding chairs about ten feet apart and was seated in the one facing the door.

"Why don't you take a seat," he said, taking out a pen and notepad.

With my back to the door, I shared my story.

"And you didn't get a look at the guy's face?"

"No. Sorry."

He shut his eyes and rubbed the back of his neck before

returning to his notes. I sat there patiently, praying for this to finish so I could be with Navil. Behind me, the other detective popped his head into the room.

"Hey, Matt, we're all set out here. You ready to head back to the station?"

"Yeah, in a minute," he replied before gesturing at me. "One thing still doesn't make sense."

"What?"

"Why were you coming here to begin with?"

His question awoke my bladder.

"What do you mean?"

He chucked me a curious look and shifted forward.

"I mean, why were you in this building? What brought you here?"

I looked away, "Um . . . I don't remember."

His eyes narrowed. "You don't remember?"

"Uh . . . no."

The other detective chimed in, "Kid, quit wasting time and answer his questions. It's been a long day."

I turned around. "Sorry, it's just—"

"Just what?"

"Everything happened so fast. We heard Jackie scream—"

"Yeah, we've got all that. But why were you here?" Gallagher asked.

I turned back around and went back and forth with him for a few minutes. He kept asking me the same question, and I'd avoid the answer.

"Matt, we don't have time for this. Let's just take him down to the station. See if a night in jail loosens his tongue."

With a nod, Detective Gallagher stood. "All right, get up and turn around."

"Why?"

"We're taking you in. Now turn around and place your hands behind your back."

"I'm under arrest?"

He yanked me to my feet and spun me around. He slapped cuffs tightly onto my wrists and mirandized me.

"Oliver Morales, you have the right to remain silent—"

"But I didn't do anything."

It didn't matter. He continued while shoving me toward the door. When Coach saw me in cuffs, he interceded.

"Whoa, fellas, hold on a minute."

"Sir, please get out of the way."

From the stage, Navil joined the fray. "Where are you taking him? *Ollie.*"

"Jesus." Gallagher sighed.

Coach placed his hand on my chest. "Why is he under arrest?"

"Are you the boy's father?"

"No."

"Then get out of our way."

Navil rushed to my side and grabbed my arm.

"Miss, please let him go," Detective Gallagher ordered. "Officer? Please?"

The cop who just stepped out of the newsroom yanked her from my arm.

"Let me go," she insisted. "Oliver."

"Navil, please," Coach chastised. "Officer—"

"Detective." Gallagher corrected.

"Sorry . . . Detective. *Please*, Ollie here is a good—"

"Then maybe you can convince him to talk."

All eyes were on me. My bladder kicked into overdrive.

"Ollie?" Coach asked. "What do they want to know?"

I caught a glimpse of Navil from the corner of my eye and couldn't throw her under the bus, so I clamped my mouth shut.

"We want to know why he and Miss . . ." Detective Gallagher looked at Navil.

"Laurent," Coach answered.

"Right. What brought them to the crime scene?"

"Well?" Coach asked us both.

She looked away, and I mumbled, "I don't remember."

Even though they asked both of us, notice who left in cuffs.

My response pissed off the detective, who began yelling, which caused Navil to scream, and soon Coach joined the fracas.

"Where are you taking him?" Coach demanded.

"Get out of the way," Detective Gallagher replied.

"He didn't do anything!" Navil yelled. "*Ollie.*"

Within seconds, they shoved me out of the exit to a waiting crowd of onlookers. Tears ran down my face as they escorted me down the steps toward an awaiting black and white cop car.

"I demand to know where—" Coach said.

"Fifth precinct," Detective Gallagher responded, handing me off to Officer Wallace.

Students whistled, and others chanted my name.

"Watch your head." Wallace forced me into the back seat.

As the door shut in my face, I watched Navil at the top of the steps, shouting my name.

"*Ollie!*"

CHAPTER TWENTY

How I didn't pee myself on that ride from hell was a miracle. The back seat smelled like the inside of a baby's diaper with a hint of vomit. I did everything I could to sit still.

Unfortunately, with my hands cuffed behind my back and Mario Andretti behind the wheel hitting every bump and pothole on the way to the station, I bounced around like a pair of sneakers in a dryer.

About fifteen minutes later, we pulled into the police station, and I somehow avoided getting a black eye when my face slammed into the thick plastic partition between the front and back seat as he screeched to a halt.

The six foot something, brawny Officer Wallace ripped the backdoor open, yanked me from the car, and shoved me toward the station.

Tears rolled down my face, thanks to the cuffs digging into my wrists and an overall sense of embarrassment that felt like a slap in the face. It didn't help that my bladder kicked into overdrive.

"Oh, quit your blubbering."

"But I need to pee."

"Hold it."

Based on all the television I watched, I expected to be fingerprinted and have a mug shot taken. Instead, Officer Asshole sealed my watch and wallet into a zip-lock bag, then walked me through the busy station to an interrogation room.

He shoved me onto a chair and told me to stay put.

Like I had a choice?

My leg bounced like a jackhammer as I nervously sat waiting for company as I took in my new environment. The cuffs continued to punish my wrists, so I tried adjusting my posture, but it only made things worse.

The room was painted a dingy avocado green and looked smaller than the ones I had seen on TV. That, or claustrophobia kicked in. The place smelled like stale cigarettes and burnt coffee. To my surprise, someone had carved *Rosanna Loves Leon* into the table, along with six of George Carlin's seven dirty words you can't say on television, or in front of my tía, for that matter.

Just as I reached my wit's end, Detective Gallagher arrived. Behind him, the other detective from school, carrying a yellow legal pad and pen, which he tossed onto the table.

"This is Detective Chao."

He smirked and got straight to the point.

"Tell us what you know."

"About what?"

They exchanged glances.

"About what happened this evening," Gallagher replied.

"I already told you. Navil and I heard Jackie scream. We ran into the room . . ."

" . . . and someone jumped out the window." He finished my sentence.

"Yeah."

Chao's nose twitched like he was getting ready to pounce.

"I'm going to ask you again. Why were you there?"

"I need to pee."

"Cross your legs."

I shut my eyes.

"What were you doing there?"

I clamped my mouth.

A heated glare. "Nothing? *Seriously*?"

Gallagher threw his hands up and began to pace.

Chao leaned forward. "You *really* have nothing to say?"

I turned away.

"I'm done," Gallagher announced.

"Want me to turn the camera off? Have a *real* conversation with him?"

My eyes widened.

Gallagher scowled at me and shook his head.

"Let's put him in a cell. See if that loosens his tongue."

Chao came to my side. "Get up."

I flinched and released a drop of pee.

He yanked me to my feet. "Jesus, I'm not going to hit you."

"I'll take him."

"You sure?"

Gallagher nodded and shoved me forward.

We walked to the back of the precinct and straight to the holding cells. The first thing I noticed was how closet-sized the cells seemed. The second was the stench of sweat and urine.

Prisoners catcalled as I was escorted to my cell.

"He's cute. Why don't you put him with me?"

"Shut the fuck up, Larry," Gallagher chided.

I'd never been more terrified.

I'd lived a sheltered eighteen years, never exposed to the underbelly of Long Island filled with scumbags, junkies, and thieves.

The moment Gallagher chucked me into my holding cell, I realized in the eyes of the law, I was no better than my neighbors.

Before leaving, he removed the handcuffs and pointed to a bare chrome toilet in the corner.

He shut the door. "You can pee over there."

The clanging sound haunted me well into my twenties.

I'd never felt so alone.

"Let's see if a few hours here will loosen that tongue of yours," Gallagher muttered as he walked away.

While it did nothing for my tongue, it sure loosened up the waterworks. After peeing, I slumped onto something resembling a cot and bawled my eyes out.

When the other inmates heard me, the taunting continued.

After what felt like millennia, Officer Wallace retrieved me from my accommodations and walked me to the lobby where Pop waited alongside a gray-haired man in a dark pinstriped suit, holding a leather briefcase.

Like a preschooler after a day away from his parents, I leaped into my father's arms.

"It's okay, Ollie. I'm here. Shhhh . . ."

Styrofoam cup in his hand, Gallagher joined us.

"Hey, we're not finished with . . ."

The guy with Pop cut him off. "Easy there, Detective . . . ?"

"Gallagher."

"Robert Eilers. The boy's attorney."

He handed Gallagher his card.

"We're not done with your client, Counselor."

"Unless you have probable cause and can argue reasonable articulable suspicion that this young man was about to, has, or would in the near future commit a crime, then you're releasing him."

They exchanged glares.

"That's what I thought. Say goodbye to the nice detective, Oliver."

"This isn't over."

Eilers waved at the empty threat and escorted us outside.

"Thanks, Bob."

"Meh." He shrugged. "How are you doing, Oliver? They didn't mistreat you, did they? I've heard *things* about this precinct."

I shook my head.

"Good." He smiled and gave me back my watch and wallet.

"Settle in the morning?" Pop asked.

"Don't worry about it. I'll have Emily invoice you." They shook hands and parted.

Once inside Pop's Caddy, snot flowed, and tears fell. After starting the car, he reached over and held me. Like a distraught puppy, I curled into his lap and drenched his scrubs.

After a while, Pop asked if I was hungry.

"Starving."

"Friendly's?"

"Yes, please."

Twenty minutes later, we pulled into the parking lot and spent the next hour or so talking about the events of the evening over burgers and strawberry fribbles.

"Why didn't you just answer their question?"

"I didn't want Navil to get into trouble."

"Oliver."

"What, Pop. She would've."

"It's better for you to go to jail than tell the truth?"

Heads turned at the mention of jail.

Embarrassed, I chucked him a look, "Pop . . ."

"Get used to it, Ollie. Until you come clean, you're going to have this hanging over your head."

And just like that, my ravenous appetite disappeared. I spent the remainder of our time staring out the window, sipping my thick shake.

On the ride home, Pop informed me that Jackie went to University Hospital, but I didn't care. I just wanted to get home and go to sleep.

Tía Carolina tried hugging me, but I walked right by her, a barking Bella, and a sleepy-looking Jaime wearing his pajamas.

"Ollie?"

"Let him be, Carolina."

I walked straight to my room, shut the door behind me, and flopped onto my bed without removing my clothes or kicking off my shoes.

My nightmares that evening were an amalgam of attacks from junkies, vagrants, and police officers.

Around 2:00 a.m., I sat up screaming. Images of a blood-soaked Jackie, looking like an extra from the movie *Carrie,* faded from my mind as Tía Carolina, Bella, and Pop burst through my door.

After learning I had a nightmare, Pop kissed my forehead, plopped Bella onto my bed, and left the room with Tía Carolina.

My dog licked my face and did her blankie dance before curling up in the crook of my spine and falling asleep.

The morning arrived quickly. Over breakfast, Tía Carolina handed me a couple of Tylenol after noticing the red marks on my wrists, thanks to the metallic torture devices.

As I ate, I learned that Fi and Navil had called multiple times.

"You know how I feel about Fiona, but I'm not so sure about that *other* girl."

I ignored her.

"Let's leave the boy alone," Pop said between sips of coffee.

She waved him off and went to the kitchen.

Instead of taking the bus, Pop drove Fi and me to school since my car stayed overnight in student parking.

When Fi saw me, she practically shattered my spine with her bear-hug greeting.

"I . . . can't . . . breathe."

"Shut up," she continued.

On the ride to school, I recounted the story for Fi.

"At least they didn't stick you with Chester the Molester."

"Jesus, Fi."

Pop snickered while driving up the school parkway. Cops still milled about the quad, so he pulled to the curb next to the Veterans Memorial Hall and dropped us off.

I stared at the police officers presumably searching for clues near the auditorium and collecting evidence as I stepped out.

Flashbacks from the previous evening played like a surreal horror movie in my mind's eye. A pit formed in my stomach, and I had to swallow back the bile that crept into the back of my throat.

"I'm just a phone call away. I have a light schedule today," Pop called.

Said the man who delivered babies for a living.

I waved back and followed Fi inside. Talk about feeling like Moses. When people saw me, they got out of my way. Some whispered and pointed, but we were left alone on our way to our lockers.

"Ignore 'em, Ollie," Fi said.

"Easy for you to say."

We turned the corner, and next to my locker stood the hazel-eyed beauty, who, when she saw me, shouted my name, and ran into my welcoming arms.

"Are you okay?"

I melted into her. "I am now."

CHAPTER TWENTY-ONE

Her hug felt like a warm towel fresh off the line. I didn't want to let go but had to, due to our stupid public displays of affection rules. The first bell rang, kicking off the daily chaos of squeaking shoes and metallic locker doors slamming shut as students ran to class. Navil ignored the madness and caressed my cheek.

"You sure you're okay?"

I kissed her palm. "I'm fine."

"I still can't believe they arrested you."

"Technically, I wasn't arrested."

She looked at me with curiosity.

"They just took me in for *questioning*," I replied in air quotes.

"Well, whatever it was . . ."

"I know."

After the second bell rang, Navil asked, "Want to play hockey?"

"Did you mean hooky?" I laughed. "I'd love to, but don't want the grief."

She smiled, and we walked to Mrs. C's class. The moment we crossed the threshold the classroom went silent. All eyes stared in our direction. My protective lioness practically snarled at the onlookers as she escorted me to my customary second-row desk. She then took the seat to my left, while Fi sat to my right. Talk about uncomfortable.

Maybe we should have played hockey.

After the last bell, I tracked down Fi. "You mind if we just head home?"

"What about Navil?"

"I think she'll understand."

What's that old saying about speaking the devil's name? As if on cue, she leaned out of the doorway.

"Are you coming inside?"

"I think I'm going to head home."

Disappointment crossed her face.

"Sorry."

She stepped outside and hugged me, "Call me later."

After receiving a kiss on the cheek, I watched her walk back inside, and saunter toward the stairs. There was something alluring about the way her auburn hair swished back and forth. It kept lock step with that perky backside.

Fi smirked when I turned back. "Ols, why don't I take the bus home?"

"You sure?"

She pointed. "She's getting away."

"Thanks, Fi." I smiled and ran inside. "Navil."

She stopped halfway up the staircase, turned, and bent down.

I dangled my car keys. "Wanna get out of here?"

Like a starburst, her beautiful face lit up. "I'll get my things."

Twenty minutes later, we pulled into the West Meadow Beach parking lot, one of my happy places. There was something about its picturesque setting and stunning views of the Long Island Sound, with Connecticut in the distance, that was so tranquil and inviting—especially at sunset. Based on the glint in Navil's eyes, I knew I had chosen wisely. The cool weather prevented us from taking a romantic walk along the beach. Instead, we snuggled up in the car and chatted for a while, mostly about our families.

I learned she spoke seven languages, was the third of five

kids, and that her father was a muckety-muck in the Belgian government.

She then asked about my mom. "Died from breast cancer about six years ago."

Compassion filled her hazel eyes. "Mon Dieu, I'm so sorry, Ollie."

"It was right after Jaime was born," I stated. "He never got to know her."

She leaned in and tenderly kissed my cheek, then rested her head on my chest. We sat quietly while the sun slowly dipped below the horizon. The Dream Academy hit tune, "Life in A Northern Town," came on the radio.

Navil immediately lit up. "Oh, I love this song."

She swayed back and forth and quietly sang along to the melodic tune. Her voice mirrored the angelic look on her face. Her beauty captivated me. If I only had my Nikon with me, I could have captured the moment.

As the song ended, she took my hand and stared deeply into my eyes. She froze me in place with her very being.

CHAPTER TWENTY-TWO

As I fell asleep that evening, I thought about this moment. How we sat and stared at one another. You could hear a pin drop as the wind blew outside the car, and the Long Island Sound gently crashed onto the beach.

I should have thrown caution to the wind, leaned over, and kissed her like that scene between Jake and Samantha, Molly Ringwald's character in *Sixteen Candles*.

Instead, I just sat there like an idiot.

"Ollie?" She leaned in.

"Yeah?"

"Why won't you kiss me?"

I flushed with embarrassment.

I wanted to lie. Tell her I was trying to be a gentleman. But the fact of the matter was . . .

"Yeah, but I-I'm . . ." I stammered. "Afraid."

Navil jerked her head back. "Of what? Of me?"

Mortified, I shut my eyes and nodded.

"Why?"

Painful humiliation seared my soul.

"Because girls like you . . ." I whispered.

"What do you mean, *girls like me*?"

"You know . . ." I gestured. "Hot . . . girls."

"You think I'm *hot*?"

"*Seriously*?" I scoffed. "Jesus, Navil, you're like the *hottest* girl in school."

She laughed, "You think so?"

"Do I . . . *everybody* thinks so."

"So, why haven't you asked me out?"

"Because hot girls like you don't go out with guys like me."

"What do you mean, *guys* like you?"

"You know . . ." I motioned toward my body.

"Mon Dieu, Ollie, I never realized you thought so poorly of yourself . . . or me, for that matter."

"I don't."

"Clearly, you *do*. What, am I too *shallow* to date a boy . . ."

"That's not what I'm saying."

"Then, what *are* you saying?"

I'd never felt more inexperienced. Where was Ernie when I needed him? As we sat there, I could feel her drift away. And if I didn't fix this, I'd lose her forever.

I sighed. "Navil, look, can we just . . . start over?"

"Fine."

"Good."

"To be clear, you *do* like me, non?"

I smiled.

"Oui."

"Très bien."

"You must be rubbing off on me . . . you know . . . like a sexy rash."

"Oh, really?" She laughed and poked my side.

"Hopefully, you're not too contagious."

"Oh, I'm contagious all right."

She placed her arms around my neck, and the air filled with excitement, along with our pheromones.

Her nostrils flared, and she nervously bit her lower lip.

Our eyes locked and, in that split second, a flash of eternity.

Navil's eyes blazed with a passionate fury.

A frightened excitement surged through me.

Like the twists and turns of a roller coaster.

The sudden adrenaline rush caused my heart to pound in my throat.

Inches apart, her warm breath mingled with mine.

Her head tilted.

Leaned in.

And just like that, fantasy became reality.

The kiss others would forever be compared.

I finally understood what Springsteen meant when he sang about an everlasting kiss. Like lighting a matchstick, a quick spark, then slow burn. Our kisses were soft and tender. Neither fought for dominance.

A periodic smile or giggle.

An awkward comfort.

The tip of her tongue slipped into my mouth.

Silky and smooth.

Like the finest chocolate.

My first French kiss . . . or was it Belgian?

I savored her.

She guided me through inexperienced territories. A slight nod here. A subtle whisper there.

"Is this okay?"

"Perfect," she purred.

I pulled her auburn hair back and slid my tongue down the curve of her neck.

"Ollie—"

I sank my teeth into her. She gasped and leaned closer.

Lights burst behind my closed eyes. Reds . . . blues . . . reds . . . blues. The fireworks of youth.

"Uh, O-Ollie?"

Something odd about her tone, but I ignored it.

"Ahem, *Ollie*."

She shoved me.

Confused, I stared into my paramour's soft hazel eyes.

Fear replaced passion.

Over her shoulder, flashing lights lit up the parking lot.

A tap on the driver's side window.

My body convulsed in shock.

Navil quickly slid to the passenger seat.

Behind me, an authoritative voice, "Roll it down."

CHAPTER TWENTY-THREE

Modern Day

"Just a couple more," Len, my physical therapist, encouraged.

A jolt of pain shot down my sciatic nerve from my left butt cheek to the back of my thigh.

"You're killing me."

"Ollie, you're doing great. Give me a few more."

Sweat pooled at the base of my spine, soaked my faded concert t-shirt for the Police that Cheryl brought me from home, along with other appropriate clothing. The timer finally went off. Allowed me to collapse back into my chair.

"Len." I waved my arms. "I'm . . . done."

"But we're just getting started." He smiled.

It felt like we'd been at it for hours. I wiped my brow and flipped him off.

He laughed. "At least you haven't lost your sense of humor."

I sucked down some Gatorade Zero.

"All right, let's get you back to your room so you can shower and change."

A half-hour later, I was back in bed, surfing the late-afternoon crap-fest on local TV.

Who watches this garbage?

I avoided the cable news and settled in with some insipid talk show featuring the latest pseudo-celeb/social influencer chatting about her new makeup line.

"I love the way this feels on my face," she shared.

The host's false platitudes made me nauseous. I turned down the sound and grabbed the dinner menu off my nightstand.

The words *low carb* were scribbled across the top in blue sharpie. My asshole younger brother struck again. Felt I needed to lose some weight. And since I was a hostage without a cell phone, I couldn't place an order with Uber Eats or Grubhub to deliver me from this misery.

A knock on my door interrupted my roadkill selection.

"Come in."

A man with a high and tight haircut, and a slightly overweight woman stepped in. They dressed plainly and flashed badges.

"Excuse me, Mr. Morales?" the mid-thirties male looking at his notepad asked. "*Oliver . . . Morales?*"

From my years living in DC, I immediately recognized their ilk.

"Who's asking?"

The pair stepped closer. The mid-forty-something-looking woman, wearing a checkered brown and tan suit and drab blue button-down shirt, introduced herself. The only thing missing from her ensemble was a coffee stain. She pushed her mask down and flipped her badge open.

There was something familiar about her. Her eyes. Jaw line. The way she stood.

"Detective Karen Skaryd, Clearwater Police Department."

"Clearwater? A bit outside of your jurisdiction, aren't you, Detective?"

With a hint of a Long Island accent, she replied, "I've been assigned to work a joint task force with the FBI."

I guess you can *take the girl out of Long Island.*

"Excuse me, Detective. Do we know each other?"

She thought for a moment and shook her head. "I don't think so."

"It'll come to me."

Her partner, Mr. High and Tight, sporting a muted gray suit, crisp white shirt, and red power tie, followed her lead and revealed his credentials.

"I'm Special Agent Benjamin Umberto, Federal Bureau of Investigation."

I didn't bother asking how they knew where to find me. Over the years, I'd come to learn if cops wanted to track you down, they'd track you down using today's technology, regardless of the *HIPAA Privacy Laws.*

So, what brings these two here?

And why's a Florida cop working with the Feds?

"What do you need?" I flatly asked.

Agent Umberto adjusted his white N95 mask. "Mr. Morales, we're here to ask you a few questions about your involvement in the recent attack on the Capitol."

Involvement?

And since when does the FBI investigate crimes at the Capitol, let alone some Florida cop? I thought all this fell under the jurisdiction of the Capitol Police, not these two.

This put me on edge. I felt the hairs on the back of my head raise. I'd been a photojournalist long enough to know you never answered law enforcement questions without your lawyer present, regardless of circumstances.

I slid my thumb onto the call button but didn't press it. Instead, I played along.

"Involvement? Clearly, *I'm* the victim here."

Umberto leaned forward. "Look, we know you were there . . ."

Skaryd raised her hand, "Ben—"

He backed off, and she took over.

"Mr. Morales, may we call you Oliver?"

"Does it matter?"

She ignored my comment. "We know you're a journalist, and we're not here to ask you about a confidential source."

I stared at her.

"We've been assigned to investigate the recent attacks—"

"And take statements from the victims. That's it," Umberto concluded.

I nodded, but still didn't trust them.

"We're hoping you can help us identify some of the rioters," Umberto claimed.

In truth, I would have loved to help them and get some justice. The challenge was, I couldn't remember diddly. There were too many gaps in my memory.

"I can't . . . help you."

"Can't or won't?" he asked.

"Is there a difference?"

"Don't you want to catch the people who did this to you?"

"Am I supposed to say no?"

"No, what you should say—"

"Ben, I've got this. Mr. Morales . . . Oliver . . . look . . ."

"If you're going to ask me if I want these assholes brought to justice, the answer is yes."

Umberto drew closer. "Then why won't you help us?"

This unexpected visit caused me stress. My throat dried, and I felt pressure in my chest. I tasted bile in the back of my throat and started breathing funny. I pressed the call button.

Over the loudspeaker, "How can we help you, Ollie?"

"Really?" Umberto chided. "You're calling for help?"

"Mr. Morales, we're not here to hurt you. We're just looking for—"

"I didn't catch that, Ollie. What did you say?" The loud-speaker asked.

"I can't help you," I replied. "Leave me alone."

Edyta entered the room and looked surprised to see my company.

"Can I help you?"

"No, we were just leaving," Agent Umberto answered.

He left his business card on my nightstand.

Detective Skaryd followed suit. "Give us a call if you change your mind."

I watched them leave my room and felt less woozy.

"Are you okay?" Edyta poured me a cup of water.

I sipped the stale liquid and crunched some ice. "I am now."

But that was a lie.

I was anything but okay.

CHAPTER TWENTY-FOUR

That evening, I choked down a sawdust-flavored chicken breast, steamed cauliflower, and wilted leaves they tried to pass off as a dinner salad.

No salt.

No pepper.

Not even a drop of barbecue or hot sauce.

Even the Granny Smith apple was mushy.

How the hell do you ruin an apple?

I pushed away my tray and flipped the TV channels as my illustrious dietician and personal tormentor entered my room.

After kissing me hello, Jaime said, "Heard you had visitors."

"Yeah. A pair of fibbies."

"Fibb—"

"Sorry, FBI agents."

"What'd you tell them?"

"The truth. I can't help them." Angry, I smacked my head. "I can't remember a goddamn thing, *Jaime*."

He grabbed my hands. "Hey, stop that."

"You don't understand."

He pulled up a chair and sat. "Then explain it to me."

"What do you want to hear? That I got the crap kicked out of me, and I now have the memory of a goldfish?"

"For starters."

I mocked him and folded my arms.

"Feel better?"

"Not really."

"Have you thought about what I said the other day?"

"About finding a new job?"

"Talking to someone."

I waved him off.

"I'm serious, Ollie. You need to speak with someone."

"I'm fine."

"Clearly."

I tried changing the subject. "How's Cheryl?"

"She's fine."

"The kids?"

"Are we *really* not going to talk about this?"

I ignored him.

"Fine." He checked out my food tray. "How was dinner?"

I flipped him off.

"C'mon, it couldn't be *that* bad."

"Really?" I pointed at the tray. "Cardboard chicken, and mulch? Remind me to nominate this place for a Michelin star."

He laughed.

"Yeah, hysterical. Has anyone turned in my cell phone or camera?"

"Not yet, no."

"I was hoping that kid would have picked it up."

"What kid?"

"You know—" I snapped my fingers. "What's his name."

He shook his head.

"The kid," I barked. "The one who followed me around that afternoon."

"Ollie, I have no idea what you're talking about," he replied. "I thought you were alone when you were attacked."

I stared at my brother like he was the one with memory issues.

"We talked about this," I stated. "Remember, I was doing my editor a favor."

"Hell of a favor."

"No shit. Anyway, she asked me to help this kid. Show him the ropes. *Tell* the story, not become *part* of it."

He shook his head.

"Really? I could have sworn—"

"Sorry, Ols."

Images swirled in my mind's eye. Pissed-off protestors in tactical vests and helmets milled about the Capitol Mall. Militia symbols adorned their garb and protective gear. In the distance, screams for justice. Gallows erected near the Reflecting Pool.

More fuel to a burgeoning insurrectionist fire. We weaved about the crowded area. I instructed this nameless face to stay close. Our press credentials swung about our necks as we captured the moment. Rioters proudly displayed hate-filled rhetoric.

From bullhorns some lectured, "It's our First Amendment right to—"

A sudden change in the crowd. Like a drop in temperature or a frothing of the mouth. People began running toward the Capitol Building. I get separated from my young charge. I ignored a looming sense of danger and searched, but throngs of rioters impeded my movement.

Echoing words, *Fake news, fake news.*

Masked men surrounded and shoved me.

"Ollie, watch out!"

I'm struck from behind.

My vision blurred.

A kick to the balls.

Like an electric jolt to the throat.

I dropped to my knees and got cracked in the skull.

Blood dripped down my face.

A punch to the jaw.

Knocked on my ass.

Curled into the fetal position.

A final boot to the face.

I screamed.

"Ollie!" I heard someone shout.

I shook.

"Oliver!" Jaime yelled. "I'm right here. You're safe."

My eyes burst open.

I white-knuckled my bed rails.

Phantom pains and dizziness subsided.

My brother elevated my bed and checked my vitals. I regulated my breathing.

He jabbed his finger into my chest. "I don't give a shit what you say."

I opened my mouth. Attempted to argue.

"Save it. Tomorrow, you're to speak with someone."

"Jai—"

"Don't *even*, Ollie. Just—"

"Derek."

"What?"

"The kid." I smacked his arm. "His name is Derek."

"I don't give a fuck."

CHAPTER TWENTY-FIVE

1986

"Is there a problem, officer?"

He blinded me with his flashlight. "License, registration, and proof of insurance."

I believe the word you're looking for is *please.*

I passed the information out of the driver's side window. He snatched it from my fingers and muttered something on his way back to his cruiser. Navil nervously chewed her manicured fingernails as she stared out the rear window.

"It'll be all right," I assured her.

The cop returned and ordered me out of the car.

"Did I do anything wrong?"

"I won't ask twice."

I stepped out and recognized him immediately.

Officer Wallace.

It was the same asshole cop who manhandled me the previous day at the police station. He sneered and shoved me to the back of the car.

"Now, place your hands on the trunk and spread your legs."

"How com—"

He spun me around, slammed me down onto the trunk, forced my legs apart and patted me down.

"I'm not going to find anything illegal, am I?"

"N-no."

"No sharp objects or anything?"

I shook my head.

He spun me back and glared at me like I ran over his dog or something. I nervously shoved my hands into my pockets to stop them from shaking.

"Keep your hands where I can see them."

I immediately removed them and stood at attention.

"Someone's been a busy boy, Oliver."

The way he said my name made my skin crawl. Shards of disgust mixed with violent intent.

"Your parents spend all that money on private school, and you *still* can't read a simple sign?"

He shined his flashlight at the entrance.

"Shit, if I were them, I'd ask for a refund."

I remained silent.

"And why exactly are *we* here this late?"

I glanced at my watch. It was only a quarter to six. He forced my chin up with the butt of his large metal flashlight.

"Look at me when I'm talking to you."

My eyes widened.

He grabbed my cheeks and got inches from my face.

"When you pulled in, did you *not* see that sign?"

"Y-yes, sir."

"Really? What did it say?"

"No parking after suns—"

"So, what are you doing here after *sunset*?"

"I'm sorry, sir. We didn't—"

"Save it."

He released my face from his vise grip and mumbled to himself. Something about kids from my school always causing trouble. He then looked through the rear window.

"She sure is pretty." He curled his lips. "Be a shame if something bad happened."

A chill ran down my spine, as he smirked and waved at Navil. She slowly became one with the passenger seat. The scumbag scoffed and tossed my ID onto the dirty pavement.

"Get the hell out of here."

I quickly gathered my things, hopped into my car, and drove away. Suffolk County's finest tailgated me with his high beams on all the way down the twisting turns of Quaker Path till he turned off on Ridgeway Avenue.

My heart pounded all the way to our student parking lot. The moment I chucked it into park, I felt like throwing up. I swallowed back the technicolor yawn, took a deep breath, and checked on Navil.

"You okay?"

"Oui. You?"

"Peachy."

"It wasn't your fault."

"It sure feels like it."

She slid over and kissed me.

"Better?"

I let out a breath and smiled.

"Walk me to my dorm?"

"I'd walk you anywhere."

Even though the evening ended differently than I wanted, I was still riding high on the events preceding our police encounter. On the ride home, all I thought about were her lips.

Her soft, perfect lips.

And that delicious tongue.

How her hazel eyes reflected the bursts of reds, yellows, and blues of the sunset.

After pulling into my driveway, I grabbed my things and strolled inside, greeting everyone before heading to my room.

As I closed my door, I overhead Pop. "Someone looks happy."

I wasn't just happy. I was ecstatic.

I couldn't wait to see Navil again.

Be near her.

Hold and kiss her.

After dinner, I grabbed the cordless and went to my room. After five tries, I got through.

"Hi, this is Ollie. Can I please speak with—"

"I'll get her," a female voice snickered.

Jeez, word got around quick, even for our school.

We spent a solid hour talking about nothing and everything. Periodically, she'd get interrupted by a dorm mate looking to use the phone but would shush her away. This was Ollie time, and no one would take it from her.

Of course, I couldn't say the same, as I received an unexpected knock on my bedroom door.

"I'm on the phone."

Tía Carolina popped her head into my room.

"We need you in the family room."

"Now?"

"Sí, ahora, por favor."

I rolled my eyes and told Navil, "I've got to go."

"It's okay, Ollie. If I stay on the phone any longer, I think Ginny will kill me."

"Stefan must be back from his trip."

"I guess."

"See you tomorrow?"

"Oui. Meet you at your locker?"

The thought of Navil waiting for me put a smile on my face. "Definitely."

"Good night, chér."

I hung up and begrudgingly followed my aunt. To my surprise, seated on the couch across from Pop was the attorney, Mr. Eilers, sipping coffee.

He placed his cup down next to a piece of pound cake, stood, and extended his hand. "Hello, Oliver. Good to see you again."

CHAPTER TWENTY-SIX

I glanced at Tía Carolina and Pop as Mr. Eilers and I shook hands.

"You must be wondering why I'm here."

He gestured for me to sit next to him, and as I did, noticed an extra plate and soda can on the coffee table waiting for me, like this was a setup.

"The police called my office today," he explained, "and asked if you would come in for another conversation."

I glanced toward Pop.

"It's okay, Ollie. Listen to Mr. Eilers."

"This time, you won't be alone. I'll be present as your legal counsel."

I chewed my lower lip at the thought of going back to that police station.

"You look nervous, Oliver."

I nodded.

"It's understandable. Keep in mind, you don't have to go. It's all up to you."

I turned to Pop for his advice.

"What do *you* think I should do?"

He shrugged. "Bob, what do you think?"

"You're eighteen, is that right?

"Yes."

"Then it doesn't matter what we think. It's your call."

You're a great help.

"If you don't want to go in, I'll call them back and tell them no. I will also order them not to contact you till they can prove..."

He droned on about something, but I was lost in thought. I couldn't stop thinking about what happened the last time I was at that precinct. I also thought about my recent encounter with Officer Wallace at the beach.

"Ollie, did you hear his question?"

"I'm sorry, what?"

The adults all exchanged looks.

"Would you give us a moment, please?" Mr. Eilers asked.

"We'll be in the kitchen. C'mon, Carolina."

Once alone, he asked, "May I call you Ollie?"

"Sure."

"Thank you. Ollie, have you heard the phrase attorney-client privilege?"

"I think so?"

He chuckled and patted my knee. "It's okay, son. You're not alone."

There was a grandfatherly warmth to his tone.

He sipped his coffee for a moment before explaining that legally, as my attorney, anything I shared with him stayed between us. The only one who could compel him to divulge private information was a judge, and that hardly ever happened.

"Do you understand what that means?"

"That I can tell you anything, and you can't tell anyone."

"Not even your aunt and father, unless you give me permission."

"Anything, *anything*?"

"Why don't we stick to the matter at hand and go from there." He smiled.

I nodded.

"What's on your mind?"

I looked toward the kitchen to make sure we were alone. Convinced of our privacy, I inched forward and told him everything.

"I see. So, you're worried that you'll get your friend in trouble."

"Totally."

"Are you familiar with the Fifth Amendment?"

"You mean like pleading the Fifth in the movies?"

He laughed. "Yes, Ollie, like in the movies. Now, most people remember the part against self-incrimination. You *do* understand what that means, right?"

I nodded.

"Good. What most people forget is it's the same amendment that presumes innocence over guilt."

"Which means?"

"In essence, your friend is . . ."

" . . . innocent till proven guilty?"

"Bingo."

I popped open my soda while digesting the information.

As I did, Navil's heart-shaped face flashed before my eyes.

Her slightly freckled nose crinkled.

Those perfect lips puckered.

That silken tongue.

Warm and playful.

Our French kiss—

French—no, not French.

Shit.

"Mr. Eilers, what if she's Belgian?"

"Come again?"

"What if she's from Belgium."

He got the same pained look Pop got when he ate ice cream too fast and received a brain freeze.

"She's *not* an American citizen?"

"No. She's from . . ."

"Belgium," he murmured. "Okay, that's a little different. I would have to consult a specialist in international law, which I'm not."

"So, what do I do?"

"For now? Nothing. Don't worry, Ollie. I'll take care of it."

"How?"

"First, I'll tell the detectives that for now we're not available to speak and will have to get back to them. Then, I'll speak with a trusted colleague."

"Mr. Eilers? Just so you know, I don't think she did it."

"That's good to know, son, but let's cross that bridge when we get to it."

"I just hope it doesn't collapse."

CHAPTER TWENTY-SEVEN

I refused to keep this news from Navil.

I wouldn't lie to her again.

I couldn't.

The moment she saw me turn the corner the following morning, she squealed and ran toward me.

After a quick hug hello, she took my hand and escorted me to my locker.

I opened it and whispered, "We need to talk."

"What's the matter, chér?"

"Not here. Too many people," I replied. "When is your free period?"

"After lunch."

"Shit. I really didn't want to wait till then."

"What's going on, Ollie? You're scaring me."

"Can you be late to first period?"

"Oui. It's French class. I'll just say I have the cramps."

Ew.

"Well, I have photography. Why don't we go to the deli?"

We snuck out the back as the first bell rang and escaped to the deli. Over large coffees, I told her everything.

"Merde, what are we going to do?"

"I don't know."

She angrily turned and walked away, muttering something to herself in French.

I caught up to her. "Hey, hey."

"I didn't do it, Ollie."

"I believe you."

She looked relieved.

"We just need to figure out who did, and why."

After school, we met at the library as usual.

"What do you want to do?"

I arched a brow and smirked, receiving a smack to the chest.

"Ollie, I'm serious."

"Sorry. Well, we can go inside and study. Or . . ."

"Or?"

I turned and gestured toward the auditorium, still off-limits to anyone without a badge.

"Do you really think that's a good idea?"

"What's a good idea?" Fi joined us.

Navil and I stared at one another.

"Okay, what are you two up to?"

I weighed my options. I've known Fi my whole life. She was my best friend, and I trusted her with my life.

"Well?"

Navil gestured toward me, so I spent the next few minutes updating Fi. The only part I left out was the make-out session at the beach.

"So, what do you think?" I asked.

She smacked the back of my head. "Are you out of your mind?"

"Ow, what?"

"Aren't you two in enough trouble as it is? Now, you want to return to the scene of the crime?"

"I just thought—"

She mimicked me. *"I just thought . . .* no you didn't, you idiot. This isn't Scooby Doo, you moron. This is real life."

"Yeah, but—"

"But nothing. Ollie, you're gonna get caught. And then what?"

"Fine. So, what do we do?"

"Nothing. Let the cops do their job."

"She might be right, Ollie."

Now you take her side?

I sighed.

"Ols, I get that you're frustrated—"

"Ya, think?"

"But something's going on here. Something . . ." Fi searched for the right words, "bigger than us."

Navil nodded.

Defeated, I turned to Navil. "Don't know about you, but I don't really feel like studying right now, do you?"

"Not really."

"Why don't you guys take a drive or something. Go clear your heads."

Navil and I smirked at one another.

Fi noticed and rolled her eyes.

"I'm going inside. I've got French to study, unlike someone else here."

"Okay. I'll swing by and grab you up around—"

"Five-thirty?"

"That'll work. See you later."

Walking past the auditorium toward my car made me think of Jackie.

"You think she's doing okay?"

"Who, chér?" She followed my eyeline. "Jackie?"

I nodded.

"You feel guilty?"

"Yeah."

She breathed out, "Every time I walk by—"

"You get a pit in your stomach?"

"Oui."

Bloody images of Jackie splashed across my mind's eye as her recent comments about not visiting her played in my ear.

"Do you think we should visit her?"

"Do you know where they took her?"

"Yeah, my father learned that she's at University Hospital, where he works."

We stared at one another for a moment, seeking silent approval.

Navil smiled and took my hand. "Let's go."

At least now she can't accuse me of not seeing her.

CHAPTER TWENTY-EIGHT

I'd been to this hospital a gazillion times. Pop had two offices. One at this hospital and another in a nearby office complex. Ever since Mom passed away, I hated coming here. Before entering, I always braced myself. The vinegary scent of the photo lab was like a bouquet of roses compared to the antiseptic blend of sickness and death of this place.

Even though it'd been years, the events of my mother's death still hit me like a kick to the stones.

Every goddamn time.

Memories from those days flooded my mind. The way cancer and chemo ravaged my mother's body. By the time she died, you could count her ribs through her hospital gown.

Any impulse to go into medicine went out the door the day she died.

"Are you okay?"

I cleared my throat. "Yeah. It's, uh . . . nothing."

"What's wrong, Ollie? You can tell me."

I didn't answer at first.

I just stared at the people milling about the lobby.

"It's just . . . every time I come here . . ."

She rubbed my back.

"I . . . think about my mom."

She pulled me close and wrapped her loving arms around me. A lump formed in my throat, but I refused to cry. Instead, I swallowed hard and thought about that innocent pain in the ass lying in bed, most likely barking out orders and driving the staff insane.

"We should go up," I whispered.

"Are you sure? We don't have—"

"Yes, we do," I replied. "*I* do."

She nodded and walked with me to the information desk.

"How can I help you?" an elderly volunteer named Evelyn asked.

"We're here to see a patient," I explained. "Jackie Woodley."

"Let me check." She searched the patient records. "Here she is, Room 405, bed number two. Just take those elevators up to—"

"Thank you, ma'am."

At the nurse's station on the fourth floor, we received directions to her room.

"Fifth door on the left. Got it," I replied.

Outside her room, I checked my breath before knocking on the door.

"Come in."

We stepped in, and to my surprise, Jackie smiled when she saw us.

"Oh my gosh, hi, um . . ."

The girl who tortured me for the past three years could not remember my name, and that reality hurt my heart.

"Ollie," I replied. "My name is Ollie. And this is Navil."

"Bonjour, Jackie. How are you feeling?"

"Okay, I guess."

I stood to the side as the roommates chatted. There was a stark contrast between the bulldog who usually bit my head off and the frail girl wearing glasses, powder blue pj's, and a bandage wrapped around her skull.

Seeing her in this state pissed me off for some reason.

Was she a pain in the ass?

Sure.

Most everyone thought so, except for the auburn-haired beauty speaking with her.

Was she nosy as fuck?

One thousand percent.

Did she deserve this?

Absolutely not.

No one did.

I glanced around the room and took everything in. Even though it'd been a while since I had stepped into a hospital room, the style hadn't changed a bit.

Olive-green walls with a hint of rubbing alcohol and disinfectant. The curtains were still as drab as the ratty bathrobe Tía Carolina wore before turning in.

Her dinner was a half-eaten fried chicken breast and mashed potatoes that looked like something you'd expect to find in prison.

"Was that your dinner?"

She scoffed, "If that's what you want to call it. I'd kill for a burger and fries."

"Seriously?"

She cocked a brow.

"I mean, we can run out if you want. Mickey D's is right around the corner."

She smiled and shook her head. "Better not. Thanks, though."

"Sure," I replied. "So, how long are you stuck here?"

"*Ollie.*"

"What?"

"Don't be so—"

"It's okay," Jackie interjected. "Honestly, I'm not sure. I'm having—memory issues."

Navil reached for her hand, but Jackie yanked it back like it was on fire.

"*Don't* touch me."

CHAPTER TWENTY-NINE

H er words chilled the room.

Navil gasped and stepped back, which caused Jackie to immediately backpedal.

"Sorry. It's just—I don't like being touched."

"I'm so sorry. I meant no—"

Unexpectedly, Jackie's mother barged in carrying a handful of magazines.

"Honey, I brought you more—oh, hello."

"Hi, ma'am."

"Bonjour."

"Mom, this is Ollie and—"

"Navil." She held out her hand. "We are . . . friends from school."

"Oh, how nice."

I found it strange that she introduced herself as a friend from school versus Jackie's roommate, but left it alone.

"We were worried about Jackie, non?"

"So, we thought we'd stop by and check on her."

"Well, that's very nice of you both." She pointed at me. "Now, do I know you?"

"Ma'am?"

She scratched her chin. "You look *very* familiar. Now, don't tell me."

"Jackie and I *have* been classmates for a few years. And we're both on the school paper together."

"No, that's not it." She shook her head. "It'll come to me."

"Mother, please."

"Fine, it's not that important. I'll just leave these . . . oh, Jackie. You still haven't finished your dinner."

Jackie rolled her eyes.

"Do you know how many starving children . . ."

Did that argument ever work on anyone?

"Then send it to them."

"You're as stubborn as your father."

"Thank you."

"It wasn't a compliment."

I caught Navil's attention and jerked my head toward the door.

She nodded.

"Hey, so, we're gonna get out of your—"

"You're not leaving already, are you?" Jackie asked.

Her look of disappointment cut straight to my heart. And to Navil's as well, apparently.

"No, mon ami, we can stay for a few more minutes, non, Ollie?"

"Yeah, uh, sure. But I do need to get you back to school and pick up Fi."

"I understand. So, you and I work on the school paper together?"

"Yep. You're the lead reporter and editor, and I'm the head photographer."

"Like Peter Parker?" she asked with a glint in her eye that made me smile.

"I'm more of a Jimmy Olsen fan, but something like that."

We bantered back and forth for a while, which felt conventionally strange. We've known each other for years but always had a combative relationship. This was our first-ever civil conversation.

I shared with her how she always walked around campus with her gold and blue notebook, searching for her next story.

"And what about you? Are you on the paper as well?" she asked Navil.

"Me? Mon Dieu, No. That's all you and Ollie. I'm more of a reader."

"You can say that again," I replied. "She reads like three papers a day."

"Wow."

"It's no big deal."

"No big deal? Please. She reads *The New York Times*, *The Guardian*, and some French paper I can't pronounce."

"Goodness, you sound like my husband, Henry," Jackie's mom chimed in. "Do you want to be an attorney too?"

"I'm not sure. I know I want to help people. Maybe work for the FPS like mon père. Are you familiar with—"

Her mom chuckled and replied in French, "Yes, young lady. I am very familiar with Federal Public Service."

I couldn't understand what she said, but her response seemed to impress Navil, who raised her brows. The pair spent the next few minutes chatting away in French while I stood and watched.

Navil told me later that Jackie's parents lived overseas for a while before settling in Maryland and working in DC.

She said Jackie's dad was an attorney for some lobbyist firm, while she spends her time—

"—hosting parties for diplomats and dignitaries."

"Bon?"

She continued her humble bragging.

"Just last week, I was telling Nancy—I'm sorry, *Mrs. Reagan*," she whispered.

Jackie cut her off. "Ollie, did you say you needed to get back to school?"

"Hmm? Oh, yeah. Look at the time. We gotta go," I said, looking at my watch. "It was nice meeting you, Mrs. Wood—"

"*Dr. Morales!*" She slapped her hands and pointed at me.

I whipped my head around. "Where?"

"No, *you*. That's how I know you."

"Huh?"

"Your father, right?"

"How'd you know?"

"Thought so." She turned to her daughter. "I never forget a handsome doctor."

"Muh-*ther*."

"What? It's true. I can see where *this one* gets it. Shame he's taken."

Somebody, please kill me now.

Jackie melted under her blankets as her mom eyed me up and down like a side of beef.

Navil covered her smile.

"Yeah, uh—we'll see ya later, Jackie. Nice meeting you, ma'am."

"Bye, Ollie. Thanks for coming."

"Au revoir, Jackie." Navil waved and received a nod.

We were barely outside the room and could hear Jackie rip into her mom for embarrassing her.

On the way to the elevator, I whispered, "Well, that was—special."

Navil chuckled.

"Now I know where Jackie gets it."

"It wasn't *that* bad."

"If you say so," I replied, stepping onto the empty elevator.

"And she wasn't wrong."

I arched a brow.

"You are handsome."

She pushed me against the wall and kissed me as the door closed.

CHAPTER THIRTY

The finger-pointing and whispers in the school hallways died down as the week progressed. By Friday, I learned of my new nickname.

Jailbird.

Real original, I know.

It was better than my former one.

Loser.

Not that anyone ever called me that to my face, but I still felt like one.

Hanging out with Navil, though, changed all that.

She gave me confidence.

I stood taller.

Even teachers noticed.

"Looking good, Ollie."

"Uh, thanks, Coach."

"Mr. Morales, new haircut?" Professor Michaels asked.

"No, sir."

"Hmm . . . there's something different—whatever you're doing, keep it up."

And *keep it up*, I did.

The remainder of the week, we visited Jackie twice. Once to deliver McDonald's and the other a few slices of pizza. Even though her mother commented on the effects fast food had on Jackie's waistline, I think she appreciated our intention. And based on the way she chowed down, we knew Jackie did.

However, by Thursday, Navil and I grew tired of playing Good Samaritans and needed to blow off steam, so during my free period, I hit the library and grabbed a copy of *Newsday*, a local paper. After reading the comics, I flipped to the movie section, found our perfect escape, and couldn't wait to track down Navil.

"What are you doing this weekend?" I asked, full of enthusiasm.

She smiled. "I don't know. What *are* we doing?"

I scanned our surroundings and made sure we had some privacy. I raised my arms, jumped to my left, and took a step to the right. I then put my hands on my hips and swiveled them back and forth, like I was twirling an invisible hula-hoop.

Her mouth shot open. "What are you doing?"

"The Time Warp."

"What?"

From a distance, I heard Fi's laugh as she approached.

"What is this idiot doing?"

Navil shrugged. "A time something?"

"Oh, my God, are you doing the Time Warp?"

I took Fi's hands and swung her around.

She resisted at first, but after a beat, joined me, peppering me with questions as we danced.

"Are you guys going to—"

"Thinking about it."

"When?"

"Saturday night. Wanna go?"

"Fuck yeah."

Exhausted, we stopped dancing and turned to Navil.

"What do you think? Wanna go?" I asked.

"Go where?"

I couldn't believe what I heard.

Has she never seen "Rocky Horror."

Zero recognition.

Fi and I exchanged looks.

"I think she's a virgin," Fi whispered.

Navil's face contorted. *"Excusez-moi?"*

"Oh, Navil. No, it's—"

Angry, she stormed off.

I ran after her.

"Navil, wait, it's not what you think," I said, grabbing her arm. "It's what you call someone who hasn't seen the movie."

Her eyes narrowed as I took her hand. I tried explaining it to her, but she didn't believe me. Over Navil's shoulder, I noticed Eddie heading toward the photo lab, so I called him over.

"Hold on, I'll prove it to you. Hey, Eddie. C'mere."

"What's up, Ollie?"

"Have you been to see *Rocky Horror*?"

"Hey, I'm not a virgin."

"See?"

Navil chewed on the comment.

Confused, Eddie asked, "What am I missing? Are you guys—"

"Yeah, we're thinking about it."

"Cool. Can I come?"

"Don't see why not."

Eddie pumped his fist. "Yes."

I turned back to Navil. "Like I was saying, the movie—"

Eddie cut me off. "Can I bring someone?"

"Sure, Eddie."

"You know, it starts at midnight—"

"I know."

"Do you think we should go out to dinner first, or—"

"Jesus, *Eddie*."

"Why don't we give them a minute." Fi grabbed Eddie and walked away.

I took a deep breath and watched the pair walk off before focusing on Navil.

"Look, first, I'm sorry about all that virgin stuff. We weren't trying to embar—"

"It's okay, Ollie. It's just—"

"It's personal."

She blushed a bit and nodded.

"Anyway, like Eddie said, the movie starts at midnight and ends around two."

"That *is* kind of late, non?"

"Yeah, but it's totally worth it."

She hemmed and hawed. "I don't think I can stay out that late."

"Oh."

Navil caressed my face.

"I'm sorry, Ollie."

"It's okay." I kissed her palm. "It was just an idea. We can do something else."

I called Fi and Eddie over.

"Hey, guys. I don't think we're gonna go."

"How come?" Eddie asked.

"The school won't let boarders stay out that late."

"What if she sleeps over at my house?" Fi chimed in.

I love you, Fi.

CHAPTER THIRTY-ONE

Saturday morning, I picked Navil up around noon and made the rounds, gathering supplies for the movie. After leaving the grocery store, we hit the toy store in the mall for water pistols, noise makers, and confetti.

As we finished, we ran into Ginny and her boyfriend, Stefan.

"Hey, guys."

"Bonjour, Ginny."

"What are you guys doing here?" Ginny asked, checking out our bag.

It's not that I had a problem with these two. I didn't. I'd known them for years, even shared classes with them. It's just we didn't travel in the same circles, and frankly, I had zero interest in changing that any time soon, especially that night.

I wanted to keep our group to a minimum. Make it a special night. For Navil and me. Particularly after the shitty week we had.

Unfortunately, Navil didn't get the memo.

She smiled and held up the bag. "We're here getting supplies for a movie, non?"

"For what movie?"

Navil turned to me.

Through a fake smile. "Rocky Horror. She's a vir—hasn't seen the movie, so I'm taking her to see it tonight."

"Oh my gosh, I *love* that movie," Ginny squealed.

Of course you do.

"Would you like to join us?" Navil asked.

"I don't know. Let me think about it," Stefan replied.

Good.

"Why don't we talk about it over lunch?" Navil asked.

"Sure." Ginny smiled.

The girls looped arms and led the way to the *Friendly's* in the mall while Stefan and I followed quietly behind. Periodically, I caught him checking out Navil's backside, which pissed me off, but I was too afraid to do anything about it.

He had me by four inches, was captain of the swim team, and strong as fuck. We wrestled once in gym class, and it only took him seconds to twist me into a pretzel, something I wished to avoid, so I swallowed my annoyance, along with some pride.

Navil wasn't the only girl he checked out that afternoon, and I wasn't the only one to notice. In addition to flirting with the hostess, he smiled at a pair of girls seated in a nearby booth and ogled our waitress as she walked away. For the latter, he received a sharp elbow to the ribs from his girlfriend.

Over lunch, Stefan eventually agreed to go to the movies with us, which pleased Ginny, who hugged him when he acquiesced. Over ice cream, I asked about his recent trip, a topic he seemingly wanted to avoid.

"So, where'd you go?"

"Oh, um . . . Ecuador."

"No kiddin'. How come?"

"A, uh, mission trip. So, what time's the—"

Mission trip. Maybe I was wrong about this asshole.

Ginny twirled his hair and cooed, "Yeah, he does them all the time."

He shrugged her off. "It's no big deal."

"I've never been to Ecuador, but I have been to Columbia and Brazil," Navil chimed in.

"You don't say?" Stefan lit up.

"Oui, mon père travels quite a bit—"

"And her family gets to go sometimes. Her passport's supposedly insane," I interjected.

"I loved Columbia. And the Brazilians are—" she kissed her fingertips.

"Ever been to Carnival?" Stefan asked.

"I wish. My sister Marie went last year. She said it was—" She searched for the right expression. "Très fou. You know, crazy, non?"

"That's one way to put it." He chuckled. "Ya definitely need to go."

Ginny chimed in, "Maybe we all can—"

Stefan rolled his eyes, ignored her, and began bragging about the twin-engine Cessna he and his brother, Royce, had parked at MacArthur Airport in Islip.

"Hell, I could take you down the coast. There's this great place right outside of DC that has the best crab cakes."

"But, Stefan, I thought that was our pl—"

"Afterwards, we can hit Georgetown. It has the best bars. This one time—"

I sat there with a fake smile, watching him blather on and flirt with my . . . I didn't know what to call her. My friend? My girlfriend? The girl I made out with. Did I have a right to tag her?

Well, whatever the hell she was, I don't know whom it bothered more—me or the one who sat there fingering her dinner knife while staring daggers at the pair. At any moment, I expected her to lunge across the table and impale Navil in the neck.

Thankfully, our waitress arrived with the check. "Will there be anything else?"

We all shook our heads.

"Will it be one check or—"

Stefan cut her off and handed her a fifty-dollar bill, which seemed to impress everyone.

Well, almost everyone.

I reached for my wallet. "I can pay for—"

"Dude, it's okay. Why don't you pick up the movie tonight?"

You mean the movie I didn't want you to come to? That movie?

Not wanting to come across as an asshole in front of Navil, I agreed. Outside the restaurant, I gave Stefan directions to my place and asked them to arrive by nine o'clock.

"We plan on hitting the diner in Smithtown before heading to the movie."

"That's cool," Stefan replied. "See you later."

Can't wait.

CHAPTER THIRTY-TWO

Modern Day

Based on the unexpected visitor who knocked on my door, Jaime must have grown tired of my bullshit and called in the big guns.

"Come in."

The man could have worn a full-body condom, and I'd still recognize those fuzzy eyebrows behind his N95 mask, not to mention the dark brown eyes. His very presence forced me to sit up straight in bed.

"*Pop*, what are you doing here?"

The last thing this mid-seventies man should have done during the COVID-19 pandemic was travel, but once he got a bug up his ass, good luck changing that mind. Tía Carolina used to call it the *Morales Syndrome*.

He now used an aluminum cane to steady his gait. From the doorway, he greeted me with a head shake and same sound of disappointment I'd received my whole life—his deep sigh. He shuffled over, slipped down his mask, and kissed me hello before examining my wounds.

I attempted to shrug him off, but he slapped my hand away. "I'm fine, Pop."

"That's not what I'm hearing, Oliver."

Jaime, you blabbermouth.

"Well, whatever Jaime told you is bullsh—"

He chucked me his don't-use-that-kind-of-language-around-me glare and raised his cane, causing me to flinch. Instead of smacking me, he hooked the leg of a nearby chair and slid it closer. Once comfortable, he proceeded to deliver another life lecture.

Pop gestured to my injuries. "I hope it was worth it. Taking pictures of those animals. You could have gotten yourself killed."

I lay against my pillow.

"Do you have any idea what you're putting us all through? The stress? And that poor wife of yours, stuck overseas—"

He blathered on for a few minutes. Any attempted interruptions or answering rhetorical questions were met with a sharp look or a talk-to-the-hand gesture.

"—and just because I'm a gynecologist doesn't mean I don't understand the male psyche or anatomy," he stated. "Do you have any idea how many parents I've counseled over the years? Lost wives. Lost infants. Cancer."

I rolled my eyes.

"*Well*?"

"No, Pop, how many?"

He leaned forward and thumped my head. "Plenty."

"Ow, that hurt."

"Good. Maybe something will get through that thick skull of yours."

"Like I said—"

He raised his cane. "Mira, if you tell me one more time that you're *fine*—"

"Okay, jeez, I *am* injured, you know."

"Trust me, pendejo, I know," he grumbled.

His continued badgering reminded me of when I quit my White House gig.

"Oliver, I don't understand. You worked at the White House.

You took pictures of the President of the United States. I can't think of a more important job."

He could never wrap his head around my role in the field, documenting the injustices of our world, versus being a mere chess piece in someone else's political game. Pop preferred the safety that came with acting like wallpaper, taking pictures of self-congratulatory men and women with their own agendas.

But when we flew to New Orleans after Hurricane Katrina hit for another round of partisan photo ops, I had enough. I pulled my director aside and turned in my White House credentials.

"You and that damn camera of yours. I should have never listened to your aunt and bought you that thing."

He started breathing harder, and his eyes began bulging out.

"Okay, Pop, calm down."

"The minute that phone rang, I knew you were hurt." He pointed an accusatory ancient finger.

"Sorry, Pop."

He scoffed at my apology. "And what's this I hear about the FBI?"

"It's no big deal."

He sat forward. "What have you gotten yourself into this time, hijo?"

"Nothing. They're investigating the riots, and they had a few questions."

"For the love of God, please tell me you spoke to these people this time. Bob Eilers isn't around to save you."

Like a six-year-old girl with a brand-new Barbie doll, he wouldn't let it go.

"That was high school, Pop. I'm in my fifties. I have kids in and out of college."

"I know how old you are," he replied. "Oh—and you're having nightmares?"

Jaime, I swear to God when I see you—

"Please tell me that you're getting help."

I turned my head and ignored him.

"Oliver?"

"I'm dealing with it my way. I have a . . . process."

His dark eyes narrowed. "Oh, *really*?"

"This isn't my first injury."

"And it won't be your last, if you keep this nonsense up."

"You know what?" I threw my hands up. "You win, Pop, okay? I'll call someone."

"When?"

"Soon."

"How about today?"

I pinched the bridge of my nose and took a deep breath.

"Fine." I gave in. "Happy now?"

"Very."

He grabbed the TV remote hanging from my bedside and flipped the TV to cable news. They were still covering the aftermath of January 6th and political fallout. He clearly didn't get the memo that this riot coverage triggered me. I feigned exhaustion and yawned.

"I think I'm going to shut my eyes for a bit."

"Get your rest. We can talk about local therapy groups when you wake up."

You're a dead man, Jaime.

Dead.

CHAPTER THIRTY-THREE

1986

If you wanted to understand the expression, "The freaks come out at night," attend a midnight showing of *The Rocky Horror Picture Show*. If that didn't work, nothing would.

Since it was Navil's first time, I decided to tone down my outfit and chose a simple t-shirt, Levi's, and sneakers. I tossed on my coat, grabbed my wallet and keys, and headed toward the front door.

"Heading out," I announced.

"Where ya headed?" Pop called from the family room.

"Movies."

"At this hour?" Tía Carolina asked.

I sighed. "Tía, it's Saturday night. A bunch of us are—"

The doorbell cut me off.

"That'll be Navil and Fi."

Jaime squealed and ran past me to answer the door, "Fiiiii."

She scooped him up and received her prerequisite kisses before stepping aside for Navil's grand entrance.

My heart skipped a beat.

She'd never looked this sexy, her auburn hair parted to the side and slicked back. Thin black eyeliner drew out her hazel eyes, and cardinal-red lipstick accentuated her pouty mouth.

She smelled great too.

I whispered, "You look amazing."

Navil blushed, came to my side, and kissed my cheek, leaving behind a subtle reminder. "Merci, chér."

Not to be outdone, Fi opened her coat to reveal her outfit. A risqué French maid outfit, push-up bra, slightly torn fishnets with fake blood streaks, and a pair of Chuck Taylor's Converse high tops.

It blew my head back. "Jesus, Fi."

After receiving my response, she sauntered into the family room to show Pop and Tía Carolina.

She threw her coat open. "You like?"

Pop spit out his coffee.

"*Hija de mi vida,* what are you wearing?" my Tía gasped.

Before she could respond, there was a knock on the door, followed by an aggressive doorbell ringing. I figured it was Stefan being an asshole since Eddie was too polite to pull that stunt. It pissed off Pop.

"I'll get it," he growled, stopping me in my place.

He yanked the door open, readying to rip someone a new asshole. Waiting for him on the other side were Detectives Gallagher and Chao, along with a sneering Officer Wallace.

Before Pop could say anything, they barged right in.

"Oliver Morales, we have a warrant for your arrest," Gallagher announced.

Pop attempted to get in their way but was shoved aside by the three, one slapping a warrant against his chest.

Once inside, Wallace made a beeline toward me and cuffed my left wrist. Chaos ensued.

Before anyone could restrain him, Jaime ran over and kicked Wallace in the shin. Not far behind him, Bella ran to my side and began barking at Wallace. It got worse from there.

When I attempted to bend down and push her away, Wallace twisted my other arm behind my back, causing me to scream from the pain shooting down my shoulder as he slapped on the other cuff.

Amidst the madness, Fi's coat flew open, revealing her intimate apparel. The sight stopped the cops in their tracks. It was like they'd never seen a half-naked girl before.

This allowed Jaime to get a final kick in before Fi scooped him and Bella up. Navil and Tía Carolina attempted to intervene in my arrest, but Officer Asshole hip-checked Navil out of the way before shoving Tía Carolina to the floor.

More screams, including Pop, whose eyes flared in anger. "You sonofab—"

Detective Chao placed himself between Pop and Wallace. Navil and Fi tended to my aunt.

Gallagher Mirandized me while Wallace shoved me out the front door for all my neighbors to see.

My nostrils flared, cheeks flushed, and jaw clenched from the embarrassment.

From behind me, Pop shouted, "Don't say a thing, Ollie. I'm right behind you."

Wallace opened the back door of his patrol car, manhandled the top of my head, and shoved me in sideways.

"You know the drill." He slammed the door behind me.

I pushed my feet against the closed door and righted myself while Wallace barked orders at my curious neighbors.

The pungent interior aroma still punched me in the face. How anyone could drive around with this stench was beyond me. I guess I'd be a miserable asshole, too, if I had to drive around in a car that smelled like a porta-potty after a New York Giants game.

Wallace eventually got in and adjusted his rearview. "What, no blubbering this time? Surprised. You seemed like such a pussy."

I glared back with a go-fuck-yourself expression but didn't

say anything. With a sneer, he backed out of my driveway and drove us straight to the police station without saying another word, while I just stared out the window.

Once we arrived, Wallace yanked me from the car and processed me. I felt like such a scumbag. I quickly learned that there was nothing sexy about getting arrested. To this cop, I was just another piece of meat to grind through the system.

After confiscating my wallet, watch, and car keys, he took down my personal information.

"I need your full name and date of birth."

I ignored him at first, but this wasn't his first rodeo. Hell, I probably wasn't even his first victim of the evening. After ignoring him a second time, he looked around for witnesses. Seeing that we were alone, he reached down, grabbed my balls, and squeezed them hard.

"I said, first name and date of birth."

Air shot from my lungs as electric pain shot up from my nether regions to my throat. I coughed out my response, placing a smile on his sadistic face.

He then put a placard around my neck, stood me against a wall with lined height measurements, and took my mug shot before moving on to the fingerprint portion of the evening.

Twenty minutes later, he hustled me into a private holding cell where I curled into the fetal position on the uncomfortable plastic cot to recover from the physical and psychological pain.

It didn't take long for the hit parade to continue.

CHAPTER THIRTY-FOUR

J ust as the walls felt like they were pressing in on me, Wallace retrieved me from my cell and escorted me to another interrogation room, this one slightly larger than the previous one and sported a large two-way mirror.

Wallace shoved me inside to the awaiting Detectives Gallagher and Chao. Chao wore a resting bitch face.

Have you ever enjoyed a day in your miserable life?

"Sit," Detective Gallagher barked.

Doing as ordered, I popped a squat on the cold metallic folding chair. They immediately peppered me with questions.

"Why didn't you tell us that Miss Woodley was recently injured at your home?"

"Is that why you went to see her? To finish the job?" Chao countered.

They spent the next few minutes building a narrative where I injured Jackie at my house before attacking her again at school.

The whole thing was absurd.

"Admit it." Chao towered over me. "You have it out for this girl. What'd she do, refuse to go to the prom with you or something?"

I made a face at the thought. "With her? Ew."

He grabbed a yellow legal pad and pencil and slid it across the desk. "Fess up, kid."

The guy was a bad caricature of someone you'd see on TV.

"If you do, the courts might take it easy on you."

I turned my face and shrank into my chair.

"Well?" Chao growled. "*Say* something."

His partner put his hand on Chao's arm. Encouraged him to sit. Instead, he stuck a cigarette in his mouth, lit it, and began pacing.

Gallagher then took a deep breath and leaned forward. "We know the truth but need to hear it from you."

I should have listened to my old man and kept my mouth shut. But these guys had it all wrong, and I'd be damned if I was going to sit there and allow them to railroad me into making a confession.

"That's not what happened."

Chao stopped pacing and grabbed a seat next to his partner, who casually leaned back in his chair like a skilled fisherman with another bite on the line.

"Then tell us what happened," Gallagher said.

Foolishly, I did.

I spent the next few minutes recounting the entire story.

" . . . and like I said, we ran in and—"

"You saw someone jump out the window, yeah, we know." Chao blew smoke in my face.

"Why didn't you tell us all this when you were here the last time?" Gallagher asked.

I sighed. "I don't know."

Gallagher's eyes narrowed, "You don't know? C'mon, kid, you can do better than that."

It was like they handed me a shovel and asked me to dig.

I whispered, "I didn't want to get anyone in trouble."

"Anyone specific?"

I shook my head.

In a caring tone, Gallagher asked, "Oliver? Who didn't you want to get in trouble?"

Just as Navil's name formed on my lips, there was a knock on the door.

"Are you fucking kidding me?" Chao shouted. "*What?*"

Wallace popped his head into the room. "Kid's lawyer's here."

I felt a huge sense of relief shooting through my body. "Oh, thank God."

Chao muttered something under his breath and left the room.

"Okay. Go get him. You got lucky, kid," Gallagher said as we waited.

We heard yelling from the hallway. "Where is he?"

When he burst into the room, we immediately locked eyes. His full of anger. Mine full of relief.

He pointed at Gallagher. "Detective, a moment, please?"

It reminded me of Tía Carolina getting ready to let us have it for making a mess. The detective slunk out of his chair and slowly followed Mr. Eilers out the door.

"You knew he had representation. Why didn't you call me to arrange this?"

"We tried that, Counselor, remem—"

"And how dare you speak to my client without counsel present."

It went south from there. Eilers threatened to have all involved up on charges. I heard words like, lose qualified immunity, internal affairs, the district attorney, and speaking to his captain, a poker buddy.

At my age, even I knew Gallagher's excuses were weak.

"We read him his rights. He knew—"

"Seriously? He's barely eighteen, and you knew he had an attorney."

I pictured Eiler's mouth frothing as his spittle covered Gallagher's face. Eventually, the yelling ended, and the door opened. Eilers joined me in the interrogation room, shutting the door behind him before taking the chair across from me.

His grim expression told me everything I needed to know but wasn't ready to hear.

"When can I go home?" I asked.

He let out a deep breath before answering. "About that . . ."

Fuck.

CHAPTER THIRTY-FIVE

"Unfortunately, you're going to have to spend a night or two."

"*Here?*"

"It's Saturday night, Ollie, and the courts aren't open tomorrow."

I slammed my hands on the table. "Damnit. This is bullshit, Mr. Eilers—"

"Just try and calm down."

Fuck you, dude. You're not the one spending the weekend in jail.

"I'll see that the charges get dropped and your record expunged."

I pulled my knees into my chest and slowly rocked in my chair. An image of Jackie's face ran through my mind. I recalled her hogging the couch that night and being a general pain in the ass.

If she hadn't come over that night.

I blamed her for everything, not knowing that the truth would avail itself in the next few weeks.

"So, I'm stuck here."

"I'm afraid so."

I slumped my head back. "This *sucks.*"

"I know. But look, I'm going to make sure they place you in your own cell, away from everyone else. The last thing we need is for you to get tossed in with gen pop."

"Gen pop?"

"Sorry, it's short for the general population. You know, the muggers and thieves. You'll be safer in your own cell."

All I could picture was Fi saying, "Chester the molester."

Mr. Eilers tried to assure me that everything would work out.

"Just be patient. By this time next week, these guys will be working on another case, and yours will be a distant memory."

"So, what you're saying is, I have to wait for someone else to get hurt?"

"More or less."

"Jesus."

"Sorry, Ollie."

Not as sorry as I am.

"Before I go, remember to keep to yourself. Don't say a word to anyone. Not a soul. Do you understand me, Ollie? You can't trust anyone in this place."

"Not a soul," I echoed.

"And if the detectives pull you aside again, tell them you want your attorney. I'm tired of these games."

Get in line.

"Just stay vigilant."

I pursed my lips and nodded.

After he left, an officer escorted me back to my cell, and although it wasn't my first time behind bars, I still couldn't get over that sense of finality the moment I heard the metallic tumbler lock behind me. Like I got dropped into a black hole.

Before walking away, the officer asked if I was hungry.

Oddly enough, I was.

"Yeah."

"Let me see if I can scrounge you up something."

I thanked him and grabbed a seat on my cot. I sat in the dank cell a while, twiddling my thumbs, before he returned with a dry bologna sandwich and pint of milk.

As I choked down my late meal, I wondered what everyone else was doing. Had they gone to the movie without me?

The gossipmongers at school were going to have a field day with this. I couldn't wait to read my yearbook superlative at the end of the year.

Oliver Morales voted most likely to be spending Christmas in Rikers.

There were no windows in this part of the building. I didn't know if that was to keep prisoners from escaping, or to encourage that aesthetic claustrophobic feeling one got sitting in these cells. Regardless, time became meaningless for me.

Just as I became comfortable with my new surroundings, the noise level increased. Neighboring cells began filling up with what I overheard one of the officers call "the weekend regulars."

One by one, men marched by my cell; some sneered, most cursed.

"What the fuck are you looking at?" a man scoffed.

Soon, a chorus of complaints echoed throughout lockup.

"Let me out of here."

"I didn't do it."

"It wasn't my fault."

That night, I heard it all and experienced worse.

Every male demographic.

Young, middle-aged, and older.

White, black, Asian, you name it. They came in wearing the same jewelry I recently wore on my wrists and were placed in similar vomit-scented cells.

It was like being at a criminal parade. The only things missing were floats and balloons. At one point, I felt like the cops were doing it for my benefit. A personalized version of that show, *Scared Straight*. To show me what happens when you break the law.

Cut to Ricky Sheridan entering my life and cell.

The twenty-something guy was a lanky six feet one, maybe two. He had me by about ten pounds and dripped of street experience. And if you searched the dictionary for the word scumbag, you'd find his unshaven mug.

He sported a shaggy brown mullet down past his shoulders and a matching cheesy mustache. He had a purple shiner emerging under his right eye which complimented the blood crusted under his nose and speckled across the front of his torn blue-and-gold-striped polyester shirt.

I don't know which hit me first, the screechy sound of his voice, or pungent scent of his cologne.

"This is bullshit, Wallace, and you know it," he yelled.

"Just keep moving, Ricky."

"I was set up."

"Yeah, yeah, get in," Wallace ordered, shoving my new cellmate into our cramped quarters.

Ricky slammed his palms against the metallic door as it shut. It created a loud boom that echoed throughout the cellblock. I jerked back on the cot and hit my head against the cement wall.

Wallace witnessed the whole thing and sneered, "Play nice, you two."

"Fuck off," Ricky snarled.

He stood, mumbling something incoherent under his breath as Wallace walked away. Without warning, he grabbed ahold of the bars on the door and let out this guttural scream, doing his best to wrench the door from its frame.

I sat, terrified, watching him throw his conniption.

I wondered once he finished with the door if I was next.

Eventually, he tired himself out. He shook his head and slumped against the door to catch his breath. A minute or so later, Ricky turned and, for the first time since entering the cell, acknowledged my existence.

"What the fuck are you looking at?"

My mouth opened, but nothing came out.

"Oh, shut the fuck up, and move," he ordered, gesturing me to get off the cot.

He scoffed as he walked past me, hopping onto the now vacant cot. He then stared intently at the door and flared his nostrils.

His cheeks soon reddened.

It was like watching a volcano simmer.

Any minute, this guy would explode.

Wanting to avoid the splash zone, I became one with the wall near the front of the cramped cell.

Mr. Eiler's words echoed in my mind. "Stay vigilant."

CHAPTER THIRTY-SIX

Modern Day

I woke up and found Pop reading something on his cell phone. I didn't know why I found it so amusing. Maybe it was because Pop was always the last one on the block to adopt new technology, like when the VCR came out. He said they were only a fad and would go the way of bell-bottom jeans.

I stared at his hands for a while, gently moving across the phone. He always said you can tell a lot about a person by their hands.

How life treated them. Were they a blue-collar worker? A farmer? Or someone who sat at a desk all day? Maybe the person was a physician, like Jaime and Pop. Someone whose hands and mind were their instruments.

Even that day, his nails were trimmed. Age spots and wrinkles did nothing to hide the power of his fingertips.

I compared them to mine and chuckled at the similarities. Like him, my fingers were my chips and salsa, just like my eyesight and mind. It was the first time I realized how alike he and I were.

It's not just Jaime, or my son, Gabriel.

All my life, I heard Pop say I was just like my mother. I not only looked like her, but I thought like her too. And like Mom, I was sensitive and wore my emotions on my sleeve. I couldn't believe I bought into that nonsense.

He and I were alike as well.

We were both artists who used our talents differently. He used his to treat patients. I used mine to showcase the events of the day. Different outcomes but similar analytics. This realization put a smile on my face for the first time in days.

"It's nice to see a smile."

I chuckled.

"Starting to feel better?"

"A little."

He put his cell in his shirt pocket and asked me about my recovery regimen.

"It's important that they get you up and move around right away. It's the same with women who've just delivered."

"So, you're saying I look pregnant now?"

He laughed and patted his belly. "You're not alone."

"C'mon, Pop, you look great."

"And you need glasses."

I shook my head.

"Can I get you anything? You thirsty?"

"I'd kill for a burger. Your *son* has me on a special diet." I handed him my menu.

He read it and rolled his eyes before taking out a pen, crossing out the blue sharpie wording, and scribbled something in the margin.

"Be right back."

He grabbed his cane and shuffled out the door, returning minutes later snickering beneath his mask.

"What'd you do?"

"Nothing."

"Won't Jaime get mad?"

He shrugged. "Meh, add it to the list."

Way to go, Pop.

On the TV, videos from the riots replayed and caught both of our attention. I shut my eyes and controlled my breathing, which didn't go unnoticed.

Unexpectedly, I felt a warm and ancient hand on top of mine. I opened my eyes and saw a worried man caring for his fifty-something-year-old son. I'm suddenly brought back to my youth, lying in a hospital bed, recovering from a stab wound to the back. Pop on one side of the bed, and Tía Carolina on the other.

"I'm all right, Pop," I whispered.

"I know."

He asked me about the riots and what I could remember. I resisted at first. I didn't want to talk about it. Not with him. Not with anyone. I wanted to put the whole damn thing behind me and move on with my life.

Just like I did with Katrina and my run-ins with the cartels in South America, and the warlords of western Africa, not to mention my gunshot wound in Afghanistan. I survived those, and I'll survive this.

"It's my process, Pop. I let them go and move forward."

He silently stared before settling back into his chair. It never ceased to amaze me how little our parent/child dynamics have changed. Regardless of our age, he still made me feel like a five-year-old.

Knowing he was just trying to help, I acquiesced and spent the next hour sharing the events of that insane day. I referenced images from the TV to fill in the gaps in my memory.

Anger filled his ancient eyes as I recounted the details. Periodically, he cursed under his breath in Spanish and said he wished he was there with me that day.

He stamped his cane forcefully on the floor. "I would have taught them a thing or two."

"Yeah, Pop, that's what we need. Two of us laid up in hospital beds. What would Carolina have said?"

A somber crease formed on his brow. "She would have called me a pendejo."

We both laughed.

"I just can't believe those people did that to you."

"I can. Look at them." I gestured to the TV.

We stared at alleged *peaceful protestors*, armed with who knew what, scale the U.S. Capitol building. They hurled everything from garbage cans to insults at the Capitol police officers. They ripped down the American flag and replaced it with their propaganda nonsense before shattering ancient windows and breaking into the building.

"Que locura."

"You think that's crazy? It was worse in person. I only wish I hadn't lost my equipment."

"And that happened when—"

"I was getting my ass kicked, yeah."

From behind Pop, we heard a familiar voice. "There they are."

"Oh look, ladies and gentlemen—Judas."

Jaime flipped me the finger before kissing Pop hello.

"How's he doing?"

"Not bad, considering."

They began speaking about me, as if I was not there. It drove me nuts.

"Ahem, I'm right here, ya know. I can hear you."

"Yeah, yeah." Jaime came over and kissed me hello. "How're you feeling?"

"Better than yesterday."

"Good."

Jaime grabbed another chair and settled in. He looked more tired than Pop, but I didn't say anything. I knew they were working him ragged thanks to the outbreak. Cheryl too. It's a wonder he even has the time to stop in and see me.

The door opened again.

It was Edyta.

"Oh, good. Dr. Morales."

They both reply, "Yes?"

She stopped in her tracks and looked confused.

Not again.

CHAPTER THIRTY-SEVEN

Pop apologized. "Sorry, force of habit."

"Hi Edyta, what's up?" Jaime asked.

"I just came on, and I noticed a change to your brother's menu. I just want to—"

He reviewed the changes. "There must be some mistake. I didn't—"

"Actually, *I* changed it."

"Pop—"

Edyta and I watched the two argue. To no one's surprise, Pop won.

"Fine, but when he has a heart attack, it's on you."

"Que dramático," Pop replied. "The menu's fine."

Jaime conceded. "You heard him, Edyta."

"Thanks, Pop."

Jaime mimicked me, "*Thanks, Pop.*"

"What are you, three?"

He poked me. "You better not have a heart attack."

Edyta left, allowing us to spend time doing what most families did when they got together. We reminisced and busted each other's balls.

"Remember that time Carolina walked in on you?" Pop laughed. "I thought she'd have a heart attack."

"I was fourteen and in the bathroom," I groaned.

Pop mimes grabbing his chest and howls, "He was—he . . . was . . ."

My ears burned from embarrassment.

Jaime laughed. "Tía couldn't look at you for two weeks."

"Yeah, well, at least my kids never walked in on me—"

Pop gasped. "*That* happened?"

Jaime shot me a look, then hid his face in his hands. "Yes."

Pop roared so hard, I checked his chair for pee. "Oh . . . oh . . . that's—"

"Yeah, yeah . . . hysterical," Jaime complained. "Cheryl cut me off for weeks."

I howled.

"Hector still can't look me in the eyes."

Pop waved his arms. "No more . . . I have to use the bathroom."

Between guffaws, he shuffled his way to the bathroom, leaving Jaime and me alone. The sound of his cane echoed across the linoleum floor. We waited for the door to close and the fan to come on before saying anything.

"Jeez, he's really showing his age," I whispered.

Jaime sighed. "I know. Cheryl and I have been talking about having him move in with us."

I digested the information.

"Would you be okay with that?" he asked.

"Of course. I just don't think he'd do it. Remember that time I asked him to move in with us after Carolina passed away?"

"I'd never seen a grown man throw such a hissy fit."

"It was worse than trying to put Gabriel down for a nap when he was little. Anyway, you have my support if he'll go for it."

We heard a volcanic flush, followed by aggressive hand washing, letting us know Pop would soon return.

The door opened, and Jaime asked, "Ready to head out, Pop?"

He nodded and slowly came to my bedside. "Listen to your nurses."

"I will. Thanks, Pop."

"Cheryl will bring him over again tomorrow before heading into work."

"Thanks, James."

He smiled and turned to leave.

"Jaime, before you go, you wouldn't happen to have a spare laptop lying around, would you?"

He thought for a moment, biting on his lower lip like he did when he was little.

"Would an iPad work?"

"Absolutely."

"What do you need it for? You're not going to surf porn, are you?"

I pursed my lips. "No, dumbass. I thought I'd catch up on some emails and stuff."

"You know . . . you may want to think about journaling. It could be cathartic."

"Not a bad idea." I nodded.

"I'll ask Cheryl to bring it." He gestured to Pop. "Better get him home before—"

"I thought we were leaving?" Pop impatiently looked at his watch.

Jaime and I exchanged looks.

"Coming, Pop."

I watched the pair leave before flipping the TV channel to a rerun of *Modern Family*, a mockumentary-style sitcom focused on a close-knit extended family.

The episode kicked off with the teenage Dunphy kids walking in on their parents having sex, and I immediately howled with laughter, thinking about my brother and his wife.

What a putz.

CHAPTER THIRTY-EIGHT

1986

Stay vigilant, my ass.

I sat there quietly watching this idiot plot his next move, simmering in whatever juices flowed throughout his foul-smelling frame.

Thankfully, he left me alone—until he didn't. Suddenly, Ricky glanced in my direction. His eyes narrowed, he smacked his lips and smirked. I felt like I had a bullseye tattooed on my forehead.

My churning stomach made noise. It seemed to humor him. The glare in his eyes foreshadowed the abuse I would shortly receive, and there was nothing I could do about it.

"What'd ya do? Forget to pay your taxes?"

I chucked him a micro-smile.

"Can't imagine it's anything too serious."

I turned slightly.

"What's the matter, Paco, don't speaky zee ingleesh?"

"The name's not Paco," I mumbled.

"It speaks. The wetback speaks."

"I'm not a wetback."

"Que? What's that? I couldn't hear you."

I cleared my throat. "I said, I'm not—"

"Like I give a fuck."

He hopped off the cot and walked to the metallic toilet in the corner. Ricky dropped trou' and peed all over the toilet, floor, and back wall.

The stench hit me like a frying pan to the forehead.

"Jesus Christ," I scoffed.

He yanked up his pants and returned to the cot, sniffing his fingers.

"Wanna whiff?"

"I'll pass, thanks."

"Ya sure? They smell a lot like your mom."

Anger burned in my eyes, but I remained silent.

He laughed some more. "Ahh, you're no fun. At least the last guy they stuck me with could take a joke. He wasn't all serious like you."

I held back a response.

"Jeez, lighten up, Paco. We're gonna be stuck in here for a while. Might as well make the most of it."

Something to look forward to.

"Suit yourself."

Tired of his new plaything, Mr. McPiss-His-Pants stretched out on the cot, shut his eyes, and fell asleep.

I sat in the dark with my spine against the gray metallic door. Listened as creaks and moans resonated throughout the cellblock as the place settled down. Between Ricky cursing in his sleep and the periodic cell checks from the police officers on duty, I spent the night doing the head-bob thing.

Eventually, I tucked my head between my knees and fell asleep. Prayed for salvation to arrive. Instead, I awoke to an overly aggressive officer shouting as he yanked open cell doors to deliver breakfast.

My new pal, Ricky, sat upright on the cot. "Did someone say breakfast?"

Before I could answer, the cell door opened, and I fell backward, slamming my head onto the concrete hallway. The overweight police officer stared down at me, furious that I was out of my cell.

"Get the *hell* back in your cell, inmate," he barked.

I yiped and shot back inside as the officer tossed a paper sack to Ricky, who caught it against his chest. Mine, he dropped onto the floor in front of me before shutting the door in my face.

I opened the bag and found a small plain Danish wrapped in plastic and a room-temperature pint of 2% milk.

As I unwrapped my breakfast, Ricky walked over and snatched it from my hand, along with my carton of milk.

"*Hey—*" I complained as he slinked away.

"Hey, what?"

With zero regard for my needs, he looked me square in the eyes and stuffed his Danish into his mouth. He then finished unwrapping mine and licked the entire top before offering it back to me.

"Want it?"

Repulsed, I made a face.

"That's what I thought." He laughed as he shoved my breakfast down his gullet.

After finishing both cartons of milk, Ricky threw his trash at me.

"All yours." He guffawed.

When the policeman returned to retrieve the trash, Ricky began yelling for his attorney.

"Hey, asshole, when do I get to see my lawyer?"

"When he gets here."

That's when his chanting began. "I want my lawyer. I want my—"

This riled up the rest of the cellblock.

"Hey, shut the fuck up."

"Fuck you, I want my lawyer."

"Quiet down."

"Lawyer . . ."

It went on like this for a while. I sat back, stunned, and covered my ears. Eventually, cops filled the cellblock and pulled the troublemakers. When they grabbed Ricky, one of the cops noticed the urine-stained walls and floor.

"What the fuck?"

"He did it," Ricky yelled as they escorted him from the cell.

With him gone, I tiptoed to the cot and inspected it for pee, or worse. Aside from the stench left behind by his sweat and cologne, all seemed fine. After a quick wipe, I hopped on and caught a quick nap.

I dreamed that Ricky got dragged to a musty old dungeon and was shackled against the wall with thick metal chains. Groans from the guilty echoed throughout the poorly lit space. In a distant corner, rats the size of church bells fed on bloody entrails of the doomed.

Unfortunately, after lunch—another dry bologna sandwich and red apple—my buddy returned.

"Miss me?" he sneered. "Move."

While shuffling to my spot against the wall, Ricky began peppering me with questions.

"So, slick. What'd I miss?"

I ignored him.

"Dude, why are you in here?"

I pressed my face onto my bended knees.

"You trying to sleep? You sleepin'? Hey, dude—"

I wanted to scream, *What the fuck do you want?*

But I didn't. I was too afraid of what would happen to me if I started yelling. I didn't want to get beat up or be labeled a troublemaker. As I sat there drowning in misery, I felt something hit my shoulder. Followed by another object landing in my hair.

Ricky snickered from the cot. I looked up and watched him wad up tiny pieces of toilet paper and throw them at me. Every time he hit me, he threw his arms up and cheered.

My ears flushed with fury.

I'd had enough of his bullshit.

If I got my ass kicked, so be it, but I was through taking his abuse.

I quickly stood, surrounded by a mound of tiny snowballs of toilet paper. My face contorted and fists clenched, ready to throw down with this asshole.

His look of surprise told me he knew I meant business. As I prepared for my attack, an officer banged on the cell door.

"Morales, you have a—" He noticed the mess. "What the fuck? *Ricky*."

"What?"

"This shit better get cleaned up by the time I get back."

"Cool your pits, Jenkins. We were just messing around. He'll clean it up when—"

"I mean it, Ricky," Officer Jenkins threatened. "C'mon, Morales. Let's go."

"Where are you taking me?"

"Hey, why does he get to leave?"

"None of your goddamn business. Now, clean this shit up."

The moment I stepped out of the cell, Officer Jenkins slapped the cuffs on me.

Ricky pressed his face against the door. "This is *bullshit*."

Jenkins just groaned and escorted me through the precinct

to another interrogation room. Pop and Mr. Eilers waited for me inside. Once my cuffs were removed, I ran into Pop's arms and bawled my eyes out.

He held me tight and soothed my emotional wounds.

"It's okay, Ollie. I'm here now."

CHAPTER THIRTY-NINE

Like chimps in a zoo, Pop picked pieces of toilet paper from my hair.

"What the hell—?" he whispered. "Bob, what's going on here?"

"I don't know."

"You assured me he'd be safe."

Mr. Eilers stormed from the room. "Be right back."

Pop and I sat at the conference table. I grabbed tissues from a nearby box and blew my nose.

"I'd ask how you're holding up . . ."

My bloodshot eyes spoke volumes.

"Yeah, okay. Look, we are doing everything we can to get you out of here."

Through clenched teeth. "Try harder."

He reached for me.

"Carolina is very worried. She would have come but—"

"Someone needs to watch Jaime. I know."

He nodded.

"Fiona and your friend practically camped out at the house."

I perked up. "Really?"

He nodded.

"They were both very upset."

I bit my lower lip.

"The girl—"

"Navil?"

"Yes, her. She kept Jaime and Bella busy while Fiona and Carolina cleaned up."

The thought of Navil playing with my brother and dog put a smile on my face. I could almost smell her perfume. And those eyes. The way they shined.

"This will be over soon. You just need to—"

"Stay vigilant, yeah, I know. Mr. Eilers already told me."

Almost on cue, my attorney returned. "I spoke with the sergeant on duty and asked him to move you to your own cell and keep you there till your arraignment."

"Which is when?" Pop asked.

"It's scheduled for tomorrow morning at nine o'clock."

I sighed. "I still don't understand why—"

"They're charging you with obstructing justice. It's all non-sense, Ollie. Just people trying to make names for themselves, that's all. I will get this thrown out, and like I said, your record expunged."

I whispered, "But I didn't do anything wrong."

Pop patted my back. "We know, buddy, we know."

Thirty minutes later, Officer Jenkins escorted me back to the holding area. Placed me in a cell across from Ricky. This didn't sit well with him.

"What's the matter, you fucking pussy? Couldn't hack it?"

I glared at him from my cell but stayed silent.

"That's right, keep staring, ya fucking wuss. I'll find you when we get out of here."

He spit loogies at me, but they missed. Painted the wall and floor near my cell, something the on-duty police officer noticed later when delivering dinner.

"The spic did it," Ricky yelled.

It took everything I had to ignore him. I curled up onto my

cot, which smelled like molded cheese, thanks to the previous resident.

Exhausted, I choked down dinner, a meatloaf sandwich—I think—and went right to sleep, only to be awakened by Officer Wallace the following morning. He banged on my cell door, retrieving me and a handful of other inmates.

Stuck in his cell, Ricky spit at me again but hit the guy shackled behind me.

"You motherfucker," the guy yelled.

He tried attacking Ricky but couldn't because of the shackles. Ricky stepped back and laughed at the guy. This pissed off an already sour Wallace, who did his best to regain control.

"Goddamn it!" Wallace yelled. "Get back in line before I start cracking skulls."

His threatening words had the right effect on all the inmates. Soon, everyone got back in line and ready for our walk of shame through the precinct and out a back entrance to an awaiting minivan. I hopped in behind a thirty-something-year-old white guy wearing a New York Mets t-shirt, jeans and smelling like sweat and stale beer.

I couldn't wait to get to court and get this over with. The silent drive to my arraignment lasted longer than my time in court. Mine was the second name on the docket.

"Oliver Morales," the bailiff called.

Pop and Tía Carolina sat in the gallery. The moment she saw me, the blubbering started. I stood next to Mr. Eilers behind a large wooden table. Across from us stood a neatly dressed brunette wearing a blue pantsuit and crisp white shirt. There was something ominous about her.

Mr. Eilers noticed me staring. "She's the prosecutor."

"Like on TV?"

He smiled. "Just like. Don't worry. We've already worked things out."

I gave him a curious look.

The Honorable Judge Harlon Turner called the court to order.

He gestured to the prosecutor. "Ms. Adderley, I understand you've come to an arrangement with the defendant?"

"Yes, your Honor."

"And what would that be?"

I leaned forward from the backseat of Pop's caddy, "So, all I have to do is cooperate, and they'll leave me alone?"

"Basically."

"And my record?"

"We're working on it, Ollie. One step at a time."

"Okay, because they took my picture and fingerprints."

Tía Carolina reached back and squeezed my hand, doing her best to comfort me with her moist grip.

I don't know who was happier for my release, her or me. I gave her a smile and then sat back. The events of the day played in my head like a video as I stared out the window.

After the judge dismissed my case, Tía Carolina ran up and wrapped her arms around me. I strongly believe, if allowed, she would have swaddled me in a blanket and carried me out of that courtroom like an infant.

As we left, a new group of inmates was escorted into the courtroom. As luck would have it, it included my old pal, Ricky, who watched Tía Carolina fuss over me.

"Aww, isn't that sweet." He laughed from his seat.

I was over his bullshit. I quietly caught his attention while everyone was busy getting ready for his case. I cupped my hand

and flipped him the finger. His eyes grew in disbelief. He bared his fangs and began yelling.

"I'll kill you, you little fucker. Kill you."

The judge banged his mallet. "Order. Order in my court. Bailiff, restrain that man."

"Yes, your Honor."

The bailiff forced Ricky to sit before receiving a lecture from the judge on proper decorum in his courtroom.

We locked eyes as the door shut behind me, putting him and this whole experience behind me like a distant nightmare, and I prayed he'd receive the maximum sentence for whatever crime he committed.

CHAPTER FORTY

The moment we stepped outside the courthouse, I filled my lungs with the freshest air I'd ever tasted. It was like God ran it through a special filter and added a pinch of sweetener just for me.

The world itself seemed, I don't know, brighter. Sunnier. The leaves in the trees more vibrant. Like they were coming to life the moment I stepped outside.

And the birds' songs were melodic. Full of hope.

I'd never more enjoyed a walk through a busy parking lot in my life.

On the drive home, Pop explained, "We're not done, by the way."

"What do you mean?"

"We have an appointment with the detectives this afternoon."

That put me on edge.

"What about school?"

"Forget about school for today."

I sat back and lowered my head.

"Don't worry, Ollie. Bob will be there with us. All you need to do is tell them the truth. The *entire* truth. Understood?"

I sighed. "Yeah."

"Good. We need to put this behind us, Ollie."

Tía Carolina nodded.

I spent the remainder of the ride home silently staring out the window. While I wasn't looking forward to returning to the police station, at least I wouldn't have to sit in another tiny cell surrounded by the dregs of society.

I guess people could have said the same about me, since I had been in there with them.

But I was innocent.

Right?

They weren't.

How could they be?

They were sitting in a jail cell.

Just like me.

But I was an innocent teenager in the wrong place at the wrong time.

"Ollie, your aunt asked you a question."

"Hmm? What?"

"I asked if you ate breakfast?"

"No."

She patted my arm. "I'll make you something when we get home."

Bella was beside herself when she saw me walk through the front door. She leaped about and barked up a storm. I thought she would have jumped out of her fur if I didn't pick her up.

Her body wiggled about as she licked my face and nostrils.

"Easy, girl, easy."

"Put her down and grab a shower. We're meeting those detectives at one o'clock."

I showered longer than I probably should have, but I needed to scrub that jail stench from my body. It was like that film you get in your mouth when you brush your teeth then have a glass of milk.

Pop banged on the bathroom door. "Ollie, wrap it up."

Waiting for me at the dining room table was a mountain of

freshly made banana pancakes, a plate full of crispy bacon, and a tall glass of moo juice.

"What? The boy looked hungry," Tía Carolina said to a silent Pop.

He looked at his watch. "Make it quick. We've got to go."

As I wolfed down four pancakes, a few strips of bacon, and the entire glass of milk, the phone rang.

It was Navil, calling me from school during her free period.

"Ollie, we don't have time—"

I waved him off, grabbed the cordless, and ran to my bedroom.

"How are you?"

"I'm ... okay."

"I was so worried about you."

"Thanks."

"Since you are home, does this mean it's all over?"

"Not quite."

"What do you mean?"

I explained how I needed to meet with the detectives and admit to everything, including—

"Just tell them, Ollie. Tell them everything. If they want to bring me in, so be it, but enough is enough. They have the wrong—"

"People, I know."

"Oui. Which means—"

"The right person is still out there, somewhere."

From the family room, Pop shouted, "Ollie, we're going to be *late.*"

"I've got to—"

"I heard. Be careful, Ollie. For me."

I smiled. "I will. You too."

"Ollie?"

"Yeah?"

"For God's sake, *Oliver*."

"I really need to—"

"Call me later, okay?"

"I will."

Pop threw my door open. "Now."

"I . . . love you, Ollie," she whispered.

"*Now*." He grabbed the phone and hung it up before I could respond.

"*Pop!*" I screamed. "*No.*"

He shoved me out the door. "Move it."

"She just said—"

"Unless the girl is on fire, I don't care, Ollie. We've got to go."

She might not have been, but I sure was. Pop tossed the phone to Tía Carolina and marched me out the front door, and I was fuming. The love of my life just told me she loved me, and my father hung up before I could respond.

I got into the Caddy, slammed the door, and buckled up.

"Easy on the door. I've still got car payments to make."

I glared at him. He ignored me and drove to the police station. On the way, he lectured me on how to act and what to say. I was too angry to respond. Plus, Navil's whisper played in my mind like an earworm.

"*I . . . love you, Ollie.*"

Meanwhile, Pop continued laying down the law. "Just remember, you're telling them the truth this time."

I just nodded.

Pop ended with, "I'm tired of this nonsense."

Get in line.

CHAPTER FORTY-ONE

We arrived at the police station ten minutes later. Mr. Eilers waited for us outside the front entrance.

Pop and he shook hands. "Hey, Bob."

"You ready, Ollie?" Mr. Eilers asked.

I nodded and followed them inside, still thinking about what Navil said.

She loved me.

Me.

Oliver Morales.

Not some pretty boy asshole with his own plane and thought his shit didn't stink.

Once we stepped into the lobby area, my reality shifted and stopped me in my tracks. I suddenly felt the weight of handcuffs around my wrists.

Pop pushed me along, reminding me of the way Officer Wallace shoved me in through the back door like a common criminal.

My stomach churned, and I felt like throwing up Tía Carolina's fantastic pancakes but choked it back.

Navil's parting words anchored me.

Gave me strength.

"We need to check in with the desk sergeant," Mr. Eilers explained.

Pop and I waited in the lobby for Mr. Eilers to do his

magic. Moments later, we were escorted to an empty nearby interrogation room.

Detectives Gallagher and Chao entered behind us and waited for the three of us to sit before closing the door and grabbing the chairs across the table from us.

I looked around the room and noticed there was something different. Unlike the others, this one felt cleaner. Less smelly. It had a refrigerator and coffee station set up in the corner. On a nearby side table sat donuts and other pastries. It reminded me of the breakrooms you see on cop shows on television.

It didn't take long, once everyone settled in, to get right to business. Detective Gallagher turned on a tape recorder, pointed the microphone toward me, and asked questions.

"Please state your name, date of birth, and address."

"Ollie Moral—"

"Your complete name, please."

I gave him my full name, birth date, and address.

"Thank you. Now, we're here today to get to the bottom of the assault on Miss Jacquelyn Woodley."

He asked me about our relationship.

"How well do you know Miss Woodley?"

"I've known her since ninth grade."

"And you get along with her?"

Does anybody?

"I mean, I guess."

"What do you mean, you guess?"

"Ollie, just answer the questions the detective is asking you," Mr. Eilers interjected.

I nodded. "I mean, yeah, we get along."

He sat back and chewed on my answer. There was something in his eyes. I felt like he didn't believe me.

"I . . . love you, Ollie."

Navil's words calmed me.

Brought me peace.

I took a deep breath and turned to my lawyer, "Can I just tell them what I know?"

He looked at the detectives.

They gave him an approving nod.

"Just start at the beginning, Ollie," Mr. Eilers told me.

"Like I said, we've known each other since ninth grade. That's when she started boarding at our school."

Detective Gallagher leaned forward. "And have you two ever been . . . intimate?"

My face twerked. "Ew—"

The adults in the room choked back laughs.

"We'll take that as a no," Detective Chao replied, taking over the interview. "Continue."

"After winter break, she got this new roommate."

I love you, Ollie.

He looked at his notepad. "Miss Laurent, is that right?"

Her sparkling hazel eyes and blazing white smile flashed before my eyes.

Rich, moist lips puckered and blew me a kiss.

I love you, Ollie.

I smiled. "Yeah—"

She craned her neck slightly to the left while doing her homework, revealing an asterisk-shaped beauty mark.

Called to me.

Begged my fangs to—

"*And*?" he barked.

He broke my trance. Detective Chao's nose twitched. I could tell I was getting on his last nerve. I shared how Professor Michaels asked me to . . .

"Tutor her in AP Calc and stuff."

"What do you mean, *stuff*?"

"You know—" I searched for the right words. "Hanging out."

The detectives nodded.

"So, you're *dating* Ms. Laurent?"

I got starry-eyed and smiled. "Yeah."

Detective Chao rolled his eyes. "How long have you been dating?"

I shrugged. "I don't know. A few weeks, I guess."

"You guess, or you know?"

"How about this . . ." Gallagher took over again. "Were you dating her when Miss Woodley was first attacked at your house?"

"No." I pursed my lips. "I mean, I *thought* it was going to be a date."

"What does that mean?"

"I invited her to come over for pizza and to watch Mel Brooks movies."

"Which ones?" Detective Chao asked.

"*Young Frankenstein* and then *High Anxiety*."

"Why not *Blazing Saddles*, or *History of the World, Part One*?"

The scene of the cowboys sitting around the campfire eating beans and farting in Blazing Saddles immediately came to mind, as did *The Inquisition Song* and many risqué scenes from *History of the World*.

"On a *first* date?"

Detective Chao considered for a moment. "Fair enough."

"I thought you said it wasn't a date?" Detective Gallagher interjected.

"It wasn't. She had three girls there with her when I picked her up."

The adults exchanged a knowing look.

"Was Miss Woodley one of the girls?"

I rolled my eyes. "Yeah."

I spent the next few minutes explaining what happened that evening, along with the subsequent events that led to Navil and I finding an injured Jackie in the newsroom.

"Why didn't you tell me this when I asked you."

"I don't know."

"Do you realize how much time we've wasted?" Detective Chao growled.

"Easy, Detective. I think the boy understands the situation," Mr. Eilers countered.

He threw his hands up. "Does he, Counselor?"

Mr. Eilers ignored the outburst. "Anything else you'd like to share, Oliver?"

Prior to the interview, Mr. Eilers advised me to apologize to the detectives if I found an opportunity.

This was it.

Picturing Bella's face when she peed in the house, I leaned forward and mustered my best apologetic puppy-dog face.

I felt like such a fraud, and they bought every second of it.

"I'm sorry. I didn't mean to cause you any trouble."

"What else, Oliver?" Pop asked.

"And I'm sorry for wasting your time."

"*And*?"

Okay, Pop, I think they get it.

"I, uh, hope you catch the guy who did this."

"Are we good here, gentlemen?" Mr. Eilers asked.

Gallagher turned off the recorder. "Try to stay out of trouble."

"I will."

"Is that it?" Pop asked.

"You're free to go," Detective Gallagher replied. "We may call you in for additional questioning."

I didn't like the sound of that, and Mr. Eilers must have read my face. He chuckled and patted my hand.

"We understand, Detective. You have a crime to solve. We'd be happy to cooperate with your investigation."

"Especially if it leads you to another client, am I right, Counselor?" Detective Chao snidely replied.

Damn.

Mr. Eilers ignored the comment and shook hands with both detectives, encouraging Pop and me to do the same.

"Here's my card. Try to stay out of trouble, okay?" Detective Gallagher repeated.

I placed it into my wallet. "I will. And Detective . . . ?"

He turned.

"I really am sorry."

CHAPTER FORTY-TWO

True to his word, the following day when dropping off Pop, Jaime's wife, Cheryl, brought over their spare iPad and charger for me to play with.

She kissed me hello. "And how is my favorite brother-in-law feeling today?"

"You mean your *only* brother-in-law."

"You're forgetting about my sister's husband, Gerald."

A self-important professor with a doctorate in modern literature. The man was a caricature. The way he kept his beard neatly trimmed and always wore a tweed sports coat with patches on the elbow, you'd think he taught at Harvard or Yale instead of some backwater college in Nebraska.

The only things missing were a pipe and John Lennon-style eyewear.

And the way he spoke.

Haughty.

Arrogant.

"How is the *good doctor* doing these days?"

"Who knows?" She stuck her tongue out. "But Katie's doing great."

"That's good. Still don't know what she sees in that guy."

"You know us Zambrana girls. We're gluttons for punishment."

I laughed.

She sat on the corner of my bed and leaned in. "Enough about them. How are you doing? And don't give me any of that Morales *I'm fine* bullshit. I can see right through it. Ask my children."

I surrendered. "I'm . . . taking things a day at a time."

"Uh-huh. And what does *that* mean exactly?"

I considered for a moment, not knowing how much honesty she wanted.

She raised both brows, encouraging me to continue.

"It means—I don't know what it means." I sighed.

She took my hands. "That's what I thought. Ollie, I know someone you can—"

"Not you too—"

"I've known her since med school."

"Cheryl, I'm f—"

She took a business card from her purse and slipped it into my hand. "She's expecting your call."

I read the card, *Dr. Cynthia Beasley, M.D., Psychiatrist.*

Cheryl leaned forward and whispered, "She helped me after my last miscarriage."

I gasped and felt the blood drain from my face.

Your last . . . what the fuck?

"When did you—"

"Three years ago," she explained. "We never told anyone."

I think back to the time period and tried to recall where I was. I was on assignment in Europe, chasing after the *Danske Bank* two-hundred-billion-euro money-laundering scandal in Denmark, considered by many at the time, the largest financial crime ever.

"I was in Europe back then."

"I recall."

"But you're doing—"

She nodded. "I am now, yes. We both are."

"Why didn't Jaime say anything? I would have come home."

"I asked him not to. We were devastated."

"Cheryl—" I took her hand. "I'm so sorry."

She caressed my face. "Thanks, Ollie. Listen, give her a call. She really helped me."

I nodded.

"Did wonders for your brother too."

"No kiddin'?"

She glanced at the wall clock. "I've gotta get to work. Before I forget, I downloaded WhatsApp onto the iPad for you so you can reach out to your wife."

I thanked her for bringing Pop and the iPad.

"Anytime. You boys play nice. And, Pop, if you need me to pick you up early—"

He waved her off. "I'll be fine."

She kissed his cheek and left the room.

"That Cheryl's something else," I commented.

Pop ignored my comment and screwed around with the TV remote.

"Jamie's lucky to have her."

"And she him," he replied defensively.

I shook my head and said nothing.

Heaven forbid you don't compliment the golden child.

I booted up the iPad, entered the password Cheryl left me, clicked on the *WhatsApp* icon, entered my wife's details, and sent her a quick text, letting her know I'm alive.

Next, I hopped on *Gmail* and downloaded a few thousand emails while Pop flipped to a rerun of *Morales In The Morning*, my wife's locally syndicated talk show.

"Oh, this is a good one," he commented and settled back.

He never missed a show. He was her number one fan.

"Good, Pop. Enjoy," I replied without looking up from the tablet.

Watching my email account populate reminded me of a slot machine. Row after row generated new messages, increasing the number of unread emails. The final tally? Four thousand, two hundred and fifty-eight.

"Jesus," I whispered.

"What's the matter?"

"Huh? Oh, nothing. Emails." I showed Pop the screen.

He squinted to read the number, then raised his bushy brows. "Wow."

"Yep. And I haven't even hopped on my work account yet."

"Can't all that wait? You *are* recovering from—" He gestured at my injuries.

He wasn't wrong. The problem was that emails were like a leaky faucet. They never stopped, so if you didn't address them, you were left with a mess.

I shrugged and ignored his advice. I was a quarter of the way through, about to open an email from my old high school buddy Eddie, with the subject line, *Check It Out,* and a link to *Facebook,* when Len walked through the door, announcing it's time for my daily abuse.

"You ready to go?" He smiled.

I groaned, "Do I have to?"

"C'mon, Ollie. You're really making progress. Let's get those sneakers on."

"Fine."

Len and Pop chatted while I got ready.

"He's really progressing?"

Len nodded. "Doing better than most, especially for a guy in his shape and age."

"*Hey,* I'm sitting right here," I whined.

They laughed, and Len looked at his watch.

"Let's go, big guy. Time's a-wasting."

"See you in an hour, Pop."

"Actually, it's going to be two hours, Pop."

"*Two?*"

"New orders."

"From whom?"

He smiled.

"*Jaime,*" I hissed.

"Your brother wants us to kick it up a notch."

"Trust me, when I see him, something's getting kicked."

He chuckled and wheeled me out the door. "You can do it."

"This is *bullshit.*"

Pop laughed as my wife's theme song played on the television. "Have fun, Ollie."

I hate you people.

CHAPTER FORTY-THREE

All I could think about on the ride home was Navil.

Her words haunted me.

I pictured her on the other end of the phone.

Auburn hair cradled her beautiful face.

A perfect combination of sadness and longing.

Hazel eyes stared deeply into the telephone handset.

Pulse raced.

Lips parted, breathing the words . . .

"I . . . love you, Ollie."

Youthful anticipation filled her soul as she awaited my response.

She leaned in.

>Click<

Pop hung up on her.

With a gasp, she wilted like a dying flower.

Spirit crushed.

Tears flowed.

An ache filled my chest.

I needed to see her.

Hold her.

Tell her that I loved her too.

Why the hell is it taking so long for us to get home?

"Ollie?" Pop called my name.

I'm pulled back to reality.

"Hmm?"

"I asked if you wanted to stop for pizza?"

"Can we, um, just head home? I really want to go to school."

"I don't think so, Ollie. Not after everything you just went through."

"But, Pop, I want to see Navil."

"You can see her tomorrow."

I opened my mouth to object.

"The answer is no."

With a huff, I folded my arms, sat back, and grumbled obscenities under my breath. The moment we pulled into the driveway, I marched inside and went straight to my room. Slammed the door behind me.

In the distance, I overheard Pop and Tía Carolina.

"¿Qué pasó?"

"Nothing happened. He's upset I wouldn't let him go see the girl."

Tía replied, but I couldn't make out what she said. They went back and forth for a few minutes till Pop concluded that he thought I needed to avoid Navil for a while.

Are you fucking kidding me?

I was fit to be tied.

Outside my bedroom door, Bella barked and scratched. I hadn't acknowledged her when I entered the house. Her whining got under my skin, so I yanked the door open and took my frustrations out on my adoring pup.

"*What?*"

With loving eyes and a wagging tail, she whimpered and rolled over so I would scratch her warm belly. I wanted to punt her across the house. Instead, I let out a deep breath and gestured at my bed.

"Go ahead."

She quickly rolled over and bebopped her way to the side of my bed so I could lift her up. I gently tossed her onto my covers, rolled her over, and rubbed her belly, all the while torturing myself thinking about Navil.

Her words played over and over in my mind.

Every word.

Each syllable.

On constant repeat.

"I . . . love you, Ollie."

I threw my head back onto my bed, covered my face with my pillows, and screamed at the top of my lungs till they burned. The veins in my neck bulged. I pounded my fists into my mattress top. A frightened Bella shot to the opposite end of the bed to avoid being struck.

Eventually, I calmed down.

I returned my pillow to its rightful place and used the back of my sleeve to wipe the tears from my face. Exhaustion plowed into me like a crashing wave. I refused to give in to the appealing siren. I yawned and plotted my escape, scanning the room for my car keys. They're not on my nightstand or desk. I teetered from dizziness.

"I . . . love you, Ollie."

I forced my eyes open and took a deep breath, filling my lungs with much-needed oxygen. Bella pawed at the covers, then made three circles before plopping herself down and shutting her eyes.

I gently slapped my face. Just enough to keep myself awake. It wasn't working. I was losing the battle. I glanced at my alarm clock.

Three hours till school let out.

Bella began to snore.

I'll just set the alarm, sneak out in a few hours . . .

CHAPTER FORTY-FOUR

My bladder woke me up around three o'clock in the morning, something Pop recently complained about, which amused Tía Carolina. I glanced at my alarm clock and noticed someone had shut off my alarm, which annoyed me. I set it for a reason, not that it clearly mattered to anyone.

My bladder stirred, and stomach grumbled. After taking care of the former, I shot to the kitchen for a bowl of cereal and glass of orange juice to alleviate the latter.

A night light and creepy sounds from our house settling kept me company as I leaned against the counter, half asleep, enjoying my late-night snack.

To masters of horror, these sounds elicited terror, but after the weekend I just experienced, they delivered unexpected comfort. From the branches scratching against our windows, to the boiler rumbling as it delivered much-needed heat to the house. Even the subtle scraping of the spoon inside my bowl held a level of—tranquility.

Normalcy.

Peace.

Unlike the moans and groans that echoed across the cellblock, full of ambiguity and mystery. Were inmates recovering from a drunken night out on the town, or was someone having his mouth covered by a cellmate stabbing them to death with a homemade knife?

Milk dripped onto my cornflakes as I stared into the nothingness of my surroundings.

These thoughts killed my appetite, so I sucked down the remainder of my OJ, and emptied my bowl into the trash before placing my dirty dishes in the sink, something I was sure Tía would complain about in the morning.

Six in the morning arrived sooner than anticipated.

I dragged myself out of bed and meandered through my morning routine, choosing to eat a second breakfast, a couple of homemade egg and cheese sandwiches.

As I choked down the second, there was a frantic knock at the front door. The hair on my forearms rose. Pop cautiously approached the front door and peered out the side window.

With a sigh and headshake, he opened the door.

"Where is he?" Fi shouted as she ran inside, spotting me at the dining room table.

Like a missile, she shot across the room and wrapped her petite yet surprisingly strong arms around my midsection.

"Fi, I can't brea—"

"Shut up," she whispered and kept squeezing, causing my mocha complexion to pale.

Thankfully, Pop intervened. "All right, Fiona. Let Ollie go."

With a final squeeze, she released me and checked me over from head to toe, like a worried mama bear with her cub.

"Are you okay? They didn't hurt you, did they?"

Her friendly attack on my personal space became too much. I stepped back and grabbed her wrists.

"I'm fine, see?"

Satisfied, she took a seat and went on a five-minute tirade, insulting everyone from our fellow classmates to the police who hauled me in.

"And those cops—Gramps always said they're assholes—"

Her colorful language irked Tía Carolina, who cleared her throat and gave her a look.

"Oh, uh . . . sorry, Tía Carolina."

She nodded, accepting Fi's apology, and kept sipping her morning coffee.

Pop pointed to his watch. "It's getting kind of late, no?"

I read the time. "Shit—sorry, Pop. I'll grab my stuff and meet you at the front door."

I ate the last bit of my meal as I snatched my gear and my jacket. Before leaving, I received a brief lecture from Pop, asking me to come home right after school.

"No dilly-dallying."

An eye roll and head nod later, Fi and I hopped into my car—still full of supplies from the movie we never did get to see—and were on our way to school.

On the ride over, I tried to focus on Navil, but Fi kept peppering me with questions. I wanted to figure out where I'd tell Navil I loved her. Would I do it in front of everyone or pull her aside before school, but Fi just pestered me.

"Tell me what happened."

"Fi, I need to—"

"Were you alone? Did you have a cellmate?"

My right eye twitched.

"How big was your cell? What'd you eat? Did you eat?"

My hands began to sweat.

"I bet it was just like *Hill Street Blues*. No—*Miami Vice*, only without the pastels and palm trees."

It took every ounce of intestinal fortitude, as Coach Connors called it, not to throw her out of the car. I knew she cared about me and meant well, but I'd just spent the last forty-eight hours in hell, and the last thing I wanted to do was relive the experience, especially when I had to figure out where and when I would tell Navil that I loved her back.

"Were all the police officers jerks? Or just the ones who—"

"Fi. *Enough.*"

She yelped and slunk into the passenger seat. For the rest of our ride to school, she didn't utter a word. I felt her large, dark eyes bore a hole into the side of my skull. I wanted to apologize but relished the quiet.

Still, the moment I parked. "Fi—I'm, sorry."

"It's okay, Ollie. I know how intense I get sometimes."

"You were worried about me."

She nodded.

"I had no right to yell at you."

She rubbed my arm.

"It's just—"

"What?"

Images swirled. A blend of my horrific weekend and Navil's beautiful face. A nightmarish amalgam formed in my mind's eye.

Ricky sneered.

Navil smiled.

Threatening shouts replaced with whispers of love.

My pulse raced and heart pounded.

"Fi—" I gasped.

A powerful wave of emotion smacked me between the eyes. Felt like a battering ram. I struggled to breathe. Began to hyperventilate.

"Ols?"

Brown knuckles turned white as my hands gripped the steering wheel. My eyes squeezed shut as I gritted my teeth and lurched forward.

Fi shook my shoulder. "Ollie, are you okay?"

A high-pitched ringing filled my ears. Coherent sentences escaped me.

"Stay with me, Ollie."

Jesus, what a week I'm having.

CHAPTER FORTY-FIVE

Classmates arriving at the student parking lot surrounded my car. Some offered their assistance, while others gawked at the geek losing his shit.

Someone shouted, "Get the nurse!"

A while later, the driver's side door opened. A rush of cool air filled the car, along with a floral antiseptic scent.

"Can you unbuckle him from your side?" I heard a woman ask as she slid in next to me.

"I think so," Fi replied.

"You're going to be okay," the school nurse whispered.

Clammy fingers pressed against my wrist and neck, checking my pulse. Distant blaring sirens grew closer as an ambulance approached.

"Make room."

"We've got him."

I scanned the growing crowd as they placed me onto a gurney. It took me seconds to locate my Belgian beauty.

Our eyes briefly locked as emergency workers took my vitals in the field, but they kept getting in the way.

"On the count of three. One, two—" The EMTs lifted me into the back of their ambulance.

As the door closed, I overheard her shout, "Where are they taking him?"

They slapped an oxygen mask over my nose and mouth

before screeching out of the parking lot in a siren-fueled ride to the nearby University Hospital Emergency Room.

As they wheeled me in, an ER nurse bombarded me with questions.

"Do you know your name?"

"Do you know what day it is?"

A penlight blinded me momentarily. Once inside the hospital, they transferred me from the ambulance gurney to a bed in the emergency room.

After drawing the bluish-green curtain, a crew of healthcare workers removed my clothes and retook my vitals.

I felt like a race car during a pit stop.

The only thing missing were those pneumatic wrenches mechanics use to swap out tires. I half-expected them to roll me over and stick a funnel up my ass to fuel me up before sending me on my way.

Instead, a tourniquet was wrapped around my right bicep, and a needle stuck into my wrist for an IV line.

In the distance, a familiar voice grew closer.

"I'm looking for my son, Oliver Morales."

"Hi, Doctor Morales—bay twelve."

Pop shoved his way past his fellow staff members and came to my side.

The last thing I remember was Pop asking, "Was he this glassy-eyed when they brought him in?"

I woke up a while later, disoriented in the same ER bay to the sound of a busy unit treating other patients on the other side of my drawn curtain. The sickly scent of antiseptic hit me like a ton of bricks.

"You had us worried."

I tipped my head back and found an upside-down Pop seated in the corner, watching over his beloved firstborn.

Half asleep, I replied, "Hey, Pop."

He walked over and checked my eyes. "How're you feeling?"

"Okay, I think."

"What's the last thing you remember?"

"I don't know. One minute I'm sitting in my car talking to Fi. The next I'm—" I gestured to my surroundings.

"You'll be okay."

I was about to ask him a question when the curtain opened, and a nurse stepped into the bay.

"Oh, good, he's awake."

"Hey, Sadie. How're the boys?"

"You know. Four and six, so, driving us crazy." She laughed. "This is your—"

"Eldest. Say hi, Ollie."

"Hi."

She began to examine me. "Don't speak."

She checked my eyes and ears before working her way down to my chest and abdomen, periodically asking if anything hurt.

"No."

Once she finished, she entered notes on my chart and pulled my father to the outside of the drawn curtain.

All I heard were bits and pieces of what they said.

"...nothing abnormal," she said.

"Test results back..." Pop replied.

"...history of panic attacks?" she asked.

Panic attacks?

Adrenaline sat me straight up. I impatiently waited for my father to return to my bedside. Fortunately, he didn't take long.

He drew back the curtain and came to my bedside with the nurse in tow.

"Okay, well . . . thanks, Sadie."

"Sure thing, Doctor Morales," she replied. "You take care now, Ollie."

With that, she smiled and left the bay.

"What's going on, Pop? Did I hear her say something about a p-panic attack?"

He switched from father mode to physician mode, pulled up a chair, and sat next to my bed. Then he scrunched his brows and looked pensive, like he was trying to solve a puzzle.

"Truth?"

I nodded.

"We're waiting on a few tests, but based on everything we know so far—"

I sat forward, anticipating the worst.

"You probably had a panic attack."

My face flushed and my ears burned with embarrassment.

"Son, they're completely normal, given the circumstances."

"Yeah, well, they're not normal for me."

He patted my hand.

"I freaked out in front of the entire school."

"I'm sure it wasn't *that* bad."

"Navil was there, and we locked eyes . . ." I stared off into space.

"If this girl cares about you, she'll—"

"She doesn't just care about me, Pop. She *loves* me."

I buried my head beneath my stale-smelling pillow and moaned. Pop gently removed it from my face and sat me upright.

"Honey, sadly, this won't be your last embarrassing moment. Try to remember what your mom used to say . . ."

I pictured her face and perked up.

"It isn't what knocks us down that defines us. It's how we react. Make sense?"

"Yeah."

"Good. Plus, what you're going through is treatable."

"How?"

"Mostly rest and exercise."

I rolled my eyes.

"—and maybe some medication."

"Great." I sighed.

"It's no big deal, Ollie."

Bad enough I'm a jailbird. Now I'm batshit crazy.

Fan-fucking-tastic.

CHAPTER FORTY-SIX

Between the sickly moans, stench of disinfectant, and a morbid sense of . . . I don't know—*death*? I couldn't wait to get the hell out of the hospital.

Just after noon, they removed the IV from my arm and sent me home with a prescription for something called *Xanax*.

"It's new on the market, and it's been working wonders for people with stress-related issues," the ER doctor informed me.

By one o'clock, I was wearing sweats and hanging out in the basement, munching on pretzels, and watching afternoon game shows.

Midway through *Match Game*, my eyelids betrayed me, and I fell asleep. The next thing I knew, my kid brother was delivering a flying elbow off the back of the couch.

The little shit knocked a fart right out of me.

After catching my, um—breath, I wrapped him in a bear hug and wrestled him to the ground. From the top of the stairs, Tía Carolina yelled at us to settle down.

"Por favor, ten cuidado. You just got home from the hospital."

Ignoring her plea, I locked in my version of a figure-four leg lock and squeezed till Jaime screamed in pain. After shushing him, we took out his Legos and spent the rest of the afternoon building and smashing till a phone call interrupted our playtime.

"Ollie—teléfono."

"Who is it?"

"Tu novia."

My girlfriend . . . oh.

"Do you have to go?" Jaime asked.

His sad, cherubic face tore at my heartstrings, but I wanted to—strike that, needed to speak with Navil.

"I'll be right back."

"Promise."

I crossed my heart and left the basement, two steps at a clip. I took the cordless and went straight to my bedroom for the call.

"Oh my God, Ollie, I'm so glad you're home."

"You and me both."

"How are you feeling? I was so worried."

"I'm feeling fine. Nothing to worry about."

She peppered me with questions, but the sound of her voice brought me back to our previous phone call. The one where she told me that she loved me. She kept asking about the hospital and doctors, but all I wanted to talk about was that conversation.

I never got a chance to respond.

"Did they give you any medicine?"

I needed to tell her that I loved her too.

And couldn't wait to see her.

To hold her.

"Ollie, are you sure you're okay?"

"Yeah, no, I mean—"

"What is it, Ollie?" she whispered.

Words and images burst through my mind.

Romeo and Juliet mixed in scenes of *Ralph and Alice* from *The Honeymooners* professing their love for one another as the musical score accentuated the moment.

My body tensed.

I had to tell her.

"Navil—" I began.

"Yes, Ollie?"

I was ready.
This was my moment.
I tugged at my collar.
My mouth dried.
"You still there?" she asked.
I blew a burp through my nostrils and got cotton mouth.
"Ollie?"
Instead of confessing my love, I—

CHAPTER FORTY-SEVEN

Splatter from my technicolor yawn rocketed across my desk and slowly dripped onto the carpet.

Dazed and ashamed, I yelled to Navil that I'd call her back and hung up before tossing the handset onto my mattress. By the second bounce, Tía Carolina barreled into my bedroom.

Her eyes grew the size of saucers. "Hijo de mi vida, are you okay?"

She immediately ran to my side and sat me down on my bed. The wave of dizziness and nausea subsided. Left behind were chunks of pretzel bits and humiliation.

"I'm fine, Tía, I'm fine."

She pressed the back of her hand against my forehead to check if I had a fever before ordering me to bed. I tried objecting, but she wasn't having it.

She ripped open my covers and pointed at my pillow. "Lay down."

After rolling my eyes, I did as I was told, snagging the phone and tucking it under my sheets. She disappeared for a moment, returning with a glass of water, aspirin, paper towels, and spray cleaner.

In less than ten minutes, all remnants of my puke were gone, replaced with a lemony, fresh scent.

"I will check on you later."

I listened for the sound of cabinet doors opening in the

kitchen before calling Navil back. I prayed that she'd answer as I dialed. The gods were listening.

"Ollie?"

"It's me. Listen, I—"

"Should you be on the phone?"

Tía Carolina could hear an ant fart halfway across the county, so I knew I only had a few minutes before she returned and snatched the phone.

"Navil, I don't have a lot of time."

She grew quiet.

"What you said to me—"

I could hear her breathing.

"The other day—"

I heard Tía approaching.

"When you called my house—"

She cursed my name under her breath in Spanish.

"I remember."

My bedroom doorknob jiggled.

I should have locked it.

Rookie mistake.

"I—love you too."

Tía Carolina burst in.

"Oliver Morales, I thought I told you to go to sleep?"

I hopped out of bed and placed my body between her and the phone.

"Oh, Ollie," Navil cried into the phone. "I love you, too."

"Dame . . . ese . . . *teléfono*."

I put my hip between Tía and the phone, but it didn't work.

"I'll—"

She ripped it from my hand and held it threateningly over my head.

"—see you tomorrow!" I shouted as Tía hung up the phone.

Huffing and puffing like the big bad wolf, she growled, *"Get in bed, coño."*

"All right, all right, I'm getting, I'm getting."

Her left eye twitched as I slipped under the covers. It looked like she wanted to smack me in the head with the phone. Instead, she shook it at me, turned, and stormed out, slamming the door behind her.

I could hear her grumbling her way to the kitchen. I also heard the basement door opening and Jaime asking for me.

"He went to bed, now—*get out of my face.*"

Sorry, kid.

CHAPTER FORTY-EIGHT

"You *do* know that my leg's broken, right?" I asked Len on my last leg lift.

"Oh c'mon, Ollie. You're doing great."

"You keep *saying* that. I don't think that means what you think it means."

Ten minutes later, we entered my room and startled Pop awake, who sat snoring in the chair next to my bed.

"You're back. How was—"

"It sucked," I whined, hopping from the wheelchair onto my bed.

Len shook his head. "Ignore him. He did great."

Pop nodded approvingly.

"Are you going to shower or rest?"

I slipped out of my sweat-drenched tee. "What do you think?"

Len ignored my attitude. "Want me to stick around, or do you—"

"I've got it," I grumbled, while Pop whispered that he'd help me.

Yeah, what could possibly go wrong? A septuagenarian with a cane, helping an overweight fifty-something-year-old with a broken leg.

That's definitely a recipe for success.

"You *may* want to stick around," I suggested.

A wink and a quick shower later, I snuggled back in bed, caught up on emails and waited for lunch to arrive. While I was away getting my ass kicked in physical therapy, I received fifty more messages.

Most were bullshit: ads, news items, and financial statements. One did catch my eye. An email from my editor. The subject line read, *Call Me*.

"That's weird."

"What's that, bub?"

"Hmm? Oh, nothing. An email from my editor. She wants me to call her."

"What's so strange about that?"

"She sent it to my personal mailbox, not my work one."

"Why would she do that?"

"I don't know. That's why I said—you know what? Never mind. Can I borrow your cell?"

Pop handed me his cell, and I stared at it for a moment. It still made me laugh that this septuagenarian who struggled to program his VCR had a brand-new iPhone. Just as funny, I no longer remembered phone numbers, like I used to, pre-cell phone days. Important numbers were on speed dial, so why remember them?

"Shit."

"¿Qué?"

I chuckled. "I can't remember her number."

"And it's not in her email?"

"No." I Googled my office number, old-school style, and left a voicemail. "It's Ollie. Tag, you're it."

I handed Pop back his phone and replied to her email with the same message, along with the phone number to my room in the rehab clinic.

"Couldn't reach her, huh?"

"No. Whatever. With all that's going on in the world, this whole thing feels so, I don't know—"

"Clandestine?"

I pointed at him. "Exactly."

Lunch arrived, so I put the iPad away and wolfed down barbecue pork, fingerling potatoes, and peaches. A half hour later, the phone rang.

It was my editor.

"How're you feeling, Ollie?"

"Not bad, given the circumstances. So, what's going on? Why the email?"

There was a long pause. "Have you heard from human resources or talked to legal?"

Strange question.

"I had *a visit*, if that's what you mean."

I heard her breathing into the phone.

"What time do visiting hours end?"

"I don't know. Why?"

"Because I can't have this conversation with you over the phone."

I could hear her teeth clenching.

"Boss, what's going on?"

"Just find out what time—"

"Hold on," I replied. "Pop, any idea when visiting hours end here?"

He shook his head.

"I'll email you."

I hung up and searched through the literature in the nightstand and found what I needed. Visiting hours were from 9:00 a.m. through 7:30 p.m. on weekdays. I grabbed the iPad, emailed her the information and received a thumbs-up emoji back.

"Everything okay?"

"I don't know, Pop. She sounded—"

"Did I hear something about attorneys?"

I nodded. "She asked me if I've talked to anyone from legal or human resources."

He arched a brow.

What the fuck is going on?

CHAPTER FORTY-NINE

I traveled the world for *these people*—put my life on the line. Hell, I was lying in a fucking hospital bed, and they *locked me out* of their system?

I jabbed the screen with my middle finger. "You've got to be kidding me."

"What's the matter, bub?"

"Hmm? Nothing."

"Doesn't seem like nothing."

"I can't get into my work email."

"And that's bad?" Pop teased. "I mean, you are trying to recover, no?"

"I suppose. Still."

"I'm sure it's just a clerical error. Back in my day..."

Pop droned on about how back in his day, the pre-internet world, he relied on administrative assistants.

"... none of this email nonsense."

I pretended to listen.

"Well, what did your editor say?"

"That she couldn't talk about it on the phone and would try and stop by after work."

He furrowed his bushy brows.

"Exactly."

"There's nothing you can do about it now. Why don't you put that thing away and get your rest."

I was a bit tired, so I snapped the iPad shut, stared at the wall clock for a moment, and shut my eyes for a few hours.

***

Just after six o'clock, Jaime stopped in after work and picked up Pop.

Jesus, this kid looks exhausted.

"Dude, you *really* need to take some time off."

"Tell that to my patients."

He stuck around for a while and caught up on the events of the day, including my plight at work.

"Sounds serious."

"We'll see. No more serious than this leg."

Jaime laughed. "Well, good luck with all that. Ready to go, Pop?"

After they kissed me goodbye, I flipped the channel to local news, and settled in for the evening. Around eight-thirty, there was a knock on the door.

"Come in."

It was my boss, Jenny.

She wore a white N95 mask, a fashionable red silk headscarf with multicolored swooping patterns covering her pixie brunette cut, and a tan raincoat. Her black leather gloves and dark sunglasses completed the mystery ensemble.

"Kinda late, no?"

"Tell me about it. I thought your family would never leave."

"How long have you been waiting?"

"Don't ask."

Due to the new COVID protocols, she offered an elbow bump instead of a hug or handshake before grabbing Pop's chair.

"I won't bother asking how you got past the guards."

She smiled. "Not my first rodeo."

"So, what's with all the cloak and dagger?"

"Plausible deniability."

She removed her outer layer, brushed her hair back, and leaned forward.

"We've got a problem."

"I'm listening."

Jenny explained that the same law enforcement team that came to my hospital room stopped by the news office to speak with her. Due to who they were, she had to get our legal department involved.

"Let me guess—a pair of assholes. One guy has a shiny bald head, and the other one has salt-and-pepper hair."

"That's them."

"That's the two who visited me. Go on."

"They flanked me during my meeting."

"Nice. And?"

"The Fibbies wanted to know what you were doing at the Mall?"

I was doing you a fucking favor.

"What'd you tell them?"

"The truth. That you were one of our journalists there on assignment."

"Anything else?"

"They asked about your personal politics. You know, *Black Lives, Antifa, MAGA.*"

"And?"

"And nothing. I told them you were a pro and kept your beliefs to yourself."

I thought of a few better responses than the one she gave but said nothing.

"Then they asked me if you had any enemies or knew your assailants."

"Why the fuck would I know the people who attacked me?"

"That's what I asked."

I encouraged her to continue.

"They claimed the attack seemed—*personal.*"

I gestured to my broken leg. "*Ya, think*?"

"Listen, I told them everything I know, which isn't much, so they handed me their cards, and legal escorted them out."

Tension spread across my back.

"What have you gotten yourself into here, Ollie?"

"*Me? I was there doing you a favor, remember*?"

She sighed. "I . . . remember."

"And why the hell am I locked out of email?"

"I was getting to that. According to my HR contact, you're locked out until you sign some bullshit agreement."

"Great," I scoffed.

"And if you take too long—"

"Let me guess, I'm fired?"

She shut her eyes and slowly nodded.

CHAPTER FIFTY

With my car stuck in student parking, I was forced to catch a ride with my father to school. We waited for Fi, but she never showed up. Apparently, she caught the bus instead, which surprised me for two reasons.

First, I didn't realize the bus still ran through our neighborhood since I began driving to school. Second, I figured even though things were weird between Fi and me, she would still catch a ride with Pop, in this case, to school.

I guess I was wrong on both counts.

Regardless, I figured I'd run into her near our lockers when I arrived at school and had Pop drop me off at Veteran's Memorial Hall. Instead, I ran into Navil. Or rather, she into me.

Literally.

She stood near my locker, and the moment she spotted me turning the corner, she yelled my name.

"Ollie!"

Students and teachers alike parted as she raced toward me. Approximately a foot away, Navil leaped, slammed me into the wall, and knocked the air from my lungs. Without a second thought, she wrapped her slender arms around my neck and planted one on my lips.

Heads turned as teachers and fellow students tried their best to ignore our breaking school policy against public displays of affection. My guess is teachers were taking pity on me while students either didn't care or had to get to class.

Regardless, our make-out session didn't last long.

"Miss me?" I breathlessly whispered.

She sheepishly smiled and spread her fingers a half-inch apart. "Un peu."

I returned her smile and recalled why I entered the building. I looked over her shoulder and searched for Fi.

Navil followed my gaze. "Who are you looking for?"

"Fi. Have you seen her?"

Navil placed her warm hand against my cheek and whispered, "Is that really what you want to talk about right now?"

Even under those dull fluorescent lights, her opulent hazel eyes shimmered with flecks of green, brown, and gold.

Hypnotic.

Caused me to forget about Fi—about everything.

Except the girl standing in front of me.

The girl I—

"I love you, Navil." I confessed.

She triggered something deep inside of me.

The words tumbled from my mouth.

Her innocent scent filled my nostrils.

We ignored the passersby and onlookers.

Unfortunately, first bell reminded us of our reality and broke us from our trance. The hallway filled with the sound of students racing to their respective classes. I glanced at my wristwatch.

Three minutes till the next bell, and AP Calculus.

"We've got to go," I stated.

"I know."

"Pick this up later?"

"Absolument." She smiled. "Definitely."

Ginny walked past and snickered.

After lunch, I spotted Fi across campus on our way to AP English.

"*Fi.*"

We locked eyes for a moment before she turned back and entered the building.

"What the fuck."

I picked up the pace to catch up, but she had a good head start and got to class before me. Instead of finding her seated in her usual spot next to mine in the middle, center row, she decided to sit in the far right corner of the spacious classroom next to a fellow senior, Clara Jenkins, a boarder from Nebraska.

I stood in the doorway and waved for Fi to join me in the hallway. We still had about five minutes before class, so I figured we could hash out our issues.

"Fi … Fi." I called. "C'mon. I know you can hear me."

Classmates slipped past me as I urged her to come into the hallway.

Well, *most* did.

As I summoned Fi, someone slipped their slender fingers between my cheeks and goosed my backside. I spun on my heels and nearly banged my head against the door jam.

I don't know who laughed harder, the people who witnessed it in the classroom, or the culprit giggling with her mouth covered, standing behind me in the hallway.

"I'm sorry, Ollie." Navil laughed. "I couldn't resist."

Red-faced, I laughed it off and escorted her into class, taking our customary seats. All through class, I kept looking over at Fiona. It saddened me, seeing her sit so far away.

Navil must have noticed. She leaned over and slipped a note into my hand with the words, "Things will work out."

I turned and offered a half-smile and head nod. After class, Navil and I made it to the hallway first before Fi, so we waited for her. She tried blowing past us, but I got in her way.

"Get out of the way, Oliver."

"Oh, it's Oliver now?"

"Move."

"No."

She shoved me. "*Mooo-ve.*"

"Not till you talk to me."

"Why, so I can *trigger* you again?"

"Fi—"

"*What*, Ollie?" she cried. "It's true. It was all my fault."

I stepped forward, but she pushed past me in tears.

Fuck.

After school, Navil and I searched for Fi, but she was nowhere to be found. We checked her usual haunts but turned up empty-handed. She wasn't in the gym, the library, or even playing Pacman at the deli, where Navil and I bought a couple of Snapples before heading back to campus.

"You don't suppose she walked home, do you?"

"Not in this weather," I replied as we crossed the street.

It was a typical dreary and overcast mid-fifties, late winter/ early spring Long Island afternoon.

Fi and I shared a ton of history. I knew her haunts almost as well as she knew mine.

In the bank parking lot, Navil took my hand. "Let's think about this, Ollie. Where would Fiona go if she had no car but still wanted to hide?"

"I don't know."

"Think. You know her better than anyone, non?"

I nodded.

"So—"

"If it were me, and I wanted to hide, I'd go to the photo lab or somewhere off campus with my camera."

"And Fiona?"

"I don't know. Fi's interests are simpler. She loves listening to music while reading romance novels."

"Like the Harlequin novels you buy at la pharmacie?"

"No, more like that stuff they make you read in school—*Pride and Prejudice, Wuthering Heights . . .*"

"Ah, the classics."

"If you say so."

"Okay, so where would you find a large selection of the classics and modern music?"

I had a lightbulb moment and snapped my fingers. "Got it. Let's go."

CHAPTER FIFTY-ONE

*B*ingo.

Fi noticed us walking toward her and rolled her eyes. "How'd you find me?"

I smirked. "Seriously?"

"Ignore him, Fiona."

Fi slid down her headphones. "I have to find new hiding places."

"Please don't," I murmured.

We found her quietly seated in the back corner of the State University library with a small stack of cassette tapes and a pack of *Twizzlers*, reading *Sense and Sensibility* by Jane Austen.

I peered into her Walkman.

She was listening to her latest music obsession, *U2*. In addition to Bono's seductive wails, The Edge's brash guitar riffs, Adam Clayton's underlying thrumming from his bass, and Larry Mullen Jr.'s unshakable drumming, she loved the social commentary found in their lyrics, and once said they spoke to her inner Irish.

"*Unforgettable Fire*? Haven't you listened to that like a million times already?"

"Said the guy who's watched that disgusting Phoebe Cates scene in *Fast Times at Ridgemont High*, like *how* many times?"

"Phoebe Cates?" Navil whispered.

"It's, *uh*, not important."

"You know—the *bikini* scene," Fi stated, imitating the scene for Navil.

Navil seemingly remembered and shook her head. "Mon Dieu, Ollie."

I turned my face.

"Don't look at me. You're dating him."

"Crazy, non?"

Nearby college students began shushing us.

I ignored the commentary. "Can we go someplace to talk?"

Fi pursed her lips and nodded.

We stepped outside into the cool evening and found a spot on a nearby bench.

I nestled between Navil and Fi.

"Fi, look—"

"No, Ols." She held her hand up. "I'm . . . sorry."

"Why are you apologizing? I'm the one who lost his shit."

"Exactly. *I* shouldn't have bombarded you—"

"You weren't bombar—"

Fi balled up her tiny fist and smacked the side of her head. "I'm just so stupid sometimes."

I grabbed her wrist. "Hey—stop that."

Embarrassed and upset, she fled from the bench, forcing Navil and me to chase after her.

"*Fi.* Slow down."

Navil caught up to her, and Fi collapsed into her loving arms. It was intimate, but not in a sexual way.

Sisterly.

Navil gently stroked Fi's raven hair and wiped away her tears. I approached but was waved off. From a distance, I watched as the pair quietly spoke.

Fi stood there, confessing whatever sins she felt she

committed, while Navil empathetically nodded along as she took in every word.

From where I stood, I could only make out a few words and phrases, like *It's okay* and *He knows.*

Eventually, they finished and called me over.

I took Navil's hand while chucking Fi a brotherly head nod. "Hey."

Sniffing back tears, she replied with her own, "Hey."

"You okay?" I whispered.

Fi sheepishly smiled. "I guess."

"Are *we* okay?"

"Were we ever?"

I thumped her shoulder.

We both smiled.

"Hungry?"

"Starving."

"Pizza?"

"You buying?"

"Don't I always."

"Not always."

"*Really*?"

"Yeah. Sometimes your father pays." She laughed.

"You're such a jerk."

"*You are.*"

"Oh?" I arched a brow and stalked forward.

"Don't . . . Ollie."

"Don't what?" Navil asked.

A sly smile splashed across my face.

"Oliver Morales, I swear to God—"

I curled my right index finger.

"I will kick you in the—"

I snatched her tiny frame in my arms and tickled Fi's armpits and ribcage. She bucked like a bronco and squealed like a pig.

"Stop it—Ollie—Hahahaha—"

Navil stood amazed as I tickle-tortured Fi to the ground. Eventually, she kicked her leg back and tagged my shin with her shoe. I let her go immediately.

"Ow! *Fuck*, that hurt!" I yelled.

"Good. Serves you right. I told you not to—"

"*Asshole*," I chided as I rubbed my wound.

"*You're* the asshole."

"Okay, you two. That's enough. You're worse than my little brother and sister."

"She *kicked* me."

"Yeah, well, he tickled me."

"You're even. Apologize to each other so we can put this silliness behind us."

"Whatever. I'm sorry I kicked you."

"Ollie?" Navil gestured.

I stuck my tongue out at Fi.

Navil smacked my arm. "*Oliver*."

"All right, all right. People need to stop hitting me."

"Apologize to Fiona."

I folded my arms. "I'm sorry."

"Like you mean it?"

"Fi—" I sighed. "I'm sorry."

"I'm sorry, too, Ollie. I really am. I didn't mean to—"

"I know."

"It's just—"

"Save it. Are we cool?"

She nodded and smiled.

"How about you give her a hug, Ollie?"

I chucked Fi a look of disgust, "Eww—"

She flipped me off.

"Guess not," Navil muttered.

"Fine, c'mere."

Fi shook her head. "After what *you just said*?"

I crooked my index finger again.

"You'd *better* not."

Navil got between us. "Okay, you two."

I escorted the pair back to our prep school across from the university.

"So, where do you want to go for pizza?" I asked.

"The usual?" Fi replied.

"I will need permission to go," Navil stated.

"That a problem?" Fi asked.

She smiled confidently. "I don't think so."

Who could say no to that face?

Twenty minutes later, we were seated in a booth at Giuseppe's pizzeria, waiting for a large pepperoni to arrive. The conversation quickly turned to my recent incarceration.

Fi broached the subject after sipping her soda. "Ols . . . you can say no . . ."

I read her like a book. "You want to know about jail?"

"Only if you want to talk about it."

Images of my time behind bars passed before my mind's eye. Along with the fear and stench, which I found strange, since I was sitting next to Navil and her tantalizing perfume.

I gave in. "What do you want to know?"

"What was it like?"

We all leaned forward like we were planning a heist, and I shared my story.

"All right. Here's what happened . . ."

CHAPTER FIFTY-TWO

Navil's hazel eyes widened.

"Christ, Ollie," Fi whispered.

"Yep."

"Here ya go, kids. One large pepperoni," Tony announced.

Nothing hit the internal reset button like a slice of Giuseppe's. Of course, it didn't hurt that I had the hottest girl on the planet seated to my right, and my best friend sitting across from us.

"Before I forget . . ." Navil said.

"Yeah?"

"Ginny asked me again if we were going to Stefan's party this weekend?"

I didn't relish the thought of going to this asshat's party. All I could picture was him spending the entire night hitting on my girlfriend while ignoring his own.

"I don't know. Do you really feel like going?"

"Only if you do. Ginny said it would be—off the hanger, oui?"

Fi chuckled.

"Hook. The expression is—you know what, never mind. Sure, we can go."

"Good. Oh, and Fiona, I'm sure you can come too."

"That's okay," Fi said. "I'm busy this weekend."

"Firehouse?" I asked.

She nodded.

"What this time?"

"Promotions."

As we chatted, a loud group of guys walked past our table, headed toward the front exit. They all wore firemen t-shirts, including the tall guy in the center. He was in his early twenties, broad-shouldered, and built like a wide receiver.

He glanced at our table and noticed Fi.

"Hey, there she is." He smiled.

Fi heard his voice and got flustered. "Oh, uh . . . hey, Tim."

"How many times do I have to tell ya? It's Timmy."

Timmy?

To my left, I noticed Navil give this guy a cool once-over. Her eyes narrowed, brow arched, and she subtly chewed on her lower lip. His stupid baritone voice, sandy brown hair, and perfect smile seemed to have mesmerized her.

"Right, sorry. Timmy." Fi chuckled.

"These your friends?"

"Hmm? Oh, yeah, this is um . . ." She stared at me and drew a blank.

Seriously?

Annoyed, I introduced myself, "Ollie."

"Are you one of the doc's kids?"

"You know my dad?" I asked as I shook his large paw.

"Heck yeah. That man's a trip. And that aunt of yours—well, I don't need to tell you."

Navil cleared her throat. "Oh, right, sorry. This is my *girl-friend*, Navil."

"Bonjour," she demurely said.

Like a dog marking his favorite toy, I wrapped an arm around her waist and slid her closer, which seemed to annoy her and amuse Fi.

"Cute accent," he stated before turning back to Fi. "Are you coming Saturday?"

"Wouldn't miss it."

"Great." He beamed.

As the pair quietly held their gaze, one of his companions walked over.

"Yo, dude, we gotta get back to the station. Oh, hey, Fi. What's up?"

"Hi, Leon."

"Duty calls," Timmy quipped. "Save me a dance this weekend?"

Fi nodded. "Sure."

"Cool. Nice meeting you guys. Say hey to your old man and aunt for me."

Neither Navil nor Fi took their eyes off him until they all left the restaurant. The look on their faces reminded me of the look Jaime got when he entered the bakery in Smithtown, only worse.

Theirs were—carnal.

And they weren't alone.

Across the way, I watched a woman as old as Tía Carolina stalk the group as they left. She gingerly dabbed sweat from her neck and brow.

Jesus Christ.

Navil bit her lower lip and playfully fanned herself.

"Tell me about it." Fi laughed.

The animated duo began speaking in French like a pair of gossips. The only words I understood were *mon Dieu* and *magnifique.*

Disgusted and a bit self-conscious, I excused myself and went to the bathroom. On my way, I overheard several women saying things like:

"Did you see those hands?"

"How about that ass?"

"They can put my fire out anytime."

I shook my head and kept walking.

After finishing my business, I washed my hands and stared into the mirror, mentally comparing myself to the hunks who'd just left, and came up short.

Extremely short.

With a slightly bruised ego, I returned to the booth and found Tony boxing up the remainder of our pizza.

"There he is. Thought we'd have to send in the Marines."

The girls chuckled.

"Will there be anything else? Maybe sodas to go?"

The girls and I said no, so I paid the check and watched Tony return to his spot behind the counter.

"You guys ready to go?" I asked, still feeling a bit dejected.

"Oui, chér," Navil replied through narrowed eyes. "You okay?"

I threw on a fake smile. "Never better."

The girls exchanged a quick glance but chose not to pick at that particular scab. Instead, we left the restaurant and headed back to school. On the ride back, Navil paid a little more attention to me than usual. My guess was she was trying to soothe my ego.

She caressed my hand and played with a curl behind my right ear.

Unfortunately, it didn't work.

I quietly pouted the entire walk to her dorm while she talked about homework and whatnot. Before reaching the front porch, she'd had enough. She pulled me aside, away from the porch lights, grabbed my lapels, and kissed me.

I could still taste the sauce and grease from the delicious pizza on her lips and tongue. The tension in my ego-bruised neck dissipated as we melted into each other.

"Better?" she asked once our lips parted.

"Much."

"You know I love you, chér, non?"

"I know."

"Bon," she said with a peck on the lips. "Walk me to the door?"

After a warm hug goodnight, I watched her go inside her dorm.

That other guy might be hot, but I've got the girl.

CHAPTER FIFTY-THREE

On the ride home, a helicopter flew overhead, heading toward the towering hospital spire with flashing red lights peeking through the forest.

It made me think of—

"Any word on Jackie?"

Fi shook her head.

The clock on my dashboard read nine-fifteen, past visiting hours. I felt a twinge of guilt that I hadn't been back to see her. I promised myself I'd fix that as the copter slowly disappeared.

The following day, life normalized. After school, a group of us gathered in the library to study. Off in the back corner, I noticed B Karlsson, the eleventh-grade genius, studying. Her blonde hair was wet, presumably from swimming practice.

At my table, Navil chewed on her pencil while struggling through our latest calculus homework. Fi smacked on cherry flavored Hubba Bubba and wrapped up her AP French assignment. Rounding out our group were Ginny and Alli, who seemed more interested in party planning than getting any work done.

As I glanced around the spacious library, watching well-dressed prep school students with noses buried in textbooks, I couldn't help but reflect on my recent incarceration and the sharp contrast it presented with my peers.

My stomach soured as I thought about my lunatic cellmate, Ricky, and wondered if he was out there somewhere wreaking havoc.

"Ollie, don't you think she should ask him?" Navil asked.

"Sorry, what?"

"Timmy."

"What about him?"

Navil looked confused. "Have you not been paying attention?"

"Yeah, no. Sorry. What are we talking about?"

"Navil thinks I should ask him out," Fi replied. "I think she's being ridiculous."

"He sounds hot," Alli chimed in.

Ginny interjected, "As my momma said, you need to lock that shit down before somebody else gets a chance."

Navil asked, "What do you think, Ollie?"

Fi's eyes pleaded for me to change the subject.

"Hey, Ginny, what time does Stefan's party start?"

"Around six o'clock, but you definitely want to get there early. Otherwise, you'll never find a parking spot."

Fi mouthed, *Thank you.* Ginny, meanwhile, spent the next few minutes bragging about the party and all the things her beau had planned. Apparently, he and his older brother were flying in goodies from "south of the border," as she called it.

"You may want to think about spending the night. Lord knows there's plenty of room," she boasted. "A bunch of us are. Right, Alli?"

"Yes, but not all of us will have a *private* bedroom," Alli teased.

"There's nothing stopping you and Giles from finding a quiet spot for the night," Ginny countered. "You too, Navil. Am I right, Ollie?"

How the hell did this turn into my nightmare?

Ginny and Alli snickered as my ears burned from embarrassment.

Navil, on the other hand, masterfully replied, "As you Americans say, we will play it by ear, non, Ollie?"

"Yeah. We'll—what she said," I stammered.

Fi was uncharacteristically quiet on the ride home that evening. It wasn't till we pulled into my driveway that she said anything.

"What do you think I should do about—"

"Fireman Timmy?"

She nodded.

"I don't know, Fi. Do you like him?"

"I mean, yeah. But—"

"So, what's the problem then?"

"You've seen him. He's all—" Fi mimed his height and muscles.

"So."

"And I'm all . . . well . . . me." She wilted like a flower.

"You're fucking kidding me, right?"

She pursed her lips and stared out into the evening.

"C'mon, Fi, you're hot."

She looked at me, stunned.

"I mean, I don't want to, ya know—"

She rolled her eyes. "You're an idiot."

"Look, all I'm saying is I saw the way he looked at you."

"And?"

"What do you mean, and? The dude likes you."

"Yeah, but he's—"

"I know—" I mimicked her previous imitation. "Who cares? And so what that he's a few years older."

"Try six."

"Whatever, a few, six, what's the worst that can happen?"

"Let's see, I get rejected so bad that I can never step foot in the firehouse?"

"You mean, the *same* fire station that your grandfather runs?"

Her face blanched. "Oh my God. *Gramps.*"

"What? He won't care."

"Really? Have you forgotten about the Artie Brennan inci-dent?"

I chuckled. "There's a name I hadn't thought about in years."

CHAPTER FIFTY-FOUR

Artie used to live down the block from us. He moved away after his parents divorced about three years ago.

One summer night, a bunch of us were hanging out in Fi's garage. There was Artie, me, Fi, Brie Levenson, a girl from around the block I had a crush on, and a few other kids.

For some reason, Artie was poking around Fi's trash and came across a bunch of empty beer bottles. The next thing you know, we're sitting in a circle playing Spin the Bottle.

Artie quickly went over the rules. "Okay, you spin the bottle. When it stops, you kiss the person it's pointing at. It's really simple. Any questions?"

We all looked at each other and shook our heads no.

"Good," Artie replied and spun the bottle.

Fi's nervousness radiated as we stared at the bottle. With every rotation, her eyes widened with a tinge of fear, and she trembled ever so slightly. To Artie's chagrin, it landed on Jeremy, one of the other neighborhood kids from around the block. Our collective laughter broke up the tension.

" 'Kay, Jeremy. Your turn."

He leaned forward and gave it an aggressive spin. We all watched as the empty brown Michelob bottle went round and round. You could hear a pin drop as it slowed and pointed at Brie.

He pumped his fist while she shrugged like it was no big deal. After removing her chewing gum, she kissed the elated Jeremy.

As she did, I caught a glimpse of her white cotton panties poking out from the top of her jean shorts. They had a flower pattern.

As she returned to her spot, she caught me staring at her backside and smiled, which caused my ears to burn from embarrassment.

Without taking her eyes off me, Brie announced, "My turn."

I gulped and watched the bottle as it pinwheeled and stopped on yours truly. I gasped while she removed her gum.

"Come here, Ollie," she ordered.

Before I could respond, Brie grabbed my shirt and pulled me in for a kiss. My chest pounded as we locked lips. After a second or two, Brie released me, and nodded approvingly, before settling back in her spot.

"Not bad," she whispered. "It's your turn, Ollie."

"Uh, that's okay. Why doesn't someone else go."

"Pussy," Artie chided. "I'll go."

Artie spun the bottle for a second time. He rocked back and forth on his haunches as he openly prayed for it to stop on Brie.

"C'mon, Brie."

Unfortunately for Artie, it landed on Fiona, whose eyes grew. He was visibly annoyed but accepted his fate.

"Fine. Let's get this over with."

Just as the pair locked lips, the garage lights flicked on. Standing in the doorway was a half-in-the-bag Gramps, holding an empty beer bottle and ready to tear someone a new asshole.

"What the hell is going on out here?"

We all scattered. Most everyone escaped, including myself, who took Brie's hand and led her to safety. Artie, on the other hand, wasn't as lucky. He slipped on an oil stain, and practically landed at Gramp's feet. I'd never felt so bad for someone in my life.

"Get over here, you little shit. Did I just see you kissing my granddaughter?"

Gramps released his empty and grabbed ahold of Artie's collar. He swung him around like a ragdoll while screaming obscenities in the poor kid's face.

"Gramps, put him down," Fi pleaded.

He ignored her and continued berating Artie, who eventually slipped from Gramp's grasp and tore out of the garage like Roadrunner, the cartoon character. As a matter of fact, I thought I heard him do the *beep beep* and leave behind a cloud of dust as he ran.

"That poor bastard will never set foot on your property ever again, not even on Halloween." I laughed.

"I thought Gramps was going to track him down and kill him," Fi chuckled. "He grounded me for like a week."

"I can still remember that look of terror in Artie's eyes."

"Worst first kiss ever."

"Hey, I thought *I* was your first kiss," I complained.

"That doesn't count. We were like seven."

"Counted for me."

My front porch lights began flashing. Tía Carolina's not-so-subtle way of letting me know it was time to come inside.

"All right. I'm coming. Geez. I can't wait to graduate and get the hell out of Dodge."

"Have you heard anything yet?"

I pursed my lips. "No. You?"

A guilty expression spread across her face.

"Oh, my God, *you have*. Who?"

"I didn't want to say anything till you heard something."

"Screw that. Who? Which college?"

"All of them."

"What do you mean, *all of them*?"

She rattled off the list of colleges and universities that accepted her college application.

"Geneseo, Albany, Stony Brook, Colgate, and Amherst."

"What about Notre Dame?"

"I never applied. Too expensive."

"Still, that's awesome, Fi."

She smiled. "Thanks, Ols. I'm sure you'll hear soon."

The porch lights flashed again.

"I better get inside before she blows a gasket."

We said our goodnights, and as usual, I waited for Fi to get home. The moment I stepped inside my house, Pop hit me with—

"Ollie. We need to talk."

CHAPTER FIFTY-FIVE

“We received a call from Mrs. Chase today.” He smiled.

“What’d I do now?”

“What makes you think you did anything wrong?”

“With my luck lately?”

“Well, you’re not in trouble. She just wanted to see how you were holding up.”

“That’s it?”

“Well—no.”

“Great.” I sighed.

“She mentioned something about a senior project.”

“What about it?”

“That she’s mentoring you?”

“Yeah. She’s helping me put on a photo exhibit in May. I told you about that.”

“Yes, well, she also mentioned that she’s pregnant—”

“And?”

“—and that’s around the same time the baby’s due.”

“So, she can’t help me. Is that what you’re saying?”

He nodded.

My shoulders slumped.

“But—”

I stared up at my father.

“What if she found someone to replace her?”

“Like another teacher?”

"Not sure. All she asked was, would you be willing to work with a substitute?"

"Like I have a choice."

"Either that or come up with a different project."

"I mean, I guess so."

"Good. That's what I told her."

"Anything else?"

"No. That's it. I've got to get to the hospital. A patient's crowning."

"Ewww."

He laughed and kissed me goodbye.

"Hey, Pop?"

"What is it, Ollie? I've got to run. Crowning, remember?"

"Yeah, gross. I just wanted to ask—any news on Jackie?"

"Your classmate? No. Why?"

I shrugged. "Just asking."

"You know, visiting hours end at eight o'clock. There's no reason you can't stop by and see her after dinner."

He wasn't wrong.

He headed to the garage. "See you in the morning.

"See ya, Pop."

After dinner, I thought about what Pop said. It was only six-forty, plenty of time for me to head to the hospital, see Jackie, and make it back in time to do homework.

The thought of seeing her alone left me feeling uncomfortable. Things were okay with Navil by my side. We could use her needing to get back to school as an excuse to leave early if things got weird.

Plus, they were roommates.

It's not like Jackie and I were friends. Hell, before her injuries, you couldn't even call us acquaintances. We were more enemies than anything. And now I was visiting her in the hospital? Alone? I pictured Navil standing over me, wagging her finger.

Fine. I'll go. But if she acts like a bitch—

Twenty minutes later, I stood outside Jackie's hospital room, weighing my options.

"You know, she's awake if you want to go in. I was just in there a few minutes ago," a nearby nurse informed me.

"Thanks."

She looked at her wristwatch. "You have about an hour."

Fuck it.

I gently knocked on the door.

"Come in."

I threw on a phony smile and crossed the great divide. I could tell she wasn't expecting me from her look of surprise as I entered.

"Hey, Jackie." I waved and smiled.

"Ollie." She pulled up her blanket and quickly fixed her hair. "What, uh, are you doing here?"

That's the same question I'm asking myself.

"Did I come at a bad time?"

"Oh, no, um, not at all." She tossed the magazine pile from the foot of her bed onto a nearby chair. "Why don't you sit here?"

I nodded and apologized for not being around to see her.

"That's okay. Nobody has."

Ouch.

"How're you feeling?"

"Better. I should be out of here soon."

"That's good," I replied, and decided to throw the skunk on the porch. "So, uh—"

She read me like a book.

"You want to know if I remember anything about my attack?"

"Am I that transparent?"

She pursed her lips. "No. It's the same question everyone asks."

"Oh."

"And to answer your question, no. The only thing I can remember is waking up in the hospital."

I reached for her hand. "I'm really sorry."

"I just can't wait to get out of this place. I feel so—"

"Trapped? Like you're in prison?"

"Exactly."

"I know the feeling."

She scrunched her brows. "You do?"

I spent the next few minutes telling her about my recent dealings with local law enforcement. It was strange not seeing her jot notes into her gold and blue notebook.

She was shocked. "But *you* were the one who found me and called for help."

"I know. Apparently, it didn't matter."

"Those bastards."

"Tell me about it."

"I am *so* sorry, Ollie. You shouldn't have had to go through all that."

"It's not your fault," I replied.

And for the first time, I believed it.

CHAPTER FIFTY-SIX

We stared at one another for a moment and empathetically shared in our mutual pain. For the first time in many weeks, there was someone who truly understood my challenges.

Sure, Navil and Fi witnessed my arrests, but they hadn't experienced the embarrassment or pain of my incarceration.

Jackie got it.

While her pain was physical, mine was emotional.

Anger flashed. "I'd love to find the person who did this to me—"

"You and me both," I interjected.

"—really make them pay."

Having been on the receiving end of her rancor, I almost felt sorry for the mystery asshole.

Almost.

She released my hand and lay back against propped-up pillows.

"How's school?"

"Meh. Homework and tests. You know. The usual bullshit."

She chuckled.

"I can't wait for this year to end."

We chatted away like a pair of old friends till visiting hours ended. Prior to that night, had someone told me I'd be bullshitting with Jackie Woodley *on purpose* for the better part of an hour, I would have told them they were nuts.

We'd known each other going on four years, and this was our first real conversation outside the newsroom. And I wouldn't call those exchanges "conversations." They were more like barking matches.

It felt like meeting her for the first time.

The real Jackie Woodley.

Not the bitch on wheels she pretended to be at school.

This version was different.

Compassionate.

Caring.

While she felt bad about my recent incarceration and had like a million questions—

I guess you *can* take the reporter out of the newsroom.

But she never made me feel bad about myself.

Less than.

The way most of my fellow classmates made me feel.

I glanced at the clock and noticed it was time to go.

She followed my eye line. "Gotta go?"

"Yeah." I nodded. "I'll be back, though."

"When?"

"Soon, Jackie."

"Call me Jack."

I popped a brow.

"It's what my friends call me back home."

I laughed.

Her eyes narrowed. "What's so funny?"

"Nothing," I confessed. "It's the thought of you and I being friends."

"Why is that funny?"

I shared with her how we usually interacted with one another.

"The only reason I treat you that way is because I respect you, Ollie."

"Ols." I smiled. "My friends call me Ols."

She returned my grin with one of her own.

"And if that's the way you treat the people you respect—"

"I know. Respect you less. I hear it all the time back home." She exhaled.

Over the loudspeaker, we heard the announcement that visiting hours were over. As I stood, Jack leaned forward and hugged me goodbye.

"I'll see you soon, Jack. I promise," I whispered.

"You better, Ols." She snickered. "You don't want to get on my bad side."

I pretended to shriek and received a laugh.

I waved goodbye from the door.

"Be careful, Ols."

"I will."

"Whoever did this to me is still out there."

"I know."

"Trust no one."

I smiled. "I won't."

"I'm serious."

"I know you are."

"At least till they catch this animal."

"I'll be careful. I'll keep my circle small. Just me, Fi, and Navil."

Her face changed at the mention of Navil's name.

Curious.

She bit her lower lip.

"What's the matter, Jack?"

She scratched her scalp. "I don't know. It's probably nothing."

"What is it?"

"It's—"

"Yeah?"

"Fi, I remember. She's your neighbor, right? That girl you hang out with all the time, that everyone swears you're dating?"

"We're not dating. Jesus, why does everybody—"

"Sorry. She's fine. It's the other one—"

"Navil. Your roommate. My girlfriend."

She pursed her lips when I said *girlfriend*.

"Her. Yeah."

"What about her?"

She shook her head slowly. "I don't know. There's something about a flower—"

"A flower?" I furrowed my brows.

"Sorry, Ols, it's just not coming to me." She sighed with frustration. "I just don't trust her, that's all."

"Look, Jackie—sorry, Jack," I replied. "I trust her—

And I am in love with her.

"She's hands-down one of the best people I know."

I spent the next few seconds rattling off Navil's best qualities.

Jackie raised her hands. "Okay, Ols. If you say so. It's getting late. I don't want you to get in trouble."

"Eh, trouble's my middle name."

She laughed. "Uh-huh. Good night, trouble."

"'Night, Jack. See you soon."

On the ride home, I thought about two things. First, that Jack was now a friend, which I never would have thought possible in a million years. Second, why didn't she trust Navil? In my eyes, the girl was perfect.

What's not to trust?

CHAPTER FIFTY-SEVEN

The following morning began like any other. Hit the snooze alarm a few times. Tía Carolina tore the covers off my bed. Ordered me to get ready for school.

Fi studied me the whole way to school. I guess she wanted to make sure I wouldn't throw another conniption. Other students did, too, as I exited my car.

Nothing to see here, folks.

Seated on a bench overlooking the parking lot, a certain sparkly-eyed stunner. Like the others, she worried about her man's return to school and wanted to be there, just in case.

The moment I laid eyes on her, my heart skipped a beat. There was something so inviting about her very presence. Jackie's comments were yesterday's problems.

Today, I had the wanton desire to be near this auburn-haired siren.

Taste her lips.

Be in her orbit.

She was the Earth and I—her moon.

Like a figure skater gliding across the ice, she sauntered toward me.

Flawless.

A patch of sunshine enveloped her like a spotlight from heaven.

"Good morning, chér," she whispered.

Due to the school rules against public displays of affection, or PDA, and the number of witnesses who could rat us out, we hugged.

While I preferred the warmth of her inviting lips, a warm embrace along with the scent of her subtle perfume were acceptable substitutes.

After whispering our love for one another, I interlocked my fingers with hers, and headed to my locker before going to Mrs. C's class. On the way, we talked about everything and nothing.

I mentioned my visit with Jackie and left out our final conversation. That would have to wait for later. When we had more time. I did, however, share how much Jackie seemed to have changed.

"It's like she's more human now," I commented.

"I told you that she was nice. You just never gave her a chance."

I laughed. "Yeah, *that's* what it was."

"Well, I'm just glad you—"

"Made a new friend?"

"Exactement." She smiled.

God, I could live in that smile.

"And next time you visit her—"

"I promise to bring you with me."

"Bon."

When we entered class, Mrs. C pulled me aside.

"I spoke with your father yesterday."

I pursed my lips. "He told me."

"Can you stick around this evening after our newspaper staff meeting?"

Like I had a choice?

"Yeah."

"Great. Okay. Better take your seat. Class is about to start."

With everything going on, I forgot about my issues with Mrs.

C. Still, I did as I was told and spent the remainder of the day splitting my time thinking about the hot girl seated to my right, and the meeting with Mrs. C after the staff meeting.

The former put a smile on my face; the latter soured my stomach. After school, I returned to the scene of the crime, so to speak—our makeshift newsroom—and took my customary seat to discuss our next issue for our school newspaper.

Gone from the room were the chalk outlines of Jackie and police tape. It was as if the incident never happened, even though I still had the emotional scars to prove it had.

The visibly pregnant Mrs. C, as always, ran the session. It felt weird not having Jackie at her side, barking orders.

As agreed, I hung out after the meeting.

"So, how're you feeling, Ollie?"

"I'm doing okay."

"I'm glad to hear it. You know, we were all very worried."

"Thanks."

"Well, about my involvement in your senior project..."

I sat there as she explained that her due date coincided with my project timelines, and if things went as planned, I should probably find a different mentor or choose a different project.

"I'd prefer to stick with doing my photography exhibit," I replied. "But how am I going to find a different mentor this late in the year?"

"I figured as much, which is why I reached out to someone on your behalf."

"Who?"

"Have I ever told you about my cousin?"

Great. Now she wants to pawn me off on some stupid relative.

"No."

"Really? I thought I had." She shrugged. "Anyway, he's a—"

As she explained things, there was a knock on the door.

"Come in," Mrs. C called.

The doorknob turned, and in entered a long-haired, bearded gentleman, looking to be in his mid-forties. He looked out of place at our school. Not many adults here wore well-worn brown leather bomber jackets, tweed newsboy caps, and blue jeans.

"Byron!"

Byron?

"Hey, cuz."

Mrs. C waddled over and embraced our new visitor with a warm hug.

I watched the pair chat and noticed there was something different about this guy.

A wisdom, like he'd seen things.

"How's my favorite cousin doing?"

"Exhausted."

"Let me look at you." He stepped back and gave her a once-over. "Gorgeous."

"Enormous, you mean."

"Hey, who's the professional here?" He then glanced in my direction. "Is this the kid?"

"It is. Ollie—" She called me over.

I walked over as ordered and politely shook his extended hand.

"This is my cousin . . ." she paused for effect. Like his name should mean something. "Byron Soladay."

Who the fuck is Byron Soladay?

CHAPTER FIFTY-EIGHT

Modern Day

Before she left, I begrudgingly asked my editor, Jenny, to contact the corporate jackals.

"Tell them I'll sign their stupid paperwork."

"I'm really sorry, Ollie."

"We both know that this is all—*bullshit*."

Her shoulders slumped. She nodded and exited stage left.

Three miserable days later, the arrogant attorneys from corporate entered my room just as I was getting out of the shower after another torture session.

I was tired.

Sore.

And in zero mood to eat crow.

No, no, come right on in. It's not like I'm standing here in my underwear.

"Don't you people knock?" Pop yelled.

"Oops, sorry," slicked-back, salt-and-pepper-hair man responded.

"We'll wait outside," Baldy added.

"Just—give me a minute." I sighed. "And, Pop, be nice."

He muttered something back at me under his breath.

"This won't take but a minute, Mr. M—" Salt-and-Pepper interjected.

"That's *Doctor* Morales."

He raised his hands. "Apologies. Meant no harm, *Doctor Morales*."

I tossed on a clean shirt and invited the pair in. "All right. Let's get this over with."

Salt-and-pepper, or Evan Seffner, as I later learned, led the way, with Baldy, or Gentry Harper, at his heels.

They again sport matching outfits—muted black suits, blue-pattern ties, black wingtips, and what I assume, were smarmy smiles under matching royal blue N-95 masks with our corporate logo.

Evans lowered his N95 and asked, "How are you feeling, Ollie?"

His question dripped with insincerity, which pissed me off, not that it mattered. These guys had me by the balls and knew it.

"I'm feeling great," I flatly responded.

He handed me a manila folder stuffed to the gills with legal paperwork.

"Shouldn't you have a lawyer present?" Pop interjected.

"It's fine, Pop."

I took my time and reviewed the content. There were three separate documents. The first was an updated three-page non-disclosure agreement, followed by a four-page non-compete which included language around podcasts, a concept non-existent when I initially signed on with the company forever ago. The last set was an eight-page liability release.

Unbelievable.

Evans pointed to the various *Post-it*® labels placed through-out the document next to the sections I needed to sign.

"You know. For your convenience."

"Uh-huh."

"They *are* taking care of your medical expenses, right?" Pop asked.

Gentry replied, "Dr. Morales, we'd *never* leave an employee in the lurch."

Smarminess emanated off him like fungus.

"Yeah, right."

"Got a pen?"

"Are you *sure* you don't need a lawyer to review it all first, Ollie?" Pop implored.

I waved him off and signed away my rights.

"Excellent. Thank you, Ollie," Evans said.

They took their paperwork and headed to the door. Paused briefly in the doorway.

"Forget something?" Pop asked.

"Yes," Gentry replied. "Moving forward, we need to be present for all meetings that involve law enforcement."

I sat up. "*Excuse me*?"

"We had a visit recently at our office. Law enforcement met with your editor, Jenny. They mentioned they'd be contacting you next. We'd like to be there when they meet with you."

It took every ounce of strength not to roll my eyes and chuck something at them.

"Fine," I curtly answered.

He pointed to my nightstand. "We left you our business cards."

"Call us if you need anything," Evans said.

"You'll be my first," I sarcastically responded.

The pair exchanged a glance and left.

Pop waited a few beats before busting my stones.

"I can't believe you signed . . ."

His lecture lasted a solid ten minutes. He blathered on about signing things without legal representation. I didn't have the strength or wherewithal to argue.

Cover the Capitol, she said.

It'll be a nothingburger, she said.
Fucking Jenny.

CHAPTER FIFTY-NINE

Two days after my visit with the corporate weasels, I regained access to over 2,000 work emails, along with my cloud storage account where I uploaded pictures when I was on the road.

"I should have listened to you, Pop."

He arched a brow. "'bout what, hijo?"

I held up the iPad. "Work. I should have left it alone."

"*Ha.* Told you so."

That's my dad.

I took a sip of water and began separating my real emails from spam. Halfway through, my PT, Len, stuck his head into my room.

"You ready to go?"

I jokingly sighed. "If I have to."

"Let's go, champ."

I said goodbye to my father and limped out the door with my walker. On our way to the gym, we spotted that female cop from Florida with the Long Island accent and her FBI partner walking toward us.

"Should I get your dad?" Len asked as they waved us down.

"No. Let's see what they want."

The pair blocked our path and pulled down their N95 masks.

"Mr. Morales, we were just coming by to see you," Detective Skaryd stated.

"Like I said last time, you're wasting your time."

"We thought that might be the case," she replied. "Still, we thought we could jog your memory with a few photos from the scene."

Umberto, her partner, held up a manila folder. "Don't suppose there's someplace nearby where we can sit?"

As I was about to say no, Len chimed in, "There's a cafeteria nearby."

Thanks, moron.

"Terrific." Skaryd smiled. "Lead the way."

We found an empty table toward the back of the spacious cafeteria. Agent Umberto slid the folder across to me and opened it, revealing black-and-white action shots they claimed were taken the day of the insurrection.

I couldn't help but view the photos with my professional eye.

I flipped through the collection. "Nice shots. Good quality."

The pictures were no different than what the media shared on television. Men and women played dress-up in makeshift military gear. Some wore light camos, while others went balls to the walls in full combat gear.

It was simply pathetic.

In the distance, I spotted smoke billowing over the Capitol Building as specks; presumably, the rioters gathered on the famous steps. I could almost hear the commotion of the crowd.

People cursed and shoved me.

Metallic bile coated the back of my throat.

Talk about a bitter pill.

"Mr. Morales?" Agent Umberto stared. "Are you okay?"

"He looks a bit pale," Detective Skaryd commented. "Let's get him some water."

Len retrieved me a cup.

The cool liquid soothed my nerves.

I took a deep breath.

The images of my corporate attorneys replaced the agitated insurrectionist. I could hear them deliver their final instructions about not speaking with law enforcement without their presence.

I closed the folder. "Sorry, guys. I just remembered. My corporate attorneys had me sign a document stating I wouldn't speak with law enforcement—"

"Without their presence." Skaryd pursed her lips.

Umberto shook his head and muttered something under his breath.

"My job's on the line here. Sor—"

She raised her hand. "It's fine. We get it."

Umberto retrieved the pictures. "I think lawyers were put on this planet to make our lives more difficult."

Skaryd jotted something down in her notepad before the pair stood and left.

On their way out, she looked back. "We'll be in touch. In the meantime—"

"Don't leave town. Yeah, I know the drill."

She nodded, and they exited the cafeteria.

CHAPTER SIXTY

That evening, I slept like shit. Every time I shut my eyes, I relived my assault. Every goddamn time. Thanks to my injuries, I couldn't take anything stronger than Tylenol PM. It worked for a few hours.

Pop showed up after lunch. I was screwing around on the iPad.

"Edyta said you had a rough night."

I let out a breath and nodded.

"Why don't you leave that thing alone. Take the day off."

"Okay, Pop."

I placed it on the nightstand and watched another episode of *Matlock*. As the episode ended, we heard a knock on the door.

I tensed up.

"Come in," Pop called out.

I half-expected the boogey man to enter. Instead, it was a slender five-foot-something brunette.

It was like seeing the ghost of Tía Carolina. Between her posture and clothing style of a conservative pink mock turtleneck sweater, blue slacks, and a classic tan peacoat.

I blinked twice.

"Can I help you?" I asked.

A sharp New England accent.

The semblance faded.

"I'm looking for an Oliver Morales."

The way she spoke.

Soothing.

"That's me." I raised my hand. "And you are—"

She walked over.

Removed her mask. "I'm a colleague of your sister-in-law, Cheryl. My name is—"

I immediately knew why she was here, and it pissed me off.

"I told her—*them*—that I'd reach out to someone *when* I was ready." I stared daggers at Pop.

"I'm sorry. I think we got off on the wrong foot."

"You're a shrink, *right*?"

"A psychiatrist, yes. My name is Doctor—"

Pop offered his chair to our new visitor.

"That's okay." She smiled. "I can stand. As long as I'm welcome."

"Of course, you're welcome," he insisted. "Right, Ollie?"

"That's very kind of you," she replied and turned back to me. "But I'd prefer to hear it from Oliver, if you wouldn't mind."

He chucked me the *don't embarrass me* look.

"Yeah, it's—fine."

Pop headed for the door. "Why don't I excuse myself?"

Coward.

"I hope you don't mind me dropping by."

Would it matter if I did?

"It's all right." I sighed.

She sat. "I understand that you've been having a bit of a rough time of late."

I laughed.

"Did I say something funny?"

"Yes. I mean no." I let out a frustrated breath. "It's just . . . I'm lying here with a broken leg, and hearing you call it a *rough time* . . . Sorry, it just makes me laugh."

I felt my blood pressure increase.

Pictured my wife telling me to calm down.

"I'm sorry if I offended you."

"Trust me, you'll know if you offend me," I sharply replied.

She nodded.

"Anyway, how can I help you?"

"Directly to the point. Good."

"I try," I smirked.

"As I tried to say, my name is Cynthia Beasley." She shared her background.

Cynthia specialized in treating people recovering from traumatic events. Her mannerisms continued to remind me of Tía Carolina. The way she moved her hands when she spoke. How she sat forward. Like she was floating on the edge of the chair. Readying to catch you in case you fell.

A softness in her tone.

Altruistic.

Motherly.

Like she was someone you could share your innermost secrets with and not worry about the consequences.

"I understand that you are a reporter?"

"A photojournalist."

Her eyes narrowed, like she was taking a mental note.

"Must be interesting work."

"Pays the bills," I replied snidely.

"Would I be familiar with any of your photos?"

"Do you mean, am I famous?"

She shrugged.

"I've won a few awards."

"And your injuries." She gestured to my leg. "You sustained them while covering a story?"

"You could say that again." I laughed.

"Work-related injuries amuse you?"

I grew tired of this back-and-forth psycho-nonsense.

"No offense, *doctor*, but I find this whole thing amusing."

"It seems I've hit a nerve. Would you like to talk about it?"

This lady just didn't get it.

"Or we can just sit here—in silence. I don't mind either way."

I took a deep breath. Her kindness killed me. I so wanted to tell this lady to fuck off but couldn't seem to find the strength.

She disarmed me.

I think it was the kindness in her eyes.

The softness in her face.

Or maybe it was the ghost of my aunt.

Who knew?

She was certainly a sharp contrast to the people who kicked my ass.

I began to hear people shouting.

Calls for my slaughter.

Beads of sweat formed.

My pulse raced.

Cynthia sat forward.

Furrowed her brows.

"Are you okay, Oliver?"

I reached for some water.

Took a sip.

Another deep breath.

I wiped my forehead.

Chewed on some ice.

"It's *Ollie*, by the way."

"Sorry?"

"You keep calling me *Oliver*. The only ones who call me that were my aunt, who passed away a few years ago, and my father."

She nodded.

"Everyone else calls me Ollie."

"In that case, please call me Cynthia."

"Can I be honest with you?" I asked.

"What's on your mind?"

"Look, I appreciate you stopping by. It's just, this whole thing feels like—"

"An ambush?"

"No offense." I laughed.

"None taken."

"I know everyone's worried about me."

"They are."

"And they certainly mean well, but—"

She patted my hand and stood. "I understand."

The moment Cynthia slipped on her mask and stepped toward the door, I pictured the outcome of refusing her services. I imagined my family standing over me. Berating me. Pointing accusatory fingers in my face.

Ollie, you will never hear the end of it.

"Wait."

CHAPTER SIXTY-ONE

ynthia paused. "Yes?"

"You made the trip. We *might* as well—"

"Make the most of it?"

I nodded agreement.

She removed her mask and returned to the chair.

"You do this a lot?" I asked.

"How do you mean?"

"Ambush your patients?" I joked.

Her soft laughter revealed slightly yellowed teeth.

"You'd be surprised where I've turned up."

"No kidding?"

"As they say, it comes with the territory."

We spent the remainder of our time getting acquainted. Her choice of words informed me that she was well-educated. Also, there was wisdom to Cynthia's approach.

Caring, but low-pressured.

Talking to her felt like I was sitting at my kitchen table eating a peanut butter and jelly sandwich with the crust cut off. By the end of our unscheduled visit, I agreed to meet with her twice a week while I was in rehab.

"So how will this work exactly?"

"Just like this," she replied.

"No. I mean, the payments."

"No different than any other physician who visits you. I bill the facility, and they bill your insurance carrier. You cover the co-payment."

"Got it. So, do I pay you now, or—"

"Let's worry about that later." She smiled.

"Okay."

She squeezed my forearm. "See you soon."

I watched her leave.

"And, Ollie?" She said from the doorway. "Thanks for not kicking me out."

I chuckled as she put on her mask and exited. Pop immediately shuffled his ancient body back into my room.

"How did it go?"

"Not bad. We'll meet twice a week."

He smiled broadly. "That's great, hijo."

"I thought you'd approve. Next time, though—"

He arched his fuzzy gray brow.

"Can we run it by me first?"

"And *ruin* the surprise?" He giggled.

I'll give you a surprise, old man.

That night, I slept like a champ. I didn't even get up to pee. The following morning, Jaime visited me solo.

"No Pop?"

"What? A guy can't stop by alone and see his *favorite* older brother?"

My eyes narrowed. "I'm your *only* older brother."

He kissed me hello. "Cheryl's bringing him later."

I gave him a quick once-over. "You look nice this morning."

"Thanks. So do you, all things considered."

"What's that supposed to mean?"

"It means, you're *old*."

I flipped him off and spent the next hour or so playing catch up. I gave him a hard time for setting me up with Cynthia, even though she and I had a good visit.

"Don't blame me. That one's purely our wives."

"Well, whoever. You're just lucky it worked out."

"I'm glad to hear it."

"Are things at the hospital getting any better?"

He brushed back his thinning hair. "Doesn't feel like it. According to the latest from *Johns Hopkins*, the COVID-19 death rates are up."

"*Jesus.*"

He sighed. "Tell me about it."

"Please tell me that you're taking precautions."

"Cheryl and I are doing the best we can. I'm just shocked neither of us have contracted the damn virus."

Jaime looked so distraught.

"We've lost some good people to this thing."

"Sorry, James."

"Me too." He tried smiling. "Anyway, I hear you had another visit from the FBI."

Just like a Morales.

Things got personal, and he changed the subject.

"Yeah. Brought pictures this time."

He cautiously asked, "And did that—"

"Set me off?" I replied. "*Ha*, a bit. Regardless, I explained to them that I'm not allowed to speak with them without my corporate weasels there."

"And how'd they take it?"

"How do *you* think?"

"Fucking lawyers."

"Tell me about it," I scoffed, and shared the details from my recent visit.

"You mean to tell me—"

"Yep."

"For fuck's sake, you're lying in bed at a rehab facility. How is any of that legal?"

"Beats me."

He shook his head in disgust.

"What was I going to do? Not sign? They have me by the balls."

"No. I get it. Still—"

"It's a scumbag move, I know."

My favorite sadist, Len, poked his head into my room, ending our time together.

"Time for rehab," he sang.

"I fucking hate this man."

Len waved me off. "Pfft . . . he *loves* me."

Jaime stood. "I'll let you go."

He kissed my forehead and left me with my torturer. A couple of agonizing hours later, I returned to my room and found Pop seated, reading the latest Susan Rogers novel with the television on.

"How did he do?" Pop asked.

"He did great. Getting stronger by the minute," Len responded.

"Go screw yourself," I jokingly hissed.

Len laughed and helped me wash up before getting back to bed.

"Missed you this morning."

"Slept in for a change."

"Good for you, Pop."

"How'd *you* sleep last night?"

"Like a rock."

Lunch soon arrived.

An overcooked burger, small salad, and green Jell-O, the lunch of champions. Between bites, I grabbed the iPad and scanned my *Gmail* account. It amazed me how much crap I received in a day. Over two hundred new messages to sort through, across three separate tabs: *Primary, Promotions,* and *Social.*

And another email from Eddie.

This one was titled, *Are You Okay?*

I clicked to open it and began reading.

"Hey Ollie, are you doing okay? I haven't heard back from you. I figured you, of all people, would have something to say about that picture I forwarded."

What picture?

CHAPTER SIXTY-TWO

1986

My teacher, Mrs. Chase, smiled at me, awaiting my response.

Her cousin's name echoed across the room.

Byron Soladay.

The name meant nothing to me.

Still, Pop taught me to be polite, so I shook his hand.

"Nice to meet you, Mr. Soladay."

"You too, Ollie. Connie here, sorry—" He corrected himself. "I mean, Mrs. Chase says you're a photographer in the market for a new advisor."

I glanced at a beaming Mrs. Chase. "I guess."

"Well, lucky for you, I'm between assignments at the moment."

Between assignments?

He looked over my shoulder and noticed the photos hanging on the nearby bulletin board. There were student pictures mixed in with historic ones, including the Vietnam War. President Carter at the Middle East Peace Treaty signing. And President Reagan and U.S.S.R. Secretary Gorbachev seated in front of a fireplace last year in Geneva.

He walked over and examined the collage.

"Are any of these yours?"

"Yes sir."

He smiled at my formality, lifted his horn-rimmed glasses, and peered closer to the various photos, and somehow zeroed in on mine.

"Mm-hmm . . . yep. Okay, I see. Interesting."

Mrs. Chase looked as excited as Jaime on Christmas morning.

"These shots here—" He called me over. "They yours?"

I came over and nodded.

"I like your use of light. And this one, nice shadow work."

"Thanks."

This was the first time I felt like someone outside of school understood my work.

He put his glasses back on and turned to his cousin. "You're right, Con. The kid's got talent. I think I can work with him. That is, if he's interested?"

"What do you say, Ollie?" she asked. "Would you like to work with Mr. Soladay?"

Before I could answer, my U.S. History teacher, Mr. Midland, burst in.

"Is *that* him?"

"It is." Mrs. Chase smiled.

He rushed over and grasped Mr. Soladay's hand. "It is *such* an honor."

I watched as he gushed over this mystery man.

"Ollie, do you know who this is?" Mr. Midland asked.

"Um, Mr. Soladay?"

Mr. Midland grew frustrated. "I'm so sorry about him."

"It's okay. I'm used to it."

I'm called back to the bulletin board. "Notice anything in common?"

I came up empty, "—that they all won a Pulitzer?"

Mr. Midland jabbed one of the prints in the bottom left corner. "Look—*again*."

Holy shit.

Photographer, Byron Soladay.

On every historic picture.

I turned and stared.

Stunned to be in the presence of someone so accomplished.

"I had no idea," I whispered.

He chuckled. "It's okay. You're not alone."

Sensing my embarrassment, Mrs. Chase came to my side as the two men began chatting.

"You okay?" she asked.

"I'm such an idiot. I can't believe—"

"It's okay, Ollie. You're in *twelfth grade*. You're not expected to know everything."

"Yeah, but Mrs. Chase—" I gestured toward her cousin's photos. "Those are—"

She nodded.

"Iconic."

I pointed to the one from Vietnam where a soldier was dragged to safety.

"*Everyone* knows that one."

And to a black-and-white print of guerrillas in Rhodesia.

"That one too."

I shook my head, ashamed and humbled.

Mrs. C placed her arm around my slumped shoulder. "I told you I knew someone."

"Not just someone, Mrs. Chase," I whispered, and pointed at the various prints. "He's—"

"Just a guy, Ollie," Mr. Soladay chimed in.

"Mr. Soladay. I'm so sorry. I had no idea who—"

He threw his hands up. "It's okay. Really. When I was your age, the only thing I cared about was the '62 Yankees."

Mr. Midland looked at his watch. "I have to run. I'd love to have you come in and speak to my class sometime."

"Sure. We can talk about it over drinks next time I'm in town."

"That would be great." He then looked over at me. "He's, uh, talking about sodas, not like, *drink* drinks."

I rolled my eyes.

"Anyway, gotta run. Good luck, Ollie."

"Why don't you two get to know one another while I get off my feet?" Mrs. C said.

Mr. Soladay and I grabbed a couple of chairs and sat across from one another.

"So, tell me about your project. What are your plans?"

I couldn't believe this master was asking me about my plans. It was like Rembrandt asking a graffiti artist what they planned to tag that evening. I never felt more like a fraud in my life.

"I don't know. I guess I'd do like a showcase. You know, put up a bunch of my best pictures."

"Do you have a portfolio?"

"Sort of."

"What do you mean, sort of?"

"Sorry, I'm nervous."

He smiled. "Don't be, Ollie. I'm just a guy a few years older than you. That's all."

"If you say so."

"Where were you planning on displaying your work?"

"Here. In the auditorium."

His eyes narrowed. "Have you thought bigger?"

"Bigger?"

"Yes. Bigger. Like the university across the way. Or a gallery in the city."

"*Manhattan*?"

"Mmm, more like The Village, but yes. I know some people."

"Sounds expensive."

He smirked. "Not with the right sponsors, but first, let's start with your portfolio."

"Yeah. Okay. When do you want to see it?"

He looked at his watch. "It's getting kind of late. How 'bout I swing by same time next week? We can review your work and maybe grab a bite to eat afterward. How does that sound?"

His offer overwhelmed me.

"Awesome. Thanks, Mr. Soladay."

"Please, call me Byron. Mr. Soladay was my father."

"Got it. B-byron."

CHAPTER SIXTY-THREE

I tore out of that auditorium like a preacher with his faith on fire.

I'd never felt so excited.

Byron-Fucking-Soladay wanted to work with me.

Me!

A nobody from Long Island.

At that moment, nothing else mattered to me.

Not my conversation with Jackie about Navil.

Homework.

Nada.

I stood in the middle of the quad and breathed in the air, which tasted sweeter than a bowl of Häagen-Dazs ice cream.

With arms raised like Rocky Balboa at the top of the steps of the Philadelphia Museum of Art, I danced about the quad, serenaded by this theme song in my mind, and a blanket of gems overhead.

From the corner of my eyes, I spotted the lights from the library windows.

Navil.

I had to share my news with her.

Prayed she'd be there studying.

I booked across campus.

I blew past the elevator, hit the stairs two at a time.

By the second-floor landing, I ran out of steam.

Doubled over.

Grabbed my sides.

Damn near passing out.

Students exiting the library came over to check on me. Some debated if they should get the school nurse. Fearful, I suspected that I was having another episode.

I held my index finger out. "I'm just . . . out of . . . breath."

Someone must have gone back inside because both Navil and Fi were soon by my side. And they weren't alone. More students piled out of the library to stare at the sideshow geek.

"Ollie, are you all right?" Navil asked.

I chuckled like a madman.

Her hazel eyes widened.

I overheard someone whisper to Fi, "I'll go get the nurse."

That shook me from my private revelry.

I called out, "No, *don't*. I'm . . . okay."

"What's going on, Ols?"

"Guys, you won't believe it."

"What, chér? What won't we believe?"

I grabbed her shoulders. "Byron Soladay wants to work with me."

The gathered students groaned their disappointment and quickly dissipated. Some headed down the stairs, and others, like Ginny and Alli, returned to the library.

"Who the hell is Bryan Solomon?" Alli whispered.

"Beats me," Ginny replied.

B Karlsson provided encouragement as she left. "Congratulations, Ollie."

"Thanks, B."

"Why don't we sit down?" Navil suggested.

She and I took a seat at the top of the stairs.

Fi stood guard behind us.

I stared into her precious eyes.

"Who is this Brian Holiday person?" she asked.

"How could I be so stupid?" I whispered. "You guys have no idea who Byron is."

"Who is he?" Fi asked.

"First of all, his name is Byron. Byron Soladay—"

I spent the next few minutes explaining everything.

"Mon Dieu, chér, that is amazing."

"Seriously, Ols, that is fantastic. Man, when you step in it—"

"Tell me about it."

"Well, I'm super jealous. The only help I'm getting on my project is from Gramps."

"That's because you're writing a paper on the history of his fire department."

"Yeah, but still—"

Navil smiled. "Maybe Fireman Timmy can help you?"

I laughed as Fi squirmed and changed the subject.

"Anyway, what are you going to do?"

I let out a breath. "I don't know. He wants to see my portfolio next week."

"Do you have one, chér?"

I shut my eyes and shook my head no.

"Don't you keep all your negatives in your lockbox at the photo lab?" Fi asked.

I followed her train of thought.

"Not a bad idea."

"What's that?"

"Ols has a ton of negatives down in the lab. He can look through them and—"

"Create a portfolio. That is a brilliant idea, non?"

"It sure is."

She took my hand and stood. "Let's go."

"You mean now?"

"As they say, there is no time like the present, right, Fiona?"

"Absolutely."

"Wow, you guys really want to help?"

"Of course, chér." She caressed my face. "We love you."

I leaned into her warm, manicured hand. "Okay."

"Let us gather our things. We'll be right back."

"All right. I will wait for you here."

I smiled, watching my two favorite people head back into the library.

You've really stepped in it, Ollie.

CHAPTER SIXTY-FOUR

They returned moments later, ready to assist me in my venture. We crossed campus and within minutes, stood outside the photo lab.

I hadn't been here in over a week, which, for me, was unusual. Since tenth grade, aside from holidays and school breaks, I spent most of my free time in this room.

I couldn't wait to step inside.

The moment I did, my heart sank.

My sanctum sanctorum was a mess.

Dried-up paper towels were left on the counter.

Dirty developer trays lay in the sink.

The trash filled with empty soda cans, candy wrappers, and other garbage.

And even the developer chemicals were left out.

"What the—"

"Ols, this place is—"

Through clenched jaws. "When I get my hands on Eddie—"

"We better clean this up," Navil stated.

"I'll grab the broom," Fi said.

It took us about fifteen minutes to tidy the place.

As a reward, I handed out the remaining soda cans from the fridge before we plopped down on the couch to catch our breath.

"Well, that was fun," I grumbled.

"I still can't believe anyone would leave such a mess," Fi said. "I thought you guys had strict rules in place."

"So did I, but I haven't been down here in over a week."

Guilt crossed Navil's face.

"It's not your fault," I stated.

"It sure feels like it. If you weren't wasting all your—"

"Hey—" I reached for her. "I'm not—"

Fi slowly shuffled away from us.

"I *love* you, Navil," I whispered.

She smiled.

"Okay?"

"Oui." She nodded and noticed Fi's discomfort. "Why don't we start reviewing your negatives, non?"

I noticed the time. "It's getting kind of late. Why don't we start tomorrow?"

We locked up and headed out.

"Give me your keys, and I'll bring the car around," Fi said.

I tossed them. "Here ya go."

We went our separate ways.

Fi toward student parking.

Navil and me to her dorm.

On our way, we took a quick detour to the shadows of her building.

Her eyes danced as she drew close.

Warm puffs of air drifted from her lips.

We drew close.

Her natural scent enveloped us.

Floral.

Innocent.

We kissed.

From a distance, headlights illuminated the area.

The arrival of my Ford Granada.

Our secluded intimacy terminated.

We laughed and headed to her front door.

Navil's parting gift, a warm hug, and another assurance of love.

My smile lit up the night.

"Someone's happy," Fi commented as I slid into the driver's seat.

Does it get any better than this?

CHAPTER SIXTY-FIVE

The next day, I spotted Eddie after second period and ripped him a new asshole.

"Seriously, dude. If I find the lab in that condition again—"

"I know. I'm sorry, Ollie. We meant to clean up."

Yoda's words from *The Empire Strikes Back* about doing and not trying immediately came to mind. I threatened to take his keys away and put him on probation.

"If it happens again—"

"It won't. I promise."

Word of me dressing Eddie down spread like measles. In my last-period class, Alli dropped a piece of paper on the floor.

Seated behind me, Ginny commented, "Alli, you better pick that up. You don't want Ollie to yell at you."

I ignored the snickering pair. After school, I met up with Fi at my locker.

"We still heading down to the lab?"

"Yeah. I told Navil we'd meet her there."

After dumping my books, we made our way to the lab.

"Hey, Fi. Can I ask you a question?"

"Sure. What's up?"

"This is gonna sound stupid."

"Most of your questions do."

"I'm being serious."

We stopped walking.

"What's up, Ols?"

It took me a moment to get my question out.

"Do you have any idea why Navil is here?"

"I'm assuming it's to make you happy, no?"

I rolled my eyes.

"You're being serious right now?"

"Don't you find it strange that she transferred in at the end of her senior year?"

"Hadn't really thought about it."

"She not only switched schools, but a whole different country."

"If you're so curious, why don't you ask her."

"I've tried, but every time I bring it up—"

"She changes the subject."

"Exactly."

Fi nodded.

"What do I do?"

"Do you want me to ask her?"

"Oh, God, *no.*"

"Okay, geez. I'm just trying to help."

"I know. Sorry."

"Let me ask you, why do you care?"

"I don't know. When I visited Jackie, she—"

"That explains it."

"Explains what?"

"Let me guess. She said something *bad* about Navil."

"I wouldn't say, *bad.*"

"What would you say?"

I shrugged. "Well, she implied that I shouldn't trust her."

Fi laughed. "You're kidding me, right?"

"That's what she said. That, and to ask her why she's here."

"Not for nothing, but let's remember the source."

"What's that supposed to mean?"

"Look, I know you're suddenly friends with Jackie now, but the girl's—"

"A gossip and pain in the ass. Yeah, I know."

"Exactly."

"So, why take advice from *Jackie Woodley*?"

Fi nodded.

"I don't know."

"Look, of the two, I trust *Navil* way more than I trust that bitch. Still, if it's *that* important to you, talk to her. Find out for yourself. What's the worst that can happen?"

"With my luck lately?"

She grinned. "You do have a point."

I smirked.

She chucked my shoulder. "Let's go check out some negatives with your girlfriend. And, while we're there, I'll find a reason to leave you two alone."

"Thanks, Fi."

A few minutes later, we came upon Navil standing outside the lab, deep in thought as she read one of her many newspapers.

After kissing her hello, I asked, "Anything good?"

"Oh, the usual. You know, crime, political corruption—"

"Don't forget sports," Fi joked.

Navil chuckled, and I groaned.

"Let's head inside before *Shecky Green* tells another joke."

"Did you speak with Eddie?" Fi asked.

"I'm surprised you didn't hear about it," I scoffed as we stepped in.

To our relief, the lab was in the same condition as we left it.

"Why don't you guys make yourselves comfortable while I grab my negatives."

Navil and Fi sat on the couch while I retrieved my lock box from the cabinet next to the empty fridge.

"Damn."

"What's the matter, chér?"

I waved her off. "It's nothing."

"He gets this way sometimes," Fi informed her. "What's wrong, Oliver?"

I shot Fi a look. "I forgot to bring in sodas for the fridge."

"And?" Fi replied.

"And I'm thirsty. It's no biggie. I'll get something later."

"Want me to hit 7-Eleven and grab something?"

"Would you? I'll treat."

I took out my wallet and Fi noticed my last twenty and snatched it.

"Hey."

"I'll bring back change." She smiled.

"You better."

"Uh-huh. Let me guess—"

"A raspberry Snapple iced tea."

"Figured as much. And you, Navil?"

"Same, s'il te plait. Merci, Fi."

"Just so you know, you're buying me gum."

"Yeah, yeah," I grumbled.

Fi leaned in. "And you can talk to her while I'm gone."

"I will. Scram."

Before leaving, Fi grabbed the *Do Not Enter, Developing Film* sign and hung it on the front doorknob.

She whispered good luck and closed the door behind her.

Thanks. I'm going to need it.

CHAPTER SIXTY-SIX

Cowardice won the battle that afternoon.

Instead of joining Navil on the sofa and asking her the question, I opened my lockbox and sorted my film collection.

Navil folded up her newspapers and joined me at the counter. She wrapped her arms around my waist and pressed her lithe body against mine.

"What would you like me to do?" she whispered into my ear.

Goosebumps ran down my spine.

Waves of saliva filled my mouth.

Any command over the English language flew out the door.

This normally reposed Hispanic photographer transformed into a horny knuckle-dragger.

Like an adolescent Cro-Magnon, I groaned as her hands ran down my sides.

Blood rushed to my extremities.

She spun me around.

Wrapped her arms around my neck.

I drank her in like sweet poison.

She leaned in.

Traced the outer edge of my right ear with the tip of her tongue.

In the back of my head, I heard an announcer state, *"Elvis has left the building."*

I pulled her in.

The tip of her tongue slid into my inexperienced mouth.

It flicked back and forth with erotic precision.

My pulse raced.

I lifted her.

She straddled me like a cowgirl at a rodeo.

Yippee-ki-ay!

We nuzzled on the couch.

"Just like that," she whispered. "Keep going. Don't stop."

Had someone told me a month ago, that I would be dry-humping the hottest girl in school in the photo lab that late afternoon, I would have said they were nuts.

But there we were.

Pheromones filled the room.

It blended with the vinegary scent from developer chemicals.

She devoured my lips and neck.

French phrases fell into my ears.

Some I recognized.

Others, forever a mystery.

"God, I love you," I moaned.

Her breathless reply, "Je t'aime aussi chéri."

Just as things turned serious, Fi returned.

Like a trained gymnast, Navil leaped off my lap.

She quickly tucked in her blouse and straightened her skirt.

I stumbled to my feet as Fi entered.

She sniffed the air.

Through narrowed eyes, she panned the room.

She spotted my shit-eating grin.

Immediately connected the dots and shook her head.

"I can come back if you want," she joked.

Embarrassed, Navil slid behind me.

Final adjustments to her clothes and undergarments.

I chucked Fi the finger and reached for the plastic bag.

"Something I said?" she smirked.

"I hate you," I quietly replied.

I handed Navil her Snapple and popped mine open, chugging down half.

After taking a few sips, Navil excused herself. "I need to use the restroom."

The moment the door closed, the grilling began.

Fi specifically wanted to know—

"Did you get any *Ollie juice* on the couch?"

"*Jesus Christ*, Fi. Eww, no. What the *frig* is wrong with you?"

"I'm just asking. I don't know what you two did. The last thing I want is to sit in it."

"*Ollie juice*? Seriously?"

"Well, what would you call it?"

She continued busting my balls till Navil returned, allowing the subject to drop and us to return to the task at hand.

"What do you want us to do?" Fi asked.

I stared at the close to one hundred photo negatives neatly boxed and sorted by year, awaiting our review.

"Ollie, I see each box has a date. What if we separate the negatives by year and category?"

"Category?"

"Oui, you know, action shots, portraits, or nature, non?"

"That makes sense, Ols," Fi commented. "It'll show this guy how much you've improved over the years."

"That's a great idea." I smiled. "Reason number fifty-seven why I love you."

Navil rubbed my back and kissed my cheek.

"Eww, must you?" Fi joked.

"I must," Navil purred.

The girls laughed at their banter while I stared at the pile in front of me.

"You guys ready?" I asked.

They nodded.

"All right. Let's get started."

CHAPTER SIXTY-SEVEN

Over the next two days, I spent all my free time in the photo lab reviewing dozens of rolls of negatives. I would love to say it was a fun process and I enjoyed every minute of it. That would be a lie.

This project consumed me.

Between my anxiety and sleeping like crap, I slowly transformed into—

Asshole Man.

As in—

"Ollie, you're really turning into Asshole Man," Fi spat.

By Thursday evening, I'd bitten the head off of any and every person that tried helping me. You name it, I chewed them out.

Navil—check.

Fi—check.

Guys from the photography group, including Eddie—check, check, and check.

What should have been a joyful process became a nightmare for everyone.

Navil affectionately rubbed my back before handing me a negative.

"What about this one, chér? I love it."

I held the negative to the light and used the jeweler's loop to inspect the film. They were pictures from a pool party at my house.

The shot she loved was of Jaime making a cannonball off the

diving board. I caught him just as he hit the water, drenching a smiling Tía Carolina and Fi standing in the background.

She wasn't wrong.

I loved this picture too.

The problem was—

"I know you're trying to help, but this isn't good enough." I frustratedly ran my fingers through my hair. "None of them are."

And like a jerk, I dismissed her.

"Just . . . go."

The way her face dropped, you'd think someone punched her in the gut. Or maybe in the heart.

I shook my head and went back to work while Navil quietly gathered her things and left the lab.

Later, Eddie handed me negatives. "There are a few good ones here."

I reviewed them and shook my head.

"For *you*, maybe," I scoffed. "Pass."

And finally, Fi.

"Ols, check out—"

I snatched the film from her fingers. "You know what? I've got this."

She'd had enough of my bullshit. "Go fuck yourself."

Fi stormed out of the lab, leaving me with the last remnants of the photography club, which stood frozen in place.

I looked at them and sighed. "Just get the fuck out."

They obliged and left me alone in the lab with my thoughts. I leaned against the counter and peered into the darkness. Wondered what was wrong with those people. Didn't they understand how important this was? That I couldn't just choose any photo. I silently cursed them under my breath and went back to work.

In the end, I chose an action shot of Jean Paul Michaels

bicycle-kicking a ball into a goal, an early morning photo of a pair of Long Island ducks paddling toward a hazy watermill in the distance, and a still shot of a wilting red rose with a slightly discolored petal floating toward the countertop.

At that moment, I knew how the flower felt.

Dejected.

As I cleaned up, there was a knock on the door.

"*What*?" I barked.

To my surprise, it was Mrs. C. coming to check on me.

"Ollie? Is everything all right?" she asked, covering her nose as she entered.

"No."

She grabbed a nearby stool and sat. "I hear you've been having a challenge."

"You can say *that* again."

"What's going on?"

I spewed all my frustrations over poor Mrs. C.

"—he's coming back next week, and all I have to show him are three lousy pictures. What am I going to do, Mrs. Chase?"

"I was afraid this would happen."

"What do you mean?"

"Ollie, take a seat. Listen, you're very talented, okay?"

"I'm glad *you* think so," I snarked as I sat on the couch.

"I wouldn't have contacted Byron if I didn't think so. Having said that—"

Here we go.

"Talent does not equal perfection."

"I never said—"

She raised her hand. "Hear me out. Do you know why this school forced its seniors to work on a special project?"

"To *torture* us?"

She laughed. "It may feel that way, but no, Ollie. It's to

prepare you for life. To be honest, I wish my high school offered this type of program back in the day."

"Seriously?"

"Absolutely. Work one-on-one with a teacher, or in your case, a world-renowned photographer, on a special project close to my heart. Who wouldn't love that?"

I felt like raising my hand but didn't.

She read my facial expression. "Ollie, you need to stop beating yourself up. Want to know the reason why I asked my cousin to work with you?"

"Because we're both photographers?"

"Well, yes, of course, but that's not the only reason. I asked Byron because you remind me of him back when he was your age."

"Really?"

She nodded. "Do you know, he didn't pick up his first camera till the back half of his senior year?"

"Twelfth grade?"

She seemingly called back a memory and chuckled to herself.

"You should have seen him. Walking around all serious, with his hair high and tight, like he was in the Marines."

My eyes widen.

That was not the picture of the casual man I met earlier that week.

"That was before he met Camille Dwyer."

The way she said her name.

With reverence.

"She was this freshman art student from the local university. I can still see him following her around town like a lovestruck puppy."

I chuckled.

"She exposed him to a whole new world."

"No kidding?"

"Nope. She was the one who noticed his keen eye for detail. Encouraged him to pick up a camera. One thing led to another and—"

Some of his award-winning shots painted my mind's eye.

"The thing is, Ollie, in the beginning he wasn't perfect. While photography came naturally to him, the same way it does with you, it took time for him to refine his gifts."

"That still doesn't fix my problems, Mrs. C. He's expecting a portfolio. All I have are—" I pointed to the pictures drying on the line.

"Would you like to know what I love most about your pictures, Ollie? What truly reminds me of Byron's work?"

My eyes widened as I leaned forward. "Yeah."

"The flaws."

"I'm sorry, the—*what*?"

She chuckled. "Ollie, anyone can take *the* perfect picture. Even a third grader."

I wouldn't say anybody.

"But that's *not* what I was looking for, and neither is Byron."

"It's not?"

"Goodness no," she replied. "He wants your flaws. How else can he help you improve your skills?"

"I don't know."

"His actual words were, 'The kid's got some talent. I hope I can teach him something.'"

"Yeah, but he's so—"

"*Gifted* . . . and so are you, Ollie."

I let out a breath and smiled. "Thanks, Mrs. C."

"Now, listen. Why don't you take the weekend to regroup? Start fresh Monday."

I nodded.

"Also, you *may* want to apologize to some people. Take them out for pizza or something. Just saying."

"Word got around, huh?"

She stood and waddled toward the door. "You think I'd step foot in this stinky lab for no reason? I don't know how you people can stand it."

"You get used to it," I replied. "Good night, Mrs. C."

"Have a good evening, Ollie."

I guess it's time to start my apology tour.

CHAPTER SIXTY-EIGHT

By the time I left the lab, it was late. Fi grabbed the bus home, and Navil was camped out in her dorm room studying. I thought about stopping by but decided to wait till the morning to talk to her.

On the drive home, I thought about my conversation with Mrs. C. She had a point. How *would* Byron help me if I only showed him my best work? As I drove up my block, I thought about pulling into Fi's driveway. Of all the people I had upset, I knew she'd forgive me.

Wouldn't she?

Across the street, Ernie's garage door was open, and the light was on. Instead of heading home, I backed into his driveway. I needed advice from the prince. As usual, doo-wop music played, and he was knee-deep inside the hood of his Corvette.

He poked his head up as I approached, "Hey, there he is. How's it going, Ollie?"

"Hey, Ernie. Getting her ready for the weekend?"

"You know it," he said, wiping his greasy hands off on a towel.

"That's cool."

He sat on a stool and cracked open a new beer. "What's this I hear about jail?"

Jesus, that was quick.

"Heard about that, huh?"

"I was home when the cops took you away. We all were," he said, referencing the entire neighborhood.

"Oh. I wasn't really scanning the crowd, if you know what I mean."

"I get it. What happened?"

I spent the next few minutes explaining everything.

"Woah. And how's the girl doing? The one who got hurt."

"Jackie? I think she's doing okay. I saw her a few days ago but haven't been back."

"Poor form, Ollie. You should check in on her. If for no other reason, to show you care."

He was right, of course.

I nodded. "I'll swing by this weekend."

"Good. How're things with the foreign chick?"

Guilt flashed across my face.

"What'd ya do?"

"What makes you think I—"

"Because you've got a dick, Ollie."

I laughed and explained my situation.

"Jesus, kid." He sucked on his beer. "You spend last weekend in jail and then throw yourself back into prison this week. Gotta be a personal record."

"So, what do I do?"

"Simple."

I leaned forward.

"Apologize."

I rolled my eyes.

Shit. I knew that already.

"That's it?"

He leaned back. "Why don't you take her out this weekend. Show her a good time."

"Well, there is this party she wants to go to."

"There you go. Take her to the party."

I nodded. "Yeah, all right."

He stood and walked to the front of his car.

"Come here for a sec."

He pointed to his pristine car engine.

"What do you see?"

Confused, I replied, "An engine?"

"Exactly. And she purrs like a kitten. Wanna know why?"

"Because you're always working on it."

"Damn right. It's no different than a relationship. Do you want things to work out with this chick . . . What's her name again?"

"Navil."

"Right, Navil. Then you need to put in the work; otherwise, you're just wasting each other's time, and you're better than that."

I exhaled.

"Do the right thing, Ollie. If you do right by her, she'll do right by you, trust m—"

The cordless phone on his workbench cut him off.

"Hold on a sec." He extended a greasy index finger. "Hello?"

I stood back to give him some privacy. An electric smile broadened his face. His voice softened.

"Hey, baby."

I've known him most of my life, and I'd never seen him like this.

Jovial.

Full of warmth.

"Of course, we're going out tomorrow. I've got something special planned." He looked over at me and winked.

I smiled and made my way toward the exit.

"Hold on, babe," he told his caller. "Ollie."

I looked over my shoulder.

"Think about what I said. If this Navil is worth it, treat her right."

"I will. Thanks, Ernie."

He returned to his call. "It was just my neighbor. Girlfriend problems."

A minute later, I pulled into my driveway. Digested the sage advice from the neighborhood prince. I needed to head inside but couldn't get Navil out of my head. I was about to put the car in reverse when Tía Carolina flashed the front porch lights.

I immediately lost my nerve and cursed myself to sleep that night.

CHAPTER SIXTY-NINE

The following day, I hoped to catch Navil before our AP calculus class, so I arrived a few minutes early. Unfortunately, she showed up before me, and seated next to her, chatting her up, was that rich pretty boy, Davis Warner. I was pissed.

Everyone and their brother knew we were going out. Aside from typical teenaged horniness, there was absolutely no reason for this dipshit to be sitting there, flirting with my girlfriend.

Navil's eyes drifted toward the doorway and must have noticed my fuming. She glanced at the clock, excused herself, and motioned for me to follow her into the hallway.

At that moment, my emotions were all over the place. On the one hand, I wanted to scream at her. Ask her why the fuck she would think it was okay to flirt with Davis when she knew I'd soon arrive to class.

On the other hand, I didn't own her. She wasn't my personal possession. Plus, I still owed her an apology for acting like an asshole. My head felt like it was about to explode.

We found a private area between the lockers, just as the first bell rang. This meant we had five minutes till Professor Michaels' class started, and the clock began ticking.

"Before you say anything, I have something to tell you," she stated.

Great, she's breaking up with me.

I fucking knew it.

Why did I have to act like such an asshole?

My lower lip quivered as I leaned back like a man awaiting a firing squad. My fight-or-flight response kicked into high gear. I felt like running away, but the hallway was full of students headed to class, some staring as they walked by, so making an escape was a challenge.

Soon, a tear fell, followed by another.

My heart pounded, and my pulse raced.

I blinked away the tears and hissed, "Just get it over with."

Her expression changed from indignation to confusion. "Get *what* over with?"

"You're breaking up with me. Just—" I pushed past her and bailed.

She called after me.

I used the back of my sleeve to wipe the snot from my face and slammed my way out of the building. I stormed past classmates and up the sidewalk toward the auditorium. In the distance, the second bell echoed, and I couldn't care less. I just knew I needed to get away from the girl who was about to shatter my heart.

In the wind, I heard a door burst open behind me, followed by Navil screaming my name.

"Ollie! Wait."

I continued my march forward and heard her running up the sidewalk. She eventually caught up with me in the quad parking lot just outside the scene of the crime, as I mentally began referring to the auditorium.

I spun around and got in her face. "What, Navil. *What*? What do you *want*?"

Her hazel eyes narrowed and blazed with fury.

Through clenched teeth, "You know what, Ollie? You can be a real—*connard.*"

I was no language expert, but the way she stuck that landing on that French word, I knew it was bad.

She poked my chest, punctuating every word. "I never said I wanted to break up with you—"

Her words hit me like a bucket of cold water. "What?"

"Although with the way you're acting—"

She threw up her hands, exhaled sharply, turned, and stormed off. My adolescent brain short-circuited as I digested her statement.

Shit.

I called after her, "Navil—*wait.*"

Her shoulders bobbed up and down as she walked away. I knew she was crying when I reached her.

"Navil, wait." I held her shoulders from behind.

After a few deep breaths, she turned to face me, confirming my fears as tears glistened on her beautiful face. Her pained expression tugged at my heart.

"Navil, I'm—" I heaved a sigh. "I'm so sorry. I'm such an asshole."

I held her tenderly, whispered apologies, and pleaded for her forgiveness. As I held her, a gentle breeze enveloped us, and I felt a warm, moist kiss land on my cheek. I released her and exchanged tearful smiles. I attempted to speak, but she placed her chilly index finger on my lips and gestured to the steps leading to the auditorium.

"Why don't we go sit down?" she suggested.

We nestled close. In the chilly air, I could see her breath. It mingled with the scent of her perfume, enveloping us in a cocoon of intimacy.

"It's just, with the way I treated you. And when I spotted you talking to that jerk, Davis, I just thought—"

"That I was breaking up with you."

I shut my eyes and nodded.

"But why, chér? Don't you know how much I love you?"

Ashamed, I turned away. "I thought I did."

She gently turned my face toward hers, smiling, "Oliver—"

CHAPTER SEVENTY

The tenderness in her voice and the warmth in her hazel eyes penetrated the depths of my soul. I felt the loving pain from Cupid's arrow as it pierced my heart. Heat emanated from her, almost visible in the air around us. We became encased in a joyful sphere cast by the gods.

"Man, I love you," I confessed.

She placed her chilled fingers in my hands and inched closer.

"We should get to class," I suggested.

"I think it's too late. You know how Professor Michaels gets."

"The man could make a nun cry," I joked.

She laughed.

"Still, we should get you inside before you freeze to death."

I stood, pulled open the doors of the auditorium, and gestured for us to go in. Navil wiped dirt from her perfect backside and followed me into the spacious lobby. We grabbed a seat on a red velvet bench near a set of vents blowing warm air.

"Navil, look—" I began. "I never meant to hurt you, of all people."

"I know, Ollie."

"This relationship thing is all new to me."

Her face softened. "You've never had a girlfriend before, have you?"

"Not really. No."

She placed her hand on my cheek.

"To be honest, I've never really been in love before. Not like this."

"No?" She smiled.

"God, no," I admitted. "I've never met anyone like you. You're so—"

She drew closer, "So?"

"—perfect."

Her eyes widened, and she let loose a guffaw that echoed around us.

"Mon Dieu, Ollie. I'm hardly perfect. Far from it." Her head shook. "I guess it's time I told you what brought me to this school."

About time!

Her facial expression changed as she folded her right leg up onto the bench.

It was solemn.

Confessional.

In a lowered voice, she divulged her truth.

"I haven't always been—"

"So prim and proper?" I joked.

She chuckled, "Oui. I was, how do you say, a bit of a rebel, non?"

I don't think her definition is the same as mine.

"How so?"

She searched for the right words.

"I used to hang out with a rough crowd."

An image of Navil dressed like one of the "Pink Ladies" in the movie, *Grease,* came to mind.

"You don't say?" I laughed.

Her eyes narrowed. "You don't believe me."

"I never said—"

She shut me up with her index finger, bent down, and grabbed her purse. From a secret compartment, Navil pulled out a bent photograph.

"This is a picture of me with friends outside a club in Bruges last year."

Astonishment splashed across my face. Sneering back at me, leaning against the wall with a cigarette dangling from her perfect pouty lips, talking to some chick with a fully shaved head was my beloved girlfriend.

Her auburn hair was a spiky raven black, matching her lipstick, and she wore a leather dog collar adorning her slender neck. Gone was any semblance of the fresh-faced girl seated next to me. In her place—a fierce badass punk.

Her luminous hazel eyes stood out beneath thick black mascara. She sported a ripped white t-shirt paired with tight blue jeans and sturdy black combat boots. Completing her look was a denim jacket wrapped around her slender waist.

"Holy shit," I whispered.

CHAPTER SEVENTY-ONE

A glint of pride reflected in her eyes as I stared and questioned everything.

"You have questions."

"Ya *think*?"

With a nod, she returned the photo to her hidden compartment.

"There's more."

"*More*?"

She looked around to make sure we were alone and lowered her blouse.

"Is that real?"

"Oui."

Hidden beneath her right shoulder blade was a tiny red poppy tattoo. I stared in disbelief. She fixed her blouse and patiently waited for my reaction.

I stammered, "Who *are* you?"

She leaned forward and whispered, "The girl who loves you."

I savored her words.

"My girlfriend, Alice, she's the other girl in the picture."

"With the shaved head?"

"Oui." She nodded. "Well, Alice got pregnant and had an abortion."

My head jerked back, but I remained silent.

"When her boyfriend found out, he broke up with her."

"Wow."

"Yeah. He was a real *connard* too." She spat.

Empathy filled my eyes as anger flashed in hers.

"One night after getting high—"

I arched a brow in surprise.

"Yes, Ollie. I used to get high. Not a lot. But every now and again. Just pot."

I fumbled for the right words. "It's, um . . ."

She laughed. "You don't need to say anything. I don't do it anymore. At least not since we started dating. Anyway, a few weeks after her abortion, we went to a local shop and got matching tattoos. Mine on my shoulder, and hers on her inner left thigh."

"Really?" I snickered.

"Yes. Mine hurt, but she almost passed out from the pain."

"I guess I understand why she got one. But why'd you get yours?"

"It's hard to explain. In your family, it's just you and your petit frère, Jaime, non?"

I nodded.

"Well, I'm the middle of five. There's my older brother, Maurice, always the dutiful one. The perfect first-born child. Went into government service, just like mon père, after he graduated college."

"Okay."

"Marie, my older sister, is in her junior year of college, studying fashion and design. When she's not in London or Paris searching for the latest trend, she's with her other obsession—Andreas, her boyfriend. She's always Andreas this and Andreas that."

"Kind of like you with me," I joked.

Navil nudged my ribs and chuckled. "You know what I mean."

"Go on."

"I got tired of my parents constantly comparing me to them." She then mimicked her parents. *"Why can't you be more like your grand frère et grande soeur?"*

The annoyance in her voice spoke volumes.

"Nothing I did was ever good enough. Not my grades. My friends. Nothing."

I pursed my lips and scoffed, "I bet they'd *love* me."

She scrunched her brows. "Actually, they would, Ollie."

"Even though I'm brown?" I pointed to my skin.

Navil shook her head. "Andreas is as black as, how do they say, the ace of spades, non. I think it's more an issue for you Americans than us Europeans."

"I'll take your word for it. I've never dated anyone from a different country before."

She caressed my cheek. "Trust me. They'd see you the same way I do."

"How so?"

"Respectable."

"Is that the only way you see me?"

"Mon Dieu, Ollie, no. I think you're *very* sexy," she whispered.

Her comment shocked me almost as much as her hidden photo.

"Seriously? Me? You think *I'm* sexy?"

"Very. I was surprised you were available."

Steam hissed from the nearby vent as I sat there stunned at her comment.

"We really need to have a long conversation about your self-confidence one day."

I bathed in the assuring beauty of her gaze.

"Anyway," she continued, "one thing led to another—"

"And you got your tattoo."

"Oui."

"Why the flower?"

Proudly she stated, "To honor ma grand-mère. No one on this planet has treated me better. Plus, it's her favorite flower."

"Do your folks know about your—"

"Oui," she scoffed. "My sister came home one weekend and walked into my bedroom without knocking. I was getting changed, and she saw it."

"Ratted you out, huh?"

She nodded.

"Were your parents pissed?"

"Beyond. They grounded me and threw out most of my outfits. All they left me with were a few t-shirts and pairs of jeans. They even got rid of my favorite boots."

"Damn."

"They threatened to send me to a convent, but Grand-mère talked them out of it."

"She really is on your side," I commented. "Is that when they decided to send you here?"

"No. The last straw, as they put it, had to do with my neighbor, Jan-Marc."

The disdain in her voice made it clear to me that this guy was a jerk.

"Winter break started, and my parents and older brother were at work. Marie was off with Andreas doing who knows what."

A picture filled my head.

"Isabel and Bo, my little sister and brother, were out back playing in the snow. I'm grounded on the couch, babysitting, watching television, and suddenly Isabel comes running inside with a little bloody nose, screaming her head off."

Navil's hazel eyes grew animated.

"I thought it was nothing. Just something got out of hand,

non? Besides, Isabel has always been, how do you say, the sensitive one?"

Having been accused of being the same, I understood and nodded.

"I tried to calm her down. Kept asking, 'Isabel, what's wrong? Did Thibo hurt you?'"

"And?"

Navil blinked slowly and took another deep breath. Her luminous spheres were so filled with rage, I could almost see flames dancing behind her pupils.

"The moment I mentioned Bo's name, she grabbed my wrist and dragged me off the sofa to the back window."

Anger bled across her face. Her slender nose twitched, and her lip curled.

"Our neighbor, Jan-Marc, was out back sitting on top of mon petit frère, shoving his face in the snow."

Her eyes narrowed, and her nostrils flared.

"Jesus. How old is this kid?"

"He is our age. Has always been the neighborhood bully, although his parents swear that he's an angel."

"I know the type."

"I ran out back in my bare feet and kicked him off Bo's back, knocking him into the snow."

"Good."

"And as I checked on mon petit frère, this *connard* . . ."

There's that word again.

" . . . came up behind me and yanked the back of my hair."

My eyes grew. "What did you do?"

"What do you think? I spun around and kicked him in—"

"His John Thomas?"

Navil's head tilted comically like a curious puppy.

"You know." I pointed to my crotch. "The family jewels."

She howled.

"Oui, I kicked him in his family jewels and then kneed him in the face."

"Chuck Norris style. Nice."

She emphatically clapped her hands.

"Then what happened?"

"I scooped up Bo into my arms, stepped over Jan-Marc, and brought him inside to clean him and Isabel up," she explained. "Well, that evening, there was a knock on our front door."

I arched a brow. "Who was it?"

CHAPTER SEVENTY-TWO

Modern Day

I opened the email and damn-near dropped the iPad.

Staring back at me was a person I hadn't seen in close to thirty years.

Dressed head-to-toe in camo.

Waving some sort of metal pipe or something.

The photographer caught her face in mid-scream, surrounded by fellow rioters on the National Mall as they prepared to storm the U.S. Capitol. In the distance, remnants of smoke grenades billowed into the blue sky.

Pop asked, "Ollie, are you okay?"

The incident replayed in my mind's eye.

My heart raced, and my chest tightened.

I gasped and released the iPad like my fingertips were on fire.

Sweat droplets formed on my forehead.

My hands trembled.

"Oliver." Pop stood and reached for me.

I grabbed onto the bed railing to steady myself.

A mix of hot flashes and chills wreaked havoc on my body.

My eyes clamped shut.

Someone held onto my back.

Prevented my rocking.

"Breathe, Ollie, breathe," Pop instructed.

I listened to his soothing words.

"In through the nose. Out through the mouth."

I followed his directions.

"That's it. Just like that."

Edyta and a crew of nurses burst into the room. "What happened?"

"I don't know. One minute he's reading—"

Pop got out of their way.

"—the next he's like this."

More hands were on me.

Took vitals.

Forced my right eye open.

Flashed a light.

Temporarily blinded me.

The same person repeated the same with the other eye.

Black dots filled my vision.

"Hold him still while I get the rest of his vitals," Edyta called. "It's okay, Ollie. You'll be okay."

A blood pressure cuff gets wrapped around my left arm. A sudden sharp pinch in my right.

I heard someone yell, "One hundred forty-one over ninety-two."

"I just gave him ketamine," someone else stated.

A slow fade to black.

A few hours later, I felt something probe and prod my body. I struggled to open my eyes.

Jaime stood over me.

Poked me.

I chuckled to myself.

Reminded me of when we were kids.

"Some things never change," I slurred.

"What was that?" Jaime asked.

"Ollie's awake?" Pop joined him at my side.

"Oh, look, it's Heckle and Jeckle."

"Yeah, he's awake."

"You scared the shit out of us," Jaime chided.

I tried to sit up and failed miserably.

"Hold on," Jaime said. "I'll help you."

He placed his arm around my shoulder and lifted me to a seated position. He then put pillows on either side of me to keep me upright.

"Thanks, James."

"You doing okay? Do you need anything? Here, why don't you sip some water."

He handed me a white Styrofoam cup with a pink straw sticking out. My throat felt as dry as sandpaper, so I took a few sips of the stale liquid.

"How're you feeling, Ollie?"

"Groggy, Pop."

I attempted to unscramble my brain by shaking my head. I wrenched my neck and gave myself a headache. The pain recalled the email from Eddie.

I searched my blanket. "Where's the iPad?"

"Why don't you try to relax and give that thing a rest?" Jaime said.

"Where the fuck is that goddamn iPad, Jaime?"

I scanned the room and spotted it on the nightstand.

Jaime got to it before I did.

"Hand it over."

"What the heck is so important that you're willing to—"

"Just give it to me. I need to verify something."

With an eye roll, he handed it to me. I opened my emails, and staring back at me was Eddie's message. To be more specific, the picture that sent me into a tailspin.

Jaime looked over my shoulder and gasped, "Isn't that—"

"I think so."

"Is she the one who attacked you at the Mall?"

"I think she's one of the people, yeah."

"Jesus."

"Tell me about it."

"What are you going to do?"

"What do you think? Call the cops."

I reached for the two business cards that the Florida cop and FBI agent left with me. Pop handed me his cell, and I called the Florida cop first, since she seemed like the one in charge.

Naturally, I received her voicemail.

"Hi, this is Detective Skaryd with the Clearwater Police Department. After the tone, please leave—"

I listened to the recording and left a message, asking her to call me right away. I did the same with the FBI agent. Next, I called my office and got ahold of the salt-and-pepper corporate attorney, Evans Seffner, who picked up on the second ring.

"This is Seffner."

"Evans, this is Oliver Morales. Did I catch you at a bad time?"

"Not at all, Ollie. How can I help you?"

I explained the situation.

"Understood," he replied. "Please don't meet with them without us present."

I mentally rolled my eyes. "Fine. Should I just have them come down here, or—"

"When they call you back, please have them contact my office, and we'll coordinate a time and place to meet."

"You mean time. I'm not very mobile at the moment, so we'll have to meet down here at the rehab facility."

"Do you know if they have a conference room or place to meet?

"I'm sure they do. Worst case scenario, we just meet in my room and ask for privacy till the meeting's over."

"That should work. Keep me posted." He hung up.

"He wants to coordinate a meeting," I told my father and brother.

"Of course he does," Pop scoffed.

CHAPTER SEVENTY-THREE

Two days later, I sat across from Detective Skaryd and Agent Umberto in a conference room that the rehab facility kindly provided, as long as we didn't leave a mess.

I'm flanked by my corporate weasels, Evans Seffner and his counterpart, the ever-bald Gentry Harper, who laid out the ground rules of this meeting to the law enforcement officers.

"We're here only to discuss the content of the email received by our client, and only the content, specifically the photo. If you ask about anything outside the scope of this, we're shutting this meeting down pending a subpoena, which we will appeal."

Or as Woody from Toy Story said, "Play nice."

"Understood, Counselor," Detective Skaryd nodded.

All eyes then fell on me.

"Mr. Morales, may I call you Oliver?" she began.

"Just call me Ollie."

"Fine. Ollie, what can you tell us about this photo?" she pointed at a printout of the picture.

I proceeded to tell her everything I knew.

"Can you confirm, then, that this is—"

"Easy, there, Detective. He just said he thinks this is. *Thinks,*" Gentry warned.

She took a beat. "Ollie, what makes you think this is—"

"Look. I'm a professional photojournalist. I get paid for seeing the details."

"And what is it you see here? I mean, this person is almost completely covered up. All we can see, from this angle, are—"

"Okay, do you see the way she's holding this pipe? And her eyes. I'd recognize them anywhere."

"Where have you seen these eyes before?"

"Easy with your answer, Oliver," Gentry instructed.

"High school."

"I'm sorry. Did you just say high school?" Agent Umberto chimed in.

"Uh-huh."

"No offense, but how long ago was this?" Agent Umberto asked.

I quickly did the mental math. "About thirty-five years ago."

The agent swore under his breath, "Are you f-ing kidding me."

His comment disrupted the meeting.

Evan Seffner stood. "I think we're done here."

"Wait a minute, Counselor. We're not done with—"

"We're done. If you don't like his answers, get a subpoena. Otherwise, you have all the information you're going to get from our client," Gentry informed them.

"Good day, Detective, Agent," Seffner said. "Let's go, Ollie."

I silently mouthed an apology and discreetly signaled Detective Skaryd and Agent Umberto to call me later,. While Umberto waved me off, the detective caught it and responded with a subtle nod.

Numbnuts one and two then escorted me back to my room, reminding me the entire way of our corporate agreement.

"Remember," Seffner stated. "If they try to get ahold of you again, call us immediately."

I hid my hand and crossed my fingers. "Will do."

Pop asked me how things went after the pair left. I pursed my lips and answered with a blank stare.

"That good, huh?"

"I need to pee."

While I relieved myself, the events of that day began playing in my mind's eye. I met up with the intern, Derek, at a local coffee shop. Discussed the ground rules. We photographed congregating attendants at the first rally, then followed a pack up to the Capitol lawn.

The temperature of the crowd changed.

Defiant to deadly.

Chants for the heads of the Vice President and Speaker of the House rang out. Gallows and a lazy swinging noose erected in the distance.

I instructed the kid, "Stay close, and keep alert."

Suddenly, we were surrounded.

My heart rate increased.

As did my breathing.

I steadied myself.

Calm down, Ollie.

The woman from the picture became one with the crowd.

I was attacked from behind.

Derek's innocent face went white with fear.

More violence.

I shut my eyes.

Amidst the chaos, the soothing sound of my therapist's voice pierced through.

"Whenever you're feeling overwhelmed, go to your happy place," she advised.

Waves crashing lightly onto a sandy beach replaced the angry mob. Seagulls squawked overhead in the distance. The heat from the sun baked my aging face. Tastebuds soothed by the salty seawater and sweat dripping down my cheek.

I rocked my head back and forth.

Loosened my neck muscles.
My heart rate and breathing normalized.
Opened my eyes.
I was back in the bathroom of my rehab facility.
Flushed the toilet, then washed my hands and face.
The cool water felt good against my skin.
Slicked back my graying hair.
Smiled at the old man staring back at me in the mirror.
Thank God, I've got the shrink this afternoon.

CHAPTER SEVENTY-FOUR

She stared at me, so I asked the question again, "Who was at the door, Navil?"

After an unsteady pause, she continued. "Jan-Marc, his parents, and the police."

"They called the cops?"

"Oui." She nodded. "Apparently, I broke his nose when I hit him with my knee."

"Serves him right."

"I agree, but his parents did not." She sighed. "Nor did mine."

"But you were defending—"

"It didn't matter. Mon père said if I had done a better job watching my little brother and sister, none of this would have happened."

"Yeah, but—"

"I know."

"Unbelievable. What happened next?"

"They forced me to apologize to that—"

"Conman?"

She tossed me a strange look.

"You know. That word you used. Sounded like conman."

"Connard?"

"That's the one."

She chuckled. "Oui. He's definitely un *connard*."

"What does it mean?"

"You know—*asshole*." She swirled her index finger toward the ceiling.

I laughed.

"After that, mon père dealt with the police through one of his connections." She sneered.

Must be nice.

"I thought things were over, but I was wrong. About a week later, my parents sat me down. They said that I had become an embarrassment to the family."

"They said that?"

"To my face."

I struggled to picture Navil being an embarrassment to anyone.

"They told me starting in January, they were shipping me off to America to finish out my last year of secondary school."

"Secondary?"

"That's what we call high school back home."

"Ah."

"I did everything I could to change their minds. Even mon grand-mère, Mémé, intervened, but their minds were made up."

Her story pained me. "I don't mean to sound like a broken record, but—"

She caressed my face. "Thank you, chér."

I kissed her palm and encouraged her to continue.

"A week before leaving, Mémé took me clothes shopping. Bought me all my new outfits. Told me to use this time to *reinvent* myself."

You've definitely done that.

"So that's why you dress and act the way that you do?"

She nodded.

"On the plus side, if they hadn't sent you here, we wouldn't have met."

"Very true," she said with a kiss. "And I for one, couldn't be happier."

The school bell rang, signaling the end of first period.

"We better get to our next class."

"Oui. I don't think we can get away with skipping two."

"I've got U.S. History. What do you have?"

"French." She snickered and took my hand.

I rolled my eyes. "I still can't believe you get away with taking that class."

Before leaving the building, she turned to me. "Ollie?"

"Yeah?"

"Please don't tell anyone about—" She gestured to her tattoo.

"Of course not. 'Sides, who would I tell?"

Fi's face flashed before my eyes.

"This secret dies with me," I promised.

She kissed my cheek. "Merci, chér."

After lunch, I ran into Fi, and she was *still* pissed off at me.

"C'mon, Fi. Give me a break. Talk to me."

"Fine. *What?*"

I opened my mouth and came up short.

"Seriously? You've had *all day*, and that's what you come up with. A shrug?"

"Sorry. I don't know what else to say."

"How 'bout thanking me for trying to help—"

"Thank you, Fi."

"—and for putting up with your stupid ass, and not punching you in the face."

I nodded. "And thank you for not punching me in the face. Anything else?"

"Give me a minute. I've got a list."

"Are we good?"

She rolled her dark eyes. "Fine. I've got a lot of things on my mind anyway."

Her expression turned dour, and she turned away from me. Something was wrong.

"What's going on, Fi?"

"You wouldn't understand."

"What are you—pregnant?" I joked.

It landed like a lead balloon.

"You're hysterical. You should go on tour."

"Just trying to lighten the mood. Seriously, what's going on? You know you can tell me anything."

"I know, Ols. It's just . . ."

I raised my arms. "Just what?"

"It's embarrassing."

"Okay, if you're not pregnant, then what's the problem?"

"It's Gramps."

"What about him?"

"You know how he likes to gamble on the horses?"

"Yeah. He hits the OTB on Sundays, right?"

"Well, apparently, it's not just Sundays anymore."

"What do you mean?"

She looked around to make sure no one would hear her and leaned closer.

"It's more like every day."

"Damn."

"And he's been on a losing streak."

"How bad?"

She pursed her lips.

"That bad?"

Tears ran down her face, "He's gambled away most of my college money."

"But that's the money you inherited when your parents died. That was *your* money."

"I know."

"Fuck. What are you gonna do?"

"Beats the shit out of me," she replied. "I've been busting my ass at this place for the past four years, and for what? So I can graduate high school and then get a job at McDonald's if I'm lucky?"

"There's gotta be something you can do. What about scholarships? Or college loans?"

"With the way things are going, Ollie, I'll be lucky to finish out the school year here. I've got to get to class."

As Fi turned and walked away, heaviness settled in the air and cast a shadow over her. She appeared sadder than when she stood in the window overlooking my backyard after her parents' plane crash.

I needed to talk to Pop. Unfortunately, when I got home that night, he got called into work, Tía Carolina went to Manhattan for the weekend, and I got stuck babysitting Jaime for the evening.

I hate my life.

CHAPTER SEVENTY-FIVE

Pop got in late that evening, so I took care of Jaime and Bella the following morning. After taking the dog for her morning walk, I poured her bowl of *Purina,* and my brother *Cheerios,* even though he wanted French toast.

"It's this or nothing."

"Fine," he scoffed.

After breakfast, Jaime ran off to the basement to watch cartoons, while I cleaned up the mess he left behind.

Just as I finished wiping down the kitchen table, Pop strolled into the room.

"Don't suppose you made any coffee?" He yawned.

I shook my head. "Sorry, Pop."

"It's okay." He smiled and grabbed coffee grounds from the cabinet.

"How was work?"

He rubbed his unshaven face. "Emergency cyst."

I made a face while he fixed his java and joined me at the table.

"Remember, tonight, I have—"

"A party, I remember."

"What time are you planning on heading out?"

"I'm supposed to be picking up Navil in a couple of hours. We're planning on spending the day together before heading to the party."

He sipped his coffee. "Need cash?"

I smiled.

Pop shook his head, "Go grab my wallet."

After handing me sixty dollars, I took a quick shower, threw on a polo shirt, jeans, a splash of *Obsession for Men*, and headed to the front door with my camera gear.

"Where's your brother?"

"In the basement watching TV."

"Have fun."

"I will."

"Not too late, okay?"

"Promise."

The Lord must have known today we wanted a special day. The birds were chirping, and nary a cloud in the sky. I stepped outside, took a deep breath, loaded my car, and exited stage left, as they say, before anyone could ruin things for me.

Heading to school, I flipped on the radio and listened to Linda Ronstadt sing her hit tune, *Blue Bayou*, and imagined Navil and me living out the song.

Just the two of us, wearing tropical garb, exotic drinks with umbrellas in hand, strolling down a white sandy beach at sunset. In the distance, sailboats and dolphins navigated the waves, as a warm breeze blew feathery palm fronds in nearby coconut trees.

As I pulled up the parkway and Linda hit her crescendo, I pictured the perfect kiss under a blanket of stars.

I couldn't help but smile as I stepped out of my car and found my beloved Belgian girlfriend on the porch chatting with a few girls from her dorm, tiny purse in one hand, stylish valise with a change of clothes in the other.

The moment she saw me, her face lit up.

Her smile as bright as the sunlight reflecting off her black-framed Ray-Ban sunglasses.

She leaped down the steps and jumped into my arms with a squeal.

I don't know who was happier to see the other person—she or me.

Our clothed bodies seemingly became one as we hugged hello.

"Bonjour, chér," she whispered.

Her voice.

Like a feather floating on the wind.

I didn't want to let her go.

Had we been alone, I wouldn't have.

"Ready to go?" I asked.

With a crinkled smile, she nodded. "Oui."

We hopped into the car and drove to a nearby mill pond, home of my Long Island ducks picture and old watermill.

I had everything planned.

CHAPTER SEVENTY-SIX

The meadow was quiet that morning.

Hardly a soul.

I found a primo parking spot right up against an unmanicured field of grass and set us up about fifty feet away from my car. Navil helped me spread out the blanket and placed the snacks and drinks on the corner so it wouldn't blow away.

"Good thinking," I commented.

I took out my camera, loaded it with a new roll of film, new batteries, and even changed the lens.

Navil looked up at me with inquisitive eyes. "So, what do we do first?"

I surveyed the area and felt like an old-time Midwestern settler.

"C'mon. We'll start by the water and work our way back to the blanket."

I helped her up and smiled to myself as she brushed the seat of her pants, then we walked toward the large pond up ahead.

Navil sported a relaxed outfit that day, opting for a cozy light sweater layered over a stylish designer t-shirt, paired effortlessly with blue jeans and comfortable sneakers.

Her auburn locks were gracefully held up in a clip, a style choice I adored because it revealed a delicate star-shaped beauty mark nestled at the nape of her graceful neck.

Whenever I stood behind her, I couldn't help but wrestle

with the irresistible urge to press a gentle kiss on that uniquely shaped mark.

She looked like a modern-day character from either *Summer of '42* or *American Graffiti*, two of my favorite movies.

Even her perfume reminded me of days gone by.

Light.

Floral.

For someone who once dressed like an anarchist, she sure took her grandmother's words to heart. Transformed herself into a latter-day fashion plate.

As I snapped a couple of photos of the old mill in the distance, Navil spotted a family of ducks cruising across the pond.

"Ollie, get them," she whispered.

I bent down. Adjusted my telephoto lens to a nice tight frame and captured the waterfowl in motion as they swam in sync toward the beach on the other side of the mill pond.

Navil remained close as a gentle breeze danced around us. Each time I stooped down to capture a shot, she was right there at my side, drawn to my warmth as if absorbing my body heat.

After about an hour of snapping pictures, I felt a shift in my focus. Instead of the scenery, my attention turned to a different subject entirely—Navil.

I figured I had the prettiest girl on the planet with me.

It would've been foolish not to immortalize her on film.

The ever-modest Navil held her hands up in protest. "Ollie, I look horrible."

"Not possible," I whispered.

She hemmed and hawed but eventually gave in to my request.

"Okay. Just a few."

I carefully positioned her by the water's edge, ready to capture her radiant essence through the lens. Demurely, she bent down on one knee, placed her chin in the palm of her hand, looked directly into the lens and smiled.

Her subtle beauty took my breath away.

"Whoa," I remarked, causing her to smile.

With careful precision, I positioned Navil so that the sun framed her head in a luminous halo. The gentle glow accentuated her features. We wandered through the meadow for the next forty-five minutes. Navil's vibrant energy filling the air.

"Can you do a cartwheel?" I inquired.

Her eyes sparkled with playful enthusiasm.

"You mean like this?" she replied, breaking into a graceful cartwheel that filled the air with laughter and joy.

Navil gracefully extended her arms. Her lithe body twisted through the air as she cartwheeled to her left with ease and precision reminiscent of Mary Lou Retton's legendary gymnastic routines at the Olympics.

With a soft thud, she landed flawlessly, her movements as effortless as they were breathtaking.

After catching her breath, she asked, "What next?"

She climbed trees. Got in the rocky sand. You name it, she did it. Eventually, I got her to lie in a field of red, yellow, and violet wildflowers.

"Pretend like you're making a snow angel."

Navil complied. She removed her hairclip and let her auburn locks cascade freely in the breeze. Her hair danced like flames in the wind as I eagerly snapped away, each click of the camera captured the eternal moment in mere seconds.

She slowly lowered herself onto the grass and flapped her arms and legs in imitation of making a snow angel. I stood over her and clicked furiously, capturing every fleeting expression that crossed her beautiful face—smiles, eyes closed, a turned profile—each one a testament to her radiant perfection.

Sunlight bounced off her pearly whites and illuminated the warm hazel flecks surrounding her iris. Navil stopped mid-motion and gazed up at me with a look that spoke volumes.

In that moment, her love shone through the lens. Created a memory that would last a lifetime. Its intensity caught me off guard. I almost dropped the camera on her face. She quickly moved as I snagged it mid-air.

"Jesus, I'm sorry."

She sat up and laughed. "Are you okay, chér?"

"Yeah, I, uh—"

Our eyes locked.

Endorphins raced.

Receptors activated.

Saliva filled my mouth.

Her eyes narrowed slightly.

A sly smile.

She lay back invitingly.

In a swift motion, I placed the lens cap on and was at her side.

Face to face in the uncut grass.

Her minty-fresh breath merged with mine.

Our mouths and tongues became one.

I pulled her close.

Felt the heat of her body against mine.

My hand slowly navigated to her backside.

A gentle squeeze.

A slight gasp.

I rolled on top of her.

Manicured fingertips dug into my lower back.

Sent shivers down my spine.

Her legs spread.

Slightly at first.

Exploration continued.

Her mouth.

Her neck.

As delicious as Sunday morning pancakes.

Flowery perfume blended with an earthy meadow.

Quacking ducks serenaded us in the distance.

Soft moan in my ear.

Followed by another.

"Ollie," she whispered.

My manhood stood at attention.

Begged for release.

The faint sound of car tires crunched on the gravelly parking lot.

A hushed whisper, "Ollie—"

She pressed herself against me.

The squeal of brakes.

"Oui, right there. Don't stop."

A car door forcefully slammed.

Navil and I gasped.

Footsteps approached.

I quickly rolled off.

We turned.

You've got to be fucking kidding me.

CHAPTER SEVENTY-SEVEN

"We've really got to stop meeting like this." He smugly smiled.

Officer Wallace.

I fucking hate this guy.

We quickly stood and wiped the meadow off ourselves.

"Afternoon, Officer Wallace."

He shook his head and rubbed the back of his neck. "Mr. Morales, aren't you *tired* of getting into trouble?"

I shut my eyes and sighed. I had no answer. We'd done nothing wrong. Making out in the grass wasn't against the law last time I checked. We both had our clothes on. And there were no witnesses besides the ducks who didn't seem to mind.

As these thoughts raced across my mind, my favorite cop got right in my face and gave me a quick once-over. He nodded and sucked on a tooth while surveying the area.

"What, may I ask, are you two up to?"

Why he felt the need to ask was beyond me. He pulled up next to my car and had the perfect view of our—dalliance.

"Nothing," I replied. "Just here taking pictures."

He arched his brow and looked at Navil. "Pictures of what?"

I stepped to my left and blocked his view, which seemed to annoy him.

"Of the pond." I gestured to the water behind me.

"Mm-hmm, that's not what it looked like to me."

"We were just, uh—"

His eyes narrowed. "Taking a break?"

"Yeah."

He poked at my camera equipment.

"All this stuff is yours?"

"Yes sir."

"And you have the *receipts* to prove it?"

"Uh, well, like, not *on* me."

"Oh, not on you?" he replied. "Because there have been reports of a theft in the area."

Of course, there've been.

A two-year-old camera and a used telescopic lens.

Right.

"Well, it's all mine," I responded. "The camera was a gift from my aunt, and the lens I got from my father this past Christmas."

"All right. Calm down. How much longer you plan on being here?"

"I don't know." I shrugged. "Probably not too much longer."

"You might want to start packing up now. Just saying."

Navil tugged my arm. "Come on, Ollie. Let's go."

"I'd listen to the girl, Mr. Morales."

We locked eyes in a silent standoff, Clint Eastwood-style, till he rested his thumb on his sidearm.

"All right. We're leaving."

He tipped his head and walked to his patrol car. "Ma'am."

Navil and I quickly packed up and loaded the car. As we did, Officer Asshole hit his siren and peeled out of the parking lot. It scared the shit out of Navil and me.

"Jesus, what an *asshole*," I scoffed.

With the mood killed, we hopped into my car and waited. The last thing we felt like doing was to have another make-out session with that connard in the area.

"What do you want to do?" she asked.

I snickered and stared at the beauty next to me. She bit her lower lip and looked away.

"Why don't we swing by my place? Make sure my Pop's surviving his day with Jaime. We can grab a bite to eat if you want. You can change, and then we'll head over to the party."

"And while we're there, I can go next door and check on Fiona. See if she needs help getting ready for her event this evening."

"Cool."

CHAPTER SEVENTY-EIGHT

Modern Day

The stars finally aligned in my favor. After two weeks in rehab, I received my walking papers.

"And my brother signed off on this?" I asked Len.

"Yep." He smiled.

"Awesome."

"I thought you'd want to hear the good news."

"You have no idea."

"Of course, this doesn't mean no more therapy."

"Whatever. At least I get to sleep in my own bed."

"This is true. In the meantime, are you ready for—"

"Some early morning abuse?" I joked.

"Call it what you will. You're doing great."

"Thanks, Len."

He escorted me to the rehab center gym for our hour and a half of stretching, light cardio, and strength training. I returned to my room, exhausted and sweaty, only to find Pop seated in his chair sipping a Venti coffee, watching television.

"Good morning, Dr. Morales," Len greeted as we entered.

"Hey, Pop." I kissed him hello. "You're later than usual."

"Your brother didn't have to go into work today, so he slept in."

"Good for him. I'm surprised he hasn't burnt himself out, with all the hours he and Cynthia are putting in."

"It reminds me of my old medical school days."

"Are you going to need help showering?" Len asked.

"Nah, I've got it."

"And if he needs anything, I'm here," Pop chimed in.

Len's lack of confidence in my father's abilities painted across his face, but he didn't say anything, aside from a fake smile and nod. While I stripped down, Len shared the news of my imminent departure with Pop.

"That is great news. When are they discharging you?"

"Tomorrow," Len answered.

Pop nodded approvingly.

After showering, I settled in and waited for lunch to arrive. To keep myself busy, I grabbed the iPad and checked my Gmail. Thankfully, the good news kept coming.

"Excellent," I announced.

"What's happening, bub?"

"T-Mobile shipped my replacement cell. Looks like I'll have it in a few days."

After thanking the staff and saying my goodbyes to Len the following afternoon, I limped into my house with my cane and walking boot, with Pop on one side and my sister-in-law, Cheryl, on the other.

"When does your—"

"Wife get home? Soon. Should be out of quarantine by the end of the week."

"I can bring back Daisy tonight if you want," Cheryl stated.

My dog's name put a smile on my face.

"How's she doing? Not too much trouble, I hope."

"Not at all. The kids loved having her around."

"And Henry? Your twelve-year-old yellow lab?"

"You know Henry. Sleeps all day. Eats when you feed him."

"So, she left him alone?"

"Meh. For the most part."

I smirked at the thought of my four-year-old mini long-haired dachshund hanging with good old Henry.

"Well, hopefully, she was nice."

"Nice enough," she replied, and walked to the kitchen to check out my fridge. "Not a whole lot in here."

"It's not like I planned my recent—"

"Vacation?"

"Yeah—" I snickered. "That's what we'll call it."

She closed the fridge and grabbed a nearby pad and pen.

"Writing a list?"

"If I don't fill this fridge, your wife will kill me."

"There's always takeout, or Uber Eats."

Cheryl pointed the pen. "Not on my watch."

A few hours later, the cupboards were full, Daisy was curled up in her doggie bed by my feet, my belly was full, and I was seated in my home office on my house phone calling various DC contacts. I wanted to figure out a way to get into the prison without causing an issue.

Two days later, I received an unexpected visit at my front door.

"Morning, Detective. No partner?"

"Nope. Flying solo this morning. May I . . . ?"

"Come in." I stepped out of the way. "Coffee?"

"Please."

"Daisy, settle down," I instructed my barking dog as we walked by. "She's harmless, but just in case—"

Detective Skaryd chuckled, bent down, and allowed Daisy to sniff her hand. After scratching the dog's ear, the detective received a friendly lick, and followed me into the kitchen.

"Cream and sugar?" I asked.

"Splenda, if you have any. Otherwise, I'll take it—"

I pointed to a sugar bowl full of Splenda packets next to a variety of coffee pods. I handed her an empty mug and watched as she selected a *Starbucks* Columbian coffee. She popped it into the coffee maker and joined me at the kitchen table once it completed its cycle.

"So, how can I help you, Detective?"

CHAPTER SEVENTY-NINE

She took a sip and said, "You've been busy."

"Excuse me?"

"I said, you've been—"

"No, I heard what you said. I just don't understand the context."

For effect, she took another sip. "You've been making *inquiries*."

"And?"

"And people are taking notice."

"What people?"

"I'm here, aren't I?"

I scratched my unshaven chin and leaned away, putting distance between us.

"What's wrong with making a few phone calls?"

"Nothing, as long as they don't interfere with *my* investigation."

"And what makes you think I'm trying to interfere—"

"Mr. Morales, look—"

"Just call me Ollie. Everyone does."

"*Mr. Morales*, I can't have you interfering in an ongoing investigation. Especially one with this much—"

"National exposure?"

She nodded.

"Look, I'm not trying to inter—"

"I don't care, Mr.—Ollie. What you're doing will hamper our ability to prosecute these people."

"All I'm trying to do is—"

"Get in and see one of the people who attacked you."

I sighed. "Yeah."

"I can't let you do this. Not right now. Not at this point in our investigation."

My nose twitched.

"Look at it from our point of view. If we allow you to see this person, the defense counsel will—"

"Make a case out of it."

"Yes. To say the least."

"You don't understand. This person I'm trying to see. We have—"

"A history?"

Her reply surprised me.

"You think you're the only one with access to information?"

My eyes narrowed.

"I've done my research. I know all about your recent and ancient injuries."

I shook my head, "So much for HIPAA."

"Special circumstances."

"Uh-huh."

"Sorry to be the bearer of bad news," she stated. "But justice matters."

"So, what happens now? Where do we go from here?"

"*We?*"

I rolled my eyes.

"*We* do nothing. Agent Umberto and I, on the other hand, continue working our investigation."

The pain in my leg began to throb. It was time for my next pill.

"Excuse me for a moment." I hobbled to the kitchen for my prescription.

She finished her coffee and stood. "It's okay. I've got to leave anyway."

"I'd love to say thanks for stopping by, but—"

"Understood. Thanks for the coffee," she replied as she walked to the sink.

"You're welcome. Don't worry about the mug. I'll take care of it."

She left her cup in the sink, petted Daisy, and made her way toward the front door. I choked down my pill and followed.

Before leaving, she turned and gestured toward a family picture hanging in the foyer.

"Lovely family."

"Thanks."

"It'd be a shame if you did something stupid and lost them," she commented. "By the way, my father sends his regards."

"Father?"

"He said I should chuck toilet paper at your hair." My eyes widened as she shook her head. "I asked him to explain, but he said you'd understand."

"Wait . . . you're *Ricky's* daughter?"

"So, you remember him?" She smiled. "Good. I'll let him know."

I breathed out the words, "Remember him? He saved my life."

She chuckled, "Small world. Must be one heck of a story. I'd love to hear it sometime, but I've got to run. I'll be in touch. In the meantime, take care of that leg."

"I will."

I stood in shock as she backed her black Dodge Charger out of the driveway.

Ricky's daughter. Jesus. Talk about the apple not falling far from the tree.

Flashbacks from my youth played in my mind's eye as I washed up the coffee mugs. Thankfully, the painkillers I took began to kick in. I also replayed my conversation with Ricky's daughter as I began to think of her.

She's got to be wrong, no? How can visiting someone in prison impact her case?

I needed legal advice. I thought about the pair of assholes at my office, and immediately decided against it. The last thing I needed was to have those two up my butt. I reached out to the attorney who helped the Missus and me put together our will a few years back but got his voicemail.

"Hi, you've reached the office of Peter Perez. After the tone—"

I hung up without leaving a message. Like the youth of today, I wanted instant gratification. Immediate answers.

Damn it.

I hopped on YouTube to take my mind off my troubles, and came across a video clip from the movie, *Caddyshack*. The scene where an impatient Ted Baxter, as Judge Smails, said to Michael O'Keefe's character, Danny Noonan, as he lined up his putt, "Well, we're waiting."

As I laughed, a thought came to mind. "I wonder if he's still in the hospital?"

I hopped online, found the number, and a couple of minutes later was transferred to his room.

With a wet wheezy cough, he answered, "Hello?"

"Judge Watson?"

"This is Judge" >*cough*< "Watson. Who's speaking, please?"

He sounded exhausted.

"Hi, Judge Watson. This is Oliver Morales. We shared—"

I heard him suck in a breath. "The doctor's brother. Sure, I remember you."

I smiled.

"How can I help you?"

His ventilator hissed in the background as I explained my challenge.

"Well, Oliver . . . >*wheeze*< . . . this is a great question and one I wish others would consider before . . . >*cough*< . . . visiting someone in jail."

His constant wheezing got to me. It kept me from digesting his insight. I interrupted him midsentence.

"Excuse me, your Honor?"

"Yes, Oliver."

"I'm sorry. Listen, I can't—this isn't fair to you."

"It's okay, son. I don't mind." He paused and inhaled.

"How 'bout I stop by and we speak in person? This way, you can take your time."

I heard him chuckle. "Only if you agree . . . >*rasp*< . . . to bring me some real coffee. The stuff they serve—"

"Is awful," I interjected. "Yeah, I just got home from rehab. The first thing I did was pour myself a cup."

Another wet, raspy laugh.

"Can I stop by tomorrow?"

"Yes—" He took a deep breath. "Any time after ten."

"You've got it. I know a place with the best coffee and crullers. And don't worry, I won't tell my brother."

"You're an officer and a . . . gentleman," he joked. "I'll see you . . . tomorrow."

"See you tomorrow, your Honor."

I just hope you last that long.

CHAPTER EIGHTY

1986

A while later, Navil returned to my house from Fi's, and we hung out in the basement watching television till it was time to go to the party.

"How's she doing?" I asked as we settled in on the couch.

"A bit nervous, but she will be fine."

"Cool."

"Oui. I helped her pick out an outfit and put on her makeup."

The thought of a dolled-up Fiona crossed my mind and brought a smile to my face. "I bet she looks mint."

Navil grabbed the blanket off the back of the couch and snuggled into me. The warmth of her body enveloped us both. She casually played with my curly locks, as we pretended to watch the movie, *Murder by Death*, on HBO.

As it played, Navil leaned in and kissed my chest and rubbed my tummy with her manicured fingertips. There was such an intimate coziness in her actions. It caused a stir in my nether regions.

Just as things were about to get—interesting, the door at the top of the steps opened, and bounding down the stairs were Jaime and Bella.

You've got to be fucking kidding me.

Jaime ran to his toys, while Bella headed to the edge of the couch. She leaped about till I picked her up. And like a jealous lover, she put herself between Navil and me, rolling over till someone scratched her pink belly.

"Sorry," I whispered.

Navil took it in stride, while I stewed in my juices.

"Ollie, come play with me."

"I'm busy, buddy."

"No, you're not. You're just sitting there watching TV."

"*Jaime—*"

Navil glanced at her watch. "I think I'll go get ready for the party."

"You sure? It's kind of early."

"Well, Ginny did say we should come early if we want to find a parking spot."

I acquiesced with a nod. After a quick kiss, she walked up the stairs and out of the basement, leaving me alone with my annoying kid brother and the dog.

"Hey, James?"

"Yeah, Ollie?"

"Can you do me a favor? Next time I'm down here alone with—"

"But *Pop* told me to come down here."

Sonofabitch.

I couldn't blame the squirt. The real culprit was upstairs watching golf or some lame western, and unfortunately, he made all the rules.

"Come play with me," Jaime begged.

"All right, squirt." I replied.

We messed around with his Lego's for a few minutes before I excused myself.

"Where are you going?"

"I've got to get ready for my party."

With sadness in his pre-teen voice, "Oh. Okay, Ollie."

While I would normally grab a quick shower, I didn't want to make Navil wait. Instead, I grabbed my favorite blue, white, and aqua-striped polo shirt, Levi's, and white Nike high-tops. I fixed my hair, splashed on a little Calvin Klein's Obsession for Men, and quickly brushed my teeth, all in under fifteen minutes.

A personal record.

Navil finished changing, and patiently waited for me in the family room. She sat in the chair facing inward, with her back toward me, bullshitting with Pop about school and stuff, with Bella on Pop's lap.

I drew close, and the dog began to bark. Navil's head swiveled in my direction, and she got up from the chair. The vision in front of me literally stopped me in my tracks. How any eighteen-year-old girl could put together such a stunningly casual look was beyond me.

"Whoa," I whispered.

"Do I look okay?" she demurely asked with a hint of a smile.

I was at a loss for words. All I could do was nod approvingly. Her auburn hair was styled in loose waves down toward her shoulders. It cradled her face and accentuated her neck. She wore high-waisted blue denim jeans with a fitted silhouette, and a brown leather belt with a silver buckle.

She replaced her previous t-shirt with a crisp white cropped top with rolled-up sleeves, a loose-fit, light-washed denim jacket, and white leather Keds sneakers with no socks.

To complete her ensemble, the girl adorned herself with nude lipstick and a delicate, enticing perfume with undertones of vanilla and amber. Its aroma enveloped me as she wrapped an arm around my waist.

Over her shoulder, I noticed Pop check her out, which I found gross, but understood the appeal. Catching my eye roll, he quickly averted his gaze, clearly embarrassed.

"We're heading out," I announced.

"Okay. Have fun. Remember, not too late," Pop replied.

"I know."

Bella hopped off my father's lap and escorted us to the front door. The way she leaped about gave me the impression that she thought she was coming with us.

"No. Stay. You're not going."

Navil placed a hand over her mouth to hide her laughter.

"Au revoir, Dr. Morales."

"Goodbye, Navil," he replied. "Be safe, you two."

"Thanks, Pop. We will."

I should have taken his warning more seriously.

CHAPTER EIGHTY-ONE

Navil and I chatted the thirty minutes or so it took us to get to Stefan's party in Miller Place. Even though it was my first time driving to this part of the county, I followed Ginny's directions and didn't get lost.

His house was one of three huge homes at the end of a long and winding road, tucked in a circular cul-de-sac lined with ancient oak trees showing signs of spring. Ginny wasn't wrong about limited parking. Cars lined both sides of the street.

About five hundred yards up the block, I found a spot. "I guess we're hoofing it."

Navil slipped her hand in mine, and we made our way toward the party, which we could hear from the street. A pulsating baseline vibrated through the tree line as we approached the house.

The top of his driveway reminded me of a ski slope, long and steep. The type you'd hate to shovel as an adult but loved to sled down as a kid. At the bottom was a carport with expensive-looking cars.

"This must be the place."

Navil nodded.

"Shall we?" I asked, offering my arm.

"Merci, chér."

We walked down gravel steps, and before heading inside, checked out a few of the cars. Based on the empty red plastic party cups strewn about, I could tell we weren't the first. Next to Stefan's BMW was a cherry-red Porsche 911 with a douchey license plate frame—a jet airplane, which read, *Fly High.* Lined up next to it was a white Mercedes Benz SL convertible, followed by a black Mercedes Benz conversion van, and then a pristine aquamarine '57 Chevrolet Bel Air with a swooping white accent. The last one caught my attention.

"Wow," I whispered. "Ernie would love this car."

I spent a few minutes surveying this vehicle. The classic lines. The thick white wall tires. The beautiful two-tone leather interior. Whoever owned this thing really took pride in its upkeep. The way Navil stared longingly at the house, I could tell this wasn't her thing.

"Ready to head inside?" I asked and received a polite nod.

At the front door I took a deep breath, put on a fake smile, and entered the massive abode with the hottest girl on my arm. The first person I noticed was an eleventh grader, Mary Fergusen, who stood there sipping on a beer, bullshitting with a few kids from school. If she was there, this meant her obnoxious older brother, Kyle, wasn't too far behind.

He graduated from our school the previous year and hadn't moved on from his glory days.

"Oh, hey, Navil." Mary waved.

"Bonjour, Mary."

As if on cue, Kyle walked by with a cigarette sticking out of his face and flicked an ash in his sister's beer.

"Kyle. You asshole."

He laughed and kept on walking.

Navil chucked me the *mon Dieu* look.

"Her brother," I replied.

Mary stormed off, presumably to fetch herself another beer, with her girlfriends in tow, while we ventured further into the house. We made our way to a large circular family room with five hallways leading in various directions.

In addition, it had floor-to-ceiling glass doors overlooking a large patio and a well-manicured fenced-in backyard. Toward the back of the property, they had installed what looked like a huge built-in Olympic-sized pool.

It put mine to shame. As a matter of fact, this whole place did. It felt like someone transported a European castle and placed it right in the middle of Long Island.

I shook my head and marveled, "This place is—"

"Énorme," Navil whispered.

Throughout the museum-like family room were expensive-looking pieces of art. Freestanding sculptures mixed with furniture that didn't look used, and surrealist paintings on the wall.

One of them called to Navil, "Is that a—"

She released my hand and drifted toward the piece. Instead of following her, I stood back and watched her examine the dreamlike painting. She leaned in, read the artist's name, and nodded approvingly. Something about this artwork fascinated her in a way I hoped my photography would others someday. I strangely grew jealous of the inanimate object.

Apparently, I wasn't the only one who noticed Navil admiring the piece, or the girl, for that matter. As her lithe hand gently traced the various brushstrokes of the artist, Stefan appeared at her side and casually placed his hand on the base of her exposed lower back.

It really pissed me off.

CHAPTER EIGHTY-TWO

In a display of familiarity, Stefan leaned in, and judging her reaction, shared a humorous remark. As she cupped her mouth and chuckled, he kept his hand in place, and continued his commentary on the masterpiece before the pair.

I'd seen enough. I marched over, and the moment Stefan spotted me poised to remove his head from his shoulders, he quickly withdrew his hand.

"Oh, uh, hey, Ollie. I didn't see you."

"Chér," Navil interjected. "This is *Personal Values* by Rene Magritte."

"He's a famous Belgian surrealist artist," the douche cut in. "My mother's crazy about the guy."

He spent the next few minutes bragging about the various pieces on display throughout his colossal home. Before we knew it, Ginny found her way to our small gathering. Based on her posture and demeaner, I could tell she'd been drinking for a while. After attempting a sloppy air kiss with Navil, she placed a possessive arm around Stefan's waist.

"Isn't this place great?" she slurred over the loud music.

"Oui, you have a very lovely home, Stefan."

"Yeah, it's uh, really nice," I muttered.

Ginny took Navil's hand. "Come on, I'll show you around."

Stefan and I watched Ginny kidnap my girlfriend, who peered back with pleading eyes.

Sorry, babe.

You wanted to come.

Soon, they blended into a crowd of teens. Some I knew from school, and others were a mystery.

Embarrassed, Stefan shook his head. "Jesus. I'm sorry about that."

"No need to apologize."

"If she didn't give great head."

Did he really just say that?

"I'm sure you know what I mean. Am I right?"

He laughed and smacked my chest like we were the best of buddies. It took everything I had not to punch him in his smarmy chiseled face.

"If you're thirsty, drinks are that way." He pointed toward one of many hallways. "We've got food stations set up on the back patio and down there in the kitchen."

"Cool. Thanks."

"And if you're interested in a little—" He covered one nostril and sniffed.

This blew my hair back. I'd heard rumors, but this confirmed it.

I kept my cool. "Yeah, uh—"

"Yo, Stef," someone called from the crowd.

"Coming," he replied and turned to me. "Fucking customers. Just track me down later, and I'll hook you up. First time's free."

What an asshole.

I watched as he reached into his pocket and palmed a tiny clear envelope the size of a sugar packet, filled with a white substance.

We need to get the hell out of here.

I walked to where Ginny dragged Navil, scanning the sea of faces, but came up short. To my surprise, I caught sight of a familiar figure beside a keg nestled in a sizable *Rubbermaid* garbage can chatting up some petite, shapely brunette I didn't recognize.

"*Eddie*?" I yelled over the music.

"Ollie, what's going on?"

"Not much. I didn't know you were coming."

"You kidding me? Wouldn't miss it. These parties are legendary."

"So, I've heard," I muttered. "I don't suppose you've seen—"

The pretty brunette cleared her throat. "Ahem."

"Right, sorry. Ollie, this is Fawn. She goes to, uh—"

Real smooth, buddy.

"Miller Place," she answered with an eye roll.

"Nice to meet you, Dawn."

"It's Fawn."

"Right. Sorry. Eddie, I don't suppose you've seen Navil? Ginny dragged her off."

"Ginny? The girl from Alabama?" Fawn asked.

"Yeah, ya know her?"

She laughed. "*Everyone* knows her."

What the hell is that supposed to mean?

"Have you checked the bar downstairs?" Fawn asked.

"No," I replied. "How do I get—"

"C'mon. I'll show you. I practically grew up in this house."

The way she navigated the place, you could tell she wasn't lying. If she didn't act as my personal sherpa, I would have missed the inconspicuous door leading to the massive fully finished basement.

As we stepped in, Eddie whispered, "Jesus, this place is the tits."

Wood flooring. A fully stocked bar with red leather stools that lined one side of the room. A couple of pinball machines, a pool table, and a dartboard. In the corner, beneath Bose speakers, a twenty-two-inch television console. Plush black leather sofas strategically placed for comfort and conversation. Completing the scene, a ping-pong table currently being used for beer pong.

I craned my neck and continued my search.

Fawn grabbed Eddie's arm. "Buy me a drink."

I waved him off. "Go 'head. I'll find her."

After mouthing a thank you, I watched as she led him behind the bar and grabbed a bottle of Jack Daniels. I shook my head and wasted my time walking around the basement searching for my girlfriend. After a few minutes, I headed back upstairs to the main floor, passing Alli on the way.

"Hey, Alli."

"Oh, hey, Ollie. Navil's looking for you. She's out on the patio doing shots with Ginny."

"Really?"

She nodded. "If I were you, I'd get out there before—"

"Thanks." I cut her off and went up the stairs.

Moments later, I was outside. Sure enough, seated at a picnic table with a few other girls from school, doing shots of tequila, my beloved girlfriend, Navil. The scene reminded me of *Indiana Jones* stumbling upon *Marion Ravenwood* in the classic movie, *Raiders of the Lost Ark,* as she fearlessly faced off against a drunken fool at her bar. Ginny spotted me as I approached.

"There he is!" Ginny shouted.

After playfully waving me over, Navil licked the back of her wrist, chucked down a shot glass filled with amber liquid, winced, and immediately sucked on a lime wedge before she spat it out onto the deck.

So much for getting the fuck outta Dodge.

CHAPTER EIGHTY-THREE

I couldn't tell how many shots Navil had sucked down but judging by the way she swayed to the music booming through the speakers, it was clear she had indulged in more than one.

She beckoned me over. "Chér, come do a shot with me."

"Yeah, *Cher*—" Ginny laughed. "Come do shots."

I threw on a fake smile and took a seat.

Navil handed me a saltshaker and whispered, "Do you know what to do?"

All eyes were on me as I took the salt.

I lied. "Yeah, uh, sure."

Navil saw right through me. Instead of making fun, she placed her hand around my waist, leaned in and kissed me, leaving behind a taste of salt and lime. She then guided me through the art of doing tequila shots.

"This is how we do it back home," she began. "You lick your wrist like this—"

With the tip of her tongue, Navil moistened the tan line left behind by her missing wristwatch and then dabbed a few grains of salt.

"Open your mouth," Navil requested.

The girls seated with us snickered as I did what I was told. Navil placed a lime wedge between my teeth and told me not to move. Ginny poured a messy shot of *Jose Cuervo Gold*.

"Ready?" Navil asked. I nodded.

Without breaking eye contact, she flashed me a smile, smoothly licked the salt, downed the shot, and seized my collar, pulling me toward her. She took the lime wedge from between my teeth, sucking the juice with precision. After savoring the taste, she spat the lime into the backyard, and replaced it with her ripe lips.

Our audience whooped and hollered as we made out. Navil released me before things got too serious.

"Now, it's Ollie's turn," Ginny announced as she poured me a shot.

I wish I could say I didn't succumb to peer pressure. But the moment they chanted my name, I gave into temptation. I grabbed the saltshaker and attempted to lick my wrist, but Navil stopped me.

"Not there." Her voice teasingly soft as she exposed her slender neck. "Here."

"Body shots. Body shots," the growing audience chanted.

"What do you want me to do?" I whispered.

"Lick my neck, then sprinkle the salt."

I abandoned all gentleness and clamped down on her neck. She squirmed as I tickled her with my teeth and tongue. After releasing her, she placed a lime wedge between her teeth, and shot me a look that melted my heart and set my loins on fire.

The chants continued. "Body shots. Body shots . . ."

With an arched brow and sexiest side smile, she invited me to taste her. Flaring my nostrils, I leaned forward, eager to sample a unique blend of salt, sweat, and perfume, before tossing back the foul-tasting amber fluid, its fiery trail burning down my throat.

Navil wrapped her arms around my neck, her touch comforting and exhilarating. I placed the citrus between my teeth. Instinctively I bit down, sucked in the tart juice, and finished my first-ever shot of tequila off with a kiss. The way people whooped and hollered, you'd think we'd won an award.

Before I knew it, Navil and I finished off three more shots each which caused my empty stomach to burp up some bile. I shook my head and made a face, which Navil immediately noticed.

"Okay, I think we've had enough," she announced to a groaning crowd. "Come on, chér, let's get something to eat."

I attempted to stand and somehow missed the floor. Thankfully, someone caught me.

"Oh, hey, Eddie." I grinned.

"C'mon, Ollie. I gotcha."

CHAPTER EIGHTY-FOUR

With Eddie on one side and Navil on the other, we made our way into the crowded house.

I turned to him and slurred, "Where's that chick?"

"Went home," he quickly replied.

"She went—"

He nodded.

"Doesn't she know who you are? You're . . . *Eddie.*"

He laughed. "And *you're* drunk."

The man wasn't wrong.

They plopped me onto the first couch we bumped into.

Eddie turned to Navil. "There's food in the kitchen. I'll be right back."

"Can you bring back some water as well?"

He waved and became one with the crowd. Surprisingly, the tequila seemed to have little effect on Navil, aside from making her slightly more animated and handsy, which I welcomed. Truly a stark contrast to the hot mess seated to her right.

Eddie soon returned with cheeseburgers, hot dogs, and bunch of potato chips, along with a red dixie cup filled with ice water. We laughed and munched on the food and were joined by Alli and her boyfriend, Giles Denton, with plates of their own.

I hated to admit it, but Ginny was right. This *was* a good party. I didn't know if it was the food, water, or laughter, but the world stopped spinning, and I could now form coherent sentences.

While I shouldn't get behind the wheel, standing upright no longer seemed an issue. And had I mentioned that Navil was getting handsy?

"Wanna walk around?" I whispered.

She purred, "Sure, chér."

We excused ourselves, clasped hands, and searched for a quiet spot in a crowded house. As we climbed a staircase, I thought I caught sight of my cellmate, Ricky. Ice ran down my spine and stopped midstep.

"Chér, what's the matter?"

I ignored her and scanned the crowd.

Navil yanked my hand. "Ollie, what's wrong? I thought we were—"

"Hmm?" I replied, continuing my search.

She grabbed my face. "*Ollie.*"

It broke my trance. "Sorry, babe. I thought I saw—"

"Saw?"

Her hazel eyes entranced me and reminded me of our mission. Finding a quiet place to—

"You know what? Never mind." I smiled.

"Hey, do you want to keep going?"

I nodded and led the way. In retrospect, we should have walked out to my car and left the party. We crept down the hallway, checking for an open room. The first one we encountered had a group huddled in the center, snorting white powder off a mirrored surface held by Kyle Fergusen, who stood there yelling at his younger sister.

"For fuck's sake, Mary, man up and do it already," Kyle ordered.

"I will. Give me a minute."

The moment she saw us, Mary froze in place, as did we.

An impatient Kyle looked at me. "Dude, in or out. Either way, shut the door."

I took Navil's hand. "Uh, sorry. Wrong room."

We made a quick escape and chuckled our way down the hall. As we walked, I overheard Kyle ask who we were.

"No one important," Mary answered.

That's me.

Mr. No One Important.

The second room we came upon was locked.

The next one was free.

"Third time's the charm," I joked.

The room was adorned with an array of swimming trophies, gleaming medals, and airplane memorabilia. In an instant, I realized whose room we had stumbled upon.

"Stefan's room," I murmured.

"Who cares?" Navil responded with a shove onto his massive bed.

Game on.

CHAPTER EIGHTY-FIVE

We slowly made our way to the center of the king-size bed, Navil nestled to my left. Her porcelain-like skin a mere inch from mine, allowing me to count the freckles that adorned her petite nose and catch a hint of burger and tequila on her breath. Her auburn hair delicately framed her face, tucked behind her ear.

She smiled.

"I love you, chér."

A tender kiss.

"I love you too."

I breathed in her essence.

She rested her lithe body atop mine.

The tip of her tongue slipped between my teeth.

A salty citrus lingered. The pleasant remnant from our time choking back bitter shots of golden fire.

She was delicious.

Intoxicating.

Paradise renewed.

Slender knees placed between mine.

Forced them apart.

Slid herself between my legs.

Pressed forward.

Slowly.

Surely.

With confident purpose.

Her neck arched.
An invitation.
I glided my tongue along her curves.
Random beauty marks.
Nibbled and sucked.
Warm flesh danced beneath my fingertips.
A firm and narrow bra strap.
Parts hidden.
Her white cropped t-shirt slid up and down her torso.
Soft shoulders and lower back exposed to the air.
Goose bumps formed.
Hands cupped her flawless covered backside.
Pulled her close.
My manhood responded.
A seductive smile.
Time progressed.
We kissed, sucked—explored.
Flames of passion filled her hazel eyes.
She whispered, "Je t'aime Ollie."
Her declaration of love.
Nervous hands skated upward.
Dumbfounded by small metallic hooks.
An embarrassed chuckle.
A slight smile.
Delicate fingers took over.
The casual flick.
Glory delivered.
Her ample chest.
Firm.
Full.
Our eyes locked.

Intensity melted my soul.
An arched brow.
A hushed giggle.
"What?" she whispered.
I shook my head. "Nothing."
Intimacy enjoyed.
She sat up.
Removed her blouse.
Flesh exposed.
Indents left behind from her strap.
A delicate reminder.
Perfume and musk filled the air.
Dopamine overload.
"You're beautiful," I whispered.
A faint exhale.
A rush of saliva.
Reached for her.
Tasted her.
She arched her back.
A delicate moan.
French expressions softly spoken.
Rolled her over.
Her tattoo fully exposed.
Exquisite red and golden petals forever painted into her flesh.
Beautiful.
A slight flinch.
Another giggle.
Depressed dimples on her lower back.
A hint of a cleft.
Uncharted region.
A soft kiss.
Another moan.

She rolled over.

Leaned up onto her elbows.

Youthful rolls formed on her tummy.

Navil held my gaze.

The glow from her hazel eyes filled my heart.

We kissed.

Soft.

Slow.

Full of intention.

She whispered, "I'll be right back."

Her half-naked body sashayed across the room.

Entered Stefan's private bathroom.

I brushed my hair back.

Reveled in my good fortune.

I hopped out of bed.

Snooped around the room. A brown digital alarm clock like mine. A pale cordless phone. Jealousy filled my heart. Countless arguments with Pop replayed in my mind.

"How many times do I have to tell you no? If you want a phone in your room, you're going to have to pay for it yourself," Pop argued.

I move onto his bookcase. First place trophies bookend a few school yearbooks and various novels. In the corner, a Pioneer brand stereo system, with records neatly stacked on their side underneath. On his bureau, a nineteen-inch RCA color television.

Over his desk, two framed pictures of Stefan and his brother. On the left, the pair wore matching outfits. Hawaiian shirts, khaki shorts, and flip-flops. Stefan's brother placed his arm around his brother's shoulder. Both sport shit-eating grins, like they'd won the lottery.

They stood in front of a small jet airplane. Presumably, theirs.

In the distance, behind the tarmac, a dense jungle, lush and green.

In the other picture, a solo pre-teen Stefan, dressed head to toe in ski gear. Skis in his right hand, and poles in his left. Snow-covered mountains filled the background.

Folded on the back of his leather desk chair, a plush navy blue bathrobe, soft to the touch.

On his desk, a black lamp, various notebooks, a letter opener with our school logo, along with textbooks and—

Wait a minute.

CHAPTER EIGHTY-SIX

Tucked between an *Intro to Psychology* textbook and an AP chemistry textbook, a familiar-looking gold and blue hardcover notebook.

Can't be.

I retrieved it from the pile and opened the front cover.

Property of Jackie Woodley.

Shit.

I recognized Jackie's chicken scratch. Flipped through the pages. She had notes on everything and everybody. This must have been what she had been working on. Her grand exposé.

Stefan's drug dealing.

Check.

B Karlsson's breakup with that jerk-off, coke-snorting bully, Kyle Fergusen.

Yep, she wrote about that as well.

Navil's tattoo and abortion?

"What?" I gasped.

My head began to spin. I couldn't put the journal down. Everything she told me about her friend was a lie. She was the one who got pregnant and dumped. And after getting the abortion, went and got a tattoo as a remembrance or something.

In the distance, I heard a shower running. It had an almost white noise quality. The sound helped me to focus on recent events. Put the pieces together. I slipped on the windowsill in the newsroom. The faint scent of chlorine.

Staring back at me were various swimming trophies. It must have been Stefan who attacked Jackie at school. But why?

I flipped back to the section that detailed his drug dealing. How he and his brother flew back and forth from South America transporting coke, and all the people they paid off. He must have found out about her article and decided to take her out.

It explained who injured Jackie in my backyard. Chucked a rock to her head. But what kind of psycho sits outside someone's house, waiting for the opportune moment to strike? This blue and gold notebook was the key to this whole mystery. I needed to do something.

But what?

My heart pounded like a jackhammer. I picked up the letter opener and twirled it between my fingers. Thought about the trouble this stupid notebook caused me. An arrest and weekend in jail. That prince-of-a-cop, Officer Wallace. My asshole cellmate, Ricky. The two detectives who made my life a living hell.

Wait a minute.

I snapped my fingers. Took out my wallet, and tucked between a pair of twenties was Detective Gallagher's business card.

Yes.

I popped a squat on Stefan's bed, placed the letter opener on his nightstand, and reached for the cordless, glancing briefly at the bathroom door.

This won't take long.

I banged out the number on the card.

"This is Detective Gallagher," he answered on the second ring.

"Hey, Detective, this is Oliver Morales."

The bathroom door swung open. Billows of steam enshrouded Navil in a sensual mist. She wore nothing but her gold chain and a seductive smile.

Perfection personified.

With raised arms, she flirtatiously asked, "Want to get wet?"

Holy fuck.

In that instant, all I had just read about Navil flew from my adolescent mind. I gulped back saliva, struck dumb by the naked vision before me. My jaw dropped and eyes widened as the phone slipped to my side.

From the handset, the faint sound of Detective Gallagher, "How can I help you, Mr. Morales?"

Navil's brows furrowed as her smile disappeared. "Are you on the phone?"

"Mr. Morales," Gallagher called out. "Are you still there?"

Navil approached. Noticed the book in my lap. Accusatory hazel eyes blazed.

"Ollie, *who* are you calling?" she pointed at the phone.

From the handset. "Beats me. One sec he's there—"

She stood before me in all her flawless glory. Her ample breasts inches from my lips. I jerked my head back.

With curled lips and flared nostrils, she ordered, *"Answer me."*

Her celestial body held me captive. I sat stunned at her inviting beauty. Annoyed, she snapped her fingers in my face. Broke my trance with a jolt.

From the handset. "Mr. Morales, *are you still there*?"

The weight of Jackie's journal caught my attention.

I raised it and shouted, "Notebook*!*"

Don't know. Something about a notebook, I faintly heard Gallagher comment.

"Jackie's notebook," I shouted. "Stefan—"

Trepidation filled her voice, *"Who* are you talking to, Ollie?"

"Holy shit, I forgot." I laughed. "When you came out—"

"Never mind all that, who's on the ph—"

"The *police!*" Detective Gallagher shouted from the handset.

In a flash of panic. "Hang up, Ollie."

"Mr. Morales, if you don't answer me *this minute,* I'm going to—"

I told the detective to hold on and turned my attention back to a very naked Navil. "You're kidding me, right?"

At that moment, the bedroom door swung open. Stefan and Ginny staggered in.

"C'mon, babe," he whined. "I just want some head. 'Sides, no one's going—"

They spotted the very naked Navil and stopped in their tracks. She gasped and twisted herself into a pretzel, covering her breasts and nether regions.

Stefan smiled broadly and pumped his fist. "*Way to go, Morales.*"

Confused, Ginny slurred, "What the hell is going on here? Why is she naked?"

Navil spotted Stefan's bathrobe hanging from his desk chair and slipped it on.

"Hey, listen, guys," Stefan lectured, "I don't mind you screwing around but—"

"He found *the notebook,* you *connard!*" Navil roared.

CHAPTER EIGHTY-SEVEN

Stefan glanced over and noticed the object in my hand.

"Awesome, you found it. I was going to give it to you later," Stefan told Navil.

"*Morales*!" Detective Gallagher shouted from the phone. "*I swear to God—*"

I shouted back, "Just give me a minute, and *don't* hang up!"

Stefan asked Navil, "Why is he on my phone? Who is he talking—"

"*The police, you idiot.*"

The shock of her comment sobered up Stefan. Anger flashed. Teeth bared. He pointed an accusatory finger at me.

"Hang up the phone, asshole."

"Go fuck yourself, you drug-dealing scumbag," I shot back.

"What?" His stunned reply.

I guessed no one had ever said that to him before. Certainly, not some Puerto Rican nobody from his high school. He shoved past Ginny, who tumbled to the floor like a pair of dice and stalked toward me.

His nostrils flared. Eyes filled with rage. As he lunged for me, I hopped onto the bed, and swatted him away like a bad dog, with Jackie's thick notebook. Blood sprayed from his nose. It coated his finely painted walls and nightstand, which he fell over.

I turned my back and yelled into the receiver, "Detective Gallagher, I'm at a party in Miller—"

The bed jostled and I lost my balance. Someone leaped onto

my back. Manicured fingernails raked the back of my hand as they reached for the phone. I elbowed my assailant and held firm.

"Slow down, Morales. Repeat. Where are you?"

"I said—"

In my ear Navil shrieked, *"Get off the phone!"*

What transpired next forever changed my life.

A sudden impact, swift and true. Intense pressure followed by an electric pain. Every nerve ending in my eighteen-year-old body felt like liquid fire. My blood-curdled scream echoed as the phone flew from my hand and my skull smashed against the wall.

My assailant rode the back of my body face-first onto the bed. More yelling. More screaming. Suddenly, my attacker was yanked off me. I lay there prone. A sour, metallic taste hit the back of my throat. Blood. My blood. I coughed and misted the wall. Navil's hysterics competed with Ginny's.

"I told you to get off the phone!" Navil screeched.

Ginny stood in the middle of the room. *"Oh, my God."*

A small pool of blood slowly stained the comforter beneath me. I lay helpless. Stuck like a Puerto Rican pig roast.

Stefan dealt first with his girlfriend. "Shut the fuck up and get some fucking help."

Pain continued to radiate. I struggled to breathe. Blood dripped down my side.

Stefan turned to Navil. "Why the fuck did you—"

"He *called* the *police.*"

"Who gives a *shit?* You don't, fucking *stab* the guy with a letter *opener.*"

As the pair argued, I rode wave after wave of agony. Tears ran down my cheek.

"What do we do?" Navil asked.

"How the fuck should I know?"

The bedroom door slammed open. I turned my head. Tried to focus. People gathered. Some pointed. Others shrieked.

Mixed in the chaos, Eddie shouted, "Holy shit, is that *Ollie*?"

He ran in and came to my side. "I'm here, Ollie."

From the doorway, a familiar voice. "Get the fuck out of the way."

I recognized it immediately. My eyes widened. Chills ran down my body. He *was* here. At the party. The boogeyman. My cellmate. Ricky Sheridan. Here for the grand finale. His revenge.

With my last ounce of energy, I screamed, *"No!"*

He shoved his way in and got on the bed. "Get the fuck away from him."

I reached for Eddie's arm.

"Don't let him—"

The demon looked around the room. "Who did this?"

My tearful whimpers his only response.

He bent down, shouted in my ear, "Stay with me, Morales. I've got you!"

He *had* me all right.

Our last encounter replayed my mind's eye. As I left the courtroom, I flipped him the bird, and he lost his shit. A bailiff held him back while he swore vengeance. And true to his word, he was there to finish me off.

"Don't just sit there, you morons. Go grab me a towel," Ricky ordered.

More movement around the room. Bile crept into the back of my throat. Mixed with blood. Intense pain combined with nausea. I heard a flutter. Ricky wrapped a thick towel around his hand. Did he plan on smothering me?

"Try to relax, Morales," he whispered. "I'm not going to lie. This is gonna sting."

No countdown, just a sudden jerk followed by my scream.

Sting?

It hurt like a motherfucker. He removed the letter opener from my back, like a chef yanking a spit from a tenderloin. Ricky quickly shoved the towel into my gaping wound. Lightning shot through my body as he applied pressure.

"Has anyone called 9-1-1?" he yelled.

I drifted in and out.

"Come on, kid, stay with me," Ricky ordered. "No one dies on my watch."

I felt a small crowd gathering. More mayhem. Sentences became choppy.

"For fuck . . . Somebody . . . Hand me . . ."

Beeps from a push button cordless phone.

"This . . . Sheridan. My shield number . . ."

More applied pressure. More pain.

"Need a bus at . . ."

The thumping from my heartbeat in my throat. It slowed with every breath. A flash of movement caught my attention. Running out the door. Clothing bundled in her bloodied hands. It was a bathrobe-covered Navil.

The sorrow in her hazel eyes pierced the pending twilight of my existence. My vision narrowed. Her final words whispered through the pandemonium. Reached my ears.

"I'm so sorry, Ollie."

A tearful goodbye followed by—darkness.

CHAPTER EIGHTY-EIGHT

Modern Day

The following day, an Uber driver delivered me to the hospital for my visit with Judge Watson. I hobbled my way to the entrance, and even behind my N95 mask, the stench of death and disinfectant couldn't be hidden.

I took the elevator to the seventh floor and slowly made my way to his room, just around the corner. Outside his door stood a middle-aged man wearing a two-piece navy pinstripe suit. Like me, he wore a mask, and the moment he spotted me, waved me down.

"You must be Mr. Morales."

My eyes narrowed. At this point, I could smell an attorney a mile away.

"And you are?"

"Sorry, I'm Fred Roman," he answered. "A friend of Judge Watson. He told me you'd be stopping by."

"Yes, to see him. He's doing okay, isn't he?" I discreetly asked.

He raised his hands. "Meh, he's doing—"

"Got it," I chuckled. "I spoke with him yesterday."

"He mentioned," Fred replied. "It's why I stuck around."

"Oh?"

"You're not in trouble or anything. I stopped by to visit him, and when he told me about you, I figured it would be easier for you to speak with someone who wasn't, you know—"

"Struggling to breathe?"

"Exactly. Can I buy you a cup of coffee?"

I cautiously accepted his offer. "Sure, but I'll buy, since I'm asking the questions."

"Fair enough. After you."

We exchange small talk as we slowly make our way to the elevators. I learned he'd known the judge for about fifteen years.

"I clerked for him right out of law school."

"Oh yeah? Where'd you go?"

"Princeton."

"The Tigers. Good school. I'm a Hoya myself."

"No kidding. I was there in '89 when you guys beat us in the tournament."

I laughed. "Oh my God, so was I. That game was insane."

The whole way down to the café on the first floor, Fred and I talked about the 1989 NCAA Division I men's basketball tournament first round match between the Princeton University Tigers and the Georgetown Hoyas.

It was a collegiate classic, featuring the likes of future NBA all-stars Alonzo Mourning and Dikembe Mutombo.

"I still can't believe Mourning blocked that final shot." Fred shook his head as we waited for our coffees and scones to arrive.

"An order for Ollie?" A cashier calls out.

"Right here," he replied and turned to me. "I'll grab these. Why don't you find us a place to sit."

I nodded and trudged my way to the first clean empty table. Fred soon joined me and placed the breakfast tray on the table.

"So, what's on your mind?" Fred asked.

I removed a notepad and pen from my jacket, with questions scribbled for the judge.

"Before we start, how much background do you need?"

"I think I'm up to speed," he answered. "You were attacked at the Capitol and want to visit this person in jail. Is that the gist?"

"Pretty much," I confirmed. "What kind of impact would it have—"

"Let me stop you right there. I'm currently a deputy district attorney, so, if *I* were prosecuting this case, I'd never let you within a thousand yards of that defendant, or prison."

"How come?"

"Regardless of your intent, the defense would use the visit against the government," Fred responded. "Let me ask you something. Why do you want to visit this person in the first place? Are you seeking vengeance? Retribution?"

"That's a good question. How much time do you have?" I joked.

He looked at his watch, "I have to be in court around three thirty, so I have time."

I took a bite of my orange cranberry scone. "To be honest with you, I don't know."

"Don't you think—"

"I should know the reason behind my visit."

He nodded.

"I have so many questions."

"Such as?"

"Why?"

"Why what?"

This was starting to feel like a therapy session with Cynthia. I took a sip of coffee.

"When was the last time you saw this person?" he asked.

"In person or my nightmares?"

"That bad, huh?"

"Let's just say, it's been a long while since I've seen her."

"So, she's a person from your past."

"Yeah."

"How did things end?"

I tapped my cane against my walking boot. "How do you think?"

He chuckled. "I meant in the past. When you last saw her."

Navil's penetrating eyes and smile came to mind. As did the blood. "Not good."

"Oh yeah?"

I slowly shook my head.

"And you haven't kept in touch? Followed each other on the socials?"

I let out a breath. "Nope. Not since the trial."

"What trial?"

The words got stuck in my throat.

"After the stabbing."

Fred leans forward. "Go on."

I shared my story. My *whole* story.

CHAPTER EIGHTY-NINE

"Wow." He whistled. "Regardless, if you have a history with this person, and were attacked by her at the Mall, there's no way I'd let you see her before a trial."

Damnit.

Not the news I want to hear.

"And not just me. I doubt the prison would allow it either."

I drained the remainder of my java. Thought for a moment.

"What about after?" I inquired.

"The trial, you mean?"

I nodded.

"That's different."

"How so?"

"Let's assume she's convicted for her current activities and has to serve jail time."

"Okay."

"And she's sentenced to a federal prison."

I sat forward.

"Well, like everything else, there's a process you have to follow."

I began scribbling notes. "Go on."

Fred is very professorial with his insights. He took his time. Provided me with examples. Things to consider and avoid. Shared useful information, like websites to visit, and people he recommended I contact before I began my journey.

We shook hands, and I thanked him for his time.

"My pleasure. I'd do just about anything for Justice Watson."

"Seems like a good man."

"The best." He pridefully smiled.

While waiting for my Uber to arrive, I began planning my next steps. Step one, locate the inmate.

But first . . .

"How are we doing today, Ollie?"

"Hi, Cynthia. Nice, um, office."

"Thanks." She cocked a brow. "Everything okay? You seem—"

"Off?"

A nod.

"Yeah. I'm . . ." I struggled for the right words.

"Why don't you take a seat over here."

She gestured to a comfortably oversized chair with no scent. No perfume. Nor an ounce of cologne. Not even a hint of disinfectant. I made a mental note to ask how this was possible.

With concern in her eyes, she says, "Why don't you tell me what's going on."

"I met with an attorney today."

"Having legal trouble?"

"Thankfully, no. Not really." I laughed.

"That's good. So, why did you meet with—"

"Fred. Nice guy. Gave me a lot to think about."

She began taking notes. "Such as?"

I slicked back my graying locks and scratched my scruff. Thought for a moment and drew a blank.

"Why don't we start from the beginning."

I spent the next twenty minutes sharing my story. Periodically, Cynthia would stop me and ask a question or two. Caused me to peel back the onion of my life.

"First loves can have a lasting impact on our lives. Especially ones that ended—"

"With so much blood?"

Her face filled with empathy. "Is this why you think you're so—"

"Fixated?"

"That's one way to put it."

"I don't know. Maybe."

"And after that incident, you never heard from her again?"

"I never said that."

"So, what happened afterward?"

"After the stabbing, you mean?"

Cynthia nodded.

CHAPTER NINETY

1986

I woke up screaming in a hospital bed. My back ached and familiar hands held me down.

"Ollie, hijo, we're here!" Pop shouted over my screams.

Someone ran to my bedside.

"Do it," Pop ordered.

A rush of warmth filled my body. Everything faded to black. Time passed. Beeping noises awakened me.

"Ollie?" Tía Carolina soothingly called. "Are you awake?"

I tried to focus. Everything remained foggy. Tía Carolina and Pop stood over me. Questions from both. Their words blending with the foreign sounds from the various monitors and equipment that kept me on this side of the dirt. A sharp pain caused me to hiss.

Someone gently lifted me forward. A nurse. My hospital gown slipped down. Exposed my wound. A ripping sound from my dressing being removed. Soothing cool liquid applied below my shoulder blade. She gently patted excess fluid from my wound. I flinched.

Fresh tape and gauze reapplied, and I was delicately laid back down. Blinked away the fog. Got a good look at my caregiver. She's young. Couldn't be more than a few years older than me. A brunette. Dark eyes. Pretty smile. Reminded me of Fi.

She told me her name, and it was forgotten the moment it left her mouth.

"How are we feeling?" she whispered.

Words escaped me.

"It's okay," she said. "Rest."

I mouthed a response.

She pointed out the call button. "Press this if you need anything."

I drifted off. Time passed. Hunger pangs roused me. My stomach grumbled. Movement from the corner of the room. Pop rushed to my side.

"Hey, bub. How're you feeling?"

My mouth was dry. It was like waking up from a nightmare.

I rubbed my eyes. "Pop, what happened?"

Electric pain radiated from my wound. I shrieked at the spasm.

"Easy, Ollie," he whispered as I rode the lightning. "I've got you."

It took forever to dissipate. I struggled to breathe. He handed me a cup of water.

"Take sips," he ordered.

The cooling liquid soothed my throat and body. I took in my surroundings.

"Can you remember anything?" Pop asked. "Who did this to you, and why?"

Images from the party burst across my mental landscape. Eddie hit on some girl. Kyle Fergusen bullied his sister Mary into snorting something off a mirrored surface. Navil's loving eyes and sexy smile.

Inviting.

Perfect and pure.

The curve of her neck.

Naked breasts.

A flower tattoo strategically hidden from inquisitive eyes.

Red and golden.

"Golden," I whispered.

"What'd you say, son?"

I blinked.

Jackie's blue and gold notebook.

I gasped and sat up like a rocket. "*Pop*. We've got to call the police."

"Easy, Oliver. You'll—"

"No, Pop. I—"

My sudden movement disturbed my wound. Another current of pain. Tears streamed down my face. Raw like the flood of emotions that flowed.

Pop held me. "I've got you, Ollie."

I gathered my thoughts and found my voice.

"Pop, you don't understand—"

"No, son, you don't understand. You're just out of surgery and need your rest."

"But Pop—"

"Don't *but Pop* me. You're lucky to be alive. Do you have any idea how close that knife was to your heart?"

For the first time since my mother passed away, I saw tears in my father's eyes. I opened my mouth but held my tongue.

Through quivered lips, "I almost lost you today."

Tears fell.

"I knew I shouldn't have let you go to *esa maldita* party," he said.

I learned early to never argue with him when he cursed in Spanish.

"If that detective hadn't been there—"

"Wait. What detective?"

"Hold on. I've got his business card right here." He reached into his pants pocket. "Here we go, a Detective Sheridan."

I mouthed the name.

"He said he knew you, which surprised me."

My face twerked.

"Never heard of him. Are you sure it wasn't Detective Gallagher?"

He handed me the card.

It read like any other business card. It had his name, rank, division, department, phone number, and precinct address.

"Detective Ricardo Sheridan, Narcotics Division. Suffolk County Police Department," I read aloud. "This makes no sense. Why would—"

I gasped.

"Hijo, are you okay?"

My eyes widened.

"Ollie?"

I dropped the business card like it was on fire.

"Son, what's the matter?"

"Do you have any idea who *that* is?"

He shook his head.

"That's *Ricky*."

CHAPTER NINETY-ONE

What was that old saying, "Speak of the devil and he shall appear"? Almost as if on cue, the moment his name escaped my lips, a well-dressed Ricky entered my room.

I shrieked.

"Jesus, kid. Calm down," Ricky ordered. "I was just coming to check on you."

I pointed at him like he was death incarnate. "That's him, Pop. That's the guy who—"

"Who saved you, Ollie," Pop stated. "Hello, Detective."

Pop welcomed him warmly.

"How's he doing, Doc?"

My father replied, "He's getting there; although, I think he could use—"

"An explanation?"

Ricky pulled over a chair and kicked his heels up on the corner of the bed.

"Just so you know—"

I shrank back, eyes narrowed.

"You screwed up a perfectly good investigation."

"How so, Detective?" Pop asked.

Ricky explained that he'd been undercover for months, chasing after the Sutherland brothers and their drug operation.

"I'm sorry. Did you say—"

"Drugs? Yeah," Ricky flatly replied. "Royce and that brother of his—"

"Stefan," I chimed in.

"That's him. Those two morons flew back and forth to Colombia by way of—"

"Ecuador," I whispered.

"You've been paying attention." He sounded surprised. "Good for you."

I scoffed.

Pop shot me a look. "Sorry, Detective. You were saying?"

"They'd been transporting cocaine back and forth, and I was about to bust them at that party, when this one decided to get himself stabbed."

"Not like I asked for it," I barked.

"Ain't what I heard," he retorted.

"Fu—"

"*Oliver*. Detective. Please," Pop interjected, "continue."

Ricky smiled at my scowl.

"Not much left to say. I had a choice. Save your son, or—"

"And we all appreciate it, right, Ollie?"

I pursed my lips.

"I said, *right*, Oliver?"

"Fine, yeah. Thank you," I scoffed. "Happy now?"

"Excuse him, Detective."

Ricky stood and mouthed, "Blame it on the medication."

Pop extended his hand, and Ricky shook it. He patted my shoulder and wished me a good recovery. On his way out the door, Pop asked him a question.

"Detective. Will you still be able to—"

"Charge these people?" He shrugged. "Depends on the DA."

"What about the person who stabbed my son?"

"We're still looking for her."

That caught my attention. "What do you mean, you're still—"

"I mean, she hitched a ride back to school, and we lost track of her from there."

"Is my boy still in danger?" Pop asked with concern.

"Doubt it," he replied. "My guess—"

Pop and I leaned forward.

"She hopped a train to Penn Station and fled into the city," he stated.

I was shocked by this outcome.

"Hey, Ricky? Can I ask you a question?"

"Shoot."

"In jail. Why were you—"

"Such a dick?"

"Yeah."

He smiled. "Like I've explained to my ten-year-old Karen. We all have roles to play."

I chewed on his comment.

"When I heard we had a kid in lockup from that school of yours, I had to check you out. See if you were part of the Sutherland crew who caught a bad break."

"I'm not."

"I realized that. It's why I let you go."

"You didn't let—"

He smiled. "Ollie, if I'd found out you were part of my investigation, there's no way you would have left lockup. Gallagher, Chao, and I would have found a way to keep you there."

My eyes narrowed.

"So, they were in on it?"

"In enough."

"What about Officer Wallace?"

"What about him?"

"Was he in on it?"

"No." He shook his head. "I mean, he knew who I was, but not why I was in the cell with you. That was purely *need to know*."

I furrowed my brows. "Then how come—"

Ricky sighed, "Because the man's an asshole. They're everywhere, right, Doc?"

Pop's eyes widened and acquiesced with a nod.

"Listen, I'm running late," Ricky informed us. "Take care of yourself, kid. Put all this behind you. Go and live a good and healthy life."

"I'll try." I smiled. "And Ricky . . . I mean, Detective?"

He smiled from the doorway.

"Thanks for saving me."

My savior chucked me a half-smile and left the room. A few hours later, I received another unexpected visitor.

"Come in," a visiting Tía Carolina called out.

CHAPTER NINETY-TWO

With Navil on the loose, and all Pop's hospital clout, he asked the administration to post a security guard outside my room. The guard poked his head in.

"You have a visitor."

Behind him stood a pink pajamas-wearing Jackie, holding a teddy bear.

I waved her in. "It's okay. I know her."

As she shuffled in, I sat up and straightened my hair. "Hey, Jackie."

"I thought we agreed on Jack?" she teased.

I chuckled, "Right. Sorry. I don't know if you remember—"

"Your Tía Carolina? Sure. Hi."

After exchanging niceties, she came over and gave me a gentle hug.

"Are you okay?" she whispered.

I attempted a reassuring smile and failed miserably.

She placed her warm hand on my cheek. "I'm so sorry you got hurt."

"How'd you—"

"Hear about it?" She smiled proudly. "I have my sources."

I joked. "Once a reporter—"

"You know it." She laughed.

In mid-banter, Tía Carolina stood. "I am going to go."

"You don't need—" Jackie objected.

"I can see he's in good hands." Tía smiled. "Jaime will be home soon from school, and I need to get home and start dinner."

"Okay," I replied.

She kissed my cheek and bopped my nose. "Be nice, pendejo."

"Yeah, yeah."

"It was nice seeing you again. I hope you feel better."

"Thank you," Jackie replied. "I'm getting out soon."

Surprised, I asked, "You are?"

"Yeah. I was hoping to surprise you at school this week, but—"

I pursed my lips and made room for her on the bed.

"I'm surprised your folks aren't sending you home."

"We fought about it, but—"

"Shit, I would have left skid marks."

She laughed. "And let them win? Fuck that."

"Well, at least you're finally getting out of this place."

"I can't wait."

"I bet."

"But enough about me. I'm here to see you, not the other way around."

I rolled my eyes. "Yes, ma'am."

We held each other's smile for a moment. It was the first time I'd noticed cute freckles on the bridge of her nose. She broke eye contact first.

Jackie then grew pensive, "So, is it true what I heard?"

"Depends." I chuckled. "What'd you hear?"

She weighed her response. "That it was, um, Navil—"

I twitched involuntarily and felt a sting of pain when I heard her name.

"It's true," I breathed.

Jackie placed a caring hand on my forearm. I stared at my bedcovers. Silent. Downcast. The wound from Navil's betrayal hurt as much as the stitches in my back. My lips trembled.

"I'm so sorry, Ollie."

I bit down. Took a breath.

"Thanks, Jack."

She gently wrapped her arms around me. Held me close. We stayed this way for a while. Silent. Comforting. The only thought that crossed my mind at that moment was— I couldn't believe, of all the people in the world, it was Jackie Woodley who comforted me.

"Can I ask another question?"

I sat back. "Of course, Jack."

"I heard all this happened because of my notebook. Is that true?"

The expression on my face answered her question. Sadness immediately filled her eyes.

"I'm sorry, Jack."

She turned away.

I took her hand. "Look, it's not your fault."

"Really? Then, whose is it?"

"It's not like you gave her the blade and told her to *stab me*," I angrily hissed.

My eye twitched as my heart filled with rage. The incident replayed in my head. My breathing increased as my blood pressure soared, and my fists clenched. In retrospect, I was surprised I didn't have a stroke. My response caused Jackie to shuffle away from me.

We were both recent victims of assault, so the last thing she needed was to be on the receiving end of a violent outburst. When I noticed her reaction, I immediately calmed down and apologized.

"Jackie, I'm sorry. I didn't mean to scare you. It's just—"

I couldn't finish my sentence. I was an emotional wreck. I placed my face into my hands and cried bitter tears.

Comforting arms wrapped around me.

"Shh, you'll be okay, Ollie," she whispered. "I'm here."

Jackie rocked me gently as I soaked her shoulder. My implosive pity party lasted a few minutes.

"Better?" she asked when I stopped crying.

I nodded. "Thanks, Jack."

She wiped my tears with a tissue. "No need to thank me. It's what friends are for, right?"

"Yeah." I smiled.

She reciprocated. The room grew quiet. I stared at her lips. Full. And her eyes. Brown with tiny green flecks surrounding the iris.

I inched closer and she didn't back away. We leaned toward one another. Tilted our heads. Closed our eyes and opened our mouths slightly.

A commotion outside my room. Intimacy interrupted. The door burst open. I instinctively placed myself between Jackie and the intruder.

"I said, I know him!" The voice of my neighbor and best friend yelled. "Now get the hell—"

"It's okay!" I shouted. "I know her. You can let her in."

"See? I told you," Fi scoffed. "Jesus. It's like you're the president or something."

I shot the guard an apologetic look as Jackie slid away, and Fi pounced.

"I was so worried about you," she whispered.

"Gently," I said.

Jackie pulled at Fi. "You're *hurting* him."

"What?" Fi replied. "Oh my God, I'm so sorry. I didn't—

I held my hand up, "It's okay."

"You sure?" she asked. "If I hurt you . . ."

"Fi, I'll be okay. You just pulled on the stiches. That's all. I'm fine."

"You're not, though. That *bitch* stabbed you."

I sighed.

"When I get my hands on her . . ."

"Easy, Rambo."

"How can you joke about this?" Fi asked. "She could have killed you."

Tell me about it.

"Fi, it was only a flesh wound. Seriously, I'm—"

"If you *fucking* say that you're *fine* one more time . . ."

Jackie stood. "I think I'll leave you two."

"No, Jack. Stay," I insisted.

Fi's brow furrowed in confusion and exchanged a curious look between Jackie and me, sensing something different in the air.

"What?" I asked.

"Yeah, what?" Jackie nervously played with the drawstrings of her pj's.

"Nothing," Fi slowly answered. "Did I interru—"

I needed to throw her off her game, to disrupt her focus somehow.

"Uh . . . how'd your thing go? Did you *hook up* with Fireman Timmy?"

My question flustered Fi. Her ivory skin flushed crimson.

My eyes widened. "O my God, you *did.*"

CHAPTER NINETY-THREE

"I did *not* hook up with him." Fi's voice filled with indignation.

"Tell your face that," I shot back. "Come here. I want to check your neck."

I reached for her collar.

She slapped my hand away. "Get away from me."

I waved it around and sucked in air to reduce the sting.

"Good. Serves you right," Fi said.

Jackie chuckled. "Are you two sure you're not related?"

"He wishes," Fi joked with a slight shove.

"Yeah, right."

Her tone changed to one of concern. "Seriously, though. You're doing okay?"

I nodded. "Pop said that the surgeon did a good job."

"I still can't believe this."

I tried changing the subject. "Can we just—"

But Fi didn't take the hint.

"Why'd she do it?" Fi asked.

"I got nothing, Fi."

"You have *no* idea why she did it?"

"Like I said, one minute I'm on the phone with the cops, the next she's on my back, yelling at me to hang up the phone. Next thing you know—" I mimicked getting stabbed.

"But why were you on the phone with the police?"

I glanced at Jackie and Fi followed my gaze.

"Just tell her," Jackie said.

I sighed. "I found her notebook."

Fi jerked her head back, "What do you mean you *found it*?"

As I explained what had happened, Jackie fidgeted, while Fi grew angry.

"Wait a minute," Fi spat out and got in Jackie's face. "You mean to tell me that if you hadn't written all those things in your stupid notebook—"

I grabbed her arm. "Easy, Fi."

She yanked away. "Let go of me, Ollie."

Jackie's face filled with guilt, and she couldn't maintain eye contact with Fi.

"So, all of this is *your fault*?"

"I didn't mean to."

"Ignore her, Jackie. It's not—"

"Didn't mean to?" Fi continued. "Do you realize that he could have been killed? And for what? *Gossip*? Your grand exposé?"

Jackie's head dropped.

"Fi, for Christ's sake, calm down."

She stared daggers at me. "Don't fucking tell me to calm down."

"It wasn't her fault."

"Really? Then whose was it?"

"It was *mine*, all right?" I shouted. "Mine."

My response shocked and silenced Fi. Jackie, on the other hand, started crying. I tried to reach for her, but she ran out of the room with her face buried in her hands.

"Happy now?" I yelled at FI.

"Ollie, how can you think this was your fault?"

"Seriously?" I replied. "That's your problem with all this?"

"Ols, it wasn't your fault."

"Then whose was it?"

"Jackie's," she stated. "And the bitch who stabbed you."

I shut my eyes and let out a long breath.

"You weren't there, Fi," I whispered. "If I hadn't picked up that phone . . ."

She placed her hand on my shoulder. "It wasn't your fault."

"Yeah. It was."

The events replayed in my head. Navil stepped out of the bathroom. Arms raised. Steam billowed around her. Naked as a jaybird. Proud. Sexy. Inviting. And stupid me. Dumbstruck. On the phone, like an idiot.

A sorrowful tear fell down my cheek.

"Ols."

"I should've left it all alone. Instead of acting like a hero. Like I solved the crime of the century."

"Well, you sort of did."

"But what'd it cost me?" I asked. "My girlfriend grabs a knife and sticks me like a pig. Damn near murdered me. And for what?"

"I don't—"

"Know what to say? I'll answer the question for you. For nothing. She escapes, and that asshole Stefan and his drug-dealing brother will probably get off."

"We don't know that. For all we know, they already tracked her down, and—"

"Uh-huh," I scoffed. "With my luck, she's landing in Belgium as we speak."

"And if she is, they will arrest her when she lands."

"With her connections?" I scoffed.

"What do you mean, her—"

"Fi, her father works for their government. You don't think he has connections?"

She sat back and weighed this information.

"There's no way they're going to allow their daughter to go

down for stabbing some Puerto Rican kid back in the States. They'll find a way to blame me or claim it was self-defense."

"But she stabbed you in the back."

"You don't think I know that?"

Fi sat back and pursed her lips, while I took a deep breath, trying to calm down.

"Look. Who knows what's going to happen? All I know is it wasn't Jackie's fault."

"Okay, Ols," Fi replied. "I won't argue with you about this."

"Good. Thank you."

She nodded.

"Now, tell me about your shindig."

She smiled.

"More importantly, who made the first move, you or Fireman Timmy?"

Her eyes narrowed, "I hate you."

I laughed.

CHAPTER NINETY-FOUR

A few days later, Pop allowed me to go home. He said I'd be safer there since my aunt was always around. He wasn't wrong, I supposed.

Still.

I felt more like a prisoner than a patient the moment I got home. The two of them tracked my every movement.

"What are you doing out of your room?" Tía yelled.

"I've got to pee."

"Make it quick," she barked.

You forgot to call me inmate.

On the flipside, she was always the first person in my room whenever a nightmare woke me, which felt like a nightly occurrence.

She'd wrap me in her arms and say, "It's okay, hijo. You're safe. Tía's here."

My first night home, Fi came over. She shared that word of my stabbing spread across campus like wildfire. The rumors ranged from Navil and I participating in a weird sex game, to us getting high, and things getting out of hand. Aside from a select few, the people who knew the truth were either expelled, behind bars, or on the run.

The latter concerned me the most. For my first few nights home, I flinched every time a branch scraped against my bedroom window. I thought Navil had come over to finish the job. She became my boogeyman.

Tía Carolina blamed it on all the horror movies that Fi and I watched, like *The Omen* and *Friday the Thirteenth*. It didn't help that my room was on the ground floor, and if you wanted to break in, my bedroom window was the ideal choice.

While convalescing, I received a few pleasant and surprising visits. My headmaster stopped by, along with our jovial Dean of Students, Mr. Digman, who joked that he'd seen students go to great lengths to get out of school, but getting stabbed took the cake.

When Mrs. C visited, Tía Carolina treated her to a delicious arroz con pollo dinner.

"I let Byron know what happened," she said between bites.

Thinking this was bad news, I simply replied, "Oh."

"Ollie." She reached over and took my hand. "He's volunteered to go through your negatives and choose shots for your project, pending your approval, of course."

My eyes widened. "Seriously? I mean, yeah, I approve."

"We thought you might," she replied. "He wanted to know if he could stop by this—"

"Absolutely. Anytime."

Of course, the downside to her visit was the mountain of homework she left me.

"I figured you could use the distraction." She grinned.

With Fi's help, Pop retrieved my car from Miller Place. As if she wasn't already a fixture in my place, Fi spent most of her free time by my side. She watched over me like a hawk. Between her, Tía Carolina, and Bella, I don't know who offered me better protection.

Toward the end of the week, I received another unexpected visit. I was hanging out in my bedroom watching television, waiting for dinner, when someone knocked on my door. Given the time, I thought it was dinner, so I responded with my typical panache.

"Go away. Nobody's home. We gave at the office."

The door opened slowly, and in stepped Jackie wearing a skirt and sweater as opposed to the pink pj's she wore in the hospital.

"Can I come in?"

I straightened up. "Jack. What are you doing here?"

"I thought I'd surprise you." She smiled. "So, surprise!"

I waved her in. "Come on in."

I looked behind her, but she was alone. After an awkward hug, due to my injury, I slid over and made room on my bed for her to sit.

"How're you feeling?"

I shrugged.

"I still can't believe someone stabbed you."

"Yeah. And over what? A stupid journal?" I stated. "No offense."

"None taken, Ollie," she replied. "I'm just sorry that you got hurt."

"So am I."

She reached out and took my hand. I didn't pull away. We sat quietly for a moment. A *Crazy Eddie* commercial filled the silent void. We both laughed at the end when he said, "In-sane." It broke the tension.

"Did Fiona tell you about Ginny, Alli, and Giles Denton getting arrested?"

"No way." I playfully shoved her. "When?"

"Ginny, the night of the party," she stated. "Alli and Giles, Tuesday morning at school. All part of the drug ring."

"No shit."

"It happened right outside the dining hall after breakfast. The police pulled up with a warrant for their arrest."

"Wow." I whistled.

"Slapped handcuffs on them and took them both away."

The weight of my arrest played vividly in my mind's eye.

"The whole thing was so—"

"Surreal."

"Exactly."

"What about—"

"Stefan and his brother, Royce?"

I nodded.

"Something about an undercover cop tracked them down and took them in."

"Fucking Ricky." I smiled. "Cool."

Jackie furrowed her brows but didn't ask what I meant.

"Anyway, that's the latest," she concluded.

I smirked. It seemed like the old Jackie was back in action. Chasing down the latest story.

"Why are you smiling?"

"No reason." I chuckled. "Still no word on Navil?"

"No. She's still at large."

I let out a heavy breath. She squeezed my hand.

"I'm sure they'll find her."

Anger stirred within me. I had to look away. Noticed a spider climb up my wall. Yet another thing to worry about. My body tensed as the incident replayed in my mind's eye.

Ginny's scream echoed through the chaos. Ricky's urgent orders. Outside the bedroom door, onlookers, and pandemonium. I watched in disbelief as Navil, half-dressed, slipped away. Her parting words silently pierced the commotion. Crimson blood splattered across the wall, a grim testament to the recent violence. Throughout it all, a sharp, agonizing pain ripped through me.

"Ollie, you still with me?" Jackie whispered.

"Yeah, sorry. Every time I think about her . . ."

"You remember."

I nodded. Jackie slid forward. Caressed my face. I placed my head on her shoulders. Tears stained her sweater. She held me till Tía Carolina stopped in to invite Jackie to stay for dinner.

She smiled and said, "I'd love to."

CHAPTER NINETY-FIVE

Returning to school wasn't easy. Everywhere I turned, reminders of Navil flooded my senses, whether it was passing by the library or walking past her dorm. Classmates' judgmental gazes weighed heavily on me. Graduation couldn't arrive soon enough.

Some students, most likely clients, blamed me for Stefan and his drug dealing crew getting expelled. They argued that if I hadn't attended his party, none of this would have happened. While I couldn't argue with their logic, they weren't the ones on the receiving end of a letter opener plunged into their back.

Over lunch, Jackie shared the latest, "Have you heard?"

"What?" I asked.

"Stefan's out of jail."

"You've *got* to be kidding me," I spat.

"Something about his parent's political connections and his age."

I felt heat rising up my neck and knew my blood pressure was rising.

She continued, "Apparently, he paid a fine and moved on with his life."

Gotta love the justice system.

We soon learned that Royce, Stefan's older brother, wasn't as lucky. The authorities leaned hard on him. The local paper named him the ringleader of the drug crew and dubbed him the Prep School Peddler.

To avoid a prison sentence, Royce agreed to testify against his suppliers, and never saw Christmas that year. En route to meet with his attorney, he took two bullets to the back of the head, execution-style. The police investigated, but came up short, and the DA's office moved on to their next high-profile case.

Something about Mary Fergusen's father, Gus, and embezzlement of funds. Eventually, though, things at school settled back into place. Like before, I spent most of my free time hanging out in the photo lab with my merry band of burgeoning photogs.

And when she wasn't chasing her latest story, Jackie hung out on the old sofa next to Fi. Due to her reputation, others felt uncomfortable. Eddie pulled me aside one afternoon and questioned why she was there.

"Just give her a chance," I told him. "She's cooler than you think."

"If you say so."

Of course, that didn't stop her from busting my stones during our school newspaper meetings. Now, though, I noticed the twinkle in her eye. Our banter turned into a secret code between us.

The more she made fun of my work—"You call that photography?"

The more fun we had—"It's better than that garbage you write."

Of course, not everyone understood.

"Okay, you two," Mrs. C cautioned, "play nice."

Speaking of Mrs. C, her cousin, Byron, was true to his word. While he never stopped by my house to check on me, he did review my work. And I mean all of it.

Over pizza, he commented, "Ollie, I must say, you've really improved."

"You think so?"

"Between your junior and senior years, you really took it to the next level."

We began sorting sample shots. First up, nature shots from Tía Carolina's vegetable garden I took in tenth grade.

"These, for example. They're a bit off-center. Some are out of focus."

I was a bit embarrassed by these pictures.

"And then these—"

Pictures from a cross-country meet featuring a female student who huffed and puffed as she ran by.

"That's Nina Ruiz," I told him. "She graduated last year."

"I love the expression you captured on her face. Full of intent."

I took pride in this. The next series hit me between the short hairs.

"This one—" he paused "—needs to be the centerpiece of your showcase."

My heart ached as I stared at the photo.

"In my opinion, it's an award-winning shot."

He spent the next few minutes complimenting me on my style.

"The expression in her eyes. And that coy smile. Like she's hiding a great secret. This one's something special."

He didn't need to tell me twice.

The more he spoke, the deeper the ache.

"You can call it *The Girl with Fury in Her Eyes.*"

All I could say back was, "Thanks, Byron."

Discomfort bled out of me like a stuck pig at a Hawaiian luau. I tried to hide my pain and failed miserably.

His artistic eye noticed. "Is everything okay, Ollie? You seem—"

I let out a sorrowful breath and turned my head.

"What's the matter? Was it something I said?"

My wounded heart flared with pain.

"No," I whispered.

"Then, what's wrong?"

I gestured toward the photo, "It's—"

He immediately put two and two together.

"Is this the girl who—"

"Yeah." I exhaled.

He turned the print over. "I'm sorry, Ollie. I had no idea."

"It's okay. Not your fault."

He leaned forward. "Look. Why don't we choose—"

I shook my head. "No. You're right. It needs to be the center-piece. Especially after what happened."

"Are you sure?" he asked. "It won't be too painful?"

"Isn't that the point?"

"Pain?"

"Authenticity."

Byron rubbed his chin and considered my comment.

"I suppose," he replied. "That's a rather mature attitude."

I shrugged.

"Given all that's happened, will your school allow it to go up?"

"Like my father says, permission versus forgiveness."

He chuckled, "We'll figure it out together. In the meantime, there's a lot of good material to choose from here. Oh, before I forget—"

I arched a brow.

"I spoke with my friend, Alfonso." He smiled broadly.

"Alfonso?"

"He's the one with the gallery in The Village. Named it after himself.

"O-kay."

"I convinced him to exhibit your work."
Holy shit.

CHAPTER NINETY-SIX

My jaw hung open. I sat there, speechless. He beamed with pride.

"Of course, we'll have to get your father's permission."

"Y-y-you'll get it."

"Good."

"I don't know what to say."

He leaned back and brushed it off like it was no big deal.

"Seriously, Byron. Thank you."

"Are you kidding me?" He smiled. "I should be thanking you, kid."

"Me? Why?"

"This—exercise. It's really taken me back. Ya know what I mean?"

I began to nod, and then shook my head no.

"You will." Byron nodded. "One day, you'll be the old fart seated across from this young upstart at the beginning of his career. The sun peeking over the horizon."

The man had a way with words.

"You'll see." His eyes twinkled.

Two weeks prior to my showcase, Mrs. C delivered her son Caleb, and Byron was called away on assignment. Talk about shitty timing. I lost not one, but two of my mentors and safety nets. Before leaving, Byron connected me with his friend Alfonso, the gallery owner.

"I told him all about you. Just give Fonz a call, and he'll take care of everything."

I became a nervous wreck.

"Ols, you're worse than a stage mom at a beauty contest," Jackie said. "You've got this."

Speaking of Jackie, she asked me to the prom. We were walking out of class together when she pulled me aside.

"Ols, have a second?"

"Sure, Jack. What's up?"

Students meandered past us on their way to class. She turned her head and bit her lower lip.

"What's the—"

"Will you go with me to the prom?"

My head jerked back.

"Uh—"

Her hands fluttered. "You know what? Never—"

"Yeah, no. I'd love to."

She smiled and gave me a big hug, which I returned. And just like that, I had a date to the prom. Fi took a page out of Jackie's book and asked Fireman Timmy to escort her.

Before the prom, the four of us had dinner at *The Devil's Advocate* in downtown Port Jeff near the Long Island Sound. The restaurant had a nautical theme and was known for their overpriced burgers and serving alcohol to minors.

Jackie looked great that evening. Her hair swept up into an elegant updo, she wore a seafoam green dress with matching shoes and pearls. Fi wore her blue cocktail dress and gold cross.

Timmy and I both wore basic black tuxedos with boutonnieres matching our date's dress colors. He looked like James Bond, while I felt like a troll standing next to him. Jackie didn't seem to mind.

They had the classic French dessert, crème brûlée, on the

menu that evening. The moment I saw it, I immediately thought of Navil and grew quiet, which Jackie noticed.

"Ols, you okay?"

I lied, "Yeah, I'm okay."

She saw right through me.

"Wanna take a walk?"

"What about the check?"

She held up her father's credit card. "Already taken care of."

I shook my head and chuckled.

"Hey, guys, Ollie and I are going to take a walk."

"Everything okay?" Fi asked.

"Yeah. Just want some fresh air," Jackie replied. "I took care of the check."

"Thanks, Jackie," Fi said.

"Yeah, thanks. You didn't have to do that," Fireman Timmy interjected.

"I know." She smiled and stood.

"Well, don't get lost, you two. The limo will be back soon."

"He'll wait," I shot back.

I took Jackie's hand and left the restaurant. It was a typical busy Saturday night downtown. Locals and tourists milled about. Jackie and I stuck out like sore thumbs, dressed in our formal wear, but we didn't care. Since we were near the docks, we crossed the street and took a seat on a nearby wooden bench.

Waves gently crashed onto the shore as we huddled close to one another and enjoyed the pleasant spring evening.

Jackie broke our silence. "So, what's wrong?"

"Nothing."

"Ollie. I can tell when something's bothering you. What is it? You can tell me."

"Off the record, you mean?" I joked.

She elbowed me. I laughed. I stared off into the distance.

"It's just—"

"Navil?"

I nodded.

"Was it something I said?"

"No, Jack, no. It wasn't you."

She looked up at me with her big brown eyes.

"I still can't believe they haven't caught her."

Jackie sat silent. Allowed me to process my thoughts.

"She stabbed me," I spat. "And for what? Her stupid secrets?"

"They were pretty big secrets, Ollie."

"I'm sorry, but an abortion and tattoo are *not* worth stabbing me for."

She sighed, "You're not wrong."

CHAPTER NINETY-SEVEN

"By the way, how did you find out about all this?" I asked.

Her lips pressed together, and she turned her head.

"Jack, where did you get your information?"

She moved her head from side to side.

I grew impatient. "Jack . . ."

She faced me. "I accidently found her test results."

"What do you mean, you—"

"Remember the night of your Mel Brooks party?"

"It wasn't really a party but go on."

"Well, I ran out of socks and searched her drawers for a pair to borrow."

I stared at her.

"Well, I found a hidden piece of paper tucked beneath her bras. I guess my curiosity got the better of me."

"And?"

"Turns out it was the results of a pregnancy test. She tested positive."

"But wouldn't it have been in French?"

"They were. But I speak it fluently."

"Since when?"

"I don't know. Since always." She shrugged. "My parents have a chateau right outside of Paris in Chantilly. My mother and I spend most of our summers there."

Of course you do.

"I think it's the main reason why they assigned us to share a room."

"Makes sense."

"Anyway, she walked in on me and lost it."

"I bet."

"She accused me of snooping around in her things. Threatened to beat me up if I told anyone. Especially you."

I pictured the scene.

"I promised her I wouldn't—"

"But she didn't believe you."

"No. I think it's why she threw a rock at my head."

Holy fuck, it was her all along.

"After that I wrote about it in my journal, just in case. I told her if she tried anything again, I'd expose her."

I slumped forward. "Did she ever tell the truth about anything?"

Jackie took my hand.

"If it'll make you feel any better, I think you were a good influence on her."

"What do you mean?"

"She stopped sneaking out at night when you two got together."

"Sneaking—"

"When she first got to school, she used to sneak out every weekend."

"Really?"

"She invited me to come, but I told her no. I didn't have a fake ID."

I stared into the distance.

"She'd come back hammered. Some Sundays, I'd have to help her get dressed for morning chapel."

I couldn't believe what I was hearing.

"But when she met you, that all stopped."

Her comment put a smile on my face, till I remembered everything about Navil was a lie. Our limo pulled up behind us and blew its horn.

"Hey. Come on, you two. Time to go," Fi yelled out the window.

The last thing I wanted to do was to head over to some stupid prom.

"Ollie. Let's go," Fi ordered.

"We don't have to go, if you don't—"

I let out a heavy breath and stood.

"No. Let's go. Fi will have an aneurism if we blow it off."

"You sure?"

I nodded and took her hand. Was I the perfect prom date that night? Not by a long shot. And people noticed. Especially Fi. While I was grabbing punch for me and Jackie, she laid into me.

"Hey, Captain Grumpy Pants. What's your problem?"

I ignored her.

"Ols? Why the long puss?"

"It's nothing," I shouted over the loud music.

"Clearly, it's something."

"We can talk about it later."

She got close and loudly whispered, "Did that bitch say something to you?"

I grew tired of Fi putting Jackie down.

"I really wish you'd stop calling her that."

"You didn't answer my ques—"

"No, okay? She didn't say anything. I mean, she did, but—" I shook my head.

"You're not making any sense."

"Fi. Let's drop it. Go have fun with Fireman Timmy."

She opened her mouth, but I walked away. After the last dance, we hopped into the limo. Some students were headed to Belle Terre, overlooking Port Jefferson Harbor, to party on the beach.

"Can we go?" Jackie asked. I was about to say no, but Fi shot me a look, so I said yes. Fireman Timmy had the driver stop off at 7-Eleven for supplies, as he called them—a couple of six-packs of Budweiser and pretzels.

"Don't tell your grandfather," he joked.

Fi playfully elbowed his ribs before cracking one open. Jackie and I followed suit. The four of us toasted the evening and did our best to enjoy the remainder of our time together, huddled up next to a bonfire on the beach.

CHAPTER NINETY-EIGHT

A few months have passed since getting out of rehab. I was no longer wearing a boot or using a cane. I was on assignment in Texas, covering the border crisis. Over breakfast, I decided to hop on the website the Department of Justice set up, listing all the Capitol breach cases. I guess they grew tired of everyone asking for updates.

A few weeks back, I tracked down *Madam Mayhem*, as I came to think of my January 6th attacker on social media. She was now married, living in central Florida with her husband and children.

I typed her name into the search bar and hit enter. To my surprise, it popped up. I couldn't believe it. Madam Mayhem's name acted as a hyperlink, which I clicked, and opened another window, with a complete list of all her official charges.

Obstruction of an Official Proceeding and Aiding and Abetting; Entering and Remaining in a Restricted Building or Grounds; Disorderly and Disruptive Conduct in a Restricted Building or Grounds; Disorderly Conduct in a Capitol Building; Parading, Demonstrating, or Picketing in a Capitol Building.

Demonstrating and picketing, huh? Yeah, that's what we'll call it.

I continued scanning the site and found another hyperlink to her indictment. It contained a three-page document filled with legalese. It stated that the grand jury charged . . . blah, blah, blah.

The document referenced the legal violations, which meant nothing to me, and proceeded to provide details on each criminal count. The further I read, the quicker my pulse raced, and my body tensed.

I leaned back and drained the remainder of my java as I digested all the data. The site provided arraignment details, along with an upcoming trial date, August 6th, a few weeks away. I wanted to be there.

In that courtroom to face my attacker. My only concerns were: would the judge allow me, could I get the time off without explaining why, and, what if I was wrong? What if this wasn't her? What if it was all just a coincidence? It's not like the government site posted her mug shot, which would have helped.

I stared down at my huevos rancheros and lost my appetite, so I picked up my cell to call my editor, Jenny. While it was early, she said I could call her anytime in case of an emergency. Of course, I'm not sure she'd consider this one.

I could call my father or brother for advice, but they'd just repeat what they've been telling me for a while. Move on with my life. Well, if I can't call them, I might as well call the missus. She has always provided good counsel, along with a swift kick to the backside when I needed one.

I checked my watch. She was one time zone ahead of me, so I knew I wouldn't wake her. Regardless, she was an early riser. Always got up before the sun, and with sweeps week right around the corner, she was probably knee-deep in something. To test the waters, I sent her a quick text:

Hey, babe. Have a sec?

She immediately replied: *Sure.*

I hit the camera icon, and it dialed her up. I caught her in the car.

"Hey, handsome. Miss me already?"

"Always." I smiled.

"What's up?" she stared presumably at the road.

"There's been a break in the case."

I didn't need to explain.

"Hit me."

I provided her the details and asked, "What should I do?"

"What do you want to do?"

I hated it when she answered my question with a question.

"What do you think?" I sarcastically answered.

Someone near her blared their car horn. "Sorry, honey, what'd you say?"

Sighed. "Nothing. Don't worry 'bout it. Ping me later when you get home."

"You sure?"

"Yeah. Don't worry about it. I love you."

"I love you too. Talk to you later," she replied and hung up.

After weighing my options, I decided I would attend the trial, regardless of the job or what anyone thought. Four days, and a few thousand miles later, I headed back home after uploading my final report and sending the link to Jenny for her to download, review, and do with as she pleased.

On the drive home from Dulles International, my only focus was to strategize my next steps. Following my recent conversation with Fred, the attorney, it became clear that participating in the trial would necessitate taking the stand. I was impulsive at times. But not a moron.

CHAPTER NINETY-NINE

Spring 1986

Three days prior to my grand exhibit in The Village, I returned home from school to discover a surprise nestled between my pillow and comforter—an unmarked letter. I opened it, recognized the handwriting, and dropped it like it was on fire. I tore into the family room, panicked.

"You let her in?" I yelled.

"Slow down, Ollie. Let who in, Ollie?" Pop answered. "What are you talking about?"

I ran back to my room and retrieved the letter.

"This." I waved.

He took the envelope from my hand and began reading it. His face turned white. Pop marched into my room with me on his tail.

"Did you leave your bedroom window open?"

With a nervous shrug, I replied, "I don't—"

He slammed it shut and locked it. Navil's face flashed before my eyes. Sharp phantom pains emanated from my wound. My breathing labored. Pop noticed and wrapped his strong arms around me.

"Easy, Ollie. I'm here," he whispered.

Tía Carolina joined us. Pop handed her the letter, which she calmly read. The pair exchanged looks of concern.

"Should we call la policía?" Tía Carolina asked.

"I don't know," Pop replied. "You two wait here while I search the outside of the house. If she's still here—"

My body stiffened. "You think she's still here?"

"I doubt it, but I'll feel safer after I look around," he said before leaving.

"Hijo, why don't we sit and wait," Tía instructed.

She sat in my desk chair, while I popped a squat on my bed. While we waited, I decided to read the letter. I got as far as two sentences before crumpling it up and throwing it away.

All I'd seen was:

> Dear Ollie.
> I'm so very sorry for hurting you. I never intended
> to—

Tía Carolina went to retrieve it, but I snapped at her, "Leave it."

My ever-cool aunt ignored me and slipped it into her pocket. "We might need it for the police."

As I leaned back against my pillow, images from my and Navil's time together washed over me. beginning with her senior pictures, to when she ran half-naked from Stefan's bedroom as my blood dripped down my sides.

Outside, Pop fiddled with my bedroom window. Tried to force it open, and thankfully failed. I still couldn't believe she broke into my house. My body trembled with rage. Bella entered the room and jumped into Tía Carolina's lap. Both kept an eye on me as I processed this recent betrayal.

Minutes later, Pop returned. "I'm pretty sure she's gone."

"Pretty sure?" I asked.

He nodded. "I'll let the neighbors know to keep an eye out, just in case."

"Shouldn't we call la policía?" Tía Carolina asked again.

"I'll take care of it. Where's the letter?" Pop asked.

Tía Carolina handed it to him, and he placed it in his front pocket. From a distance, I heard the basement door open. It was Jaime, who began to whine.

"I'm hungry. When's dinner?"

Tía rolled her eyes and excused herself, with Bella close behind. Pop informed me that he'd call the police in the morning and would feel safer if I slept at a friend's house that evening, just in case.

"I'll call Fi. See if I can crash on her couch."

"Good." He nodded. "In the meantime, hang out in the family room, where I can see you."

After dinner, I went next door to Fi's. She and I have slept at each other's homes a million times, so it wasn't a big deal. Gramps joked he liked having another man in the house, which always got under Fi's skin.

Fi and I stayed up until midnight before calling it a night. She arranged a spot for me on the couch in the family room and went to bed after *The Honeymooners* ended. As for me, sleep proved elusive. I couldn't deal with Navil breaking into my house.

I can't believe she broke in. And for what? To leave me a fucking letter? Why can't she just leave me the hell alone?

Apparently, I wasn't the only one who struggled to sleep that evening. I'd never seen Fi look so tired.

"Are you okay?" I asked over breakfast. "You look tired."

"Me? What about you?" she replied. "Did you get *any* sleep last night?"

I shook my head no.

"I still can't believe she broke into your house."

"Tell me about it."

"What was she hoping to accomplish?"

"No idea."

We talked about it the entire way to school.

"Pop said he was going to call the police. Just in case she tried it again."

"If that bitch tries it again, she'll have to deal with me," Fi snarled.

I smiled, knowing that she meant it.

Over lunch, Jackie had a similar response.

"She *what*?"

"Broke into my—"

"The nerve," Jackie scoffed. "I can't believe she—"

"I know."

"And what was she hoping—"

"I don't know. Maybe just to drop off the letter."

Jackie chewed on my response, and after a few beats, shook her head.

"That doesn't make any sense. If she was all *I'm sorry*, then why hasn't she tried to do the same thing with me?"

I shrugged.

"Well, if she does, I'll be waiting for her." She smiled with a glint of vengeance.

CHAPTER ONE HUNDRED

The big day finally arrived for my first ever exhibit in The Village. The selected photos were ready, invitations had been sent out to friends, neighbors, faculty, and family members. Even the gallery owner, Fonz, as he preferred to be called, extended an open invitation in the *Village Voice*, a local newspaper known for its alternative perspective on current events, to come discover a captivating new Puerto Rican talent.

The exhibit was scheduled from 6:30 to 9:30 p.m. Tía Carolina drove Jackie, Fi, Eddie, and me into the city that morning. Pop and Jaime would arrive later, since the last thing anyone wanted was to have my little brother underfoot.

We arrived around ten in the morning, and Alfonso, the gallery owner and namesake, waited for us out front. I damn near pooped myself the moment we pulled up in front of his place. Everything that I planned for would soon become a reality. No more excuses.

Once inside, Fonz guided us through his expansive gallery showcasing various pieces of artwork, from prints to paintings to sculptures. Eventually, he led us to the two walls in the main area where my name was prominently displayed. It was on these walls that I would set up my photos.

"I put you here." He smiled proudly.

I swiped my sweaty hands down my pant leg and followed Fonz to the back. Next to his office, he had set up a staging area for us. There were tools and equipment strewn about the place: hanging hardware, framing tools, chisels and various carving knives, cleaning supplies and adhesives.

"I'll leave you to it," Fonz informed us before offering Tía Carolina coffee. "I have my own French press in my office."

A couple of hours later we finished setting up our display, and awaited Fonz's final approval. My centerpiece photo stopped him in his tracks.

"Whoa." He stood, marveling at the setup. "You took this?"

I nodded.

He rubbed his chin. Examined the photo from every angle. I stared in silence.

"Mm-hmm . . . mm-hmm," he whispered.

He then took a step back and shook his head. "This is no good."

My heart sank.

"We need to fix this." He pointed at the lighting. "Your centerpiece needs to pop."

I breathed a sigh of relief as he escaped to the back. From a distance we heard him shuffling things around, until he returned with an elaborate lighting setup. Within minutes, Fonz built an illuminated metallic frame around Navil's picture, which passersby could see from the street.

"That's much better." He smiled and looked around at the showcase. "I must say, Ollie, your work really *resonates* with me. When Byron said he found your work captivating, I thought he was exaggerating."

Slightly embarrassed, I smiled. "Uh, thanks."

"You're welcome." He clapped. "Okay. Now, who's hungry?"

Four hands shot up.

"Do you guys eat burgers?"

We all enthusiastically nodded.

"Excellent." Fonz smiled broadly. "I know just the place."

After locking up, we followed closely behind Fonz like dutiful ducklings, as Tía Carolina brought up the rear. Two city blocks north and three more east, and we arrived outside *Melanzana's* on Christopher Street. Like most places in The Village, it didn't look like much, with its dingy paint, half-torn awning, and a curb in need of repair. But once inside, our world changed.

The scent of freshly baked bread hit us the moment we crossed the threshold, which put a smile on everyone's face, including Tía Carolina. Up front, a display case was filled with bread and pastries.

Tía Carolina whispered to herself in Spanish, "We'll definitely take some home."

Yes.

After exchanging the European both-cheeks kiss with Fonz, the hostess seated us at a large table overlooking the street. Our server arrived and quickly took our drink orders. Eddie and I got chocolate shakes. Jackie and Fi got Cokes. To my surprise, Tía Carolina ordered a glass of red wine, and Fonz joined her.

I scanned the menu and tucked between the Chorizo Burger and Patty Melt was their Masterpiece Burger. Two patties with caramelized onions, applewood bacon, cheddar cheese, lettuce, and tomato served on a brioche bun, with a side of thick steak fries.

"I know what I want," I announced.

I turned to Fi, who sat to my left, and over her shoulder, I spotted an auburn-haired girl wearing a black leather jacket and tight blue jeans cross the street. Ice ran down my spine as the hair on the back of my neck sprung up.

I shot up from the table, ran through the restaurant, and

burst out the door just as the girl turned the corner. I shouted Navil's name and took off after the girl, nearly getting hit by a cab as I crossed the street.

From behind me, I heard Jackie, Eddie, and Fi exit the restaurant and call after me, but I ignored them. I turned the corner, and down the block I spotted the auburn-haired beauty. My heart raced.

I called her name one more time, "Navil."

For a moment, she appeared to pause, which stopped me in my tracks. Without looking back, she continued her trek forward, and never broke her stride as I ran and called after her. Up ahead, she took a left at the corner, and by the time I reached it, she had vanished.

Fuck.

CHAPTER ONE HUNDRED-ONE

Modern Day

After all my planning, including a request for time off, I missed the trial. My editor, Jenny, was sent to cover the United States hectic withdrawal from Afghanistan. She thought Derek was ready for the big leagues, only to be proven wrong. The junior photog couldn't handle the mayhem of this unique overseas assignment.

"Remember the last time you asked me to do you a favor?" My leg throbbed at the memory.

"I know, Ollie, but it's just for a couple of we—"

We went back and forth but eventually she played to my ego, and off I went. It turns out, it didn't matter. Due to COVID-19, they were holding trials via teleconference, so I couldn't attend, even if they allowed me to sit in the gallery, which was a long shot at best.

While sipping a thick cup of coffee, I read that Madam Mayhem struck a plea agreement with the government. She pleaded guilty to Count Five of her multi-count indictment.

Parading, Demonstrating, or Picketing in a Capitol Building, in violation of Title 40, US Code, Section 5104(e)(2)(G).

The courts dismissed her remaining charges, ordered her to pay a $500 restitution fee, and sentenced her to ninety days of incarceration at the DC Central Detention Facility, set to begin September 1st, which meant she'd be home in time for Thanksgiving and Christmas.

What the serious fuck?

The site also posted her *Statement of Offense* or written and signed confession. It detailed the events of that horrific day, including *Madam Mayhem* and her husband's participation. How they entered the Capitol Building through a broken door on the west side. Attacked police officers inside, hung out with a crowd in the *Statuary Hall Connector* outside the *House of Representatives*, and finally left through the east exit.

In total, she spent approximately three hours on the grounds, from her attendance at Donald Trump's inciting rally, to their march through the Mall where she and her cohorts beat the crap out of me, to their time inside the Capitol.

And what was her punishment for all this? A lousy ninety-day sentence and a $500 fine. It was the second time she got away with nothing more than a slap on the wrist, and it pissed me off.

This was bullshit.

What felt like an eternity later, I returned home and was greeted by an overexcited Daisy, who piddled on the foyer floor. Too tired to yell at her, I scooped her up, received a good old-fashioned face slobbering, and then wiped up the mess after which I texted my wife that I was home.

She immediately responded with a pair of heart emojis and promised to see me later. I won't hold my breath. It was the middle of sweeps month for her show, that crucial period for syndicated programs where they aired the most compelling and captivating content to entice both viewers and advertisers and influenced network decisions on continuing the show, *Morales in the Morning.*

As I unpacked, I thought about my conversation with my wife, after reading about the plea deal.

"Ols, look. You have no idea what her life's like," she commented. "For all we know, this is a worse punishment than spending time behind bars. Plus, remember what the Good Book says about repentance and forgiveness."

While I didn't appreciate her Christian logic, her pearls of wisdom made sense. After putting the laundry on, I grabbed a nap with the dog, who hours later woke me as her high-pitched barking echoed from our front door throughout our empty home.

"Jesus Christ, Daisy, shut the fuck up," I shouted.

From my bedroom door, I heard, "Is that any way to greet your wife?"

I sprang from the bed, wrapped her in my arms, and kissed her hello.

"Miss me?" she whispered.

"Just a little." I smiled.

CHAPTER ONE HUNDRED-TWO

Spring 1986

The showcase started slowly, and I was so distracted by the events of the day, every time the front door opened, I expected it to be Navil. The many who promised to come never showed up, which left me disappointed. Fonz did his best to assure me.

"It's okay, Ollie. Some very important people *have* stopped by."

I didn't know who he was talking about. I held three conversations that night, first with Pop, who arrived with Jaime right as the event began. The second was with Fi, who asked about the action shot I posted of Jean Paul Michael as he mid-air bicycle-kicked a ball deep into the net, scoring a game-winning goal. My last was with Jackie, who tried to cheer me up.

"It's early. People will come. I just know it."

I put on a fake smile and then noticed two older gentlemen standing in front of my centerpiece. The one on the right was a neatly, yet casually dressed African American man. The other, a Caucasian man wearing a blue pinstripe suit, holding an overcoat.

There was something different about them. It was the way they gestured at the portrait and chatted back and forth. Took it in from different angles. Nodded in agreement before moving on to the next section.

"You should go talk to them," Jackie recommended.

"And say what?"

"How 'bout, *do you have any questions?*"

After a not-so-gentle shove, I made my way over. The African American gentleman noticed my reflection in the glass and waited for me to make first contact. I glanced back at Jackie, who gestured for me to say something.

"Hi, uh, can I, um, answer any—"

They both turned.

In a whispered drawl, the African American man asked, "Are you the artist?"

"Artist?" I questioned.

They stared at me.

"I mean, yes. I'm the, uh, artist, I mean, um, photog-photographer."

His lower lip protruded a bit as he nodded in approval. His companion smiled slightly at my response.

"You have an excellent eye," he stated.

"I agree," said the other.

For the next fifteen minutes we walked around my showcase. They both had a gentle curiosity about them. We'd stand in front of a picture and spend the next few minutes breaking it down. They asked me unique questions.

"What filter did you use?" and "How were you *feeling* when you took this picture?"

And noticed things.

"See right here?" The Caucasian man gestured toward my photo of Dylan O'Donnell hitting a home run. "The way you captured the moment."

I leaned in and stared at my own work as if seeing it for the first time.

"You can actually see the seams of the baseball as it connects with the bat."

He was right.

"And the way the ball seems to curve into the batter," the other commented.

The way they explained things made me feel like a student attending a lecture from his favorite teachers. The phrases they used regarding photography stayed with me for a long time. Some became personal mantras.

Comments like, "Pictures are your friends."

I never considered that.

"They have a language of their own."

They weren't wrong.

"They connect the human spirit."

Their words not only lifted me that evening but inspired me throughout my career as a photojournalist.

From the corner of my eye, I noticed Byron entering the gallery. His trusty Nikon swung from his neck. He spotted us, captured a quick picture, then came right over, placing his hand on my shoulder. "I see you've found my latest discovery."

"*Byron.*" The African American gentleman hugged him.

"There he is." The other man did the same. "How're you doing, old man?"

"Who're you calling old?" Byron laughed. "I can't believe you guys made it."

"When Byron calls—" the African American man jested.

"You come." His companion chuckled.

"How're you doing, Bobby?"

"Better than I should be, my friend." Bobby laughed.

"Elias, how're things in the West Wing?"

West Wing?

He pinched the bridge of his nose, "Let's just say, POTUS keeps us on our toes."

"So, I've read," Byron joked.

I stood silently as the men kibbitzed back and forth for a few minutes. Byron escorted them around the showcase. He pointed out things in each picture that caught his attention. Periodically, they'd one-up each other.

"But how about the delicate way he captured the light in this one?" Elias said.

"He has a point, Byron," Bobby commented. "Of course, you're both missing the overall meaning behind this piece."

I shadowed them like a faithful puppy tailing his master. Pop must have noticed me trailing behind the trio, and soon came over to introduce himself.

Bobby was the first to engage with Pop. "Are you this young gentleman's father?"

"I am." He shook his hand. "Dr. Morales."

Please don't embarrass me.

"It's a pleasure to meet you, doctor," Bobby replied. "I'm Bobby Williams. If you don't mind me saying, your son is one heck of an artist."

My jaw dropped, and my eyes grew.

Pop smiled broadly. "I don't mind at all."

Elias introduced himself next. "Elias Garber, Dr. Morales."

"Nice to meet you, Mr. Garber."

Bobby modestly shared that he was a staff photographer for the Chicago Sun-Times.

"Dr. Morales, don't let him fool you," Bryon stated. "Bobby's Pulitzer Prize-winning work in the urban community continues to change people's perspectives on poverty in America along with other social issues."

Bobby waved off his commentary.

"And Mr. Garber here is the current official White House photographer."

Impressed, Pop's brows rose.

"Like this one." He gestured to Bobby. "He's known for his ability to capture intimate and candid moments of the president and his family."

The president?

"It's no big deal," Elias whispered.

"No big—" Byron shook his head. "Dr. Morales, he's captured

images of President Reagan seated at his desk as he signed bills into law, or dancing with the First Lady during a state dinner. Frankly, any image of significance that took place in and around the White House were due to his powerful lens."

A stunned Pop shook both their hands. "It's an honor to have you here."

The pair took it all in stride.

"Your son has potential," Bobby commented.

"I've been telling him that for years," Pop replied.

You have?

Byron interjected, "You have one heck of a son here."

My face flushed. "Uh, thanks, Byron."

"Byron here tells us you're in your last year of high school," Bobby said.

"Yes, sir. I graduate in a few weeks."

Both he and Elias nodded.

"Any thoughts on where you're headed in the fall season?"

I quietly replied, "I wanted to go to Georgetown, but they waitlisted me."

"Georgetown." Bobby threw his nose up as if I'd farted. "Have you given any thoughts to schools in the Midwest?"

Elias mockingly replied, "You mean like Columbia College?"

Bobby smiled. "Now that you mention it—"

"Aren't you tired of shilling for that place?"

"Says the man who lives and breathes Hoyas blue and gray," Bobby countered.

"Easy, gentleman." Byron stepped in. "There's no need to scare the boy."

"I'm just saying there are better options out there, that's all."

"Like NYU, for instance," Byron said.

Both Elias and Bobby shot him a look.

"You're kidding me," Elias shot back. "Name one halfway decent photographer that's graduated from that place."

Byron raised his hand. "What about me?"

"Oh, please," Bobby said. "You were there for three semesters. That doesn't count."

"Listen, if your son needs help—" Elias handed Pop his official White House business card.

His eyes lit up.

"Playing the White House card again?" Bobby jibbed. "Seriously?"

Elias shrugged.

"Don't listen to him . . . Ollie, was it?" Bobby placed his arm around my shoulder and dragged me away.

"Whoa, whoa, whoa," Elias called out and rushed to my side. "Where are you taking him?"

Bobby waved him off. "You need to expand your horizons."

"Broader than *Georgetown*?" Elias interjected as Byron joined us.

Bobby continued, "There's no finer education than—"

I felt like a piece of saltwater taffy getting pulled back and forth. The three went back and forth, boasting about their respective alma maters. Pop shook his head and smiled while I silently marveled at this heroic trio.

Byron pulled me away from Bobby. "Pay no attention to these two, Ollie. The minute they get in the same room together, it's like thunder and lightning. And if there's scotch around, it's worse. Trust your mentor."

Both took umbrage with his comment.

"That's not true," Elias stated.

"How can you say that?" Bobby asked.

"Really?" Byron countered. "Must I remind you of our last fishing trip?"

They both laughed.

"I still say that wasn't my fault," Elias said.

"Oh, so the boat tipped over by itself?" Byron asked.

"And just as I was reeling one in too," Bobby said.

"You wouldn't pass me the bait."

"So, you decide to capsize the boat?" Bobby teased.

"No. I tried reaching for the bait bucket and—"

This joyful interaction would soon be eclipsed by an event that forever shaped my life. Byron noticed it first. His eyes tracked people slowly walking to the front window overlooking the street.

From outside the gallery, I heard a familiar voice screaming. The doors were closed, so I couldn't make out the details. I excused myself and pushed toward the commotion. Jackie cursed someone out on the sidewalk at the top of her lungs. Eddie and Fi soon joined me.

I craned my neck. "What's going on?"

Eddie shrugged. "No idea. One sec, she's hanging out by the door, the next—"

Fi said, "Who's she yelling at?"

Suddenly, it felt like there were a million people gathered inside the gallery. And outside, locals blocked our view as they stopped to enjoy the free show. I peered between a pair of heads and caught my first glimpse of the recipient of Jackie's tirade.

An auburn-haired girl in a black leather jacket and tight-fitting blue jeans, with her hair neatly tied up into a high ponytail.

I gasped.

CHAPTER ONE HUNDRED-FOUR

The more Jackie yelled, the more people gathered. I noticed Pop standing by the door. His face turned white, seemingly confirming my suspicions. He found me in the crowd.

"Back away from that window, Ollie," he ordered. "Get to the office. *Now.*"

Ignoring his command, I shoved my way through the crowd. As I reached the door, a fist wrapped around my collar and yanked me backward.

"I told you to go wait in the office."

"Is it her?"

He stared and didn't answer.

"Pop. Is that Navil?"

Tía Carolina came to my side with Jaime on her hip.

"Why don't you take your little brother into the back?" she calmly suggested.

Are you out of your mind?

"You do it," I sharply replied. "I'm going out there."

Pop spotted Fi. "Fiona, take him to the back."

She nodded and took hold of my arm. "C'mon, Ols. Let's—"

I jerked loose, "Get the fuck off me. I'm—"

People got out of my way as I tore outside. Jackie's voice grew louder. Out of control.

"Oh my God, she has a knife," someone screamed.

Jesus, was she here to finish the job?

Pop was on my tail.

"Somebody call the police!" another shouted.

In the distance, the faint sound of police sirens approached. My chest pounded. I pushed past an onlooker. Pop snagged my collar again. I squirmed free. Shoved my way past another stranger.

"Move!" I shouted.

Like Jaime snaking his way around a crowded toy store, I bobbed and weaved through the crowded sidewalk.

Pop screamed for me, "Ollie, get back inside!"

I ignored his pleas. Pushed my way forward. Made it to the front of the encircled onlookers. Skidded to a halt. My pulse raced. Eyes widened. Icy terror ran down my spine. Before me in her black leather jacket and form-fitted blue jeans. My betrayer.

I shouted her name, "*Navil*!"

She turned. Our eyes locked. She mouthed my name.

"*Ollie.*"

Her face softened. Defensive anger replaced with loving grace. She'd returned. The love of my life was back. My heart leaped, and so did Jackie.

"Don't you turn your back on me, you bitch."

She yanked Navil's ponytail. Threw her to the ground. Kicked her neck and shoulders. Navil curled into the fetal position. Tried blocking each blow and failed miserably.

"Jackie, stop!" I yelled.

She temporarily paused her onslaught. Searched the crowd. Spotted me.

"Leave her alone," I shouted.

Jackie's eyes filled with fury. Navil suddenly twisted around. Swung her leg. Caught Jackie in the ankle. Caused her to trip and smack her head on the concrete sidewalk. A shiny metallic object slashed the air.

Navil got to her knees. Her face was feral. She leaped at her downed opponent. Fists flew. Navil punched her in the jaw. Jackie countered with a blow to the side of Navil's head. Manicured nails raked across cheeks. Blood spilled. The pair went back and forth. Blow for blow. Cherry lights and sirens drew near. The encircling crowd cheered on the teenage combatants.

"That's it, honey. Hit her in the face."

I attempted to intervene, but strangers held me back.

"Let go of me. Navil. Jackie. Stop," I begged.

I needed to put an end to this. I bit down on the hand atop my shoulder. Its owner cursed and shrieked in pain. I took a step forward. It's as far as I got. Strong arms suddenly wrapped around my arms and chest. Held me in place. I attempted to wiggle out of them, but to no avail.

It was Ernie. The prince. Like a crane, he lifted me off the ground.

I kicked and screamed, "Put me down! Let me go."

He tossed me toward my father. I landed sharply on my knees. Pain shot up and down my body. Tears filled my eyes. I stood and turned. Attempted to escape. Both he and Mr. Digman blocked my path.

"Get out of my way."

"Sorry, champ," Mr. Digman replied. "You're not going anywhere."

"Please," I pleaded.

In the same manner he used when disciplining Bella, Pop shouted, "Ollie. No."

Eddie and Fi came to my side. Held me back. I tried to shrug them off. Police cars screeched to a halt. Cherry tops reflected off dirty brick buildings. They lit up the gallery.

From the crowd, a high-pitched scream followed by an unfamiliar voice.

"Oh my God, she stabbed her."

My heart sunk to my toes.

Not again.

CHAPTER ONE HUNDRED-FIVE

Modern Day

"How was your flight?" My wife asked with an affectionate smile.

"Meh, same. Long."

She caressed my face. "You look tired. Have you eaten?"

"Not yet. You?"

She shook her head.

"Thai?"

"Sure. Order me the usual," she replied over her shoulder on the way to the bathroom with Daisy in tow.

I grabbed the menu in the kitchen and placed our customary order. For her, Amazing Eggplant in peanut sauce and brown rice. For me, a spicy chicken Panang with jasmine rice, and an order of spring rolls.

"It'll be here in about an hour," I announced on my way back to our bedroom.

As I turned the corner I came to a complete stop. In the doorway stood my beloved with her arms raised, wearing nothing but a smile.

"An hour, huh? Should give us plenty of time," she purred. "Why don't you get over here and give your wife a proper hello."

Even though we'd been together forever, she still knew how to stun me silent. If I had a tail, it would have wagged as I gulped back a mouthful of saliva and obeyed her command, but not before locking our now whining Daisy outside our bedroom.

One of the many positives of being in a long-term relationship was knowing each other's shortcuts, especially the intimate ones.

I quickly disrobed, joined her in bed, and marveled at her beauty and my good fortune.

"What?" she whispered.

I smiled and stroked her body. "Simply amazing."

She rolled her eyes. "Okay, tough guy."

Throughout our time together, we learned to take our time. Enjoyed one another. Allowed the flame to slowly burn. Build on our passion. I could still picture our first time together in my one-bedroom loft near Georgetown. It was early in my second year working at the White House, and my freshman year at college. *U2* was playing RFK stadium for their multi-platinum album, *Joshua Tree*. Knowing it was her favorite band, I scored tickets and invited her to fly down.

After the concert, we went back to my place and had a few drinks. We were both single at the time. One thing led to another, and we've been together ever since.

An hour or so later, the doorbell and Daisy's bark jolted us back to reality. We dressed, retrieved our dinner from the front porch, made our plates, and sat adjacent to one other at the kitchen table.

"I'm surprised to see you home so early," I commented between bites. "I figured you be home around midnight."

"Yeah, well, when I told them you were coming home today—"

"They let you go?"

She smiled. "Something like that."

We chatted about her upcoming interview with a congress-man trying to make a name for herself with the DC movers and shakers.

"They say she's positioning herself for a Senate run."

"What do you think?"

She sat back and sipped her merlot. "Has as good a shot as any, I suppose, given the competition."

"That bad, huh?"

She chuckled, "Could be worse. She could be our represent-ative."

As I laughed at her joke, she spotted my backpack hanging from the back of my chair instead of in my office.

"Submitted your pictures?"

"Before I got home."

"Good."

The thought of my laptop caused me to think of the case and make a face. She spotted it immediately.

"What's the matter?"

"Hmm? Nothing. Why?"

The downside of a long-term relationship was that your significant other, especially this one, knew all your idiosyn-crasies. She stared at me over her wine glass and saw right through me.

"What?" I innocently asked.

She popped a brow. "Seriously?"

"All right."

"When are you going to stop obsessing over this?"

"Babe, you—"

She raised her hand. "Please don't tell me I don't understand."

I attempted to say something, but she cut me off.

"You keep forgetting I was *there,* Ollie."

"Not the last time you weren't," I groused.

"Just because I was stuck overseas in January doesn't mean—"

"Honey, I know. It's just—"

She stood and wrapped her arms around me. "Ollie. You have to let it go."

I shrugged her off and stood. "Don't you think I've tried?"

Her face filled with empathy.

"Do you have any idea how frustrating this is?"

"Some idea," she whispered.

I let out a breath. "Not only was she the cause of everything that happened to me back in the day, and got away with it no less—"

"Only because she had connections."

"Trust me, I remember."

I grabbed the laptop from my backpack. Booted up the website and pointed at the screen.

She came to my side.

"And now she's getting away with it again," I scoffed. "Check out this bullshit."

She read the details of the plea agreement.

"Can you believe that shit? I get my ass handed to me, spend time in the hospital plus rehab, may have to get corrective surgery when I'm older, and what does she get?"

"She's still going to jail." She turned and stood.

"Please. Three lousy months. She could probably do that standing on her head."

My wife stared silently at her agitated hubby pacing back and forth like an idiot. Daisy began to whine at her feet. She didn't like it when her mommy or daddy were upset.

I gestured toward the dog. "Just pick her up."

She lifted her canine baby and nestled her in her arms while I shut down the laptop and escaped to the bathroom with my cell phone. Over the years, it had become my sanctum sanctorum whenever I wanted to be alone.

From outside the door. "I cleaned up and am turning in."

"Okay."

"I love you, Ols."

"Love you too."

CHAPTER ONE HUNDRED-SIX

That fall, Jenny had me back covering the crisis at our southern border. This time, I started in San Diego, California and worked my way east toward El Paso, Texas, home of great Tex-Mex and my favorite minor league baseball team, the El Paso Chihuahuas, with the cutest mascot, a pup named Chico. I informed Jenny that I have to head home for the weekend.

"Gabriel's on break between semesters and decided to grace us with his presence," I explained to her.

"Nice. Does this mean you're having another one of your famous Morales shindigs?"

"You tell me," I responded. "Check your inbox."

There weren't too many things that excited my boss. Parties at my house were one of them.

I heard her reading the email, " . . . starts at six o'clock. Perfect. What do you need me to bring?"

"Why are you asking me? Reach out to the boss."

"Every time I do, she tells me to just bring myself and Sam."

Sam was her wife.

"So, there you go."

She sighed. "We'll bring some wine."

"Even better."

I hopped a flight from El Paso to BWI Marshall Airport with a one-hour layover in Houston, which gave me enough time to pee and grab a quick snack for the three-hour flight home.

Between flights, I purchased a thirty-three-ounce Smart Water bottle, and a bag of Rold Gold pretzels. I pinged my wife before boarding the plane.

"Hey, babe."

As usual, she was on the go.

"Hi, honey. At the airport?"

"Yeah. Getting ready to board. See you in a few hours."

"Okay. Please be safe and play nice with the flight attendants."

"If I have to," I joked.

"That or they kick you off the plane and put you on the no-fly list. Your choice."

"You're no fun."

"Tell me that later," she cooed.

I smiled. "I love you."

"Love you more. There's some lasagna in the freezer from Casa Firenze."

"Did you get the meatballs too?"

"Don't I always?"

"You *do* love me."

"Sometimes. Listen, I've—"

"Gotta run, I know. See you tonight."

We blew each other a kiss and hung up. I tossed the pretzels into my backpack, headed to my gate, and boarded the flight. A few hours later, I pulled into my garage and to my surprise, my wife was home.

Guess she wasn't kidding about later.

I grabbed my things and was greeted by a barking Daisy.

"Okay, settle down. Let me get inside," I instructed her. "Hey, babe. I'm home."

"I'm in here."

I wheeled my luggage in and spotted her still in her work

clothes, seated in her lounge chair with her laptop open, sipping a glass of red wine.

"Hey, bub. What're you doing home so early?" I asked after a kiss hello.

She took a sip of wine. "You may want to sit down."

The hair on the back of my aging neck stood to attention.

"What's wrong? Is it the kids?"

"No, honey, the kids are fine, your father's fine, and so is your brother."

"Then, what's wrong? Something with your show?"

She drained her wine glass. "No. The show's fine, or as fine as it could be."

"Then what's going on?"

She clicked her keyboard and turned her laptop toward me. "Here."

"What am I reading?"

She took my hand. "She's gone, Ollie."

"Who's gone?" I replied, before reading the screen.

It was an obituary notice. Blood drained from my face as I read the screen.

"What? When?" I asked in disbelief.

"Keep reading."

Her obituary explained she passed away due to COVID-19. On the next tab over, my wife showed me an article detailing the impact of the virus on the state and federal prison system. Due to overcrowding and limited resources, close to twenty-five hundred held in state and federal prisons died of COVID-19-related causes.

I sat back in disbelief.

"But she was just—"

"I know."

"She was only supposed to spend—"

"Ninety days. I remember the plea agreement."

"I still don't understand how this—"

"Honey. COVID-19 is no joke. And when you have people packed together like sardines—"

"I get it. It's just—"

"Wasn't supposed to end this way."

I nodded. "Yeah. I mean . . . where's the justice?"

"Ollie. She died in prison. Left behind a family."

I digested the information. Images from my youth played across my mind's eye. Our many interactions, including the final time I saw her. After the stabbing. Her hands soaked in blood. Eyes wild with a fearful rage.

" . . . her funeral is next week."

"Hmm?"

"I said, according to the obituary, they're having a funeral for her next week."

"Where?"

"Some town called Dunedin, Florida."

I nodded and stared in disbelief at the information on the screen. My wife got up and sat me down. Placed herself in my lap. Wrapped her arms empathetically around my neck. Rested my head on her shoulder. I breathed in her calming presence.

"I still can't believe Jackie's dead."

CHAPTER
ONE HUNDRED-SEVEN

Spring 1986

"Oh my God, she stabbed her."

Those words echoed into the night like a nightmare. The mob gathered outside the Greenwich Village gallery scattered. I yanked away from Eddie and Fi. Shoved my way through the throng of scrambling witnesses. My eyes widened at the horror.

"*No.*"

The scene shocked me to my very core. A madwoman straddled atop her victim like an enraged cowgirl. Her clothes splattered in crimson. Hands, face, and hair strewn with blood.

"How does that feel, huh?" Jackie screamed as she stabbed at Navil.

Navil struggled to defend herself.

Another puncture. "You like that?"

More gore.

"Everyone, get back," an officer ordered as he approached, his pistol drawn. "Drop the knife."

Jackie just smiled as she plunged the blade deep into Navil's chest.

Blood drenched Jackie's face.

"For fuck's sake, somebody, call an ambulance," someone shouted.

Jackie raised the bloody knife again. The officer, still steps away, repeated his warning to drop the knife. His pistol was leveled, but he didn't have a clear shot. He couldn't take the risk in the crowd.

My adrenaline surged. I leaped forward and tackled her off Navil. The curved blade flew from her grasp.

Jackie flailed. "Get the fuck off me!"

Before I knew it, a strong pair of hands tossed me off Jackie like a ragdoll. I tumbled and landed on my face. Jackie squirmed as the cop placed his knee on her lower back. His partner was right behind him, and he slapped cuffs onto her blood-soaked wrists before yanking her to her feet.

Jackie howled as they escorted her away, "Let me go! That bitch had it coming!"

I hobbled to Navil's side and knelt in her blood. Her eyelids fluttered open. She smiled and reached for me.

Her blood-soaked fingers brushed my cheek, then gently slipped down my face to her side like a leaf falling from a branch. The fire in her eyes slowly dimmed.

"Navil," I whispered loudly. "I'm here. Stay with me."

Blood dripped from the corner of her mouth. She coughed and sprayed red mist on my face. Instinctively, I jerked back, but I still inhaled the gore. The taste of hot pennies hit the back of my throat.

As I wiped my eyes with the back of my hand, Pop came to her side. Navil exhaled then shut her eyes. Pop began to administer CPR.

From behind me, the sound of work boots as they hammered the pavement, rushing toward the scene. The EMTs had arrived, one male, one female.

"Out of the way, people. Out of the way," the male EMT shouted.

His female partner shoved me aside, and they got to work. Pop quickly informed them he was a surgeon and gave them the rundown.

"Thanks, Doc," the male medic said. "We'll take it from here."

Pop stepped back, allowing the pair to do their job, while I came to his side. Behind us, the cops were securing the scene.

In mere moments, a blood pressure cuff and mask were secured onto Navil. Next, the female EMT flicked a syringe and injected something into Navil's right arm, while other one took her vitals and prepared her for transport.

Pop tried explaining what they were doing but I waved him off as I watched them place Navil onto a gurney and wheeled her to the back of their awaiting ambulance.

Without thinking twice, I ran after them.

"Ollie, *wait*," Pop shouted.

Navil reached for me as they opened the back of the vehicle. I took her hand and shot a quick glance at the medics, who were exchanging looks.

"You've got twenty seconds. We're heading out," the woman EMT said as she and her partner prepped for departure.

I stroked Navil's pale cheek.

"I made it, Ollie," she wheezed. "Saw your invitation."

I questioned. "What invitation?"

"The newspapers," she rasped.

The female medic waved me away. "Okay. That's enough. We've got to get her to the hospital.

I let go of Navil's hand, and she said, "I'm so . . . sorry, chér."

"Okay, one, two—"

As they slid her into the ambulance, Navil slipped off her oxygen mask, and our eyes locked. Before the door shut, she kissed her fingertips and mouthed her final words to me.

"I love you, Ollie."

The ambulance roared to life. I chased it for two blocks, shouting at the top of my lungs, as its sirens echoed through the narrow streets of Greenwich Village, "I love you too, Navil!"

From the distant police car, Jackie screamed, *"No!"*

Pop eventually caught up to me, and I collapsed into him like a wave dissolving a kid's sandcastle. Remnants of Navil's blood mixed with my tears, staining Pop's finely tailored blazer. Behind us, Byron's camera flashed, capturing my pain and his next award-winning photo as the EMTs vanished into the neon-lit Greenwich Village evening.

In mere moments, they were gone.

And so was Navil.

Dead on arrival.

CHAPTER
ONE HUNDRED-EIGHT

Modern Day

After a direct flight into Tampa International Airport, we took the shuttle to our rental car, a red Nissan Rogue with all the bells and whistles. An hour later, we pulled into the JW Marriott Hotel on Clearwater Beach, grabbed our luggage, and handed the keys off to the valet parking attendant.

"Checking in, sir?"

"Yes, we'll be here for a few days."

"Very good, sir." He handed me my ticket. "Our number's on the back. Just call it whenever you need your car, and give us—"

"Twenty minutes?"

He nodded. "Fifteen, twenty."

Once inside, my wife excused herself while I checked us in. Eighteen minutes later, we stepped into our spacious twenty-fifth floor suite. Gulf Coast sunlight flooded the room. Revealed a spacious haven of luxury filled with an ocean-inspired décor.

Sandy hues, driftwood accents, and floor-to-ceiling windows framed the turquoise Gulf waters below. It was a shame we were there for a funeral. I stepped out onto the balcony. A warm, salty breeze greeted me. Sunshine coated my aging face. Painted the crystal clear skies with shades of gold.

Behind me, warm arms wrapped around my waist. Pulled me close.

I smiled. "We're definitely not in Kansas anymore."

"Pretty view," she whispered.

"Wanna explore, or do you need to lie down?"

I sucked in the ocean scent. Stillness washed over me.

"I wish we had a hammock."

She peered over the balcony onto the beach. Noted numerous private cabanas and lounge chairs with our hotel logo dotting the silky white sands.

"Want me to call down and reserve us one of those cabanas?"

"Sure. When in Rome . . ."

She kissed my shoulder and found the hotel phone. Half an hour later, we lay next to one another in our cozy retreat by the shore. Cushioned seating and a thatched roof provided comfort and protection from the hot Florida sun.

A gentle Gulf breeze carried the soothing sounds of waves, seagulls, and families enjoying their time in the sand and warm coastal waters. I turned to my bikini-clad beloved and smiled.

"All good?" she asked.

I reached for her. "Better than good."

She snuggled into me. We kissed and breathed in the salty air. I slowly drifted off. Time passed. An afternoon rain shower awakened me. We grabbed our things and made a run for it. Our laughter echoed down the hallway leading to our suite. She fumbled for our room key.

"I've got it." She placed the plastic key against the sensor.

With a green light and click, we entered and made a beeline to our bedroom. We flopped onto the bed and spent a wonderful time together. That evening, we had dinner in the hotel restaurant. The hostess placed us at a window overlooking a pair of swaying palm trees. If I didn't know better, I would have sworn we were living inside a postcard.

"Beautiful view," my wife noted.

I looked across at her and smiled. "It sure is."

She rolled her eyes. "Didn't you get enough of that a little while ago?"

I chuckled, "What can I say? I'm addicted to you."

"You're something," she joked.

The service was the following morning at eleven. According to Google Maps, we were about forty minutes away from the funeral home. My wife and I enjoyed a pleasant dinner. Sea bass for her and a twelve-ounce sirloin for me. After dinner, we kicked off our sandals and strolled along the beach.

I so enjoyed Florida Gulf Coast sunsets. Almost like the Lord himself painted the perfect scene. Hues of orange, pink, and gold blanketed the sky. Gentle waves reflected the heavenly vibrance. Just off the beach, I noticed an ice cream parlor.

"There's always room for ice cream."

Fi patted my belly. "Are you sure?"

CHAPTER ONE HUNDRED-NINE

I ordered two scoops of Rocky Road while she got one scoop of raspberry and another of mango sorbet. We spotted tables on the sidewalk and took our evening treats there.

"Ready for tomorrow?" she asked.

"As ready I'll ever be," I replied as ice cream melted down my cone. "We won't have to stay long."

"I know, honey. We can stay as long as you want."

"Thanks. I know you weren't a fan of hers."

"Was anyone?"

"Ouch."

"Sorry. That was mean."

I shrugged. "Mean, but honest."

"Still. That was forever ago. For me, at least."

"No, for me too." I groused.

"Well, I just want to put this all behind us. Move on with our lives, Ols."

"Agreed."

"If there's one thing I've learned over the years, honey, is we must let go of the past. Learn from it, sure. But break free, like Beth Moore says."

"You and your Bible studies," I chuckled.

"I attend them because I enjoy them, and they work."

I chose not to argue.

"Anything else?" I asked.

She swirled a spoonful of sorbet into her mouth before continuing. "You need to stop worrying so much."

"I don't worr—"

"Ols, I've known you my entire life."

"And?"

"And sometimes, you're that same lonely, worrisome little boy I used to watch from my bedroom window."

"I wasn't worrisome."

"Please. I used to sit there and watch you in your backyard. All alone. Worried about getting dirty or something."

"That's so not true. I just hated the snow. Besides, you were the lonely one. Staring down at me like that." I pantomimed her. "Hell, it's the reason I invited you down to play with me."

She laughed. "Okay, fine. We were both lonely."

"Anything else?"

"You sure?"

I licked my ice cream. "I picked the scab. Go ahead."

"You have to stop trying to find your happiness in others. You need to learn how to find joy in yourself. In your surroundings. When we were younger, you used to find it in your photography."

"I still like what I do for a living."

"And I'm not saying you don't. All I'm saying is, you used to find *joy* in it. I can still remember watching you develop your negatives. You'd spend forever marveling at a bee floating above a flower. Or children playing with their parents."

"Yeah, but—"

"Today, it's just a job. Something you're good at."

"Some might say great."

"Good. Great. Doesn't matter. You're not finding joy in it, honey. You haven't for a while now."

I digested her insight and stared at a young couple passing by.

"After the Capitol, I thought for sure you'd retire."

"And do what?"

"Whatever you want. I make more than enough money to keep us going."

"Making you what, my sugar mama? I'd be your kept man?"

"No, Oliver, you'd be my *husband*. Honey, you're my best friend. I've been in love with you my entire life. You're stronger than you think."

I sighed.

"Just think about it. Start small. Take fewer assignments. Maybe teach photography somewhere. I'm sure if you called Georgetown, they'd love to have you teach a course."

Her suggestion piqued my interest. "You think so?"

"Oliver Morales, you're an alum, and a Pulitzer Prize-winning photojournalist. They'd be crazy to turn you away."

"Food for thought."

We were up early the following morning. Hoping to blend in and not overdress, I put on a pair of slacks and blue and white striped button-down, while Fi wore a knee-length black dress with matching heels and a set of pearl earrings.

Forty minutes later, we pulled into the gravel parking lot of a rundown-looking O'Brien's Funeral Home and Crematorium. The landscape was overgrown with misshapen bushes, uncut lawn, and moss-filled trees. It was worse than some of the third-world countries I visited.

"Jesus," I whispered.

The lot was full of old cars and pickup trucks. Our rental stuck out like a sore thumb. I backed into a spot and stared as people entered wearing jeans and t-shirts.

"I think we're a bit overdressed," my wife stated.

"Ya think?"

EPILOGUE

Inside, the place was rather serene. Muted tans and browns with floral arrangements strategically placed throughout the foyer and hallways. A young family of four gathered outside of what appeared to be a chapel of some sort. They greeted us with a smile and asked if we were there for Jackie's funeral.

"Yes." I nodded.

Presumably, the wife and mother of the two young men standing in their Sunday best, pointed out a sign-in book on a table adorned with pictures of a forty-something Jackie. Gone was the bitchy, confident girl from high school who summered in France. Staring back at me now was a rural woman of limited means making the most out of her life.

After Fi signed the book, we were escorted to the third to last pew by one of the youngsters. He handed us a copy of the program and went back to his parents.

The décor on the inside of the chapel was no different than the rest. Dated wood furniture with worn-out cushions. Subdued lighting encouraged mourners to quietly contemplate their loss and mortality.

Some attendees took notice of Fi. I heard whispered, "What is she doing here?" and "I didn't know Jackie knew a celebrity?" As usual, Fi took it all in stride, ignoring the comments, and did her best to blend in.

At the front of the chapel on a large wooden easel was another photo of an adult Jackie, reminiscent of the ones available at discount department stores. She wore a green print dress, a coffee-stained smile, and a simple gold cross necklace.

A deep cobalt blue ceramic urn sat atop a nearby podium. Its glossy finish shimmering in the subdued lighting. Somber organ music quietly created a mood for solace and remembrance. The place soon filled with mostly casually dressed mourners.

Button-down collared shirts, jeans, and sneakers for the men. Knee-length summer dresses for the women. From a side door, a man in a brown suit, presumably the funeral director, stepped out and nodded to someone behind us. A quiet processional march replaced the organ music.

A man in his mid- to late-fifties with a raggedy graying beard and a dated blue suit entered the chapel. Behind him, a girl in her late teens to early twenties. Unlike most of the others in attendance, she wore a calf-length black dress with matching black shoes and a string of white pearls.

She escorted Jackie's mother, in similar garb, along with a black hat and cane. Fi and I must have stuck out, because the girl glanced in our direction as the pair slowly walked past us. I offered a sympathetic smile and received a head nod. She was the spitting image of Jackie down to the intense eyes

"The apple didn't fall far from that tree," my wife whispered.

Gravity and the weight of time seemed to have taken a toll on Jackie's mother. She appeared shorter and had the slightest hump. This once former doyenne of the DC Beltway now took measured and deliberate steps, oftentimes leaned on her cane to steady herself as she scanned the fading red carpet ahead of her.

After a traditional eulogy, attendees offered remembrance of the recently deceased. Her daughter, Anita, shared warm stories from her youth, growing up in nearby Pinellas Park, before moving north to live with her widowed Mee-Maw.

After the service, Fi and I made a beeline for the exit, stopping periodically for her to sign autographs, which I found distasteful. She just shrugged it off, as par for the course.

Outside, a few feet from our rental, Jackie's daughter, Anita, shouted for us, "Excuse me, sir? Ma'am?"

We stopped and turned.

"Hi. Sorry for yelling."

"It's okay, sweetheart," Fi replied. "We're so sorry for your loss."

"I'm sorry, but you're Fiona Morales, from *Morales in the Morning*, right?"

"Guilty as charged."

"Then you must be—"

"Oliver Morales, her husband." I offered my hand.

She nodded knowingly. "My mother used to talk about you all the time."

I arched a brow. "Oh?"

She shared Jackie's tales of woe before fumbling for something in her purse.

"I have something for you." She handed me a sealed envelope.

My name was written on the front in cursive.

"She dictated it to me while she was in, well, I'm sure you know."

"Should I read it now or—"

She shrugged. "Whenever. She made me promise to give it to you."

I pocketed it for later as Fi, and I offered our final condolences.

"I better get back inside," Anita said. "Mee-Maw hates coming to Florida."

We hugged her goodbye and wished her well. Once behind the driver's seat, I cracked it open and read the letter.

Dear Ollie,

I'm writing this to you from a prison of my own design. No words will ever justify the pain I caused you, both in the past and recently in DC. My actions were thoughtless and inexcusable, and I take full responsibility and am committed to making amends.

I still can't believe I attacked you at the Capitol and placed those ads in those newspapers years ago just to lure Navil to your exhibit and confront her. That night will forever haunt me.

I pray you will find it in your heart to accept my sincerest apology and in time maybe earn your forgiveness. I'm so very sorry, Ols.

Yours truly,
Jack

A wave of forgiveness washed over me, as memories from my youth flooded my mind's eye. From the many times Jackie and I argued, to our cuddling on prom night at the beach. A time where she and I turned a corner and became friends. Maybe more so. We'd never know.

Fi placed her loving hand on mine and with an empathetic smile, "You, okay?"

"Yeah. I think I finally am."

Fi and I took the scenic route back to our hotel. Between her love, the Gulf of Mexico, and U2's inspirational song, "Beautiful Day," on the radio, my body felt lighter, as heavy burdens slowly drifted from my soul. An albatross forever gone, replaced with memories, forgiveness, and the sweet taste of freedom. A beautiful day indeed.

ACKNOWLEDGMENTS

I am profoundly grateful to the many people who have supported and contributed to the creation of this book.

Vega Street Team

Angela Albertus, Corinne Costanzo, Tina Donovan, Karen Gargiulo, Pepper Hust, Barbara Leibold, Karen Nelson, Sally Orwig, Jennifer Readby, Susan Ressa, Susan Rogers, Nicole Spence, Dan Terrell, JoAnn Vorndran, Lindsey Vorndran.

Legal Advice

Fred Green, Luis Roman

Writers Group

To the Pinellas Writers & Authors Group, your writing critique and feedback have sharpened my axe and elevated my work.

Family

To my beloved wife Jeanette, whose continual encouragement moves me forward, and to my four sons, William, Phillip, Michael, and Devin, who inspire me daily.

My Fans

Your feedback and reviews motivate my creative endeavors and drive me to improve with every book.

My Editor and Publisher

Janet Fix, thank you for all you do to help us put out our best work possible. Your dedication and expertise are invaluable.

Thank you all for being an integral part of this journey.

ABOUT THE AUTHOR

Award-winning romance author Phillip Vega is a born storyteller who found his true calling later in life when he began putting his vivid imagination onto paper. Juggling his fervor for writing alongside a successful career in software sales, Phillip finds solace and inspiration in his Long Island upbringing, enriched by his Hispanic heritage. Now living in the vibrant landscapes of Florida, he draws upon his memories of summers on Long Island to craft gripping romantic narratives that captivate readers.

Vega's literary journey began with *Last Exit to Montauk* (Manhattan Book Awards Winner, 2020), followed by *The Captain & the Queen* (Top Shelf Dual-Finalist, 2020), and *Searching for Sarah* (Book Excellence Awards Winner, 2021). In his latest novel, *Fury in Her Eyes* (releasing summer 2024), Vega delves deeper into the intricacies of human emotion and the complexities of relationships. Versatile and engaging, Phillip thrives in interpersonal settings, including guest appearances, interviews, and book signings, always eager to connect with his readers and share his love for storytelling.

Follow Phillip on his website **www.phillipvega.com** where you will also find his social media handles. His books are available in both digital and paperback formats at your favorite book retailer.